FENDER BENDERS

FENDER BENDERS

BILL FITZHUGH

WILLIAM MORROW

75 YEARS OF PUBLISHING

An Imprint of HarperCollins*Publishers*

HarperCollins books may be purchased for educational, business, or sales
promotional use. For information please write to Special Markets Department, HarperCollins Publishers Inc., 10 East 53rd Street,
New York, NY 10022.

FIRST EDITION

Designed by Nicola Ferguson

Printed on acid-free paper

Library of Congress Cataloging-in-Publication Data has been applied for.

ISBN 0-380-97757-5

01 02 03 04 05 RRD 10 9 8 7 6 5 4 3 2 1

To the songwriters, who can say in a three-minute song what I struggle to say in three hundred pages.

And to the musicians, who can convey more with the right four chords than I can in an entire book.

And to Kendall, who is a song unto herself.

ACKNOWLEDGMENTS

My thanks to the following people who graciously shared their expertise and time: First and foremost, to my old Jackson pals J. Fred Knobloch and Bill Simmons, who answered a thousand questions and got me hooked up all over Nashville. If there is a single true note in this book, it's thanks to them. James Stroud not only allowed me to pick his brain, he also let me sit in while he mixed a single. Colleen Miche joined me at the Bluebird Cafe and told me things about Nashville I would not have known otherwise. Also, Tom Dupree, editor and music lover, and my sister, Liz, both of whom keep trying to make me a better writer. Don't stop now.

Others who helped: Bruce Feiler provided industry insights and a lot of material I just plain stole from his fabulous book *Dreaming Out Loud*. Janine Smith gave critical early ruminations. Tutti Westbrook went beyond the call of duty. Jeff Weber weighed in on the producer's p.o.v. and royalty calculations. Professor Rebecca Brown of Vanderbilt Law School was kind enough to answer questions for no other reason than her generosity. And thanks to Paul Scholten at County Q Studios for letting me attend that session.

Fender Benders is a work of fiction. In reality there are no dishonest record producers or lawyers in Nashville or anywhere else. In real life there are no calculating artists, cheating spouses, or fickle lovers. In the real world men don't hang out in honky-tonks drinking too much, none of them drive pickup trucks, and they certainly don't own guns. And if they did, they'd never use them to kill other people. All of those characterizations are bald stereotypes, the origins of which are unknown and which have never been proven to exist in nature.

FENDER
BENDERS

_1_

F red Babineaux was halfway between Morgan City and Houma when he decided he had a brain tumor. He couldn't think of anything else to explain the king-hell of a headache swelling inside his skull. It was a tumor, he was sure of it, a tumor the size of a pink Texas grapefruit.

Fred was driving south on a narrow stretch of highway that traced the spine of a levee separating two cane fields thirty feet below on either side of the road. He was heading for Terrebonne Bay to meet with a man who wanted to buy a boat from the manufacturer Fred represented. The sale would mean a fat commission, but at the moment Fred would have forfeited that plus two months salary to make the headache disappear. He picked up the can of Dandy's Cream Soda that was sweating in the cup holder. He held it to his head for a moment hoping the cold would soothe the pain. When that failed, Fred thought maybe the problem was dehydration or low blood sugar, so he gulped half the can.

The fields below on both sides of the levee were lush with a young crop of sugarcane flourishing in the promising Louisiana heat. It was hot for late April and humid. A couple of snowy egrets stalked the edge of the cane fields stabbing orange beaks at their lunch. Here and there the familiar smear of armadillo slicked the road. Fred identified with one whose head had been reduced to the consistency of a thick roux.

His dehydration and low blood sugar theories disproved, Fred took his hands off the wheel and steered with his knee so he could massage his throbbing temples. The radio was tuned to Kickin' 98, "Classic Country for South Louisiana, playing a mix of the old and the new, because a song ain't gotta be old to be a classic." They were playing a ballad at the moment, soothing close harmonies Fred hoped might ease his pain. By the end of the song, however, Fred knew he required pharmaceuticals.

He leaned over for the glove compartment when, suddenly, he heard what sounded like an airplane landing on the roof of his car. Startled by the abrupt roar of the thundering engine, Fred jerked his hands back to the steering wheel, narrowly avoiding a long plunge off the road. "Sonofabitch!" Adrenaline poured into his system. His heart rate soared, turning his already bad headache into severe unilateral periorbital pain. Fred looked out the window and saw the crop duster raining Gramoxone onto the sweet young cane. *Maybe that's what caused my tumor,* he thought. He'd been up and down these roads so many times over the years there was no telling how many gallons of herbicides and pesticides he'd absorbed. That had to be it. You could strap Fred Babineaux to the bottom of one of those noisy old biplanes, poke a few holes in him, and spray a field with whatever came out. Kill anything it hit.

Fred looked to make sure the plane wasn't coming again, then leaned over and popped open the glove compartment. He grabbed the familiar yellow-and-red box of Dr. Porter's Headache Powder, an aspirin product sold only in the deepest parts of the South. He'd bought this particular box at an EZ Mart in Shreveport the day before. To Fred's relief, the usually impenetrable plastic shrink-wrap on the brand-new box sloughed off easily and he quickly fingered out one of the folded rectangular sheets of wax paper that held the powder like a professionally packaged gram of something else entirely.

With one throbbing eye on the road, Fred unfolded the two ends of the rectangle and then the long top. He held one end closed and, with a jerk, tossed his head back and poured the bitter powder into the back of his throat. He chased it with the remainder of his cream soda and, wincing slightly, swallowed the solution to all his problems.

In no time flat, Fred forgot about his headache. Sadly it wasn't due to the fast-acting nature of the medicine. At first his face went numb and his breathing became irregular. He considered pulling to the side of the road, but the shoulder was only four feet wide before dropping sharply into the cane fields below. The eighteen-wheeler bearing down from behind prevented him from simply stopping in the middle of the road.

Moments later, with no warning, Fred threw up violently, spewing his fried lunch onto the windshield. Panic set in as his body realized he was dying before his mind could grasp the fact, let alone ask why. Desperate to see the road in front of him, Fred wiped at the vomit covering his windshield. Smearing it only made matters worse. As if his compromised vision didn't make driving difficult enough, Fred began to hear sounds that didn't exist. His heart lapsed into what would best be described as irregular cardiac activity. But at least the headache wasn't bothering him anymore.

Fred's mind fixed on why he suddenly felt like he was dying. His wheels drifted onto the gravel shoulder, kicking up a spray of rocks that scared the snowy egrets into the sky. Had Fred been listening to the radio, he'd have heard the DJ introducing an old Dorsey Dixon song. "Here's a classic country flashback on Kickin' 98!" But Fred wasn't listening to the radio anymore. All he could hear was what sounded like a chorus of outboard motors in his head. The auditory hallucinations were part and parcel of the process taking place throughout his body, namely, the total cessation of his cellular metabolism. His central nervous system was so compromised that it was shutting down, and not temporarily.

Roy Acuff was singing about blood and whiskey mixed with broken glass strewn across the highway.

Struggling to keep his car on the road, Fred began to convulse, and suddenly he couldn't breathe at all. He began to shake like a dog shittin' peach seeds. Increased amounts of unsaturated hemoglobin in his blood turned his mucus membranes a bluish tint. His body suddenly jerked straight as a board, causing him to floor the accelerator. His head pitched backwards, and a moment later, Fred's car soared off into the cane field just as the crop duster passed overhead heading in the same direction. Fred's soul had been called to the hereafter.

"*. . . and I didn't hear nobody pray . . .*"

FORREST COUNTY, MISSISSIPPI

Mr. T's was just off Highway 49 a few miles south of Hattiesburg. The place was named after the owner, Buck Talby, a mean old coot with an ulcer. From the outside Mr. T's looked like it might be a dump, but inside it was a genuine shithole. A wooden plank floor littered with peanut shells, cigarette butts, chewed tobacco, and the occasional cockroach was lit by three neon beer signs and a flickering fluorescent tube over a pool table. The clientele consisted of farm and forestry product workers wearing baseball caps touting brands of outboard motors and oil additives. There were also a few yahoos from nearby Camp Shelby, a National Guard training facility. Grease-stained work shirts and T-shirts with yellow armpits met the dress code. It was Saturday night and the men were gussied up in the hopes of picking up on a little something the wife wouldn't have to know about.

It was in this context that Eddie Long stood on the tiny stage with his guitar. He was tall and lean and handsome. He was lost in his music, playing the hell out of a rocking version of "Ring of Fire." Eddie had tuned out his indifferent audience long ago and was channeling anger into his performance, substituting a torrid run of notes for the mariachi horns of Cash's version of the song. Every time he bent a note his face bent with it like his life was attached to the strings of his Fender DG21S. He wouldn't dare bring his big flat-top Gibson into a place like Mr. T's. Damn thing cost too much. The Fender was his road guitar but no less dependable because it cost less. It was Indian rosewood with a solid spruce top. It produced a sturdy bass and a brilliant treble that Eddie rode like a racehorse.

Eddie's anger stemmed from the crowd's neglect. He wanted them to pay attention, to hear what he was doing. He wanted them to be enthralled, though he would have settled for vaguely inter-ested. But they weren't either one, and there was nothing Eddie could do but use his time onstage to practice until he found himself in front of a crowd that cared.

What Eddie failed to notice was a guy named Jimmy Rogers, sit-ting in the back, enraptured by the performance. Jimmy had a pen and a pad of paper and was poised to write. But he hesitated when it occurred to him, not for the first time, that it was impossible to describe the sound of music with mere words. Still, he shook his head and took a stab at it. *Can't win if you don't play*, he figured.

Eddie reached the midpoint of the song, snarling and distorting his good looks. He wouldn't be doing it tonight, but when Eddie smiled it was so beguiling you couldn't look away. His eyes were the same Cadillac green as a 1958 Gretsch Country Club Stereo guitar, and he was a right dresser too. He was wearing Wranglers, pressed, with a white T-shirt under an open, untucked denim work shirt. A dark pair of sideburns dropped from underneath his silver belly Stetson, tapering to point down at a pair of cowboy boots that had been selected to convey a heritage that didn't look nearly as store-bought as it was. Halfway between the hat and the boots was a shiny silver belt buckle the size of a butter plate. The result of all this was a sort of disinfected rodeo look. It was the latest in a series of styles Eddie had tested for his stage persona.

Eddie was on the last chorus when he looked down and noticed a change in the expression of the National Guardsman at the front table. The guy'd been drinking boilermakers all night and had just finished eating an oyster po-boy and a side of tater-wads. Suddenly he had the look of a man who couldn't hold it down anymore. Eddie would have gotten out of the way except the stage was the size of a bath mat and if he jumped off he figured he'd get pelted with a beer bottle. It had happened before. So he just kept playing.

A moment later the guy's mouth opened like a yawning dog. What followed was a pleasant surprise, relatively speaking. A single oyster, still intact, popped out of the man's gaping maw and landed on one of Eddie's Durangos. Eddie didn't miss a beat. With a deft flick of his boot, Eddie launched the oyster back at the guardsman, missing his mouth by mere inches. The man wobbled a bit, then, wearing an oyster eyepatch, landed facedown on the table. Eddie just kept singing. *"I fell into a burning ring of fire . . ."*

This wasn't the worst gig Eddie had ever played, but it ranked. He'd been playing bars like this one throughout the South for the past seven years, paying his dues. He hoped to move up to the Mississippi casino circuit and eventually to Nashville, but his immediate goal was to finish this set, get his money, and get the hell out of there. Eddie had decided he was going to do whatever it took never to have to play at a Mr. T's again.

Eddie lived in Hinchcliff, up in Quitman County in the Delta, the birthplace of the blues, but he was a serious student of all things country, especially Nashville fashions, grooming habits, and music trends. He subscribed to *Country Weekly* and *Billboard* and had his satellite dish aimed plum at TNN. It was all part of Eddie's plan to become a country music star.

In the meantime Eddie worked and took classes part-time at

Quitman County Junior College. At twenty-seven, he was the oldest guy in his class. He'd taken a few years off after high school and had resumed his education only after figuring out what he wanted to do with his life. Eddie was a good student, taking business courses with an emphasis on marketing. He could have taken electives in composition or music theory down at Delta State, but the way he figured it there was more to becoming a superstar than playing the guitar or being a good songwriter. You could hire people for that sort of thing—"outsourcing" is what they called it in his business management class. There were talented people who supplied those services. And those people in turn depended on the stars for their own livelihoods. It was symbiotic, like many host/parasite relationships, though in the music business it was sometimes hard to tell who was which.

Eddie had picked up the guitar pretty quickly and, thanks to some lessons, he was good and getting better. He practiced daily, though he tended to use practice as an excuse to avoid doing the things he didn't want to, like getting what his wife called a regular job. But that wasn't to say Eddie didn't work. He brought in money from his singing gigs and from working part-time for nearby property owners. He helped out on the Hegman farm during harvesting, and during the spring and summer he tended a small peach orchard owned by the Lytle family. But, to his wife's eternal aggravation, Eddie was far more dedicated to his dream than to hers.

Her name was Tammy, and lately all she wanted to do was start a family. But that hadn't always been what Tammy said she wanted. Before they married, she had promised to support Eddie until he made it as a singer. "I believe in you, Eddie," she used to say.

Eddie took Tammy at her word, and over the past nine years he had hustled together a string of clubs in Mississippi, Louisiana, Alabama, and Arkansas where he performed on a regular basis. He was also hot on the college circuit, playing frat parties at every university in the Southeastern Conference. He was especially popular at Ole Miss and Auburn University. His repertoire was limited but smartly chosen. In addition to some originals, Eddie played classics from the pop and country charts. He had a good voice, too. It didn't make you bolt up and marvel at its qualities; rather it was a country-lite tenor, perfectly suited to the songs he chose.

But the folks at Mr. T's didn't care about any of that. Eddie was just background noise for their Saturday night. Most of them talked straight through his sets, and nobody was afraid to yell out their order to the bar in the middle of a ballad. It was the sort of thing that usually pissed Eddie off, but tonight he was past caring. He'd done this for too long and was too good to have to put up with this kind of shit anymore. He finished his song and got off the stage as fast as he could, heading for Mr. Talby's office to get his cash. He'd been counting heads for four nights and by his reckoning was due at least three hundred dollars.

"Hey, Eddie!" a familiar voice called out.

Eddie turned and, for the first time that night, saw a friendly face, the one he'd missed earlier. It was Jimmy Rogers, a freelance writer he knew from Jackson. Jimmy had reviewed several of Eddie's shows. "Hey, how you doin'?"

"Not bad," Jimmy said with a shrug. "I heard you were playing down here, so I convinced the *Hattiesburg American* they should hire me to write a review." Jimmy had been following Eddie's career for several years and had become something of a fan. "Lemme buy you a beer?"

Eddie looked toward Mr. Talby's office. "I'd like to, but I'm driving back home tonight. Can I get a rain check?"

"Sure, no problem." They shook hands. "I'll send you a copy of the review."

"Thanks, man. Say nice things about me."

Eddie turned and headed for Mr. Talby's office. It was a cramped space with liquor boxes and stools stacked around the perimeter. Mr. Talby was sitting behind a desk in the middle of the room looking every bit like the fat sixty-year-old mean-ass backwoods cracker that he was. He was pouring milk into a glass of ice and scotch when Eddie walked in. Next to the glass was the tray from a cash drawer, a rotary phone, and a .38. Sitting on the edge of the desk was a bouncer who answered to the name Hummer.

Mr. Talby looked up at Eddie standing on the other side of the desk with his guitar case in hand. "I suppose you're here for some of my money." There was nothing friendly about the way he said it.

"Just what I'm owed," Eddie said. "By my count it's about three, three-fifty, somewhere around there."

Mr. Talby's head jerked backwards. "Three-fifty! You must be seein' double or something." He took a gulp off his drink and winced. "Hummer, what was your count?"

Hummer shook his head. "More like two hundred."

"That sounds more like it." Mr. Talby peeled ten twenty-dollar bills off a stack and held them out to Eddie.

"Two hundred?" Eddie couldn't believe it. He looked at the money, then at Mr. Talby. "That's not right. Can't be." He pointed out toward the main room. "I counted every night." He pointed at the cash register tray. "It's at least three."

Mr. Talby put the two hundred dollars back in the stack. "Well now, what're you sayin', son? You callin' me a cheat? 'Cause I don't take that kinda bullshit from faggots like you." He slid his hand over to the gun, pulled it toward him. "You want the two hundred or you want Hummer to show you the fuckin' door?"

QUITMAN COUNTY, MISSISSIPPI

Eddie and Tammy Long lived in northwest Mississippi, in a two-bedroom brick house not far from the Tallahatchie River. The living room was appointed with a rent-to-own sofa, love seat, and press-board entertainment center. There was a "God Bless This House" needlepoint on the wall by the front door. Over the sofa was a watercolor of a cow in a cotton field, done by Eddie's aunt Theda, who lived down in Greenville. The master bedroom was given over to Tammy's grandmother's four-poster bed, a dresser, and a vanity, all in naturally distressed pine. The window air conditioner worked nonstop from May till mid-October.

The kitchen, which was also the dining room and laundry room, was tight as the skin on a sausage. The avocado-green fridge pressed against the rust-brown stove. The washer and dryer were squeezed over by the back door, preventing it from opening all the way. The dishwasher was on wheels and hooked to the sink faucet. A large table and four chairs were wedged into the corner, forcing you sideways to get past.

Eddie was in the kitchen and was in a good mood for the first time in a coon's age. It had been three months since he got ripped off by Mr. Talby, and he hadn't had much work since then. But he'd just received news so good it made him feel like writing a song. Eddie sat on the edge of the kitchen table with his feet on the seat of a chair. He hunkered over his pride and joy, a Gibson SJ-200 Reissue. It was an instrument of unrivaled beauty both in looks and sound. And that beauty hadn't come cheap. Eddie had dropped nearly three thousand dollars on this baby. Its gleaming body of solid flamed maple and spruce lent instant artistic credibility to whoever held her close.

Eddie focused on the bound Madagascar rosewood of the fingerboard and the creamy dollops of rainbow radiating from the mother-of-pearl inlay. He rearranged his fingers and tested a new chord. Six strings of honey. He tried his newest lyric, "I'd cross a double yellow line to get to your heart." Chord change. "You know I've loved you like that right from the start."

Eddie smiled and pulled the pencil from behind his ear. As he wrote the lyrics on the pad of paper at his side, Tammy shuffled into the kitchen in her pale green housecoat. She stared at the dishes stacked near the sink. "I thought you was gonna do these," she said.

Eddie peeked up from under his cowboy hat. "Hang on, sugar britches. I think I got one here." He looked back at his lyric sheet. "Uh, get to your heart, right from the start, uh . . . let's load the cart . . . I need a spare part . . . I want your cherry tart . . ."

Tammy muttered, "Who gives a fart?" She turned on the water full blast and threw the dishes in hard enough to chip one of them.

Eddie gestured at the sink with the head of his guitar. "Just leave 'em, sugar, I'll get at 'em later." Eddie didn't see Tammy turning a nasty shade of red, but the thing was, he didn't need to see it to know it was happening. It seemed to happen a lot lately. He knew it would pass just as soon as—

A plate whizzed by his head and shattered against the wall. "Jumpin' Jesus!" Eddie looked up just in time to see the second plate leave her hand. He twisted his torso to shield his precious Gibson from the flying dish. "Ow! Shit! That hurt, puddin'."

"You don't know about hurt, buster!" Tammy set her jaw and squinted in a way that only rural women can. "I'll show you hurt!"

"Whoa, sugar, let's talk about this." Eddie scrambled off the table and ducked behind the solid-backed chair. "Whatever it is."

Eddie and Tammy had been high-school sweethearts with no long-term plan. They were just young and ultimately incautious. As Eddie's Aunt Theda had said, they'd been eatin' supper before saying grace, and sure enough Tammy pulled up pregnant the summer after graduation. So they got the justice of the peace to tie the knot before Tammy's dad found out and tied a knot around Eddie's sweet neck. A few weeks later Tammy miscarried. That was nine years ago. Things had been tense as a D-string ever since.

With her long blond hair and dreamy, half-shut eyes, Tammy had always been languid and slinky, but ever since her "misfortune," she carried herself like a dying succulent, a thirsty blond houseplant with a terminal case of the vapors. So it surprised Eddie more than somewhat when she managed to throw the heavy serving bowl across the kitchen like she did. Crash!

"Sugar, wasn't that the bowl your Cousin Minnie gave us?" Eddie had an easygoing Southern country accent, not too twangy, not too flat.

Tammy began screeching. "Shut up, Eddie! I am sick of you and your songs and having to do all the work around here, and bringing in all the money in this house on top of it all! If you don't take that job Daddy offered you, I'm gonna pack my bags and move right out and then who you gonna find to pay your rent? Huh?"

Tammy's daddy owned the Dollar Store in town and was ready to give Eddie what passed for a decent job in this part of the country. Eddie would never say it, because he liked the old man, but the truth was he'd rather have a catfish bone stuck in his throat than put on one of those polyester vests with the smiley-face button on it. Eddie knew you didn't become a country music sensation standing on the sales floor of the Dollar Store in Hinchcliff, Mississippi. "Sugar, I thought we settled this before we got married. You promised me—"

Thwick! A steak knife lodged in the wall behind Eddie. "That's right, you just keep throwing that in my face," Tammy hollered. "I got the right to change my mind if I want, especially after what I went through." When it suited her needs, Tammy used the miscarriage as an excuse for neglecting everything from her appearance to the promises she had made. "I gave you all the time you needed," she said. "You just ain't done it, and you ain't man enough to admit that you ain't got what it takes to make it in Batesville, much less Nashville."

"Now, sugar, let's be fair," Eddie said in his sweetest voice. "Even Elvis had to leave Mississippi to get discovered."

"Elvis?" Tammy raised her voice a notch. "You ain't Elvis, Eddie, and you never will be! Do you even hear what's comin' outta your mouth? You got a perfectly good job just waitin' for you and instead of takin' it, you're hiding behind the kitchen table comparing yourself to the King. When are you going to give up on this nonsense and do right by me?"

Eddie poked his head out from behind the chair. "Sugar?" Another plate flew by, knocking Eddie's hat off. He ducked back behind the chair, wondering how come his life had turned out so bad. He put up with Tammy the best he could, but he was running out of patience. Episodes like this one made him want to slap her clear into Coahoma County, but his long-term plans prevented him from giving in to that temptation. Eddie picked up his hat and held it out to see if it would draw fire. A John Deere coffee cup flew past and bounced off the wall. Eddie knew he had to calm Tammy down before she ran out of dishes and went for the gun, even if it was just a .22. He pulled the Gibson into playing position, strummed a familiar chord, more slowly than it was usually played, and sang in his softest voice, "*Stand by your man . . .*"

"Stand by where?" Tammy shrieked. "In the damn welfare line?" She hurled a cast-iron skillet Eddie's way. "I've had about all of this I can take, Eddie. It's time for you to start taking care of me the way a man's supposed to."

"Tammy, sugar, that was a real good throw. Now listen, I was going to surprise you with the news tonight, but I guess now's as good a time as any to tell you . . ."

Tammy had another steak knife raised over her head ready to throw. "Tell me what?"

Eddie strummed the guitar, flamenco-style. He spoke like a big-city radio announcer, rising slowly from his crouch as he spoke. "Starting *this* Wednesday at the Gold Coast Extravaganza Casino in Biloxi, Mississippi, for five straight nights, ladies and gentlemen, the next superstar of Nashville, Tennessee—Mr. Eddie Long!" He ended with a flourish on the guitar.

A second passed as the news sunk in. Suddenly Tammy squealed and began hopping on one foot. "Eddie!!!"

"I'm talkin' regular paychecks for six weeks, Sugar. Playing the casinos from Biloxi to Lula." Eddie pushed up the brim of his hat with his index finger. "What do you say to that?"

There was a pause as Tammy put her hands over her mouth in amazement.

"Careful with that knife," Eddie said.

Tammy slid her hands from her mouth to her cheeks. Her voice took on a sudden sweetness as her eyes went wide. "Eddie, how much?"

Eddie strummed the Gibson. "Three-fifty a week."

Tammy laid the steak knife in the sink, real gentle. "Before or after taxes?"

"That's take-home, sugar. I'll be sending most of that back to you." Eddie picked a couple of notes and improvised a lyric. *"I'll be sending you the money, 'cause I love you so much honey . . ."* Eddie put the guitar down and crossed to where Tammy was standing. There was one more thing he knew she wanted to hear, even if he didn't want to say it. "And I tell you what." He pulled her close. "You come up when I'm playing the casino in Lula and we'll get started on making those babies."

Tammy squealed again. "I knew you were going to make it, Eddie! I told you I believed in you, didn't I? Haven't I always said that? You are going to be such a star!" She kissed Eddie's neck while hopping around squealing. Then she suddenly stopped. Her mouth opened wide. "Eddie, I just had the best idea! Let's drive up to Memphis and go to that Chinese place I like. I think we need to celebrate!"

Eddie thought about it for a moment before a smile crossed his face. "Yeah," he said. "That'll work."

LEE COUNTY, ALABAMA

It was three o'clock on a stifling afternoon. The air wasn't moving. The heat was battling the humidity to see which could do the most damage. Sheriff Bobby Herndon of the Lee County Sheriff's

Department was driving north on County Road 147 with his windows sealed and the air-conditioning chilling the cruiser.

Having lived in this part of Lee County all his life, Sheriff Herndon knew the 147 was lined on both sides by cotton fields even though he couldn't see them. All he could see was the tall bushy shrubs the Highway Department had planted along the property lines most of the way between Auburn University and Gold Ridge.

For the past hour Sheriff Herndon had been testing the new UltraLyte laser gun, but traffic had thinned out and everybody was doing the speed limit, so he switched the gun off, sat back, and tried to enjoy the drive. He was gazing down the road thinking about where he was going fishing that weekend when his peripheral vision suddenly picked up some movement in the tall shrubs on his right. As he turned to look, a bright red 1995 Massey Ferguson 8150 with the big 18.4R42 duals in the back came roaring through the bushes, hell-bent for crossing the road about thirty yards ahead.

Sheriff Herndon could see the driver struggling terribly inside the tractor's big glass-encased cab. The man's face was red and twisted as he fumbled desperately to open the door. The sheriff recognized the man as Hoke Paley, one of the richest men in Lee County. He owned half the land that bordered the 147. Mr. Paley was famous all across Alabama for his business dealings. Word was he had screwed half the people in the county without having sex with a one of 'em. He was a mean, hard man who didn't lack for enemies.

Sheriff Herndon hit his lights and brakes at the same time as the big red tractor lurched onto the road. Hoke managed to open the door, and, looking skyward with his hands clutched around his own throat, he stepped out of the tractor's cab as if to walk a plank. Unfortunately he was eight feet above the ground and there was no plank. He tipped over like a cartoon character and landed flat on his terrified face.

The big red tractor continued, driverless, across the road,

through the shrubs on the other side, and on through the field. The sheriff called for an ambulance, but it didn't matter. Mr. Paley was already dead when the sheriff rolled him over; several of his teeth were on the pavement. His face was covered with pinkish spit and gravel, and there was a box of Dr. Porter's Headache Powder poking out of his shirt pocket.

2

J immy Rogers was a member of the fourth estate, but only in the loosest sense of the word. He was really just a freelance writer with a fondness for music and a girl named Megan. Jimmy had been a reporter for a couple of the state's newspapers but had quickly tired of the assignments they foisted on him—puff pieces on this year's debutante fashions, that sort of crap. He knew the only way to get the assignments he wanted was by surrendering the security of a paycheck and going freelance, so he had resigned and started writing concert reviews and artist profiles.

Jimmy had been doing it long enough to become the unofficial official reporter-and-photographer covering the entire Mississippi music scene. At one end of the spectrum this meant reviewing the occasional big concert at the Coliseum in Jackson or the one in Biloxi. At the other end of the continuum he covered small clubs, like Mr. T's, where local talent got its start. But he spent most of his time at the state's thirty-some-odd casinos.

On any given night, 365 days a year, there was at least one

"newsworthy" concert somewhere in the state. He covered any show he wanted, wrote reviews, then tried to sell them. Regional magazines and newspapers occasionally hired him to do interviews or review specific shows, and the tabloids were always interested in photographs—preferably scandalous ones—of anyone approaching celebrity status. The *World Globe* had once paid Jimmy $2,500 for a photo of a drunk Jim Nabors impersonator throwing a punch at a woman who had heckled him at a show in Vicksburg. "Faux Nabors, Real Punch!" was the headline. The casinos, which had descended on the state like a plague in the early '90s, were Jimmy's bread and butter.

As a kid, Jimmy had been a devotee of the old James Bond movies—the ones with Sean Connery. It was through these films that Jimmy had formed his image of what a casino should be like. They were elegance and sophistication, royalty and worldliness. Casinos were glamour palaces filled with beautiful, witty people and debonair espionage agents drinking martinis and surrounded by alluring decor.

So Jimmy was understandably disappointed the first time he walked into one of the casinos on the Mississippi Gulf Coast. There wasn't a tuxedo or a martini in sight, and Jimmy would have bet his own mother's life that no one in the building was associated in any way with the intelligence community. The place was ten million watts of tackiness with all the glamour of a neon-lit cockfight. But it was where he plied his trade, and tonight was no different. He was there to cover Eddie Long's first appearance at the Gold Coast Extravaganza Casino in Biloxi.

Jimmy had asked Megan, his girlfriend of three months, to join him. As they walked through the casino's main room, he turned to her. "Is it just me, or does it feel like we're inside a giant *Dukes of Hazzard* pinball machine?" Despite being a native, Jimmy sounded only vaguely Southern.

"Granted," Megan said, "it's not Monte Carlo." She stopped at a slot machine. "But it's still fun." She dropped four quarters into the slot and pulled the arm.

Just then a man walked past wearing a *Who Farted?* T-shirt and a big smile. Jimmy wondered if the man had hit a jackpot or if he was just happy he still had those three teeth. "Look at these people." Jimmy's tone was more sympathetic than condescending. "They can't afford to throw their money away like this. Hell, I can't afford it."

"I don't see a gun to anybody's head. And how do you know they can't afford it?" The bell on Megan's machine dinged a few times and then two quarters dropped into the tray. "Ha! Look, I won fifty cents."

"No, you lost fifty. You put in a dollar, remember?"

"Well thank you, Mr. Negativity." Megan plowed the fifty cents back into the machine and pulled the lever. It made some cheerful electronic noises before displaying the results. Cherry. Orange. Bar. "Ohhh, poot." Megan banged the front of the machine with her fist, then reached into her plastic bucket of coins and continued feeding the machine. "You know, I am so tired of hearing people talk about the evils of gambling and how it takes money from those who can least afford it and blahblahblah."

Jimmy smiled at her "blahblahblah." She never said "blah, blah, blah," like three words. It was always "blahblahblah," real fast, like she was in too much of a hurry to express the et cetera in whatever she was talking about, and it was a lot easier than actually making a point. Megan wasn't stupid, but she'd never been accused of intellectual industry either. She was ambitious and had every intention of ending up on top of the heap before all was said and done. She didn't have a specific plan, but she was adept at seizing opportunities.

But none of that mattered to Jimmy. He was too smitten to care. He stood there watching her, still astounded by his dumb luck. He'd met Megan at a media convention in Jackson some months earlier. She was representing the radio station where she worked as an on-air personality. Jimmy was there networking. Her unconventional-for-Mississippi looks caught his eye immediately. She was twenty-seven with purposeful cheekbones and a downy complexion that had come by way of a beautiful Irish grandmother. Like something out of *Mirabella*, she was wearing a black silk charmeuse shirt, wool-silk trousers with a silk cummerbund, and black patent stiletto pumps. Her eyes were Liz Taylor violet thanks to tinted contacts. She was crowned with a bramble of wild reddish-orange hair that looked unkempt and expensively styled at the same time. In a state filled with blond pageant beauties, Megan was a head-turner of a different sort.

Jimmy had approached her immediately. "Hi, I'm Jimmy Rogers," he said. "I love your radio show. Especially your character voices." He smiled.

She smiled back. "Thanks," she said. "Which one's your favorite?"

He pretended to think for a moment. "That would have to be the Sweet Potato Queen. Very authentic. You really capture the spud-ness of the character."

Megan fingered the white glass necklace circling her throat. "Yeah, she's one of my favorites." She glanced across the room and waved at someone before returning her attention to Jimmy. "So, you were saying?"

Jimmy gestured at her apparel. "Love your outfit too."

"Thanks. It's Michael Kors, except the shoes, of course." She kicked a foot out to show off one of the pumps. "Manolo Blahnik."

"Of course." Jimmy kicked out a foot, mimicking her. He was wearing cheap, scuffed penny loafers. "Men's Warehouse," he said. "Fifty percent off."

Megan looked. "No. Those? And they look so . . . JCPenney."

"You just have to know how to shop," Jimmy said. "But I compensate for my lack of fashion sense by being cute."

Megan stepped back and gave Jimmy the once-over. He was a boyish twenty-eight with an aversion to suits. He dressed to accommodate his image and his income as a writer—tan Dockers, white button-down shirt, occasional sports coat. He had thick dark hair and a thin nose surrounded by a constant look of bemusement or confusion—it was hard to tell which. His eyes were trustworthy, lending him an aspect of decency. "Still," she said, "cute as you are, you might want to consider shopping somewhere that doesn't have the word 'warehouse' in the name."

They flirted for an hour or so before slipping away from the conference and going for drinks at Nick's, where Jimmy tried to talk her into becoming his fashion consultant in exchange for his being her sex slave.

Now, three months later, while Jimmy was still marveling at her beauty, Megan lost her bucket of quarters in the slots. "Oh well." She glanced at her watch. "Show starts in ten minutes. Let's go on up." They went upstairs and were seated at a table in the middle of the room. Jimmy pulled a spiral notebook from his coat pocket and laid it on the table next to his camera.

When the waitress came over, she pointed at the camera as if it were a snake. "Sir, you can't have a camera in here. It's casino rules." Jimmy pulled out a stack of laminated press credentials. He had one from Harrison County Civil Defense, one from the Associated Press, one from the *Sun-Herald,* one of his former employers, and one from the casino's PR department. Jimmy handed her the last one. "Okay," she said. "I just have to check." She handed the card back and took their order.

Jimmy had seen Eddie perform almost thirty times in the past several years, and he had written reviews of every show. In fact, Jimmy had written the first published account of Eddie Long in concert. It was a positive review that Jimmy sold to the paper in Natchez. Since then, Jimmy had sold several more reviews in addition to a short interview. Eddie showed his gratitude for all the good exposure by buying a great many rounds of drinks. Between the liquor and the mutual admiration, they'd developed a friendship.

As a writer Jimmy aspired to more than writing concert reviews and lurking in the shadows hoping for disgraceful photo ops. He wanted to write something more substantial, though he didn't know exactly what—a book, a play, something, as long as it was about music or musicians. Jimmy hadn't hit on it yet but he was looking.

The waitress arrived with two draft beers and a deep-fried Cajun onion bloom just as the lights went down. An announcer's voice came over the loudspeaker system. "Ladies and gentlemen, the Gold Coast Extravaganza Casino is proud to present a rising star in country music. Please put your hands together for Mr. Eddie Long!"

The crowd gave an enthusiastic round of applause as the curtains parted in the darkness. All they could see was the silhouette of a tall, Stetson-topped figure stepping up to the mic stand. Eddie let the room settle until all they could hear was the faint ping-ping-ping of the downstairs slot machines. Then, through the hush, came the sound of Eddie tapping the soundboard of his guitar as he counted down to the start of the first song. "One . . . two . . . uh one, two, three." The spotlight lit him up like a rocket launch. And when Eddie let the big flattop Gibson sing, it was like he'd closed an electrical circuit. A current surged through the room, charging the crowd. Hair stood on end as Eddie held the guitar tight up under his right arm while leaning left, tilting the head of the guitar just a bit downward. He cocked his head the way he'd seen in a picture of Hank Williams and smiled his way through an up-tempo honky-tonker that brought the crowd to its feet. Megan was the first to stand. She'd seen Eddie a few times with Jimmy, and she liked what she saw.

Eddie sounded better than he ever had. His playing was assured, his voice was strong and clear, and his stage presence was undeniable.

The power of music never ceased to amaze Jimmy. He picked up his camera and squared Eddie in the viewfinder. When Eddie turned and looked to the middle of the room, the light jumped under the brim of his hat and caught his face at the perfect angle. That's when Jimmy noticed Eddie's smile for the first time. It was perfect and winning. Jimmy adjusted the focus and took a series of photos. Click, whirr. Click, whirr. Click, whirr. Jimmy's mind suddenly began spinning like the motor drive of his camera, and after about five shots an idea formed. The last shot in particular—Eddie seeming to look straight into the lens—stuck in Jimmy's mind like a thumbtack. He laid the camera on the table and looked around, measuring the faces in the crowd. They were mesmerized. Eddie owned them. At that moment Jimmy realized what he wanted to write. He grabbed his pen and started scribbling on his notepad.

Megan barely noticed. She was riveted by Eddie's smile and his performance as he worked through his usual set, a perfectly paced roller coaster of ballads, mid-tempo traditional country, and upbeat Texas swingers. He ended his set with an up-tempo country rocker that brought the crowd to its feet and elicited a dozen rebel yells. The stage was thirty feet wide and Eddie used every inch of it.

He was at one end of the stage as he neared the end of the last song. With one hand holding his hat and the other holding his guitar, Eddie started running. He fell to his knees and slid to a stop in the center of the stage, where he leaned back and hit the closing licks. Anyone not already standing shot up. Bathed in the spotlight, Eddie held his arms out to the side and shut his eyes, smiling all the while. He was something to look at, all right, and he got a standing ovation. After a minute, he got to his feet, tipped his hat, and took a bow. "I wanna thank you folks for coming out and having some fun with us here at the Gold Coast Extravaganza."

A woman in the crowd screamed, "I love you, Eddie!"

Eddie smiled. "Why, I love you too, ma'am," he said, tipping his hat again. "I also love everybody in the upstairs office for having me here this week. I really do appreciate it." He winked knowingly at the crowd. "And so does my wife." He got a good laugh with that. "Ya'll have a good night," he said, wrapping things up. "And remember, friends don't let friends gamble at the other casinos." With that, Eddie spun on his boot heel and disappeared behind the curtains. A moment later, the house lights came up and the canned music came over the house speakers.

Megan sat down and popped some fried onion into her mouth. "Wow. I can't believe he doesn't have a record deal." Megan felt she was a fair judge of musical talent. She was, after all, the assistant music director at the radio station in Jackson in addition to being on the air. "That's the best show we've seen him do, don't you think?" After several years in radio, Megan had purged much of her Southern accent. She could call it back in a flash, and she did so regularly in service of some of her radio character voices, but on an everyday basis she spoke with a geographically nonspecific broadcast intonation.

Jimmy nodded, but didn't speak. He was preoccupied, scribbling in his notepad. He was hunched over the table, his hair hanging down, obscuring his face. Megan was about to say something when she felt a hand on her shoulder. "Hey, good-lookin'."

Megan turned and looked up. "Eddie!" She turned her head and offered her cheek, which Eddie kissed in a gentlemanly fashion. "What a great show!"

"Thanks." Eddie spun a chair around and sat in it with his arms resting on the back. "I tell you what, it sure felt good."

Megan put her hand on Eddie's arm. "I just told Jimmy I can't believe you don't have a record deal yet. But I just know it's gonna happen for you. I really believe that."

"I appreciate that, I really do." Eddie scanned the room. "I heard some A&R guy from Nashville's supposed to be down here doing some scouting, but"—he shrugged—"nothing yet."

Jimmy, still lost in his writing, hadn't acknowledged Eddie's arrival. Eddie looked at Megan. "Man, you'd think he might at least look up when a guy kisses his girlfriend and sits down at his table. Hell, I'da already punched somebody." He winked.

Megan smiled and lapsed into the exaggerated Southern Belle character she used on her radio show. "Why Mr. Long, you'd defend my honah with violence?" She fanned her face, then put the back of her hand against her forehead. "I believe I might swoon."

Eddie shook his head in mock disdain. "Miss Megan, I declare, you deserve better than this shabby treatment. Why don't you come live with me?"

"You mean, aside from the fact that you're married?"

"Yeah, aside from that." He nodded toward Jimmy. "What's he doing?"

Megan shrugged. "Don't know. He's been working on it since your first song."

Jimmy suddenly looked up. "And you're not going to be disappointed, either." He extended a hand to Eddie. "Great show."

"Thanks, man."

"And stop hitting on my girlfriend."

"My bad," Eddie said as he tried to get a look at what Jimmy had written. "You're not writing another review, are you? I don't think there's a newspaper left for you to sell it to."

"I think you're right." Jimmy pulled his hair back and smiled devilishly.

Megan reached for the notepad, but Jimmy wouldn't let her have it. "Ah-ah-ah. Not yet." Jimmy folded his hands over the pad and looked at Megan, then at Eddie. "Not five minutes ago I had what I believe you'd call a revelation. Actually I had two."

Eddie held his hands up to testify. "Well then, amen brother! Twice."

"C'mon," Megan said. "Just tell us."

"I finally figured out what I'm going to write," Jimmy said. "My master project."

"Well, don't tell me it's songs," Eddie said. "Songwritin' ain't as easy as you think. I just make it look that way."

Jimmy got serious. "All right, now you have to see this as a long-term project, okay? No telling how long it's going to take." He turned and pointed to Eddie. "That depends on you."

Eddie tipped his hat backwards on his head and threw up his hands. "I give up."

Jimmy opened the spiral notebook and put it on the table for Eddie and Megan to read. There in large block letters were the words THE LONG AND SHORT OF IT: THE EDDIE LONG STORY. "I'm going to write your biography." Jimmy sat back with his hands behind his head. He was beaming.

Eddie broke into a huge, flattered smile. "Damn, son. You serious?" He looked at Megan, then at Jimmy. "I think it's a great idea." He turned to Megan. "What do you think?"

Megan couldn't help but smile. She knew Jimmy was miserable reviewing Little River Band concerts, and she could see how enamored he was of this idea. "I think it's perfect."

"I do see one small problem," Eddie said. "Seein' how nobody knows who the heck I am, why would anybody want to publish my life story?"

Jimmy pointed at Eddie. "Because my second revelation was that you are going to be famous."

"That was your other revelation?"

"Yessir. And who's been following your career from the beginning? Who better to chronicle your development from struggling singer-songwriter to Nashville superstar?"

"I think he's right," Megan said, reaching over to touch Eddie's arm again. "You're too talented not to succeed." She let her hand linger.

Jimmy nodded. "I've seen you, what, thirty, forty times? Something made me keep coming back to see you, right?"

"I thought it was 'cause I kept buying you drinks."

"Didn't hurt, but that's not it," Jimmy said. "I watched the crowd react to you tonight, and it struck me plain as all get out that you have what it takes to make it in the business. Your performance gets better every time I see you. You're good-looking, you're talented, and you're a pro. Look, it's no skin off your nose, right? I'm the one taking the chance. Whaddya say?"

Eddie shrugged. "What the hell."

"I think it's a great idea," Megan repeated, her hand still on Eddie's arm.

"Me too," said Eddie. "Seems like a helluva lot of work, though."

"Hey, if anyone can do it," Megan said, "it's you."

"Thanks." Jimmy appreciated the comment, but he noticed Megan was looking at Eddie when she said it.

* * *

Tammy had inherited the four-poster bed from her grandmother. It was a queen with five wooden slats underneath to support the box spring and mattress. It had had six slats originally, but one got lost in a move about twenty years ago. And now, in a moment Tammy had been looking forward to since Eddie announced his road trip, those old slats were being sorely tested.

Tammy dug her heels into Carl's back and urged him on. "Oh, baby, yes! Find the spot! Find the spot!" She tended to direct the action as much as participate in it. "Right there, baby! Now give it to me!" Carl didn't mind. It was better than trying to guess what she wanted, the way he had to do with his wife. "Rock me, baby! Yes!" Carl was screwing to beat bobtail and thrusting so furiously that he soon worked the slats out of place, causing one side of the box spring and mattress to crash to the ground, leaving the lovers at a precarious angle.

"Whoa!" Carl grabbed the headboard.

"Don't stop!" Tammy hollered. "I'm almost there. Go! Go!" Carl hung on and, after another minute of turbulence, finally delivered the goods. Tammy trembled and jerked and made a noise that sounded like a yodel. "Oh, baby," she cooed afterwards. She let out a sigh and closed her eyes.

For Carl, the guilt always came right after he did. It never showed up in time to keep him from doing wrong, so he always did it, and he always felt bad right after. Carl was lying there at a forty-five-degree angle, fretting about the potential consequences of sleeping with another man's wife, when Tammy nudged him. "Carl, honey, be a sweetheart and fix the bed, would you? I'm gonna get something to eat."

"Bring something back," he said. As long as he was breaking rules, he thought, he might as well go all the way. His own wife didn't allow eating in bed. Carl climbed out of the bed, put on his briefs, and put the slats back in place. A minute later, Tammy came back carrying three cardboard food containers. "Whacha got there?" Carl asked.

Tammy held the boxes up one at a time. "Orange beef, mu shu pork, and shrimp in garlic sauce." She handed the shrimp to Carl.

"The hell'd you get Chinese food?"

"Me and Eddie went to Feng Shang's in Memphis coupla days ago. I always order way too much so I can have leftovers." Tammy climbed in bed and started in on the orange beef.

Carl looked dumbstruck. "You didn't bring no beer?" Tammy didn't respond; the answer seemed too obvious. Carl grunted as he got out of bed. He headed for the kitchen.

"Hey, puddin'?" Tammy called from the bedroom. "Bring me one too, okay?"

Carl gritted his teeth, grabbed two beers, and went back to the bedroom. He climbed back in and started nibbling around the broccoli stems in the shrimp dish. "You know who's working the register today?"

"I think it's Mary Jo, why?"

"No reason, just curious." Carl and Tammy worked together at the Dollar Store. He was in sporting goods. She was in the young women's department. Carl finished off the shrimp, then tilted the box to drink the last of the garlicky juice.

Tammy looked at him, then tapped her chin with a finger. "You got some sauce on you."

Carl wiped his mouth with the sheet, burped, then started in on the mu shu pork. "Hey, lemme have a bite of that orange beef," he said.

Tammy shook her head and jerked the box away. "You didn't share none of yours," she said. "So don't you come sniffin' around mine." Tammy made quick work of the remaining beef, then put the container on the bedside table. While Carl chewed up the bits of pork and egg and green onion, Tammy shut her eyes and started rubbing her temples.

"This is good stuff," Carl said, finishing the mu shu. He glanced at the clock on the dresser and saw that they had about two hours before they had to be at work. Carl drained the rest of his Bud and dropped the can on the floor. He reached over to Tammy. "Hey, you know what? I'm thinking I might want me some seconds, puddin'. Whaddya say?"

"I got a damn headache," Tammy said, pushing his hand away.

Carl gritted his teeth again. If he'd wanted a woman with a damn headache he could've stayed at home. Tammy got up and padded into the bathroom. "I need an aspirin," she said. Carl lay in bed wondering if he ought to make a quick exit or wait and see if Tammy was willing to give it another go after she medicated herself. After a moment he decided to get out of there. He was looking for his pants when he heard a crash in the bathroom. It sounded like Tammy had raked everything off the shelves in the medicine cabinet. "You okay?" He waited a second but Tammy didn't answer. Then he heard an odd gurgling noise. With one leg in his pants, he hopped toward the bathroom to see what had happened.

Just as he reached the door, Tammy staggered toward him, her face frozen in horror. She was spitting pink mucus and she couldn't breathe. She lurched forward, grabbing Carl, nearly pulling him to the floor.

"Holy shit!" Carl had no idea what was happening. He had never seen such terror in anyone's eyes. "The hell's wrong?"

Tammy convulsed and managed to say, "Carl." Then she collapsed. Carl was paralyzed as he watched Tammy's face lapse into a hideous twitching seizure. He thought about giving her mouth-to-mouth, but quickly decided against it. He could tell this wasn't about needing air. And the pink foam gathering around her mouth was damn unappealing. It seemed like he stood there for an hour watching her die, but she actually stopped moving within a couple of minutes. Carl squatted down and felt for a pulse, but there was nothing. She had died all at once. Carl got a terrible feeling in the pit of his stomach. *Fuck! The Chinese food's poisoned! I'm going to die! With my pants half on!* He raced into the bathroom and tried to make himself throw up, but he couldn't do it. After a minute he tried to get a grip on himself and assess his health. Other than being scared sick, he felt fine. *Maybe it was just the orange beef.* He was suddenly glad Tammy had refused to share.

Carl's mind raced as he considered his options. *What the hell do I do now? If I leave her here, someone will eventually find her, and God knows I left plenty of DNA evidence. I shoulda used a damn rubber. Plan B? If I call the cops and tell 'em what happened, Eddie and my wife will find out we was screwing around, but at least I'll be less of a suspect, since suspects don't usually call the cops, do they? Hmmm, that's a plan of last resort. Plan C? What if I dump her body in one of the big lakes? Sardis? Arkabutla? Enid? Hell, there's no time for that, I'd be late getting to work, besides which there's bound to be a hundred people at every lake in the state this time of year. Plan D? What if I make it look like somebody killed her? No, wait, somebody did kill her, right? Or did they? Why the hell is she dead? Wait a minute! Plan E! Best idea yet.* He thought it through the best he could and decided it was the right thing to do, all things considered.

Carl knew he had to act quick. He didn't think the plan would work if Tammy started to get cold. First he ran into the kitchen and put on a pair of bright yellow rubber gloves. They were two sizes too small but they'd prevent the further spread of fingerprints. Next he ran back into the bedroom and grabbed the .22 pistol Tammy kept in the dresser drawer. He stopped for a second to think about everything he'd ever learned from television cop shows, then he put the gun in Tammy's hand, put it to her head, and helped her squeeze the trigger. He looked the other way and got as far away as he could so nothing would splatter on him. Pop! The .22 kicked a little when it fired. Carl was relieved to see it wasn't too messy on his side of Tammy's head.

He left the gun in her hand and watched her for a minute. *Dammit!* He'd waited too long. There was hardly any blood coming from the wound. Without more blood, even the dumbest cop would know she had died before she was shot. Carl decided to give her some CPR to pump some out. Once he'd coaxed some blood onto the floor, he started to wipe his fingerprints off everything he'd touched. He went into the bathroom and put everything back into the medicine cabinet, including the box of Dr. Porter's Headache Powder. He looked at the clock. Thirty minutes before he and Tammy were supposed to be at work. Just one thing left.

Carl took a piece of paper and a pen and wondered where to begin. He had never written a suicide note. What would she say? *Wait a second, I can't write the damn note. Eddie'll know her writing. Quick, Plan B? Uh, got it!* Carl rummaged though drawers until he found some scissors, some glue, and a couple of *People* magazines. Like a frantic kidnapper, he cut letters out of big-print ads and story headers. After a few minutes he took the glue and pasted together the shortest suicide note in Quitman County history. It said, simply, "Depressed." He put Tammy's fingerprints all over it and propped it up against the flower vase on the dresser.

Fifteen minutes till his shift started. Carl made the bed, then ran back to the kitchen, where he grabbed a plastic garbage bag. He gathered the Chinese food to-go boxes and the beer cans, then he stopped and looked around for anything he might have forgotten. It looked good. He put on one of Eddie's baseball caps and snuck out the back door.

*   *   *

Henry Teasdale had political ambitions. They weren't big ones, but they were ambitions nonetheless. The Teasdales had lived in Quitman County for five generations and, over that period, had evolved from a clan of clay-eating peckerwoods to a family of social standing. Henry was well known throughout the county as a successful businessman. He had a controlling interest in a large catfish farm, owned significant tracts of arable land, had some oil and gas holdings, and owned the county's largest retail business, the Dollar Store in Hinchcliff, Mississippi.

Recently, after his district's incumbent was convicted of taking kickbacks from an FBI agent posing as a culvert contractor, Henry had decided the time was right for him to run for a seat on the County Board of Supervisors. With the election still five months away, Henry still spent most of his time managing the Dollar Store. It was the best way to keep his employees from robbing him blind, and it was also the easiest way to campaign. He just roamed the store pressing the flesh and handing out twenty-percent-off coupons to anyone who agreed to vote for him.

Carl had been at work for about an hour when his boss walked into sporting goods. Carl was nervous as a frog on a busy road with a busted jumper but he tried to remain calm. There was no way Mr. Teasdale could know anything, right? Still, Carl was afraid there was something about the way he looked that might give away his terrible secret. He feared Mr. Teasdale could see his heart pounding beneath his polyester vest. Carl knew sleeping with the boss's daughter was against company policy, but, as Carl knew better than anyone, that wasn't the worst of it. *Just relax*, Carl told himself. *Take a deep breath. Speak.* "Hey, Mr. Teasdale, how you doin'?"

"I've felt better," Mr. Teasdale said, "but it cost me more."

"Yes, sir. Me too." Carl fiddled with a display of aluminum baseball bats, trying to look busy and worth having as an employee.

"Carl, you got any idea where that useless daughter of mine's at?"

Carl swallowed hard and acted ignorant. It was the easiest thing he'd done all day. "I thought she was working." He looked over in the direction of women's wear.

"No, she didn't show up for her shift. I called over to the house but got the damn machine." Mr. Teasdale leaned an elbow on the shelf with the catcher's mitts and rubbed at his forehead. "How the hell am I supposed to run a business if my employees don't show up, huh? Tell me that, Carl."

Carl shook his head and shrugged, hoping his anxiety didn't show. "I don't know, Mr. Teasdale. It's not like her to miss a shift."

Henry nodded. "I guess I'll ride over to her place and see what's going on."

"Yes, sir." Carl almost broke down and told his boss he'd been with Tammy just a few hours earlier and that she had died suddenly from a bad serving of orange beef and that in his panic he'd made the whole thing look like a suicide and Lord knows he was sorry. But somehow Carl managed to keep his mouth shut. He knew if he let that cat out of the bag, the rest of the litter would follow. If it was known Carl was present at the time of Tammy's death, the coroner might go poking around in areas that would lead to certain foreign bodily fluids and, what with Eddie being out of town and all, Carl would be in the awkward position of having to give some blood. And that would lead to Carl's losing his wife, his job, and, depending on how jealous a husband Eddie was, possibly his life.

* * *

Henry Teasdale didn't want to believe his tormented eyes, but there she was, lying on the floor, too dead to skin. "Oh honey," he whispered. "Why'd you do it?" It was a terrible sight, the sort of thing no man should have to see, but Henry'd seen it and there was nothing he could change.

Or was there?

You ask anybody in Quitman County and they'd tell you Henry Teasdale was nothing if not practical. Yes, he had emotions and feelings and such, but he had become successful not because he was in touch with his inner child, but because he was a pragmatist. So after the initial shock wore off, he got to thinking about things he could fix. He couldn't fix the fact that Tammy had killed herself and, in so doing, had committed a terrible sin, but he could fix whether it looked that way.

His daughter was dead and he'd have to grieve, but that could wait. God would pass judgment on what Tammy had done, but unless Henry did something about what lay in front of him, every voter in his district would pass their own judgment on Henry and his suitability for the Board of Supervisors. After all, this would be the third Teasdale suicide in fifteen years. The rumors, already bad, would become unbearable. Henry knew he'd never get elected if his opponent started raising the question of insanity in the family gene pool. He had to do something. He decided to make it look like murder.

He went to the kitchen and got the rubber gloves. They were small, but he managed to squeeze his hands into them. He returned to the bedroom and pocketed the suicide note. Next, he wiped the gun clean. Then he wondered what to do with it. Henry decided to take it with him and drop it off the Tallahatchie Bridge. That was fine, but still, something seemed wrong. But what? Oh. Tammy wouldn't have just stood there and let the intruder shoot her. She'd either have something under her fingernails from putting up a fight, or her hands would have been tied or something. Reluctantly, Henry went to the backyard, pulled down the wash line, and returned to the bedroom.

After wrestling Tammy's stiff arms behind her back and tying them, Henry set about making it appear Tammy had walked in on a burglar with anger-control issues. He rifled through all the drawers, throwing stuff on the floor, overturning lamps, taking jewelry. Having achieved the desired walked-in-on-a-burglar effect, Henry picked up the phone and dialed 911.

3

NASHVILLE, TENNESSEE

Whitney Rankin sat in Owen Bradley Park wide-eyed and wondering if he'd come to the right place. He was an unknown songwriter, just arrived in Music City after spending years honing his skills in thankless places. He was sitting at the north end of fabled Music Row, directly across from the original Country Music Hall of Fame. It wasn't there anymore, having moved downtown a year or two ago. Whitney wondered if that was symbolic of anything.

His tight-lipped smile was in conflict with the vague sense that he was in the wrong place at the wrong time, but he wasn't sure where else to go to do what he did. "Damn," he whispered as he looked around. "Now what?"

Whitney knew Owen Bradley was one of the most important producers in the history of country music, having made Patsy Cline and Brenda Lee huge stars by applying to country the songwriting and production techniques of pop music. Depending on your point of view, Owen Bradley was the man who deserved either credit or blame for having paved the way for what became known as the Nashville Sound. Whitney gave him credit. He didn't subscribe to the notion that one type of country music was better than another. They were just different. They were all part of the music's evolution where the worst thing that could happen was stagnation. So it was no wonder to Whitney they'd honored the man with a park of his own, even if the park itself wasn't much to speak of. It was small and unassuming and brought to mind Hal Ketchum's notion about how country music was just three chords and the truth. It consisted of some trees, several pine-straw-lined flower beds, a few concrete benches, and a life-size bronze sculpture of the man himself seated at the piano. It was a nice little patch of calm, Whitney thought.

He was twenty-nine and dressed like a songwriter who'd never had an appointment on Music Row, which was okay since he'd never had an appointment there. The standard dress code up and down the Row was country-club casual and golf-course ready. Every now and then you saw someone wearing a suit and tie or dressed in full country regalia, but not as often as the tourists expected.

At first glance Whitney looked more or less like he belonged. But on closer examination he somehow looked . . . different. He was six foot three and, as his mama used to say, he was so skinny he had to stand in the same place twice to cast a shadow. He wore tight black Wranglers, a black T-shirt with a dark gray vest over it, and a worn pair of black Tony Lama ropers. There was a ragged piece of an old red bandanna tied around his wrist. He had a turquoise stud in one ear and a dangling silver earring in the other. His hair was long and dark and dangerous as it fell from under a black Resistol Lancer with a thin leather lariat hatband with a small red feather in it. He had a dark patch of stubble on his chin but it wasn't enough to spoil his narrow boyish face. It added up to an off-kilter country look that tended to draw queer looks, but, having always been a little different from others, Whitney was used to the stares.

He hopped to his feet to stop a woman who was walking by.

"Excuse me, ma'am." He sounded Southern as fried okra. "I'm sorry to bother you, but could you do me a favor and take my picture?" He handed her a disposable camera. "Over here by the statue? I appreciate it." Whitney was creating a photo chronicle of his journey to wherever it was he was going. The woman took Whitney's picture, then smiled. She saw his guitar case and knew why he was here and what he was up against, especially dressed the way he was. "Thank you, ma'am," he said as she went on her way.

Whitney was alone in the world, but he was all right with that. He figured every good songwriter needed his share of bad fortune. Whitney's mom had died two years ago and his dad had disappeared long before that. He didn't know much about his father. His mom had told him only that he was a good man, but troubled. She had remarried, to a man named J. C. Rankin, who adopted Whitney and gave him a new last name, but that was about all he'd given. He hadn't wasted much gas on being a father to the boy. Whitney was all right with that too; after all, J. C. hadn't fathered him, so it was enough that he'd fed and housed him until he was seventeen. And he'd rarely hit him. You couldn't ask more than that from a stranger, really.

Whitney had grown up with a guitar in his hands, a guitar that his father had left behind. Whitney could play it too. Ever since he was fourteen, he'd been writing songs. He had a suitcase full of them, but, like many songwriters, Whitney had one in particular that was his favorite. He couldn't wait to play it for somebody in Music City. He hoped his mama was looking down, watching him. He wanted to make her proud.

Whitney was sitting on a concrete bench, so uncertain about his future that all he could do was look around and say in a funny way, "Oh boy." He didn't know exactly what to do next, but it was time to do something. So he stood and picked up his guitar case. Just as he about to leave he heard a splash come from behind the tall wooden fence that bordered the south end of the park. Whitney wandered under a magnolia tree and looked for a spot in the fence where he could see through. He wedged the toe of his boot between a couple of slats in the fence and pulled himself up to look over the top. What Whitney saw sent a tingle up his spine. It was the crystal-blue water of a swimming pool in the shape of a great big guitar. He shook his head slowly. "Well, check it out," he said slowly. It even had strings painted on the bottom.

# # #

The Mississippi Highway Patrol did the decent thing, sending a patrolman out of the Gulfport substation to break the news. Eddie was in his hotel room working on a new song when the knock came to his door. "Mr. Long, I'm afraid I've got some bad news."

Eddie blanched when he heard Tammy had been shot. Of all the things he might have imagined the patrolman saying, that his wife had been shot would have been way down on the list. The patrolman reached out to catch him when it looked like Eddie's legs might give way, but he made it to a chair and sat down. "She was shot?" He couldn't believe it.

Eddie canceled the rest of his shows and made the long drive back to Quitman County. The whole way back he thought about what his future held now that Tammy was gone.

It was bleak in the Mississippi Delta when they laid Tammy to rest, overcast, with thunder rolling in the distance. The air was dead still and thick as two dogs' heads.

Eddie did his best to be strong. He walked on one side of Mrs. Teasdale offering support while Henry was on the other. There was a good turnout at the church. The preacher kept it simple and let anyone speak who was of a mind to. Carl sat in the back of the church with his wife and toddler. He kept his mouth shut and felt guilty about everything he'd ever done.

After the funeral, family and friends gathered at the Teasdales' home just outside of Hinchcliff. Everyone agreed, it smelled good up inside that house. The kitchen was thick with green bean casseroles and fried chickens. And the pies! The flakiest crusts, the best fruit and nuts, butter, lard, and shortening. Pure comfort for the mournful in a ton of saturated fat.

A group of women gathered around a vat of Miss Lexie's pineapple casserole, a unique combination of sweet tropical fruit, sharp cheese, butter, sugar, and a pile of Ritz cracker crumbs. They ate the entire thing straight from the dish.

Another group of women stood to the side of the room making derisive comments about the diameter of certain thighs over at the casserole. They also talked about how great Eddie looked in his all-black suit. They knew it was tacky, what with the dirt still being fresh on top of his dead wife and all, but they couldn't help themselves, and they meant it in the nicest possible way. He really did look good in his grief.

Carl was there, still with his wife and toddler. He had surrendered to what he assumed would be a lifetime of guilt and fear of exposure. He was drinking bourbon by the tumbler and weeping uncontrollably. The sheriff was there too. He had come as a friend to express his condolences, but at one point late in the afternoon Mr. Teasdale pulled him aside. "What can you tell me about the investigation?"

"Now, Henry, I'm not here on business," the sheriff said. "But if you insist, I'll tell you what I can."

Henry looked him in the eyes. "Let's step outside."

They went to the back porch and lit cigarettes. "Henry," the sheriff said, "I gotta tell you, this is got me stumped. I got evidence indicating both murder and suicide." He lowered his voice. "And I don't mean to be disrespectful, but not too long before she died, Tammy had sexual relations with someone other than Eddie."

"What're you saying?"

"All I'm saying is this thing ain't on all fours."

"It sure ain't." Henry looked away, ashamed that his daughter had sinned by cheating on her husband and had compounded the matter by taking her own life.

"I can't make head nor tails out of it, Henry." He dropped his cigarette on the ground, stamped it out. "Now, the medical examiner hasn't finished all the toxicology tests, but I tend to think the simplest explanation's the best, and that gunshot wound in the head's as simple as it gets. I'll know more in a few days, but for now I'm telling the district attorney it's an open murder investigation. We got no useful fingerprints and no weapon." He hesitated a moment, then looked at Henry. "Did Tammy own a gun?"

Mr. Teasdale nodded as he flicked his cigarette away. "She had a twenty-two. A pistol."

"Hmm, 'at's the caliber what killed her, but there weren't no gun at the house. That's what got me thinking it was a murder. You know, like someone broke in the house and found the gun and then Tammy walked in on him . . ." He rolled his shoulders to say "you know the rest."

Mr. Teasdale looked off at the horizon and squinted. "You said you got evidence of suicide too. What's that about?" Henry thought he'd cleaned things up pretty good. He didn't like hearing the word "evidence."

The sheriff folded his arms and looked to the ground for a moment. "Well, like I said, I was thinking it looked like an open-shut murder case right up until we found some clippings from a magazine in the trash can, then we found the magazine with letters cut out of it, you know, like a ransom-note situation? Once we figured out what letters were missing, we pieced 'em together and came up with some options, but do you know the only one that made any sense was the word 'depressed'? That's what got me thinking about suicide."

"Is that right?"

"Henry, I know it's happened before in your family, and I just want you to know that I'm not saying it was suicide because, well, like I said, this one ain't on all fours. I don't wanna be calling it something it's not, especially if it's gonna hurt your family."

"I appreciate that."

"So I'm trying to figure out why somebody would cut out a bunch of letters from a magazine to spell the word 'depressed' but then not do anything with it. Know what I mean? On the other hand, if Tammy cut out the letters for a suicide note and then killed herself, where's the note and where's the gun? I suppose an intruder could have stumbled into the house after she killed herself, if that's what happened, and he'da taken the gun, but why take the note, assuming there was a note, you know?" The sheriff shook his head. "Like I said, it's got me stumped."

"That's a mess all right. Just don't make much sense any way you look at it."

"No. It don't." The sheriff turned to go back inside. "I'll let you know soon as we find anything out." He stopped and put his hand on Mr. Teasdale's shoulder. "Henry, I'm real sorry about all this. Let me know if there's anything I can do."

Henry nodded, said thanks, and went back inside.

*   *   *

A few hours later, when most of the mourners were either gone or drunk, Eddie and Henry were off to the side of the living room having a heart-to-heart. "Son, I'm hurting pretty bad," Henry said, "and I suspect you feel the same or worse. I wish there was something I could say, but I can't improve on anything the preacher said, and he didn't do much to make me feel any better."

"I appreciate that, Mr. Teasdale. I'm real sorry I was gone. Maybe if I'da been here, none of this would've happened."

Henry put his arm around Eddie. "Don't do that to yourself, son. If you'da been here, you might be dead too." In truth he was thinking that if Eddie had been here, then whoever it was Tammy had been sleeping with might be the one who was dead, but Henry wasn't going to tell Eddie about what the sheriff had said in that regard. Henry reckoned Eddie'd been hurt enough.

Across the room, Carl's wife was offering her condolences to Mrs. Teasdale. Carl had finally stopped crying, but he was clinging like a vine to the fear that he would be exposed at any minute. He stood at his wife's side with puffy red eyes and a nervous twitch.

Eddie looked at the floor, then at his father-in-law. "Mr. Teasdale, I've been giving it some thought and I decided I can't stay here." Henry looked like he might have expected this. "I appreciate your job offer, but you know I've been wanting to get my music career going, and, well, maybe this is God's way of telling me it's time to move to Nashville and get serious about it."

Mr. Teasdale nodded. "Maybe you're right, son. Maybe you're right."

* * *

Blacks were to Nashville what Charley Pride and Stoney Edwards were to country music—rare, but there was no sense denying they existed. The geographic center for Nashville's black population revolved around a series of presidentially named roads—Van Buren, Garfield, Monroe, Harrison. As was the case in many Southern cities, one of Nashville's favorite restaurants was located in this area, on a rough cut of asphalt just off Jefferson.

The sign out front said Estella's Shrimp Joint, but to hear the locals say it, you'd have thought it was Estella's Swimp Jernt. Estella's had been open for thirty years, serving the best fried shrimp plate in the state of Tennessee, mostly after midnight. Estella's was the place to go in Nashville when everybody else stopped serving. It was a beacon in the darkness for the city's nightcrawlers—black and white alike—and for everybody who worked the late shift and who wanted a drink after the statutes said it was illegal to get one. In fact, after hours on any given night of the week you were likely to find at least one state legislator washing down his fried shrimp with a pint of bourbon.

Estella's was two deluxe mobile homes pushed together side by side on a raised foundation. The interior was worn and friendly with red Naugahyde booths, four-top tables, and a long service counter with soda-shop seats. The floor was tan linoleum flecked with red. Pale blue shag carpet covered the lower half of the walls. Above that was a sort of brown fabric-corded wallpaper which gave the place terrific acoustics. In the corner by the door was a jukebox with an old hand-lettered sign reading "Three selections for fity cent." Estella's was the only place in town where you were liable to hear La Vern Baker, Ivory Joe Hunter, Solomon Burke, or King Curtis. The place was an R&B clearing in a pedal steel jungle.

Otis and Estella Frazier were the sole proprietors. Estella was somewhere in her sixties; she wouldn't say exactly where. She had mostly gray hair and was a little short for her 180 pounds. A few years ago Estella had had a heart attack, "but it was jes' a small one," she said. After a battery of tests, her doctor told her she had to stop smoking, stop eating fried food three times a day, and start getting some exercise. Estella swore she would change her ways, but soon decided the doctor was overreacting.

Estella had long known she'd never be rich, so she decided she'd be comfortable instead. She wore loose-fitting blue jeans and a baggy old pullover shirt with long sleeves, always covered with a knee-length white apron. A pair of reading glasses dangled from a string around her neck, but she used them only while at the cash register. Estella took orders, ran the register, and went table to table chatting up the clientele no matter if they wore cornrows or cowboy hats. Everybody loved Estella.

Otis was a couple of years older than Estella and built just the opposite. He was a rumor of a guy with brown eyes that understood your problems. He had a silvery mustache streaked with black that curled sweetly at the corners of his mouth. A tuft of gray sprouted just under his lower lip. He wore a black leather beret and open-collared shirts, and his expression—a sort of suppressed smile—made it look like he was waiting for you to get the joke. But Otis's calm and amiable face belied a troubled past.

* * *

It was two-thirty on a Saturday morning and the place was about three-quarters full. Estella snapped a scrap of paper into one of the clothespins hanging in the window between the service counter and the kitchen. "Three swimp plates and a cheeseburger," she said, ringing the little bell.

Otis looked up from the deep fryer to glance at the order. "Three swimps and a cheese." He tossed a meat patty on the grill, then pulled the shrimp from the fridge, where they were soaking in milk and paprika. He drained half a pound and began to dredge them in the flour.

"Otis," Estella said with a gesture. "Who's that over at fourteen?" Otis couldn't see table fourteen through the service window, so he went to the kitchen door and looked out. Estella met him there, wiping her hands on her apron. "He's steady been actin' funny since I carried him that gin," she said.

Otis shook his head a little, shrugged. "Never seen him." He went back to the kitchen knowing that if the guy was up to no good, Estella was the better one to deal with it. Otis lowered the basket of shrimp into the deep fat fryer. Greasy steam escaped into the vent.

Otis came from Clarksdale, Mississippi. He had discovered early that he had a gift. At nine, he was soloist in his gospel choir, and by the time he was in his late teens, he had a popular late-night radio show on which he played "race" records and occasionally sang a song or two, accompanying himself on the guitar. His show ended at two in the morning when the station went off the air. After that Otis and some friends used the production room as a recording studio. Otis sent some of the tapes to a Memphis-based record label and eventually signed a recording contract and got a manager by the name of Bill Herron.

Otis's first record, "Lookin' for Ruby," was on the R&B charts for twenty-two weeks, peaking at number sixteen. It also crossed over to the pop charts, hitting number thirty-nine. His second record, "Don't Let Me Go," soared to number two R&B, crossing over to become a number twelve pop hit. Otis looked to be on his way to the top. But, as Otis was quick to point out, things ain't always what they appear to be.

Over the next couple of years, a good deal of money passed through his hands on its way to buying cars, whiskey, and women. Money problems followed, as they tend to, and Otis was soon in need of another hit if he was going to maintain his lifestyle. But his next two records stiffed and Bill Herron dumped him and screwed him on a fair amount of royalties. Otis started drinking and soon ran afoul of the law. But all of that was a long time ago and Otis chose not to dwell on it.

Still, Otis was thinking back on that night in Memphis when suddenly there was a commotion out in the main room. He heard a table overturn, plates and flatware crashing onto linoleum. Otis craned his head out the service window just as Estella yelled, "Somebody better call a amalance!" It sounded more like a threat than a plea for help. Otis watched Estella charge out the door with the small cast-iron skillet she kept behind the cash register. She was quick for her size.

Otis shook his head as several customers gave chase. Otis just went back to his deep fryer. No point in letting the swimps burn. Besides, it always happened like this. Somebody would try to skip out on their tab, Estella would chase 'em down, several customers would pull Estella off the customer before she did too much damage with her skillet. She'd get the money she was owed and they'd all go back inside laughing while Estella carried on about how that fool was lucky they pulled her off before she got a good swing at him.

Tonight, Estella had a man pinned against his car. She had the skillet raised over her head when a young black man and an older white guy in a cowboy hat caught up with them. The cowboy hat restrained Estella while the young black man kept the gin drinker from going anywhere. Estella was hollering, "Lemme go! He's stealin' from me and he's got it comin'!" The cowboy hat was snickering. He told Estella to calm down. "Calm down nothin'! This nigga's gonna find out what it means to—"

"Hey, Estella," a man called out from behind the crowd. "How you doin'?" The man asked it like he was passing her on the sidewalk on a Sunday afternoon. The crowd parted as a tall man in a tuxedo walked to the center of attention. Franklin Peavy was a white man, but a dark one. With his chestnut complexion and his black-dyed hair done up in a militant bouffant style, Franklin looked like the demon child of Conway Twitty and Johnny Mathis.

Estella knew who it was before she saw him. "I'm good, Mr. Peavy, how're you?"

"I'm fine, Estella." Franklin reached up and removed his clip-on bow tie.

"You sure looking fine," she said. "Where you been all dressed up, another one of them awards ceremonies?"

"Yeah, the Big Pick Awards were tonight. One of my clients was nominated. Didn't win, though."

"Thass too bad," Estella said. "Maybe next time."

"That's right, there's always next time," Franklin said. "So. What's going on here?"

Estella struggled against the man holding her. "This fool tried to run out on his bill," she said, nodding at the fool in question.

The gin drinker shook his head, wide-eyed as a stereotype. "I was fixin' to get my wallet out of my ride," he said, gesturing at the old Chrysler. "I was gonna pay."

Estella pulled away from the cowboy hat and lunged at the gin drinker. "You lyin'!" She landed her skillet against the man's ribs. Everybody heard the cracking sound. The cowboy hat struggled to keep from laughing as he grabbed Estella and pulled her back.

"Estella, you're gonna end up like Otis, you're not careful," Franklin said.

"We's both justified." Estella couldn't have looked any angrier.

"Court might not see it that way." Franklin reached over and pulled a wallet from the gin drinker's pocket. Both of them feigned surprise. "What's this?" He handed the wallet to Estella.

"You got no bidness reachin' in my pocket! You got a damn search warren or somethin'? I'll have you rested for civil rights vilations."

Franklin Peavy smiled at the man. It wasn't a friendly smile. Franklin's white teeth stood out like little square Klansmen in the context of his nut-brown face. "Got any witnesses?"

"Everybody here's a witness," the man insisted.

Franklin looked around at the crowd. "Anybody see what happened?"

"I didn't see nothing," the young black man testified.

"I saw this man run off without paying his bill," the cowboy hat added.

"He attacked Miss Estella, but she defended herself real good," a woman in the back of the crowd said.

"This a frame-up!" The gin drinker pointed a greasy finger at Franklin Peavy.

"That's gonna be hard to prove in Nashville-Davidson County," Franklin said, leaning close to the man. "I should know, I'm a lawyer."

"He's a good one too," Estella said.

This was true, as far as it went. But Franklin Peavy was actually a partner in a well-known artist management firm, so his practice was confined almost exclusively to music industry contracts. He hadn't been in a criminal court since handling that matter for Estella's husband a few decades ago. But there was no need to explain any of that to the gin drinker, so Franklin just turned to Estella and asked if she had got the money she was owed.

"Sho' did, and a good tip too." Estella handed the wallet back to Franklin, who stuck it back in the gin drinker's pocket. Franklin took the skillet from Estella, then put his arm around her shoulders and led her back toward the club. "Estella, I think I need a plate of your shrimp and a little bit of personality."

"What kind you want, Mr. Peavy?

"Scotch'll be fine."

* * *

Two days after seeing Eddie in Biloxi, Jimmy dropped by the radio station where Megan worked. While she finished her shift, he sat in the newsroom reading stories as they came over the AP wire. "The twenty-four-year-old daughter of Delta businessman Henry Teasdale was found dead in her home in Quitman County," one story opened. At first it caught Jimmy's eye because of the tender age of the deceased. The name Teasdale didn't mean anything to him, but he was curious about the death, since most twenty-four-year-olds found dead in their homes have died of something more interesting than old age. Jimmy was disappointed to find the cause of death was still under investigation, but he continued reading until he got to the part that said, "She was the wife of popular local entertainer Eddie Long."

"Oh my God." Jimmy felt an empty, sinking sensation. He read the story again. It was awful. He tried to imagine how he'd feel if Megan died. It sickened him. But then something happened. The sick, sinking feeling was replaced by something more pleasant, which bothered Jimmy somewhat. Yes, he felt bad about what had happened, but what could he do? It wasn't his fault. It was a

tragedy, sure, but the fact remained that Tammy's death was a blessing in disguise if you happened to be writing Tammy's husband's
biography.

Jimmy waited until Megan finished her shift before telling her
what had happened. She took the news with slack-jawed shock.
They debated whether they should attend the funeral. Megan
wanted to go, she said, to see Eddie and to offer condolences.
Jimmy argued they'd be strangers intruding on a private family
event, since he knew Eddie primarily on a professional basis. In the
end it was a moot point, as Megan had a shift change at the radio station and had to work. The day of the funeral came and went. Megan
sent flowers and a card. Jimmy called to convey his condolences.

*   *   *

A week later, Jimmy started work on a magazine article he'd been
hired to write. He also started to worry about his relationship with
Megan. There was something about the way she had looked at
Eddie that night in Biloxi that left Jimmy insecure. He wanted to
talk to someone about his feelings, so he turned to the King and
asked his advice.

Elvis sneered at Jimmy as if to say he never had any problems
with women. Elvis was wearing his white high-collared Eisenhower
jacket, all spangled with sequins and glitter. His guitar strap was a
bandoleer draped across his chest. His right hand pulled the microphone close. His eyes smoldered and stared straight into Jimmy's.
Elvis would be this way forever, or at least as long as Jimmy kept the
plastic statue glued atop his computer monitor. It was a piece of
kitsch he'd bought at Graceland while doing research for a magazine
article. Elvis brought a little atmosphere to Jimmy's office but he
didn't offer any solutions for Jimmy's problems.

Perhaps it was just that Megan had been captivated by Eddie's
performance that night. God knew he was good-looking. And standing onstage in the spotlight with that beautiful guitar and that damn

smile of his, well, Jimmy couldn't compete with that. It made him wonder if he really had a chance with Megan. Writers weren't sexy the way musicians were, especially unknown writers. No one wanted to watch a writer perform his craft, since it pretty much looked like typing. But girls did like a handsome man with a guitar. For that matter, they seemed to like any sort of man with one. Even Keith Richards had groupies, for Christ's sake.

Jimmy sneered back at Elvis. Maybe he wasn't giving Megan the sort of attention she deserved. That was probably it. It was a simple problem with a simple solution. He made a note to take Megan flowers the next time he saw her. With that, he returned his attention to the article he was writing. It was a piece on the Mississippi Delta Fried Catfish Blues Festival. He'd finished a first draft, about fifteen hundred words. Now all he had to do was cut a third of it. He stared at the screen for ten minutes, but he couldn't concentrate. Dammit. He had the distinct feeling, an instinct really, that the problem with Megan wasn't going to be solved with flowers. He started to wonder if Megan was thinking about him or Eddie. He started to replay the Biloxi scene in his head. Was she being polite to Eddie because he had just finished a show or was it more than that?

The next thing Jimmy knew he was dialing her work number. He got voice mail and thought about hanging up, but then he made the mistake of saying, "Hi, it's me." Then he froze, couldn't think of what to say. *Try to sound relaxed,* he thought, *like none of this matters, like you could take her or leave her.* "Uh, you know, I've been wondering if you . . ." Jimmy stopped. He couldn't believe it. He'd almost asked if she'd been thinking about Eddie. "Uh, this is going to sound weird, and maybe I shouldn't leave this, but I was wondering, the other night at the casino, was it just me or, I guess what I'm asking is if you're more interested in, well, oh, hell, I never should have started this. Forget you heard this. Is there a button to erase this shit? Uh, call me." He hung up. He felt like such an idiot.

■ ■ ■

When the toxicology reports came back, the sheriff called Henry Teasdale and Eddie. He asked them to come down to the jail. They sat in the sheriff's office. Eddie looked like he was still in shock. He had the dazed countenance of a lottery winner who didn't think he deserved to win. He responded to questions with nods and shrugs and an occasional "yeah" or "I don't think so." Henry shortstopped most of the questions, thinking there was no reason for his cuckold son-in-law to go through more than he already had. But there were some questions Eddie had to answer, like whether he knew Tammy was having an affair.

Eddie looked up, wounded and confused. "No, sir. I didn't." His voice was small and distant. He still couldn't believe things had ended the way they had.

"Well, I'm sorry to be the one to tell you, but we know for a fact she was. In fact, she'd been with someone the day she died." He looked down at his hands folded on his desk. "Now if we knew who she was seein', we could compel a blood test and that might help us clear some things up, but if you don't know who it was . . ."

Eddie shook his head slowly. "I didn't know." He continued staring straight ahead, remaining expressionless even as the sheriff explained that Tammy had died of poisoning and that she'd been shot after she was already dead. Eddie didn't react other than to blink a few times. The sheriff turned to Henry and asked if he had anything to add to his previous story. Henry shook his head, ashamed of what all he'd done.

"All right, Henry, I understand," the sheriff said. "Here's what I think happened based on the facts I got. You stop me if I get something wrong." Henry just looked at the floor and nodded. "You went looking for Tammy, just like you said. When you got to the house you found she'd killed herself with the poison and you found the note. You couldn't stand the thought of your family's reputation suffering further, so you took the gun, made it look like a murder, and then you got rid of the evidence, including the note. Is that pretty much it?"

Henry nodded even though it wasn't the truth. It was close enough and he just wanted this to be over with. He said he was sorry.

All of this was news to Eddie. Up until now, he'd thought the intruder story was the truth. He'd thought someone had shot her. He hadn't known anything about the affair or a suicide note or that his father-in-law had tampered with evidence in the hopes of protecting the family name, or that Tammy had really died from the poison. It was such an incredible set of facts Eddie didn't know what to think, so he just remained silent.

"My guess," the sheriff said, "and it's just a guess, you understand, but my guess is that Tammy was feeling guilty about the affair she'd been having. Since Eddie was out of town, this fella had come over and they'd . . . well, you know . . . and afterwards, after this fella left, the guilt just got to her and she took the poison." He paused a moment. "I've seen it before."

Henry looked up, squinting as if he had a new theory. "Maybe this fella she'd been seein', maybe he's the one who poisoned her and then made the note."

The sheriff shook his head. "Well, Henry, I suppose the suicide note—if that's what it was—it mighta been intended to mislead investigators, but since we don't have it we can't say for sure, can we?" He looked Henry in the eyes. "Do you have it? It might help us answer some questions."

Henry shifted in his seat and looked out the window. "It's gone."

"Okay." The sheriff was patient, as if he was involved in a negotiation with a child. "I guess I expected that." The sheriff steepled his fingers and looked from Henry to Eddie. "If it helps any, the medical examiner said she died quick." Eddie looked up at the sheriff, but didn't speak. "Now, I considered some other possibilities, but they just ain't flush with the facts."

"Like what?" Henry asked.

"Well, like you said, it's possible her lover gave her the poison and then shot her. But why would he shoot her if she was dead already, which she was?"

"Unless he thought the poison hadn't killed her."

"Well, yeah, but that still leaves me wondering about the letters cut out of the magazine. Why would she write a note? Did it say 'Depressed,' Henry?" Henry nodded, confirming the note's existence. " 'Course it's possible there was something more sordid going on, like if she was having some sort of affair with two men or a man and another woman, but if we go down that path, well, that's a can of worms I don't wanna open," the sheriff said. "About all I know for sure is that poison was in her before the bullet was and, according to the medical examiner, if she took this poison, she wouldn'a been able to shoot herself. Of course, somebody coulda slipped her the poison, but there'd be no reason to shoot her afterwards." The sheriff held his hands up. "I can't make sense outta this except for the way I said."

"I could see that," Henry said.

"I'm real sorry to have to tell you this, Henry, but I'm gonna write it up as a suicide."

"Well, now, wait a second."

"I've got to, Henry. I'm real sorry, but without further evidence, I don't have a better choice. We got no third-party fingerprints, otherwise we might be able to find out who she was seein' and then we might be able to compel a blood sample, but without that note or the gun—" The sheriff tilted his head slightly. "You don't have the gun, do you, Henry?"

Henry shook his head again. "It's gone too."

The sheriff let out a long breath. "Without that, I'm stuck," the sheriff said. "It's either a suicide or I have to open up a murder investigation that I already know don't go anywhere. And then I'd have to drag you into it for tampering with evidence and such, and I don't wanna do that, Henry. I think this other's the best way." He stood and walked Eddie and Henry to the door.

"I understand," Henry said. "I'm sorry I did what I did, but . . ."

"I know, and I can't say as I blame you." The sheriff put his hand on the doorknob, then stopped and looked at Henry. "Unless you got anything to add, I'm closing the case."

Henry shook his head.

"All right then," the sheriff said. He opened the door.

Henry started out of the room, but Eddie just stood there, silent, staring at the floor. "Eddie?" Henry said quietly as he touched his son-in-law's shoulder. "Eddie, let's go. It's over."

With that, Eddie looked up and said, "Good."

4

For the most part, Nashville's fabled Music Row consisted of a
three-quarter-mile stretch of two unassuming one-way streets
running parallel to each other. 16th Avenue ran one way north
while 17th Avenue ran one way south. Looking north from the south
end of either avenue, one would never guess the business resulting
in ninety percent of the country music consumed in the world was
conducted in this generally sleepy mile and a half of road, a stone's
throw from Vanderbilt University. But such was the case.

Many of the publishing companies, recording studios, law firms,
and record companies were quartered in the houses and other simple buildings that fronted on the magnolia-lined streets. But of
course not everyone worked out of these quaint dwellings.

There were several large structures of courageous architectural
design on Music Row, primarily at the north end. When the country
music industry hit it big and the money started pouring in, the
entertainment conglomerates began building on Music Row. When
they did, it appeared they were not hindered by any covenants,
codes, or restrictions in terms of architectural styles or the unity

thereof. For example, the Gaylord Entertainment building looked like something out of a 1950s science fiction movie. On the other hand, Reba's corporate headquarters, just up the street, offered a more modern design, almost churchlike in its motif, while the MCA building, just off the Row, presented a facade reminiscent of a Seattle Brew Pub or an enlarged Ray-O-Vac battery.

The largest of all the structures on Music Row belonged to the two main performance rights organizations. The ASCAP and BMI buildings were so immense as to make songwriters and publishers wonder if they were getting all the money they were owed.

Somewhere on 16th Avenue, not far from Sony Music headquarters, was a two-story house that had been converted for business purposes into Herron & Peavy Management, an artist management firm. Downstairs was the reception area and all the administrative functions. The upstairs featured two large offices with views onto Music Row.

One of the offices contained a small legal library, some fine art, and a beautiful maple desk and credenza on which sat the most up-to-date computer equipment available at any given time. This was the office of Franklin Peavy, Esquire and technophile. Franklin was a serious over-clocker with a Celeron Socket 370 super-heatsink fan combo for keeping his gear cool. His CPU always had the most memory, fastest processor, biggest Zip drives, and latest video and audio cards on the market. He had a wireless mouse, a mounted digital camera for video e-mail, a thirty-six-inch monitor, and every other cutting-edge peripheral available. "Wireless application protocol connects me to the universe" was his motto.

The second office consisted of three walls covered with framed platinum records, gold CDs, and cassettes of artists the firm represented. There were photos of the artists accepting awards, blown-up charts from *Billboard,* and racks of compact discs. It was in this office that Big Bill Herron, co-owner of Herron & Peavy, sat at his desk flipping urgently through a paper. It was the new issue of

Nashville Scene—the one with thc annual list of Nashville's Power 100. Big Bill needed to know where he stood among "The Most Important People in Country Music."

Big Bill was in his mid-sixties and liked to joke that he was suffering from biscuit poisoning. He wasn't quite five eight, 220 pounds, but he was close. His gut was the first thing you noticed after you stopped staring at his spectacularly round head. It was a fleshy beach ball. In fact, all of Big Bill's features were so unusually bulbous that many people in the business referred to him as Tennessee Ernie Borgnine.

"Goddammitall!" Big Bill threw the magazine on the floor, mad as a pig on ice with his tail froze in. "I don't believe it! That can't be right." He snatched the magazine up off the floor and turned back to his listing. Sure as God made little green apples, he was number ninety-nine. It was a comedown, and a bad one. Less than ten years ago, Bill had been number seven, and now he was number ninety-nine? "Well shitgoddammitall!"

Like many people in the business end of the music industry, Bill had started out as an artist. But it quickly became clear he was better riding gain on the microphone than singing into it. Over the years he established himself as successful producer as well as an artist manager. He had a good ear for a song, and he had hooked up with a good attorney, Franklin Peavy, to form a business exploiting their respective talents as well as the talents of others.

That wasn't to say Big Bill robbed his clients blind. You didn't stay in business long if all your clients went broke. You had to be careful how and where you got that lagniappe. You had to know the intricacies of publishing, recording, performance, and merchandising contracts. You needed to know what songs were hits and which ones were filler and who was willing to give up some of their publishing just to get recorded. You also had to know when to give up some of your own points and to whom. These were the things Bill and his partner knew as well as anyone. Given that, Big Bill wondered why he was so close to being off the damn list.

Big Bill knew the music industry was voracious. It chewed up and spit out talent as well as those who managed and produced it. The machine had to be fed. And with fresh meat arriving every day, there was always someone to feed into the teeth. But Big Bill was used to doing the chewing. He wasn't used to being the meat.

Once a powerful and successful management firm, Herron & Peavy was now just getting by. They blamed it on the current state of country music. After a huge surge in popularity in the 1990s, which had translated into record-breaking sales and staggering income for more than a few, the industry had gone into a slump. In fact, if you believed all the whining on Music Row, you'd have thought everyone in the business was losing money. Still, Herron & Peavy had a marginal stable of artists and songwriters, and there was a steady trickle of old producing and publishing money coming in. But Big Bill needed more, and being dropped to ninety-nine on the Power 100 wasn't going to help.

Bill was his own worst enemy, financially speaking. His accountant liked to say Bill's spending habits were out of line with his income. He maintained a ten-thousand-square-foot home in Belle Meade, complete with a half-million-dollar recording studio, which, unlike every major studio in town, didn't have a computer or a piece of digital equipment in it. Big Bill was dangerously devoted to analog technology, arguing that it gave a warmer sound than the crisp, isolated 0's and 1's of binary sound reproduction.

Big Bill also wore tailor-made clothes. Not that he was a connoisseur. He was just trying to compensate for his looks. As someone once said of him, "Big Bill was born ugly and had a bad setback." He also threw his money at car dealers. He figured if it was true that one was a lot more handsome with a C-note in his pocket, then imagine how good-looking he must be when he pulled up to the valet in one of his Mercedeses, or his decked-out Excursion, the largest model of compensation made by the Ford Motor Company. And as if the car payments weren't enough, Big Bill was sending alimony checks to three ex-wives along with child support for six children and the lawyers they rode in on. Things had gotten so bad lately that Bill had been forced to sell his house in Aspen. Despite his six-figure income, Big Bill Herron was, as they say, in a bad row of stumps.

*   *   *

It was noon on a Thursday when Bill's partner appeared in the doorway. Franklin was wearing his usual office attire: black mock turtleneck, sports coat, dark slacks. He was a graduate of Vanderbilt Law School and a good attorney, but more and more he'd been thinking what he really wanted to do was produce. Unlike Big Bill, Franklin was enamored of digital studio technology, especially the computerized systems by Alesis, Tascam, and Fostex. But, like everyone else in the business, Franklin above all favored Pro Tools by Digidesign, considered by many to be the ultimate system for digital audio production.

Franklin looked up from the sheaf of phone messages in his hand. He could see Bill was irritated, and he knew why. "I see you managed to hang on to the hind tit of that list," he said in his Southern gentry lilt. Franklin had grown to hate Big Bill more than he could say. There were a lot of reasons for the hostility, but what chapped Franklin's ass the worst was how Big Bill got all the glory and Franklin just dotted the *i*'s and crossed the *t*'s. Of course, Bill hated Franklin too. The two of them would rather not have to work together one more day, but since the names Herron and Peavy were worth a far sight more together than either name by itself and since they both felt they were too old to go out and start from scratch, they stuck together like a hateful old married couple afraid of being alone.

Big Bill tapped the face of his thin gold watch. "We open too early for you today?" His voice had the twangy stress of a mean good old boy.

"I was out late," Franklin said, returning his attention to the phone messages. "Went to Estella's after the awards, kept her from killing a man, had a few drinks."

"That's very touching. I'm happy for you both." Bill held up the magazine. "Now what the hell we gonna do about this?"

Franklin shook his head in contempt. "Nothing to do. The magazine's out, you're on the list, stop your whining." Franklin walked away leaving Bill to stew about his decline in Music City's power structure. One of the phone messages triggered a thought, and Franklin pulled his digital recorder from his pocket. "Reminder. Call Ken at Swerdlow, Florence to discuss controlled composition clause."

As soon as Franklin turned his back, Bill flipped him the bird, mouthing the words *Stop your whining*. He stood, went to the door of his office, and slammed it. Bill turned to look at the wall of gold records he had produced and wondered how and when things had gone so wrong. When Bill came into the music business all you had needed was a microphone, a room with padded walls, a two-track reel-to-reel, and somebody who could sing and play guitar. Now everything was 24-bit, integrated digital recording, editing, processing, and mixing systems. Big Bill had seen things go from 45s to LPs to eight-tracks to cassettes to CDs. And now the compact disc was about to be replaced by something called a flash memory device. Then there was something called music streaming and a computer file compression code called MP3 and Napster. What the hell was that all about?

Before long, record company executives and artist managers were going to be out of the loop entirely and the damn artists would be in control of everything. This was not the kind of world in which Big Bill was equipped to live. One minute he was at the top of the charts, the next he was an eight-track tape in a digital download world. It wasn't supposed to end this way, he thought. He just wanted to get across the finish line with some dough in his pocket, but he'd gotten lazy and fallen behind. He looked again at *Nashville Scene* and knew he couldn't let it end like this. He had to find somebody to help get him out of this mess.

*   *   *

Two days after the funeral, Eddie was still in an emotionally blunted state. He packed his car and headed to Nashville. He got a motel room his first night there. The next day he found a one-bedroom unit at the Country Squire Manor Apartments complex, a sprawling series of cheaply constructed apartments offering three floor plans. Eddie took apartment 9, the smallest available. He signed the documents and paid his deposit. He moved his stuff in and drew the curtains. Five days later, Eddie was still inside with the curtains drawn. He hadn't arranged for phone service or cable. He had a pizza or two delivered, but otherwise he was a recluse. The only way his neighbors could tell he was there was the sound of his guitar.

Eddie was troubled. In his mind everything had gone to pieces. Nothing made sense. His emotions were all over the road, like George Jones behind the wheel of a lawn mower on his way back from the liquor store. He felt abandoned, cheated, guilty, violated, confused, remorseful, anxious, and saved, all at once. Eddie didn't know how to deal with the emotional chaos, except with his guitar. He was scared half to death and he knew he had to find words for his confusion or it would consume him. But words wouldn't be enough; the emotional turbulence had to be set to music. The dissonance in his mind had to be translated into melody. Minor chords seemed inevitable.

Eddie couldn't sleep more than an hour at a time. When he did, he dreamed of Tammy, twisted and choked by the poison. The shot to the head would jar him awake and he'd pick up the guitar and try to pry the thing out from inside him.

By day five, Eddie was in the grip of a powerful force and he knew what it was. He just hoped he could survive it. He wondered if this was what songwriters suffered every time they wrote a great song. Eddie remembered an interview of a writer whose work he admired. She said, "A lot of us have good songs inside. The trick lies in getting one to come out. Every time I manage to get one out, I'm immediately struck by the terror that I'll never be able to do it again. Or worse, that I will."

Late on the fifth night, the song poured out of Eddie like hot oil. The words, the melody, the lonesome harmonies. It was sorrow set to music. It wasn't a blues, but it was in the neighborhood. It was a requiem, a confession, and a guilty celebration. And it had a great hook.

It was over in an hour. Eddie seemed to wake from a fugue state. He looked around, unsure of where he was. He set his guitar down and wiped the sweat from his fingers. There was a pad of paper in front of him. There was a song, written in Eddie's hand, though he only vaguely remembered writing it. He stood and stretched his muscles. Eddie felt a relief he couldn't describe. He felt cleansed and purified, but it was more than that. It was a purge. It had to be what women felt upon giving birth. Or maybe it was what Tammy felt when she finally died after suffering through the poison and arriving at relief.

Eddie knew he'd just forged a great song out of emotional turbulence, and suddenly the pall lifted, whatever had happened was over, and the air was calm and clean. It was just past dawn. Eddie went to the curtain and pulled it back. He saw trees and sunshine and he knew he had a song that could launch a career. Now he just had to take it out for a test ride.

■ ■ ■

Buddy Glenn wrote a beauty back in 1974. He called it "Good Old Daze." Carson Fletcher recorded it on his debut album with Big Bill Herron producing. It went to number one on the country charts and crossed over to become a number one pop hit as well. Carson Fletcher's career took off and soared for six years until he had a heart attack in 1980 and retired.

After "Good Old Daze," Buddy Glenn spent the next twenty-seven years trying to write another hit. Yet despite his prolific output, Buddy never wrote another song that earned him more than a few thousand dollars. He wrote a lot of good songs during that period, but, as sometimes happens, nobody recognized them. Fortunately Buddy had retained his half of the publishing rights and "Good Old Daze" still brought him about $15,000 a year from radio play and record sales. But that was about all Buddy had coming in, and lately nobody was particularly interested when he had a new batch of songs to plug. "Too old-school," they said.

All of this chipped away at Buddy's spirit, eventually crushing his confidence and stealing his gift. But things had really fallen apart a year ago when Buddy's wife, Lynn, was diagnosed with cancer. They didn't have any insurance and they ate through their meager savings in short order. Buddy took a second on the house to cover medical expenses. He started giving guitar lessons and working as the night manager at Shoney's, but it wasn't enough. When the money ran out he turned to his publisher for a loan. The terms were simple. Big Bill loaned Buddy $10,000. Buddy agreed to pay it back in a year with $5,000 in interest. If he was unable to repay the loan with the interest, Big Bill would take ownership of Buddy's half of the publishing on "Good Old Daze." Now the loan was due.

Buddy walked into Big Bill's office that afternoon drawn and tired. He'd aged badly in the past few years. Lynn was at home dying and just about everybody had stopped returning his calls. He'd recently sold his last two guitars.

"Hey now!" Big Bill said, gesturing at a chair. "Come on in, take a load off." Big Bill sat down behind his desk. "How's Lynn doing?"

Buddy sat down and took off his hat. He couldn't look Big Bill in the eyes. He just worried the rim of his hat as he spoke. "Not real good," Buddy said. "The tumors didn't respond to the last round of chemo."

Big Bill frowned slightly. "Mmmm." There was an envelope in front of Big Bill. He picked it up and began tapping it on the top of the desk.

Buddy tried to sound optimistic. "But we just heard about a new, experimental treatment that might help."

"Well all right," Big Bill said, pointing with the envelope. "Sounds like things are startin' to turn around for ya."

Buddy shook his head. "Problem is they can't do the treatment here 'cause the FDA hadn't approved it yet. We gotta go down see this doctor in Mexico. He does the treatment at this special clinic. It's real expensive."

Big Bill nodded. "Boy, I tell you, they get you comin' and goin', don't they?" Bill casually opened the envelope and removed the document inside. "Look," he said, "I know you wanna get back so you can take care of Lynn, so let's just go ahead and do this and then you can head for the border." He gestured toward the south.

"Bill, I ain't got the money." Buddy just blurted it out.

Big Bill sat there, expressionless. "You ain't?" He said it real flat, almost like he knew already. "Well. Hmmm." He unfolded the piece of paper and glanced at it.

"The bank won't do a third on the house," Buddy said. "Fact, I'm a couple months behind and they're gonna take it if I don't catch up by the end of next week." Buddy's voice was wavering, like he might crack if he had to talk about it any more. "Lynn's real sick, Bill. I gotta keep that publishing. I need that money real bad."

"That's a shame," Big Bill said flatly. "I'm real sorry, that's the truth."

Buddy finally looked Bill in the eyes. "I'm begging you. I need your help. Lynn's gotta get that treatment or I'm gonna lose her." He looked back at the floor. "Ask yourself what Jesus would do and I know you'll do the right thing. That publishing money's the only thing I got left."

"That's tough all right," Big Bill said. "But listen, this ain't Bible school and I really don't appreciate you dragging all the personal stuff into this. It's unprofessional. I mean, you don't hear me pissin' and moanin' about all the bills I gotta pay, do you? All my personal problems? And believe me, I got more'n I can say grace over."

Buddy put a hand to his face to hide his tears. "I'm sorry, but I don't wanna lose her."

Bill held up their agreement. "Buddy, we're just gonna do what we agreed on," he said. "That's all. Only thing left to do here is figure out the multiple." The multiple was a factor used when determining the value of the publishing rights on a catalog of music, though in this case it was just for the one song. Depending on the marketplace, the multiple typically ranged anywhere from three to fifteen times the current annual revenues the publishing generated. The agreement stated they would negotiate the multiple according to the market as of the due date of the loan.

Buddy hated to do it, but he didn't have much choice. He just hoped Big Bill would consider his situation and help him out. He took a moment to compose himself, setting his jaw, steeling himself for the business. "Well now, I've been asking around," Buddy said, "and just about everybody I talk to agrees 'Good Old Daze' has got some legs on it, and, well, I think we oughta be talking about a multiple of at least ten."

Big Bill shook his head like a disappointed teacher. "Ten, huh?" He scratched the back of his neck. "I guess me and you talk to dif-

ferent folks, 'cause my survey says it's more like a one. It's not getting the radio play it used to, nobody else is recordin' it, and Lord
knows Carson Fletcher's records ain't selling much anymore. Things
is just flat out there, Buddy. You ask around town, nobody's making
money on anything."

Buddy looked up, startled. "One? One's not a multiple! Stop
horsin' around with me, Bill. You know that song's worth a lot more'n
that."

"I sure wish the market was in better shape," Big Bill said. "Just
bad timing, I guess, but I don't think I can go any higher. I'll give you
fifteen grand for it right now."

"I can't take that, Bill. That don't get me outta my hole, much
less get me down to Mexico to get Lynn her treatment. I can come
down to nine, but that's it. I just can't do it for less than that."

"Well, damn, that leaves us about a hundred 'n' twenty thousand
dollars apart."

"Bill, if you can't do nine, you gotta let me go across the street
with it. I know I can get nine from Johnny Rae and that'll let me
pay you back with the interest and I can still take Lynn for that
treatment."

Big Bill face drained of all humanity. He picked up the agreement and read for a moment before thumping the page with his
finger. "Says here I got thirty days to come up with a counteroffer,"
he said. "So I guess I'm gonna need some time to think it over." He
folded the agreement and slipped it back in the envelope, then
he stood up. "I'll call you at the end of next month." He smiled.
"How's that sound?"

Buddy swallowed hard. Visions of Lynn's funeral passed his nar-
rowing field of vision. "I ain't got thirty days. Doctor said Lynn's only
got a couple weeks without that treatment, and even then he can't
say for sure."

Big Bill nodded. "Well, my offer for fifteen grand still stands. You can take that right now." He winked at Buddy. "Either way, it's up to you."

*   *   *

The Dirty Dawg Howse in Starkville, Mississippi, catered to fans of the Mississippi State Bulldogs. The walls were covered with team pennants, game schedules, and neon beer signs.

Boomer and Skeets were second-string tackles. They were at the Dirty Dawg Howse drinking beers with a couple of girls they'd just met. Naturally the two big boys were trying to impress the coeds. "What the hell you tryin' to say?" Boomer hammered a fist on the tabletop. He demanded an answer, and at six foot four, 280 pounds, you'd think he'd get one pretty quick.

But Skeets was six-five and 275, so he wasn't particularly intimidated. In fact he just sat there, smirking, peeling the label off his bottle, wondering if he was getting laid tonight.

"Don't just sit there grinnin' like a barrel of possum heads," Boomer said. "You sayin' I don't know what I'm talkin' about?"

Skeets leaned onto one of his beefy forearms. "I'm sayin' you can't measure a snake till it's stretched out dead. What are you, from Alabama or something? I'm speakin' English." He looked at the girls and winked. They giggled.

Without taking his eyes off Skeets, Boomer turned his head slightly and spit some tobacco juice onto the floor. "Shit, boy, you better put it down where the goats can get it if you expect anybody to understand what—" Boomer didn't get to explain his point fully because Skeeter suddenly hit him upside the head with a beer bottle. All hell broke loose as the two behemoths exploded into one another, sending bottles and ashtrays crashing to the floor. The girls jumped up from the table, squealing, tickled that two rutting bucks would put on a show just for them.

Then, out of the blue, a screeching chaos roared over the house loudspeakers. "Hey, goddammit!" a voiced howled over the sound system. Everyone in the place stopped and turned to look at the small stage in the corner of the room. There they saw Eddie Long standing with his guitar and his eyes burning. He had a bottleneck wedged on one of his fingers which he ran up and down the neck of the guitar while torturing the strings into a caterwaul. The place fell silent, all eyes on Eddie. "Now, I'm here to play some music. You two wanna play Gladiator, go somewhere else." There was a pause before the crowd applauded Eddie's command of the situation. They laughed and hooted some more as Boomer and Skeets and the two girls were escorted from the place.

Eddie had booked a weekend gig at the Dirty Dawg Howse. It was his first since Tammy's funeral. He thought a college crowd would be a good focus group for the new song. He opened his set with "Dixie National," one of his upbeat honky-tonkers, then went into his usual repertoire. About fifteen minutes into his set, Eddie saw familiar faces at the door. Jimmy and Megan had driven up from Jackson. They worked their way through the crowd and found a table in the back. Megan tried to make eye contact with Eddie while Jimmy ordered beers.

Eddie was working through his version of "Act Naturally." The crowd sang along with the one line in the chorus everybody knew. Eddie looked great in the bright light, wearing his black jeans and white T-shirt with an unbuttoned work shirt over it. He moved like nobody's business up there, and by the end of the song, the audience was his. "Thank you," he said. "Thank you very much." Eddie made eye contact and acknowledged Jimmy and Megan with that subtle upward nod musicians onstage share with their close fans.

Eddie pulled a barstool over to the mic and sat down for the first time that night. He dropped out of his fun-guy persona. "If you folks don't mind, I'm gonna slow things down just a bit and do something new for you." His tone was somber, almost confessional. The lights dimmed as Eddie prepared for his big moment. He slid the capo down a fret and strummed the guitar slowly once, then again. He tuned one string, then another, stretching things out and building the anticipation.

When Eddie looked up from his guitar, the crowd saw a changed man. The hundred-watt smile had been turned off and there was something sad about his body language and his gaze. Eddie was serious, wounded, shocked, and ready to confess. Having seen Eddie's show so many times, Jimmy sensed this more than anyone. He'd never seen Eddie put on this mask. He felt something of consequence in the air, so he clicked his pen, ready to write.

Eddie was still strumming the guitar slowly, a chord change here, a chord change there. "This time last month," he said, "I got the notion in my hard head that I pretty much knew how things were going to turn out in my life, like I was in control of things. I had a wife. I had some gigs lined up playing my music and figured it was just a matter of time 'fore I hit it big." Eddie cracked a wry smile and shook his head. "To quote a famous Mississippi songwriter, 'Have you ever seen a bigger fool than me?' " He bent a note and tried to look ironic. "Well, it turns out I was wrong. Turns out this is the only gig I've got lined up in the foreseeable future. I don't know if I'm ever going to make it to the big time, and even if I do, I won't be able to share it with my wife, because . . . because she died not long ago." He strummed a minor chord, beautiful and sad, and let that sink in. The place was silent; even the bartenders had stopped to listen.

Eddie resumed strumming the guitar slowly. "She was beautiful and I loved her, I gotta say that, but she's gone now and . . . well, it just goes to show you . . ." He shook his head. It looked for a moment like he might cry, but he kept it together. "Anyway, after she died, I moved up to Nashville, where something happened I can't really explain. I can't put words to it, but one night, it was late and I was struggling with all my emotions about what had happened and—" Eddie stopped playing and he leaned forward onto the body of the guitar. "And all the sudden, a song just . . . I dunno, it just sort of poured out of me. Like I said, I can't explain it. It just . . . happened." He resumed playing. "Anyway, I know her soul's in this song and I'd like to do it for you now. This is the first time I've played this for anybody, so bear with me. I hope you like it. It's called 'It Wasn't Supposed to End That Way.' "

Most of the women in the place were crying before Eddie started to sing. Megan was in tears and Jimmy was on the verge, wiping his eyes so he could see enough to write. He wanted to get that speech verbatim. The song opened in a medium slow tempo, a bar or two of lament. It put Megan in mind of a sad hymn with each change softly chosen. Then he started to sing, and it came straight from his soul.

When the song was over, there were no dry eyes in the house. Jimmy was astonished. This was as close to perfect as a song got. Eddie soaked up the applause and thanked the crowd. His melancholy smile conveyed appreciation as well as a sadness appropriate to the moment. The crowd's response confirmed that Eddie had that rare and valuable thing known as a hit. After a moment, he got off the stool, took a bow, then resumed his usual set. He got the house rocking with a Steve Earle cover followed by an original. Then he played himself off the stage with Lefty Frizzell's "She's Gone, Gone, Gone." He got a standing ovation and came back out for a second bow, but he didn't do an encore. He left them wanting more. Eddie took off his guitar and held it up. "I'm gonna take a little break, folks. I'll be back in about twenty minutes, so stick around and be sure to tip your waitresses."

After his set, Eddie joined Jimmy and Megan at their table. Megan jumped up and wrapped her arms around him. "Eddie, I am so sorry about Tammy," she said. "The song is beautiful."

"Thanks. I appreciate that." He held on to Megan, enjoying the feel of her sympathy. "And thanks for your note and the flowers. That was real nice."

As Jimmy waited for Megan to unwrap herself from Eddie, he wondered about the etiquette of grief hugs. Weren't you supposed to keep your pelvis away from the other person's? Megan obviously didn't think so, and Eddie didn't seem to mind. Jimmy thought hugging Eddie would be the emotionally correct thing for him to do, but the Dirty Dawg Howse seemed like the wrong place to do it. Besides, he wasn't sure they were quite that close. When the time came, he opted for a firm left hand on the back side of a regular handshake, a sincere-minister sort of thing. "I'm really sorry," he said. "How're you doing?"

Eddie shrugged. "All right, I guess. All things considered." They sat down and a waitress brought a round for the table. Megan reached over and put her hand on Eddie's. "I wish you had a recording of that. I'd love to play it on my show."

Eddie smiled. "Really?" He gave Jimmy a *How about that?* look. He turned back to Megan. Her hand was still on his. "That'd be great," Eddie said. "I mean, I think it's the best thing I've ever written. But when someone in the business, I mean, you're a professional radio programmer—"

"Look, I'm just the assistant music director, but my boss listens to me."

"Still, that means a lot, coming from you."

Jimmy wrote something in his notebook, then looked up. "It really is a great song. You really have something there. I mean, seriously, that's a hit."

"Thanks, man, I appreciate that. But I tell ya, if that's what you gotta go through for a great song, I'm gonna have to find a new job."

Jimmy nodded. "How long did it take to write? You said it just poured out of you—what was that like?" He was poised over his notepad.

Eddie smiled. "You're really serious about writing that book, aren't you?"

"Hell yes I'm serious. I've already written about thirty pages," Jimmy said. "It's a little scattered and I'll have to go back and get some information about your 'formative years,' but yeah, I'm serious.

And I'll tell you, after hearing that song, I'm more convinced than ever you're going to make it."

"I appreciate that," Eddie said, "I really do, but—"

"Oh, wait a second," Jimmy said. "Maybe you can answer this." He flipped back a few pages in his pad. "Do you know who said, 'Writing about music is like dancing about architecture'?"

Eddie thought about it a moment. "I think it was Elvis."

Jimmy shook his head. "I don't think so. That's a little out of the King's range."

"No," Eddie said. "Costello. But I wouldn't bet on it."

"Hmm, that's the first time his name's come up. Megan thinks it was Frank Zappa." He wrote Elvis Costello's name under Zappa's. "But neither one sounds right to me."

Eddie watched Jimmy writing in his notebook until Megan gave his hand a tender squeeze. When he looked over, Megan's violet eyes were all his. And then, subtly, she winked at him.

Jimmy was too involved in his writing to notice. He knew others would come along to write about Eddie, but Jimmy's would be the definitive biography. He was the only guy who'd been there from the start. His would be the only book to have Eddie's first speech about "It Wasn't Supposed to End That Way." His imagination started to run away. *Rolling Stone* might preview a few chapters in a feature article, and from there, who knew what could happen?

"Here you go, Eddie." Jimmy looked up and saw the club's manager standing by the table holding out a cassette. "Great set," he said, slapping Eddie on the back.

"Is that what I think it is?" Megan reached for the tape.

Eddie pulled it out of reach. "I had 'em record it off the board," he said. "I'm sending it to some publishers and artist managers." He smiled as he felt one of Megan's hands dancing lightly on his thigh. "And I'll make one for you, too."

5

et it, girl!" Doreen hollered as she watched Estella bump and grind to the funky percussion coming from the jukebox. Estella was dancing to Slim Harpo's 1966 hit "Baby Scratch My Back." Otis was out there with her, clapping his hands as he circled Estella's big wiggling planet like a skinny little satellite. His choreography was starchy, his steps painful and economic due to arthritis. The ache informed his dance, resulting in a style that was pure Otis.

Toward the end of the song, Estella lapsed into some final frenzied gyrations. "That's it, that's it," Otis said, backing out of the way until she was done. "Mmmmm-lawd! Yes! Nobody move like my sweet baby," Otis said.

Estella was laughing hard when the song ended. She plopped down at the table next to her old friends Doreen and her husband, Maurice. "Child, it's too hot in here be dancin' like that," Doreen said as she dabbed at her forehead with a napkin. "I ain't even movin' I'm all wet."

Maurice pushed a cold beer over to Doreen. "Cool on down with that, Mama." He said it like Don Cornelius or something, a real smoooove operator, sort of Barry White by way of Billy Dee Williams.

Estella picked up a menu and fanned herself. "I'm tellin' you," she said. "I know I ain't dance like that in a long time." She laughed and pulled Otis into her big lap. "But I still got it!"

"Yes, baby, you do," Otis said, patting Estella's thigh. "And you always will." He turned around and kissed her cheek, and they both laughed some more. It was nearly four in the morning. There were only three customers left in the joint, and they were just drinking. Otis had closed the kitchen hours ago, and until he got up to dance, he'd been sitting with Doreen, Maurice, and Estella just talking about the old days.

Maurice started chuckling. "I know you 'member that show down in Baton Rouge . . ." He ducked his head and started giggling so hard he couldn't finish the sentence.

"You talkin' about that night the police came backstage and caught that funny boy playing with hisself . . . ooohhh child! And that promoter throwin' a buttonhole on that half-and-half." Doreen slapped a hand down on the table. "Liked to never stop!"

They all hooted and still acted as shocked as they'd been when it happened. They were younger then, by about forty years, and innocent in the ways of a wider world. They had all traveled together while Otis was having his moment in the sun. Estella and Doreen were backup singers. Maurice played tenor sax. He was smoooove back then too.

"Whatever happened to the man what opened that show?" Doreen asked. "Great big fat mother."

"Old Chubby Dykes?"

"Yeah, what become of him?"

"He moved back to Georgia long time ago," Maurice said. "Sure could sing."

"Sure could," Estella agreed. "I be surprised if he's still alive,

though, big as he was. Probably had a heart attack by now. I know
he had the high blood."

"You one to talk," Doreen said. "And you ain't done halfa what
that doctor told you. You ever quit them cigarettes?"

Estella waved a hand in front of her face. "Lawd, yes, child, I
quit. Takes me a mumf to smoke a pack now."

"Well that's good," Doreen said. She nudged Otis. "You know
who I was thinking about the other day? That white man you used to
run with."

"Who you talkin' about?" Otis took off his beret and wiped his
glistening head.

"You know, played guitar on Ray Charles's country records, you
know, 'I Can't Stop Loving You,' and them. He had a couple sides of
his own got pretty big."

Otis nodded. His face creased, all serious. "You talkin' 'bout
Chester Grubbs," he said.

Doreen pointed at Otis. "That's him. Where's he at now?"

Maurice shook his head. "I heard all sorts of things 'bout that
man. Either drunk hisself to death out in Texas or maybe it was
heroin, I forget, but I heard he'd passed."

"That's a shame," Doreen said. "He sure had it going on for a
while. Yes he did."

Otis looked off into space, thinking about his unlikely friend
Chester Grubbs. The two of them had hit it big at the same time.
Both based in Nashville, they played on some of the same bills
when Otis's records were crossing over to a white audience and
Chester was playing with Ray Charles. They shared a taste for livin'
high on the hog and they rode their respective waves to the top
before things went bad for both of them. Their friendship was like a
struck match, flaring up hot and fast and going out before the whole
stick was consumed.

For Otis, it was the confluence of jealousy, liquor, and knowing
he'd lost most of his money. He'd had his early hit, but they'd

stopped coming just as quick as they'd started. But Otis thought the money would never stop coming in, so it had never stopped going out. Before he knew it, he had to trade his Cadillac for a Chevrolet. When Bill Herron dropped him and took most of his royalties, Otis was forced onto the chitlin' circuit, where he started drinking too much. Otis could see the writing on the wall, and it left him in a foul mood. One night, out back of a club in Memphis, drunk and angry, Otis pulled a knife when he caught a man trying to force himself on one of Otis's backup singers. The man said he wasn't taking no for an answer from the woman, so Otis did what he had to. He killed the man. Stabbed him to death. "Don't nobody mess with my woman," Otis said as the man bled out at his feet. The woman was Estella. She and Otis had been married less than a month at the time.

The Memphis police might've written it up as justifiable, except the dead man was white. Otis was looking at a one-way ticket to Fort Pillow State Penal Farm, so he called the only lawyer he knew, one Franklin Peavy, Esq. Franklin was a young white attorney who hadn't partnered up with Big Bill yet. He had negotiated the contracts of several R&B artists Otis knew from the concert circuit. The two had met in Birmingham, backstage at a show headlined by Percy Sledge. Franklin told Otis that his song "Lookin' for Ruby" was one of his all-time favorites. He gave Otis a business card and told him to call if he ever needed a lawyer for anything. Of course, Franklin was thinking more along the lines of contract work, but when Otis called from jail about fifty dollars from being broke, Franklin agreed to handle the case pro bono, and he did a good job.

Otis was sentenced to eight years for manslaughter, an unimaginable sentence for a black man convicted of killing a white man in Tennessee in the 1960s. And Otis knew it. Just before they took him from the courtroom after sentencing, Otis turned to Franklin and said, "I owe you, Mr. Peavy. If there's ever anything I can do for you . . ." Then they took him away.

Estella was faithful to Otis while he was gone. She visited him and she went to church. And she went to night school to learn book-keeping. She'd saved all her money, and without Otis knowing, she'd saved some of his too. She bought a little piece of property in Nashville and put a mobile home on it. She lived in the back and ran Estella's Shrimp Joint right out of the kitchen.

Otis got out in five years for good behavior. He went back to Nashville and joined Estella, and had been fryin' swimps ever since. But Estella would tell you Otis was never the same after prison. He'd been plenty crazy when he was younger, but now he was quiet, maybe even a little philosophical. Standing over that deep fryer night after night, Otis reflected on all the things that had happened to him and all the things he'd let get away. One of those things was his friendship with Chester Grubbs. He wondered whatever happened.

* * *

Franklin was in his office reviewing royalty statements. *God, this is depressing*, he thought. The money wasn't coming in the way it used to, and that had Franklin worried. He hadn't made as many invest-ments as he might have when the firm was on top, and the ones he'd made had turned out to be bad. Like many day-traders, Franklin had managed to screw the securities pooch during the biggest bull mar-ket in America's history. On top of that, he took expensive vacations and put four kids through private colleges. And now, with retirement looming, it was becoming clear Franklin wouldn't be able to main-tain the lifestyle to which he'd become accustomed, unless some-thing changed.

He slipped on his brand-new Q375 Technologitronic wireless phone headset and turned to look at his reflection in the window. It didn't change his financial situation, but he liked the way it made him look—on top of it, technologically hip, superior in a cutting-edge sort of way. If nothing else, he had that.

As Franklin returned his attention to the royalty statements, Big

Bill started the tape for the umpteenth time. Despite being able to hear only muffled noise through the wall separating their offices, Franklin could tell his partner had been listening to the same thing all afternoon, and it was driving him nuts. He yanked the headset off. "Bill, turn that shit down!" he yelled.

Big Bill ignored the request. He was leaning forward, his head positioned between the two speakers mounted on the far corners of his desk. Lids closed over his bulging eyes, he moved to the music and mouthed the words. He looked like a toad doing karaoke. When the song ended, he reached over and hit rewind again. He turned and yelled at the wall, "Hey, Franklin, come in here! You gotta hear this!"

"In a minute!" Franklin yelled back. "I'm trying to run our business!"

Bill turned to the wall and made some sort of angry Italian gesture he'd picked up from a movie. "The hell you think I'm doin' in here, lap dancin'? I'm working on the part that actually brings in money! Now come listen to this!" He lowered his voice slightly. "You prick."

"What was that?" Franklin thought he heard the word "prick" seep through the wall. Who the hell did he think he was? Franklin had put up with a lot of shit from Bill over the years, but he wasn't about to put up with name-calling.

"I said come here quick! You're going to want to hear this!"

Franklin mocked his partner under his breath. "You're going to want to hear this . . ." He snatched the royalty statements off his desk and went over to Bill's office, waving the papers as he walked in. "Hey, you're the broke dick with the cash-flow problem. The sooner I go over these things and review the allocations, the sooner you'll get your dough. God knows you need it." Franklin enjoyed pushing Bill's money button.

Big Bill sat there, glaring at Franklin, his finger poised on the play button. "Shut the fuck up and listen," he said finally. He pushed the button and the song played. Franklin stood there, impatient at first, but halfway through the chorus he sat down and started to pay attention. After another verse he looked at his partner. Big Bill smiled, nodding. "What did I tell you?" He slapped his desktop. "God, I love this business!"

"Shhhh!" Franklin looked toward the ceiling and listened. It was the sound of money.

Big Bill jerked a finger into the air, waiting for something. Then, cued by a chord change, he pointed at one of the speakers. "Mandolin solo right there," he said, already mixing the final version in his head. "Pedal steel comes in here, way in the back." He tilted his head slightly. "And right here, a low fiddle part, no, maybe a cello, just underneath the whole thing. You'll hardly notice it, but it'll make you cry." The song ended and all they could hear was tape hiss.

Franklin looked at Big Bill. "Who the hell is that?"

Bill held up a glossy eight-by-ten photo. "Name's Eddie Long. Good-looking kid, just moved here. According to his letter, he's looking for management." He arched his eyebrows.

Franklin took the photo and studied it. "That's quite a smile."

Bill snatched the photo away from Franklin. "Yeah. The only problem is we ain't got it under contract yet."

Franklin knew Bill was right. That was a hit country song with serious pop radio crossover possibilities. "Any other songs on the tape?"

"Mostly filler, but not bad."

"Publishing?"

"Doesn't say, but I betcha dolla he's still looking."

"You call him yet?"

Bill held up Eddie's letter. "Didn't give a number. Just invited us to come hear him Monday night at the Bluebird."

"Can't go Monday," Franklin said. "That's the Country Music

Confederation Awards. We got somebody nominated for Best New Countrypolitan Act Appealing to Women."

Bill pushed the rewind button. "That's very touching. Send a proxy. We gotta get this kid, or at least that song." Bill looked at Eddie's cover letter. "He says if he doesn't get picked to play onstage, he'll play for us in the parking lot." Bill grinned. "You gotta like that."

"Whatever." Franklin shrugged. He pulled out his digital micro recorder and held it to his mouth. "Reminder. Print out standard contracts for artist Eddie Long."

*   *   *

Whitney had been driving around for quite a while when he saw the "Room 4 Rent" sign in the front yard of the house on 16th Avenue. Ten minutes after knocking on the door he was signing papers on the place. He couldn't believe his luck. First off, the room came at a fair price. But the price didn't tickle him half as much as the location at the south end of Music Row. Literally on the Row. He could just sit on the front porch in the shade of the magnolia tree and play his songs, looking up occasionally to see if any of the big shots were driving by. "Man," he said to the landlord, "this is some town."

The next day Whitney went looking for work that would allow him to pay his bills while pursuing his music. The help-wanted ads led him to a job waiting tables at the South Side Smoke House. Situated halfway between Music Row and Vanderbilt University, the place was always filled with music industry people and good-looking college girls. The job wouldn't make Whitney rich, but it was enough and it was close to home.

Whitney was driving back from the Smoke House, humming the melody of his favorite song, when something started to grind under the hood of his old truck. "Hang on," he said as he patted the dashboard. "We'll get you fixed up." Whitney loved his truck. It was one of the few things that never let him down. He turned and headed to

Broadway, where he'd seen some auto repair places. The mechanic
said he'd get to it as soon as he could. Whitney sat in the greasy
waiting area wondering how he was going to pay for the repair. If
worse came to worst, he'd leave the truck until he got a few paychecks under his belt. He could walk to work. It wasn't that far.

Whitney looked through the magazines on the table. *Guns &*
Ammo, Field & Stream, and *Road & Track* held no appeal for him.
Over by the door was a tall stack of *Nashville Scene*, a free local
alternative newspaper. The front cover screamed at Whitney:
"Nashville's Power 100—The 100 Most Influential People in the
Music Business!" It was exactly what Whitney was looking for, and
he didn't even know he was looking for it.

Flipping forward from the back of the paper, Whitney immediately came across the name of Big Bill Herron at number ninety-
nine. Whitney read the names of the performers and songwriters
that Herron & Peavy had managed and/or produced over the years.
There were some true legends on the list. Big Bill Herron was
quoted as saying, "We're in the talent business. We're always looking
for new songwriters and performers. There's nothing more gratifying
than taking a raw talent and guiding them, helping them find their
sound or their voice. It's the best job in the world." *These fellas seem*
like the sort I should talk to, Whitney thought. *Might help me with*
the ropes. He'd make an appointment to see them soon as he had the
truck back.

"Gonna need a new water pump," the mechanic said as he
wiped his hands on a blue shop rag. "Gonna run about three hundred dollars."

Whitney tried not to look poor, but three hundred was a lot more
than he'd ever had. He twisted at the ragged bandanna tied around
his wrist. "Be all right if I just left the truck until I get the money to
pay for it?"

The mechanic shrugged. "All right, but this ain't no damn stor-
age facility. You don't come back by next month, I'll part it out."

"Yes, sir, I understand," Whitney said. "I'll be back soon." He turned to leave, then stopped and turned around, holding up the copy of *Nashville Scene*. "Okay if I keep this?"

"It says 'free' on it, Jethro."

On the walk back to his place, Whitney read the list of the industry's power brokers. He was surprised at how many he'd never heard of. Whitney didn't notice, but the most telling aspect of the list was the ratio of lawyers and executives to songwriters. He focused more on the names of people he recognized and anyone from his home state. He figured any of those folks might be glad to help him, but still he was going to start with Big Bill Herron and Franklin Peavy.

Thirty minutes later, Whitney was almost home. As he stood at the corner of 16th and Horton waiting for traffic to pass, he got to thinking. With the exception of the busted water pump, the news was all good. Nashville was all right. It was green and there were hills and it smelled more like the country than the city. It'd do for now. Five minutes later, when he got back to his place, Whitney sat under the magnolia in the front yard with his writing pad. He wished he had someone to write a letter to, but he didn't, so he wrote a song instead.

*   *   *

Megan held the razor between finger and thumb, unsure if this was what she really wanted to do. Her indecision was compounded by feelings of guilt for thinking about leaving Jimmy this way. Would he understand? Did she owe it to him to talk it over? It wasn't as if they were engaged. Sure, they'd dated for a couple of months, and yes, she had feelings for him, but, big deal. They obviously weren't strong enough to stop her from doing this. She looked at the clock and saw it was four-thirty. If she was going to do it, she had to do it now.

This week's *Radio & Records*, the radio industry's *Wall Street Journal*, was on the table next to the old Ampex reel-to-reel where

Megan was editing her air check tape. The *R&R* was open to "Opportunities." One ad was circled, for a radio station in Nashville. They were looking for a female air personality with strong production and promotion experience. This had Megan's name all over it. She had to do it, right? She was chasing her dream, right? This was about her career. This wasn't about chasing Eddie Long. Who ever said it was? She looked again: four thirty-five. She had to get the tape edited, dubbed, and to the post office before five, so she made the first cut. She rolled the tape ahead until she found the other mark she'd made with her stubby grease pencil. Megan carefully laid the tape in the editing block. The door to the production room squeaked open just as she was about to cut the tape. She didn't look up to see who it was.

"Surprise . . ." When Megan heard Jimmy's voice she almost sliced through a knuckle. She looked up and saw him pull some flowers from behind his back. "Pistils and stamens for my radio sweetheart," he said, smiling like a child who'd done a magic trick. He hoped the flowers would make romance appear out of thin air.

Oh God, she thought, *not flowers.* Megan already felt bad enough, and now she had to proceed in light of a bouquet. *But as long as he's bringing flowers,* she thought, *why bring such cheap ones? Don't I deserve a dozen yellow roses?* "Jimmy . . ." Her inflection implied he wasn't supposed to do that sort of thing on account of the fact she wasn't really serious about their relationship. "That's very sweet, thanks."

"You're welcome." He looked around for an impromptu vase. Megan hoped he wouldn't notice the ad she'd circled for the Nashville job. Of course, if he brought it up, she could say someone else was considering the job. Just because she was in the same room with a circled want ad didn't mean she was leaving town, right? Megan didn't want to lie, but she also didn't want to get into a big heart-rending discussion about why she was applying for a job in Nashville and what did that mean about her feelings for Jimmy and blahblahblah. She only had twenty-two minutes to finish what she was doing and get to the post office on time. "What're you doing here?"

Jimmy leaned over the mixing console and looked at the notes Megan had made about her tape. "I was at the library doing some research for the book, was in the neighborhood, decided to drop by." He turned the notes slightly so he could read them better. "What're you working on?"

Megan ignored the question. She made the second cut on the tape and spliced the ends together. "This is so primitive," she said, nodding at the reel-to-reel. She imagined herself in an all-digital production room of the station in Nashville. "What were you researching?"

Jimmy admired Megan's soft hands as they deftly manipulated the tape. "I was looking for newspaper accounts of Tammy Long's death. There wasn't much written about it, so I guess I've got to go up there and interview some people. The sheriff, coroner, that sort of thing."

"Right," she said. "Great idea." *This is good,* Megan thought. Jimmy was really getting into the book. Maybe he'd get so caught up in his writing and research that she could use it as an excuse to end things with him. *All you ever think about is that book!* she could say. *What about me? What about my needs?* That wouldn't be a bad approach. "I know I've said this before, but I think the book's a great idea."

Jimmy was pleased by her endorsement. "It's coming along," he said. "I've got my notes organized and I put together a chronology for the 'early years' chapters." He paused. "That reminds me." He pulled out his pad and made a note. "I need to call Eddie and get his early impressions of Nashville." He put the pad down and glanced again at Megan's handwritten notes. "So what're you working on?"

The lie came to her suddenly. "Oh, yeah," she said brightly. "I was going to tell you, but I wanted to hear about the book. I got the wildest call this morning. The program director from a station in Nashville called, completely out of the blue, said he heard me do a shift when he was driving down to New Orleans for the Me-Oh-My-Ohs."

"The whats?"

"The On the Bayou Country Music Awards. They're new. The little trophies they give out are called Me-Oh-My-Ohs. They're little statues of Hank Williams standing in a pirogue. Anyway, this PD was going on and on about how he loved my voice and my banter. It was really flattering and he wanted to have a tape and blahblahblah, so I decided to send him one, just so he could have it on file, you know, just in case."

Jimmy felt like he'd been hit with a nine-pound hammer. "You're moving to Nashville?"

Megan saw his eyes drifting toward the open *Radio & Records* so she dropped her grease pencil on the floor by his feet. When Jimmy bent to pick it up, Megan swept the *R&R* into the trash can. "Nooo," she almost chortled. "I'm not moving to Nashville. Well, it's not up to me, anyway, is it? He just asked me to send an air check tape. He didn't even say they had a job or anything. And who knows? The guy'll probably be working in Buffalo by the time this tape gets to Nashville. You know how radio is. But still, working in a larger market would be a great career move for me, don't you think?"

"Well, sure, but I just . . . it never occurred to me you might want to leave . . . Jackson."

Megan rewound the reel-to-reel, then popped a cassette into the deck. "It's not that I want to leave Jackson." She cued up the tape and started dubbing. "In fact, it'd be great if Jackson suddenly became a medium-size market, but I don't think that's going to happen. So—look, it's no big deal," she said.

Jimmy sagged a bit. "It'd be a big deal to me if you moved." He seemed wounded. "Who would I give flowers to?" He looked at Megan and smiled as hard as he could, but he started to get an empty feeling, like he was one date from the old I-think-we-should-see-other-people speech.

Megan struggled to look sympathetic. It's not like she wanted to hurt him. All she wanted was, well, she wasn't really sure what she wanted. But she knew whatever it was, it wasn't in Jackson and it wasn't with an unknown freelance writer with limited financial prospects. "You're right," she said, "it would be big deal, I'm sorry. I don't mean to—I don't know what I mean." She waved a hand, hoping to make it all go away. "I wouldn't worry about it."

"Yeah, well, easier said than done." Jimmy leaned against the wall, arms folded. He didn't say anything, he just looked at Megan.

Megan couldn't look at him. He was in love and she wasn't. And even if she was, she figured she could do better. And didn't she owe it to herself to try? Why couldn't Jimmy just get the clues and let her go easily? Why did someone, specifically her, always have be the bad guy in these scenarios? She didn't like breaking his heart or anyone else's, but it's not like you marry everybody you date, right? She felt the pressure from Jimmy's stare, and suddenly it just shot out of her mouth. "It's just—I feel like I'm stagnating here." Megan thumped the Ampex machine with a finger. "I don't want to get stuck here where everything's still analog. I want to go someplace digital, you know?" She finally looked up at Jimmy. All he could do was shrug. "I don't want to spend the rest of my life making ten dollars an hour doing live remotes for every doughnut shop that opens out on County Line Road." She held a hand up. "Not that there's anything wrong with that. In fact, it's such an honorable calling I think I should move on so someone else can have this opportunity." She faked a laugh, hoping to lighten the moment.

"So you're just thinking of others then." As soon as he said it, Jimmy regretted the sarcastic tone.

Megan snapped back, "It's just an air check tape, Jimmy."

"Okay," he said. "I'm not trying to stand in the way of your career. I guess I just thought there was more to us than this."

"This has nothing to do with us," Megan said as the cassette rewound.

Jimmy absorbed the comment. "That pretty much says it all, I guess." *The bad news about loving someone,* Jimmy thought, *is that they don't have to love you back.*

Megan had ten minutes to get to the post office. "Look, don't try to make me feel bad about this."

"That's not what I'm trying to do," Jimmy said. "Besides, I'm not sure that's possible."

Megan stuffed the cassette in an envelope and sealed it. She stood and looked at Jimmy. "Listen, I gotta go."

*   *   *

It's a generally accepted fact that it takes years to become an overnight success in Nashville. About the only folks who don't accept this are the ones who just got to town. They were the big fish in their own small ponds who decided it was time to share their gift with the world. They were pretty sure all they had to do was knock on a couple of doors, let somebody hear a few of their songs, and, quick as you could say "Grand Ole Opry," they'd be opening for Shania Twain.

When that failed to happen, they either went home blaming their failure on Nashville or they got serious. For those who got serious there were plenty of opportunities to be heard. Bellevue Station, the Broken Spoke, Douglas Corner, and 12th & Porter were just a few of the Nashville clubs that featured an "open mic" night.

But of all the clubs in Nashville, one in particular had become the Mecca for aspiring singers and songwriters. The Bluebird Cafe was a small, unassuming place several miles south of Music Row. They served food and drink like any other modestly priced cafe in the South, that is, with more cholesterol than regard. But it also served up music, and this it served with reverence. In fact, the club had a motto printed on T-shirts to reflect this respect. It said: *Shhh!* The food, it had to be noted, didn't get a slogan.

Tucked into a shabby strip mall on Hillsboro Pike, the Bluebird Cafe was famous for being the place where a lot of stars got their big break. Artists like Vince Gill and Sweethearts of the Rodeo were said to have been discovered here, and the artist formerly known as Chris Gaines was alleged to have secured a recording contract with one of his Bluebird Cafe performances.

The Bluebird had two open mic nights, one on Sunday, one on Monday. Sunday night's required an audition and so usually had a higher level of talent. Monday night, however, was luck-of-the-draw, and the performances ranged from pleasant surprises to don't-quit-your-day-job. Every Monday afternoon around five, the hopefuls arrived in the parking lot. The doors opened at five-thirty and those wanting to perform rushed in to sign up. The names were all dropped into a hat, and twenty-four of them were chosen. Starting at six o'clock, each person got to sing two songs and hope for the best.

It was Monday night, and the Country Music Confederation Awards were getting under way across town at the Ryman Auditorium. This was good news for Bill Herron and Franklin Peavy, inasmuch as it meant there would be plenty of parking at the Bluebird and there would be few competitors scouting the open mic talent.

Franklin arrived first and snagged a good table. While he waited for his partner, Franklin nursed a scotch and played with his new toy, the latest wireless application protocol Internet connection device. He was as fond of digital gadgetry as Big Bill was averse to it. Franklin goaded Bill about this, suggesting a connection between technophobia and Bill's diminished status among Nashville producers. *That idiot would bring a club to a gunfight*, Franklin thought as he used his toy to get some stock quotes, make a few bad trades, and check his e-mail.

Franklin was logging off when his partner arrived. Despite Big Bill's plummeting to ninety-nine on the Power 100, the staff at the club still treated him with a certain respect. He could hardly get across the room without one of the club's regulars stopping him to pay respects. "Excuse me, Mr. Herron, I'm a big fan," they'd say. "I bet I've got every record you ever produced."

Franklin watched all this from his table, his eyes narrow and bitter. The thing that galled him most after all his years in the industry was that no one ever stopped him to pay respects. They'd all scurry over to that fat, bug-eyed partner of his, scraping and bowing and hoping for a word or two, but they never acknowledged Franklin. It wasn't fair. Franklin had been involved with as many hit records as Big Bill, if only in the contract negotiations. And he knew all the big stars, or at least their attorneys. How come he didn't get any damn adoration? Because he was a lawyer, that's why. The guy who wouldn't be eaten by a shark out of professional courtesy. Yeah, yeah, he'd heard 'em all, and they weren't any funnier coming from Travis Tritt than from some twice-divorced car salesman dissatisfied with his custody arrangement.

This hadn't always bothered Franklin, but as he approached the end of his career, he'd begun to crave recognition. To this end, Franklin had lately been thinking about producing records himself. He'd been to hundreds of recording sessions and watched Big Bill practice his craft. It didn't seem to amount to much more than telling the engineer to make the drums louder or to put some echo on the vocals. Anyone could do that, he thought. And by God, if that's what garnered respect in this town, then Franklin was ready to do it. The only problem was, all their clients had signed contracts making Big Bill their producer. Now all Franklin had to do was figure out how to get around that niggling detail. But how hard could that be? After all, he was the one drawing up the contracts.

Bill arrived at the table, chuckling. He could tell by Franklin's expression what was going through his mind. Bill held his hands out, palms up. "What can I do?" he said. "I'm a famous producer, you're a lawyer." He said it the same way he might say "hemorrhoid." Residual celebrity status was the one thing Big Bill had that Franklin didn't, and rubbing it in was one of the few pleasures left to him.

Franklin looked up, eyes mad as Merle Haggard on a jag. "Oh, I meant to tell you this afternoon, but I forgot . . . go fuck yourself."

Big Bill laughed as he sat down across the table from Franklin. "I understand." They ordered drinks and sat there, not speaking, just waiting for the music to start.

The first act was a stunning blonde whose arrangements seemed influenced primarily by Trini Lopez. When she finished she was approached by several men, each claiming to have access to important A&R executives for major labels. False promises were made and phone numbers exchanged. The next two acts were as earnest as they were unpolished. One appeared to be doing a poor imitation of Robert Earl Keen while the other was an uncomfortable cross between Jimmy Dale Gilmore and Little Jimmy Dickens.

The rest of the candidates were out in the parking lot in front of the Bluebird. A pair of speakers mounted under the eaves allowed them to hear the performers inside. Eddie Long was out there, sitting on a low concrete wall, tuning his guitar. His name had been drawn tenth, so he still had thirty or forty minutes before he was up. In the meanwhile, he was listening to and criticizing each performer that came before him. Every now and then he looked out from under the brim of his hat at the others who were waiting. Some were cool, leaning against trucks, smoking cigarettes. Some were pacing, nervous, having second thoughts. One kid seemed to be saying a prayer. Eddie smirked at that and shook his head.

An employee stuck her head out the door, looked at her clipboard, then called for the next performer. "Whitney Rankin?"

He finished his prayer and looked up. "Yes ma'am," he said. "I'm right here." He picked up his guitar and followed her inside. Whitney waded through the crowd and stepped up to the microphone, scared to death. The dark-haired skinny kid drew the queer looks he was used to, but he shook 'em off. Still, he was afraid to open his mouth at first for fear he might throw up. Too afraid to speak, he quickly slipped on his harp rack with his Honer 565 Cross Harp. After a deep breath and a glance at his audience he attacked his guitar. It was a dark country rocker with renegade overtones and something evil bubbling just under the surface of the harmonica. His voice was sure and the song was as smart as it was angry. Before he was halfway through, the queer looks were gone. When it was over, some even looked ashamed as they applauded.

"Thanks very much." Whitney smiled and took another deep breath. "Man, am I nervous." The crowd laughed with him. Whitney twisted at the bandanna around his wrist as he looked out at the room. "I guess I've written a hundred songs or more, but out of all of them, this next one's my favorite." He tuned a string. "It seems like I've known the song all my life, even though I only wrote it a few years ago." He shrugged. "Anyway, I call it 'Night's Devotion,' and, uh, well . . . here we go."

The first chords stilled the room, taking everyone by surprise. It couldn't have been any more different from the first song, like a lullaby following Steppenwolf. When Whitney started to sing, Big Bill felt the strangest sensation. Judging by the expressions of the others, he wasn't alone. Big Bill couldn't explain why, but he suddenly felt like a child being loved. He couldn't remember the last song that had made him feel like that. Could this song possibly be so good? Bill looked at his glass. It was only his second drink, so it wasn't the alcohol. No, this was a good song, pure and simple. Maybe even a great one.

During the soft harmonica bridge, Bill found himself thinking of the word "lovely"—an adjective that hadn't crossed his mind since who knew when. He pulled out a couple of business cards and wrote "Whitney Rankin" on the back of one.

There was silence after the song ended. Whitney thought he'd bombed, thought his favorite song was crap. But the crowd suddenly snapped out of their dream state and gave him the sort of applause usually reserved for craftsmen who had just performed an acknowledged gem.

Big Bill nudged Franklin and nodded at the stage. "That'll kill cotton knee-high," he said. Whitney stood in the spotlight, relieved, surprised, and pleased. He smiled, thanked the crowd, then headed for the door. As he passed the table in the corner, Big Bill reached up and handed Whitney a business card. "Hey, kid, give me a call."

Whitney paused to look at the card. He recognized the name from the list in *Nashville Scene*. "All right," he said. "I sure will." He floated into the parking lot feeling like he'd just signed a record deal. He would have stayed to hear the other performers, but it smelled like rain and Whitney had a long walk in front of him, so he headed home, not even thinking about the hole in the sole of his boot.

The other singers stared as Whitney headed out to the road and started walking east with his guitar case, a new man in black, different and fearless, they thought. The woman stuck her head out the door and called the next name on the list. The guy just shook his head. "I ain't going up there after that," he said. She shrugged, called the next name. There was no response, but a Ford driven by a recently discouraged singer screeched out of the parking lot heading south.

Eddie stood up, tilting his hat back. "I'll go," he said. The others turned and looked, wondering who the hell this guy was. The woman stepped aside, holding open the door. Eddie walked through the crowd with his big flattop Gibson held above his head. He stepped into the light, looking down at first, then slowly tilting his head back to reveal his face. "They said I could do two songs," he said, "but I think I'm just gonna do one, so everybody else'll have time to do theirs." He strummed the guitar once, then again. "I wrote this song not too long ago, after my wife died," he said, grabbing everyone's attention. "It's called 'It Wasn't Supposed to End That Way.' " And then he sang the song.

Just as it had in Starkville, the song left the room breathless. Looking out at the stunned faces, Eddie knew he'd kicked some ass. He thanked the crowd as he slipped the guitar strap over his head, then he headed outside.

Big Bill brushed Franklin's arm as he stood up. "C'mon," he said. "Let's go have a talk with our boy." They caught up with him in the parking lot. "Hey, Eddie," Big Bill called out. "You got a minute? We'd like to talk to you."

"Sure thing." Eddie held out his hand. "Eddie Long. What can I do for you?"

They shook hands. "Eddie, I'm Bill Herron and this is Franklin—"

"Big Bill Herron, the producer? Are you kiddin' me?"

Big Bill smiled and looked straight in Eddie's crystal-green eyes. "No kiddin'."

"I sure didn't expect to see you here. I figured you'd be at the CMC Awards."

Franklin elbowed his way past Bill. "By the way, Eddie, I'm Franklin Peavy. Bill and I work together."

"Nice to meet you, Mr. Peavy." Eddie pointed at him knowingly. "Hey, you negotiated that big recording deal for Luther Bridges, didn't you? That was a helluva deal!"

Franklin puffed up a bit. "That's right," he said, "You must read the trades pretty close."

Eddie scuffed his boot on the asphalt. "Oh, I just try to keep up with both ends of the business, that's all." Eddie leaned his guitar case against his car, then pushed up the brim of his Stetson. "So what do a couple of big shots like you want with little ole me?"

Big Bill smiled. "Son, we'd like to talk to you about your career."

6

nder normal circumstances, Bill and Franklin would have taken Eddie to the Sunset Grill to discuss career possibilities. The Sunset Grill was Nashville meets Hollywood with deep fried spinach served by hip young waiters dressed in black. Using flattery and the big-city atmosphere of the place, Herron and Peavy found they could get most new-to-town artists to sign almost anything. But with the CMC Awards wrapping up, it would be too crowded to get within a block of the place, so they decided to go elsewhere.

Big Bill was at the wheel of his Ford Excursion. Franklin was way the hell over in the copilot seat and Eddie was two yards behind them in the first row of backseats. Eddie was leaning forward, hanging on their every word. Two big-time music industry vets telling war stories.

Big Bill and Franklin got along fine when it counted. And nothing counted more than signing new talent with an unpublished hit song. They'd done it so many times it was a dance. One minute Bill would lead, then Franklin would take over. They two-stepped on the fears and egos of the uninitiated, and they rarely stumbled.

"Seriously," Eddie said, "you really think it's a good single?"

"A good single?" Bill looked in the mirror at Eddie. "Hell, son, it's way more than that. You put that song on the worst disc you ever heard and I betcha dolla it'd go gold, maybe platinum. You got any idea what a song like that's worth?"

"Not really."

Big Bill smiled inwardly. "Let's say you sell five hundred thousand units, okay? That's good, but not as good as I think this song is, but let's just use it for an example. A gold record brings in four million for the label." Big Bill paused to let the seven figures sink into Eddie's imagination. "Now, you don't get all that," he said with a smile, "you gotta share some of it with your producer. But even if you're not very good at math, you can tell you gonna do all right."

"That's a lot of money," Eddie said. He sounded almost suspicious.

Franklin actually said, "You ain't just whistlin' Dixie. You come out of the gate with a hit single like we're talking and the record company's gonna wanna keep you happy, right?" Eddie nodded. "Sure, they got the option on your next seven discs and a greatest-hits package, but trust me, they'll renegotiate. Probably increase your royalty rate from the standard eight percent to, say, ten percent, maybe even better if you let me handle it."

"Better than ten percent?" Eddie smiled like he'd just been let in on a secret. "You've done that before?"

"I'm the one who did it first," Franklin said. "I've renegotiated some of the best contracts in country music history. Trust me, I can get you a higher royalty than anybody in town." For the next fifteen minutes, Peavy and Herron spun wild stories of success and financial excess they had personally witnessed. They gave one example after another about the artists they'd handled and the money they'd made. "You shoulda seen that girl's face when she saw that check for a hundred thousand dollars. I thought she was gonna faint." It was a sales pitch they'd made a hundred times, and it sounded mighty tempting. Sign with Peavy and Herron and get the keys to the kingdom.

During a lull in the pitch, Eddie glanced out the window. He'd been in Nashville long enough to recognize what neighborhood they were in. He leaned forward and tapped Franklin on the shoulder. "You mind if I ask where're we going?"

Franklin reached into his coat pocket and pulled out his global positioning satellite receiver, showing it to Eddie. He pointed at the map on the screen. "We're here, right?" He pointed again. "Place we're going to is there. It's called Estella's. Best fried shrimp you'll ever put in your mouth."

"Plus they got a great jukebox," Big Bill said. "If you like old R&B."

Eddie smiled and nodded. "Sounds good." He didn't care about the jukebox or how good the shrimp were. His just wanted to get down to business.

As he pulled into the parking lot, Bill looked in the rearview mirror at Eddie. "You like old R&B? I'm talking Little Milton, Jackie Wilson, that sort of thing."

"That's a little before my time."

"You know, I managed some of those R&B acts when I first started." He shook his head. "Boy, that was a *long* damn time ago," he said with a laugh. "Produced some hits too. Also did some concert promoting." Big Bill found three parking spaces near the front door and took them all. As soon as they got out they could hear the jukebox.

"Hey," Eddie said, cocking his ear toward the music. "Tyrone Davis."

Big Bill gave Eddie a shove. "You rascal. Before your time, my ass. I been had!" He chuckled. He was starting to like this Eddie Long.

Eddie smiled. "Well, you know, I heard a little of this and that."

Big Bill reached the door first, opening it for the others. The smell of tobacco and fried shrimp hooked them and drew them in, where they were greeted by Estella. She was perched on her stool, her upper body heeding the call of Tyrone's song. "Well, well," she said as the three men came through the door. "If I could turn back the hands of time . . . Come ooon in!" Estella eased up off the stool and slid three menus off the stack in front of her.

Big Bill stepped up and slapped the top of the podium, an old man acting foolish. "Who do I see about gettin' a table at this establishment?" He forced a laugh, causing everyone else to do likewise.

"Hello, Mr. Herrons." Estella had a habit of putting an *s* on the end of his name. "How you doin' tonight?" Not that she cared. She didn't like the man. Didn't trust him any further than she could comfortably spit a rat, but there was no point in acting it out. There was nothing wrong with his money. "Good to see you."

"We're all right," Big Bill said. "We just come to get our mouths greasy."

"You come to the right place, then." Estella had long suspected Big Bill of stealing money back when he was Otis's manager. It was just a hunch, of course. It wasn't something she could prove, so she just kept him at a polite distance. Estella looked at Franklin and gestured with the menus. "You want the booth, Mr. Peavy?"

"That'll be fine, Estella," Franklin said as Estella led them toward their table. "You doin' all right tonight?"

"Oh yeah, ain't complaining. How 'bout you?"

"Good, good, we found us a new talent here and decided to fatten him up with some of your shrimp." Franklin clapped Eddie on the back and winked.

Estella led them to a corner booth and pulled out the table so they could squeeze in. "Well all right. Everybody just set down here." After pushing the table back in, Estella took their drink orders, then left.

Bill leaned back in the booth, arms spread wide across the back of the seat. "You know, Eddie, I been in this business a long time and I've come to be a pretty good judge of talent. And I gotta tell ya, when I got your tape, I said to Franklin, I said, 'Betcha dolla this boy's goin' places.' " Bill gave a quick nod to confirm he was speaking the truth.

"I appreciate that. But here's the—"

"So," Big Bill interrupted, "where're you from and how long you been in Nashville?"

Eddie leaned forward and fixed Bill with his eyes. "Mississippi and long enough," he said. "If you don't mind, Mr. Herron, I'd like to cut to the chase on this." Big Bill and Franklin wouldn't have looked more surprised if Eddie had stood and pissed on the tabletop. They glanced at one another, curiosity replacing surprise. "No disrespect," Eddie said, "it's just that I ain't much for small talk and I kinda take a business approach to things. That's all. I hope you don't mind."

Franklin and Bill looked at each other again then laughed. "Well all right, then," Bill said. "Let's cut to the chase." He gestured at Franklin. "Show him the contract."

Franklin pulled a document from his coat pocket and handed it to Eddie. "This is a standard artist-manager contract. It has all the usual clauses detailing our percentages for the different types of deals you might enter into, touring, recording, publishing, et cetera." His tone was relaxed and meant to imply that there was no reason to even read the thing it was so standard. "Why don't you go ahead and take a look at it while we have our drinks."

When Estella brought the drinks to the table, she saw Eddie looking through the contract. She was tempted to warn him against selling his soul to Mr. Herrons, but it wasn't any of her business, so she held her tongue. "Mr. Peavy, ya'll wanna go ahead and order?"

"I think we'll have three shrimp plates, if that's all right." Franklin looked at the others to get their approval. Big Bill nodded.

Eddie never looked up from the contract but made a vague wave of his hand. "Yeah," Franklin said, "three of the plates'll be fine."

Estella took the menus and went back to the kitchen. "Three swimps," she said as she came through the swinging door.

Otis went to the refrigerator and pulled out the large metal bowl. He set it on the counter and turned to Estella. "This Mr. Peavy's order?"

"Uh huh. He's over there with Mr. Herrons, 'bout to get some boy to sign papers." She looked out the service window at the booth where they were sitting. "That man is ugly as a stumpful of spiders and twice as crooked."

"Man can't help the way he looks," Otis said. He plunged his hands into the big bowl of cold milk and paprika and he gathered extra shrimp the way he always did for Mr. Peavy. "And you don't know he's gettin' his hooks in that boy's pocket any more'n I do. Now just do like me and let it go." He lifted his hands out of the bowl and let the juices drain between his fingers.

Estella put her hands on her hips and looked at Otis. "That's right. That's 'xactly what you did." Her head jerked from side to side as she spoke. "You just let it go and he just went right on down to his bank and made a gret, big deposit with all yo' monies."

Otis smiled serenely, forcing the little gray tuft of whisker under his lip to point outwards. "Jus' let it go," he said as he worked the wet shrimp into the spicy flour. "Bye, bye."

Estella turned and headed for the door. "Hmmph." She loved Otis, but she could never understand his peace of mind and the way he accepted his fate. There was no denying that he had stabbed that man in Memphis, but the way Estella figured it, Big Bill Herron had put the knife in Otis's hand. When she walked by the booth, Estella looked at Eddie and hoped things would turn out better for him.

Eddie didn't notice Estella. He was absorbed in the subparagraphs of the clauses in the contract. Somewhere on page seven he stopped and looked up. "What's this?" He turned to Franklin. "You coproduce everything I do?"

It was hard to say who was most surprised by this question, Franklin, who never expected some hick kid to actually read the contract, let alone understand it, or Big Bill, who, up until this moment, had always been the sole producer listed in the contracts they issued.

"Oh, that's just a credit," Franklin said, trying to remain calm. "It's nothing, standard stuff." He tugged on the cuffs of his shirt and inspected a button closely. He hoped Big Bill had suddenly gone deaf and that Eddie would drop the matter.

But Bill's hearing was fine. And despite the web of veins in the whites of his bulging eyes, so was his sight. He stared across the table at his partner. The sonofabitch was sneaking shit into the contracts. Bill wondered how long that had been going on. He wanted to say something about the knife twisting in his back, but he didn't want Eddie to know there was dissension between the partners, so he acted like this was business as usual. "Oh yeah." Bill tapped his forehead with his fingers. "That's the credit-only clause we discussed adding to the new contracts? I'd completely forgotten about that." He emphasized the word "completely."

Franklin looked at the red veins in Big Bill's eyes. "Yeah, credit-only, like we discussed." He'd begun to sweat like a pedophile on a playground.

Eddie flipped ahead a page and pointed at something. "Well, here in paragraph six, sub-b, doesn't that trigger this producer royalty?"

"Let me see what you're pointing at." Franklin took the contract and pulled some reading glasses from his pocket. Head tilted downward, Franklin pretended to read what he already knew was there. "Well, I can see how you might misread that, yes. It's a complicated clause and perhaps not as artfully written as it might—"

"Well, let's lose it all," Eddie said flatly. "No offense, but I'm only

going to agree to have Mr. Herron produce the record, all right?" He
flipped forward to review the last pages of the contract without waiting for a response.

This was a first. Big Bill and Franklin didn't know what to say.
Bill was tempted to laugh, since Eddie had just pulled the rug out
from under Franklin's attempted coproducing scheme. And Franklin
was tempted to reach across the table to strangle him for doing it.
But neither of them said anything. They just sat mute, waiting, as if
under Eddie's spell. He had taken control of the situation and the
two veterans were willing to let him, for now. Eddie had a song they
wanted. It was a hit, plain and simple. They figured the best way to
get it was to play along until the kid was in so far over his head they
had to bail him out. Then they'd show him how they renegotiated
contracts.

Eddie gauged the reactions on their faces. "Don't get me wrong,"
he said. "I want you guys to handle things for me, but let's get one
thing straight from the get-go. I've done my homework. I know
about compulsory licenses, producer royalties, synchronization
rights, and mechanicals. I also know about MP3 files, I-drive, and
Internet marketing strategies. The bottom line, fellas, is that we can
have a mutually beneficial relationship only if we don't try to fuck
each other at every turn. Know what I mean?"

Franklin and Bill were dumbstruck. They'd never met a young
artist who seemed to know so much about the business. Artists usually didn't know this much till they'd been screwed several times,
lost their record deal, been through detox, and ended up in court
with the IRS. Herron and Peavy could only stare across the table at
this prodigy. This kid was going places.

"Here's what it boils down to," Eddie said. "You want me and my
song, you're gonna have to do it my way." He shrugged. "Otherwise
I'll find somebody else."

Each of them had a reason for agreeing to Eddie's terms. Big Bill
needed the money he knew the song would fetch. Franklin just

wanted to be associated with a hit. He figured it would go a long way toward earning him the industry respect he so coveted. Bill and Franklin looked at each other with what-do-you-think expressions. They'd worked together long enough for each to know what the other was thinking. Finally, they both nodded. "What the hell," Big Bill said. "We'll try it your way."

Eddie's face didn't light up the way most young artists' did when their deal closed. In fact, if there was any change at all in his demeanor, it was that he seemed to grow a little darker. "Oh, yeah, one more thing." Eddie leveled a knowing finger at Franklin. "The standard royalty rate for a new artist is twelve percent," Eddie said. "Not eight. Twelve." He looked off toward the kitchen, then back at the stunned lawyer and his partner. "After we eat, I'll tell you about my marketing plan." He turned and looked back toward the kitchen again. "Now where's this shrimp plate you've been bragging about?"

*   *   *

Megan was doing her best to forget about Jimmy. *Clean breaks hurt less, right? Is that true both of bones and of broken hearts, or is it just bones? Wait a second, it's clean cuts that hurt less than ragged ones. That's it. Paper cuts hurt more than—Christ! Why am I worried about paper cuts?*

Megan knew Jimmy was in love with her, but she didn't think she bore any responsibility for that. All she did was go out with him. Sure, she laughed when he told a joke, and she'd met a few members of his family, but that didn't mean anything, did it? And, yeah, they'd had sex, pretty good sex, come to think of it, but so what? They screwed more than they made love, or at least that's what Megan'd been doing. Jimmy would probably tell the story differently, but he tended to be a romantic about those sorts of things. Was it Megan's fault that guys just tended to fall in love with her? It's not like she asked them to.

She couldn't worry about that right now. She was running out of time. She was at the radio station clearing out her desk. She was due in Nashville in two days to start her new job. Between now and then Megan had more to do than she had time to do it. She was in too much of a hurry to worry about neatness, so she dumped the contents of a drawer into the liquor box she'd brought for packing.

As she slid the drawer back into the desk, Ken Hodges, the station's general manager, appeared in the doorway. He looked like a weasel wearing a bad hairpiece. It wasn't really a rug, but his hair was done in such a rigid Trent Lott style that it looked like one. "You can't just quit," he said. "You gotta give me some notice."

Megan pulled out another drawer. "I gave you notice an hour ago, Ken."

"C'mon, Megan, that's unprofessional. I need a couple of weeks. Just do your shift for two more weeks. I'll give you a little raise."

Megan dumped the contents of the second drawer into her box. "Starting to wish you'd given me that contract last year when I asked, huh?"

A sigh of resignation seeped out of Mr. Hodges. He needed to keep Megan on the air. She had terrific numbers, and up until now anyway, Ken hadn't had to pay her much more than minimum wage. "All right," he said. "We can talk about a contract, if you want. But—"

"There's no point in talking about it now, Ken. You're too late."

Mr. Hodges assumed a fatherly tone. "Megan, you've heard the expression 'The grass is always greener on the other side'? You might want to think about that. In fact, you know what? I got a file full of résumés from jocks in places like Nashville. They all hate working in markets where they live from book to book, their job completely dependent on ratings. They all want to come here where there's security and more of a family atmosphere. Isn't that what you really want?"

Megan stopped what she was doing and turned to face Ken. "Do you remember what you told me every time you refused to give me a contract or even a small raise?"

He thought about it for a moment. "No. I mean, about what?"

"You said the real value of working here is that it's a springboard to bigger markets. That's how you justify your piss-ant wages. You said this was a training ground for moving up. The thing you always said I should aspire to."

Ken shrugged, unembarrassed by his lies. "Well sure, what do you expect me to say?"

"You're right," Megan said. "By now I should just expect you to lie. I suppose you don't have any other skills to rely on."

Ken gestured at the flowers Jimmy had given Megan. "What about your boyfriend?" he asked. "Is he moving or are you leaving him too?"

"He's not my boyfriend," Megan insisted. "He's just a guy." Megan paused, surprised by how easily those words had shot out of her mouth. But she meant it. Jimmy was just another guy standing between her and something better. Sure, she liked Jimmy in her own peculiar way, but she wasn't in love with him. She'd never said she was. *More important*, Megan thought, *yeah, the grass has got to be greener*. If nothing else, she owed it to herself to take a look on the other side.

Ken knew he wasn't going to change her mind, so he decided to try something he'd been considering for a while. He glanced up and down the hallway to make sure no one was watching, then he slipped inside the small office and closed the door behind him. Click. He locked it. The next thing Megan knew, he was standing directly behind her with his hands on her ass. "You know, I was just thinking I might be able to come up with a real nice severance package for you."

The clod was kneading her ass like pizza dough. And his tone wasn't that of just another idiot good-old-boy making a clumsy sexual advance. He sounded more determined than that. Megan scanned the desktop. Her options were a letter opener, a stapler, and a pair of scissors.

Ken fumbled with his zipper. "Whaddya say we tear off a quick piece and I'll see about a couple weeks' pay as your parting gift?" He leaned against her, trying to pin her to the desk.

Megan selected the best office supply for her needs and reacted with remarkable swiftness. Grabbing the large stapler with both hands, she opened it like a set of jaws, spun around, and closed it within an inch of serious pain. Ken was stunned not only by her quickness and her accuracy but by the viciousness of her proposal. If she finished what she'd started, the next time he peed it would look like a gimmicky lawn sprinkler. "Okay, okay," he said putting his hands in the air in surrender. "But you don't know what you're missing."

Megan shook her head. "I can't even believe you said that." Then she stapled him.

Ken screamed like a baby.

Megan handed him the staple remover, then shoved him aside. And on her way out the door she snatched Jimmy's flowers and tossed them in the trash.

* * *

Jimmy knew he'd screwed up. Instead of the yellow roses, which he knew Megan loved, he'd made the mistake of operating under the assumption that it was the thought that counted, resulting in the chintzy $6.99 grocery store arrangement. But in a world where upgrades are always available, who can blame a girl for wanting to improve her position? Jimmy figured it was unfair to expect Megan to lower her standards just because he was a broke-dick writer. Better that he improve his own financial position and pop for the roses next time.

Once again he thought about calling Megan to apologize. He

knew the worst thing he'd done was to buy cheap flowers, but he was still considering an apology. *Christ*, he thought, *this sensitive guy thing's got a death grip on me. I didn't do anything wrong. Why should I always be the one to try to smooth things over? Would it be any skin off her perfect, slightly upturned nose to pick up the phone and call me with a little sweet talk and an 'I'm sorry'? I mean, how tough would that be?*

All this was running through Jimmy's head as he sat staring at his computer. On the screen was a tentative outline for the opening chapters of *The Eddie Long Story*. But Jimmy hadn't written anything lately. The momentum of his great book project had petered out, owing largely to the fact that Jimmy was spending most of his time trying to figure out a way to make Megan fall in love with him. Jimmy looked up at plastic Elvis for inspiration. "Give me a sign," he said. "Tell me what to do." Jimmy jumped when the phone rang. He stared at it a moment before picking up. "Hello?"

"Hey, man! You workin' on my book?"

Jimmy smiled. "Hey, Eddie, how you doin'? I was just about to call you."

"And I bet you promise you'll pull out in time too." Eddie laughed the way guys do when they retell old jokes. "Listen, Mr. Hemingway, I was just callin' to let you know that I got your next two chapters. It turns out yours truly has signed a contract with Herron & Peavy Management."

"Holy shit! As in Big Bill Herron? Damn. Congratulations!" Jimmy opened a new blank document and started typing. "Details, man. What's the deal?"

Eddie told the story of his performance at the Bluebird. "After I played the song," he said, "I just walked out of the place. Left 'em with their jaws on the tabletops." He told Jimmy how Herron and Peavy had approached him afterwards, and how they had sealed the deal at Estella's.

Jimmy pried the particulars from Eddie. He knew there was a

good anecdote in the scene where Eddie negotiated changes in his contract over a plate of fried shrimp with Joe Tex singing in the background. Now that Eddie had signed with one of Nashville's most storied producers, Jimmy suddenly felt new momentum gathering on his own project.

"All right," Jimmy said, "so you signed with Herron & Peavy. What's the other chapter?"

"My marketing plan."

Jimmy paused. "Your marketing plan?" He stopped typing. "I don't think so. But here's an idea," he said brightly. "Maybe you could write a song about it. A real honky-tonker about direct mail and targeted demographics. I can hear it now." Jimmy started singing in a twangy baritone. "Come 'n' listen to a story 'bout my marketin' plan, gonna do some advertisin' and establish me a brand."

Eddie summoned a dark chuckle, then lapsed into his own exaggerated country accent. "Well shoot me for a billy goat if 'at ain't the funniest thang I ever heard!"

"You're the one with the funny ideas," Jimmy said. "The book's supposed to be about the rise of a populist singer-songwriter, not a business plan."

"And if it was still nineteen-fucking-sixty and I was just handing my career over to a producer and his shyster partner, I wouldn't even bring it up. But times've changed and one of the things you're gonna wanna put in there is how I took charge of my career from the get-go. And to tell the truth, I bet this'll be one of the better chapters."

"Yes, as the marketing section of most musicians' biographies tend to be," Jimmy said.

"Look, smart-ass, you don't have to use it, but you oughta at least hear it."

"All right, what's the plan?" Jimmy sat back and propped his feet on the table.

Eddie took a deep breath. "We're creating a character," he said. "A very mysterious character. A guy with a tragic background. And once we've generated sufficient interest in this mystery man, we're going to look for him. And then we're going to find him. And then we're going to sell him to the public."

Jimmy sat up. He had no idea where this was going, but it wasn't what he'd expected. He put his hands back on the keyboard and listened as Eddie explained the plan. They had already put the first part into play.

"We set up a website attributed to a woman named Frances Neagley," Eddie said. "She lives on a farm somewhere in the Tecumseh Valley. Her website is dedicated to an unknown musician, the identity of whom Miss Neagley is trying to discover. According to the information on her website, this unknown musician—apparently a young man—is the artist behind the most beautiful song Frances Neagley has ever heard." Eddie sounded like he was sitting around a campfire telling an old story.

The story, as Miss Neagley related it on her website, was that she was surfing the Net one night looking at the websites of the country music artists she liked when she stumbled on an otherwise unidentified site called endthatway.com. According to Miss Neagley, the mysterious website had very little text and one small MP3 file free for the downloading. "Here's a song that came from within my heart," the mysterious musician had written at endthatway.com. "Please listen to it and pass it on if you like it." Miss Neagley downloaded the file but promptly forgot about it as she continued surfing that night.

A week later, according to the story, she remembered the file and listened to the song. What she heard was so moving she could hardly believe her ears. She sat there at her computer, mouth agape, as this stranger probed the aching parts of her heart. She felt like he was singing to her the song she would have written about her worst heartache if she could ever write a song. Her sense of wonder at all this suddenly turned to shock when, halfway through the refrain, the song stopped cold.

At first, Miss Neagley wrote, she thought she'd accidentally hit a wrong button or something. She played the song again, and just as it had the first time, the song ended abruptly when it was half over. Miss Neagley assumed she had done something wrong in downloading the file. She immediately went online searching for endthatway.com. But the site was gone without a trace, as if it had never been there.

" 'I listened to this fragment of my heart over and over that night,' Ms. Neagley writes."

"Now wait a second," Jimmy interrupted. "Is this for real? How did you find this woman?"

Eddie laughed. "There is no woman," he said. "Well, there is a Frances Neagley. She's a friend of mine, she'll be the webmaster for the site, but the rest is just storytelling."

"All right, all right, keep going." Jimmy had been sucked in.

"She was so haunted by this song that she's been trying ever since to find out who and where the mystery musician is and where she can get a complete version of the song, because she has to hear how it ends," Eddie said. "Now, somewhere on her site, Frances gets a little confessional, and she tells us about herself. She's a woman in her late thirties, raised in the country, moved around a bit over the years. Had her share of relationships, good and bad, but she finally met the love of her life. They got married and bought a small farm and on their first anniversary her husband was killed in a tragic accident. Frances had no other family and she was left with little more than a mortgage and a hard heart. After her husband died, she thought her capacity for feeling had died with him. Until she heard that song."

"We're talking about 'It Wasn't Supposed to End That Way,' right?"

"Of course," Eddie said. "At any rate, she'll start writing letters and e-mails to country music radio stations asking about this unknown artist, citing lyrics from the song, asking if anyone knows who the musician is." Eddie paused again. "Are you gettin' all this?"

"Yeah," Jimmy said. "This is the best chapter so far."

"Like I said." Eddie continued with mounting enthusiasm, "Okay, in the meanwhile, music directors and programming consultants in other parts of the country are going to start getting letters and faxes from the general public asking about this MP3 file that's been floating around the Net. They want to hear the whole song, they'll say. People will start writing to country music magazines and record labels, and sooner or later, somebody in the business is going to have to hear this song."

"What if nobody writes these letters?"

"Jimmy?" Eddie sounded like he was speaking to a child.

"Yeah?"

"Wake up! We'll be the ones writing the letters, people we hire. They'll mail the letters, and send the faxes, and zap e-mail from all over the country. It won't cost much more than the price of stamps and some ISP charges."

"Clever boy." Jimmy had never thought of Eddie as devious, but this was in the neighborhood. It was an inspired deceit, but it raised a question. "How ethical is this?"

"This is a marketing campaign. What's ethics got to do with it?" Jimmy snorted a laugh. "Anyway," Eddie continued, "assuming this works and we get the attention of the record companies, we'll bring the parties together and let the bidding begin."

"Interesting," Jimmy said. He was impressed by the quirky possibilities of the plan, but he was skeptical of its viability. He thought about it for a minute. "It's different, I'll say that. But I don't think that's how record companies work. I mean, I guess I'm having a hard time imagining that a record company would sign an artist based on Internet buzz."

Eddie paused a moment. "I've got three words for you, Jimmy. *Blair. Witch. Project.* Remember that a few years ago? No major Hollywood film distributor would ever consider picking up and releasing a feature shot mostly on videotape by a bunch of nobodies from Florida, right? Never happen, right? Not in a million years. But it did happen, and the damn thing made over two hundred million dollars."

"Well, I'll give you that."

"We're just trying to find a new way to skin the cat, that's all. If it doesn't work, we can still take our tape to the record labels, we just won't be in as good a negotiating position. No big deal. See, even though the Internet's ready as a means of music distribution, the general public isn't ready to use it that way. But the public is already using it to get information, even if the information isn't genuine, so that's what we'll use it for."

"Maybe you're right," Jimmy said. "Could be a great way to get the labels' attention."

"That's the plan," Eddie said. "So what about the book? How's it coming?"

"It's shaping up," Jimmy said. "Especially now. I mean, you getting hooked up with Herron and Peavy, well, I know it doesn't guarantee anything, but that's a major step. Right now I'm still working on the first three or four chapters and I'm heading up to your old neck of the woods to find out about the young Eddie Long. You know, interview some of your old teachers, friends, and neighbors, that sort of thing."

"Oh?" Eddie's tone changed suddenly. He sounded unenthused.

"Yeah. Who's most likely to tell embarrassing stories on you?"

"No shortage of folks to do that," Eddie said. "Most of 'em'll make shit up if they think it'll get their name in a book. Fact there ain't no tellin' what kind of crazy shit you'll hear about me from those folks. Best advice I got is, don't believe everything you hear."

7

immy felt like someone had plugged him in. He pushed back from his desk and spun around in his chair a few times. Then he leaned back and closed his eyes and let things take shape in his mind. He could see the cover for the book—a tall backlit figure wearing a Stetson, arms outstretched with a guitar held aloft in the right hand, a glint of light starring off the pearl inlay of the fingerboard. The title stretched boldly across the top: *The Long and the Short of It: The Eddie Long Story* cut a path through the middle of the backlit figure. Finally, in a larger typeface across the bottom, the author took his place: *Jimmy Rogers*.

Someone called his name. The curtain pulled back. Jimmy strode onto the stage to warm applause. "Oprah! So nice to see you," he said, bussing her cheek. No, it wasn't really an Oprah book, was it? "Dave!" Nah. "Jay!" No, none of the network shows ever promoted authors. "Charlie Rose, such a pleasure." Unlikely. PBS was probably too snooty for the book. "Crook and Chase! So nice to be here!" Syndication was better than nothing.

But what if Eddie didn't make it? What if he was a complete fail-

ure? Jimmy couldn't afford to waste a year writing a book about a
guy no one ever heard of. Unless he recast it as a work of fiction.
Hmm. On the one hand, if Eddie succeeded, Jimmy had a great
biography. If Eddie tanked, Jimmy simply had to add a few small
elements, a murder or two, perhaps some sex, a little betrayal, and
voilà! He had a novel. It was a great story either way, and Jimmy
could end the fictional version however he wanted. Country superstar rides off into the sunset or failed artist dies by his own hand.

Inspired by the possibilities, he spent the rest of the afternoon
writing. He fell into a state as everything Eddie told him emptied
out of his head. Jimmy had never been to the Bluebird Cafe, so he
added some imagined details. He wrote up Eddie's account of the
negotiation at Estella's, softening Eddie's portrayal of Herron and
Peavy as obsolete country buffoons, rendering them instead as
crusty old music industry sages.

Jimmy then got into the chapter on Eddie's marketing plan. The
more he considered the details, the more he came to see how canny
the idea was. An alternative fictional ending abruptly presented
itself: Eddie fails in Nashville, then moves to New York and
becomes the most successful marketing strategist in the advertising
industry. Nah, if he failed, it was better if he hanged himself. Dra-
matically speaking.

Several hours later Jimmy came out of his state. His eyes were
red and dry, his neck hurt, and he longed for Megan. He wanted to
call her while still exhilarated from his writing. He wanted to tell her
about Eddie. He wanted to tell her he loved her and he needed to
hear her say it back, so he picked up the phone and dialed. *No
apologies this time,* he told himself. *No one's to blame.* He'd just ask
if she wanted to go down to George Street for a drink. He'd casually
mention his idea about writing the book as a novel if it didn't work
out as nonfiction. He wouldn't make it sound like he was seeking
her approval, of course, just another idea he had, no big deal. He'd
been wanting to write a novel for years anyway. *Maybe if she started*

thinking of me as a novelist, he thought, *then she'd start taking me seriously.* He smiled. Things were going to work out just fine. He could feel it.

After the fifth ring he started to think she wasn't home. And sure enough, a recorded voice came on the line. "I'm sorry," she said, though she didn't sound like she meant it. "The number you have reached is no longer in service." *What? That's impossible.* "If you feel you have reached this recording in error, please hang up and dial the number again." Jimmy looked at the number pad. *Must've dialed wrong,* he thought. He dialed again, concentrating on the digits this time. "I'm sorry," she repeated. Jimmy hung up. A lonely feeling grew in his heart, and it made him desperate for an explanation. Maybe some psychotic radio fan had gotten Megan's number. Sure, and she'd been forced to change it. That had to be it. No problem. Jimmy would just call the station.

"Yes, I'd like to leave a message for Megan Taylor, please."

"Miss Taylor no longer works here," the receptionist said. "She got a new job."

Jimmy grew desperate. "Really? Like over at Z-102?" He asked the question without conviction because he knew the answer. He just couldn't bring himself to say it. So the receptionist said it for him.

"No, some station in Nashville. I don't know which one."

Jimmy hesitated. "Yeah, okay, thanks." He hung up, shaking his head. What a schmuck. He could hear Megan's voice. *Nooo, I'm not moving to Nashville. Well, it's not up to me, anyway. He just asked me to send him an air check tape. He didn't even say they had a job available or anything. And who knows? The guy'll probably be working in Buffalo by the time this tape gets to Nashville. You know how radio is.*

Yeah, Jimmy knew. Radio was famous for disloyalty. You give your heart and soul to a station, then you come to work one day and find the locks changed, the format abandoned, and the request line no longer in service. It reminded Jimmy of somebody he knew, or someone he thought he knew. He wondered if she was already there, wondered what she was doing. Was she thinking about him? He wished he could read her mind, just for an hour.

He sat there thinking about her for a long time. Segments of their relationship popped into his head. He remembered the time she got the hiccups from laughing so hard at something he did, and he thought about that day in Vicksburg. God, he'd never forget that. He pulled an envelope from his desk drawer. It held photos Jimmy had taken at a party a month or so ago. He flipped through the photos until he found one of himself with his arm around Megan. He was smiling like a fool drunk in love. Megan looked like she was waiting for the moment to pass. He hadn't noticed that before. Now that he did, he knew it was over. She was gone. Maybe she'd never wanted to be there in the first place. She'd dumped him. And now he was alone, sitting in a small room in a small apartment in a small town feeling sorry for himself as the broken-hearted are wont to do.

Like far too many people in this state of mind, Jimmy started to think his brand of heartache was special and would make a great song. He came up with a title: "The Number You've Reached (Is No Longer in Service)." But what rhymed with "service"? Nervous? Purvis? No good. Back to the drawing board. How about "If You Reached This Recording in Error (Please Hang Up and Dial Again)"? No, that was too long. He struggled with the idea late into the night but he couldn't make it work. Rhymes were hard to come by, and those that came didn't say what he wanted.

Outside it was dark, but Jimmy didn't notice. He was preoccupied by his own darkness, a black melancholy that tended to make him melodramatic and fatalistic. His girl had left him and he couldn't even come up with a song title to express his anguish. Oddly, that's when he saw a faint glimmer. All things considered, Jimmy realized he wasn't as bad off as he could be. At least he still had the book, nonfiction or otherwise. Maybe he could win Megan back with that.

Jimmy stood and went to pack. He'd be leaving for Quitman County in the morning.

* * *

Whitney called Big Bill the Monday after his open mic performance at the Bluebird, and to his surprise, Big Bill invited him to dinner to discuss his career.

Even though his mama had warned him against it since he was little, Whitney allowed himself to feel a little more important than he'd allowed the day before. He'd have bet not everyone got invited to dinner with Big Bill Herron and Franklin Peavy. He just wished his mom was still alive so he could tell her the news. The restaurant wasn't far from Whitney's place, probably a ten-minute walk. Since his truck was still at the repair shop and the hole in his boot wasn't getting any smaller, he was glad Mr. Herron had picked a place close by. A guy just couldn't get any luckier than that, Whitney thought.

He cut out a new piece of cardboard and slipped it into his boot. Then he put on his black Wranglers, a dark plaid shirt, and his dark gray vest. He stood in front of the mirror as he put on his black Lancer. He took a good look and told himself things were going to work out, then he headed over to the restaurant.

Whitney stopped cold on the sidewalk across the street from the restaurant. The moment he saw the Mercedes pull up to the valet, his outsider status was reconfirmed. He hadn't dressed for this sort of place, and it was too late to turn back. Inside the hostess took one look at him and tried not to smirk. She'd seen an untold number of hopefuls come through here looking for their future, but she'd never seen one dressed so *mal à propos*. Sometimes she wished they'd just stop coming to town. All they did was muddy the water for real singers and songwriters like herself. "Can I help you?"

Whitney took his hat off and ran his fingers through his long hair. "Yes, ma'am. I'm here to meet Mr. Bill Herron and Mr.

Franklin Peavy." He could tell by the way she looked at him that she disapproved.

The hostess smiled mechanically. "Right this way." She took Whitney to the table where Herron and Peavy were waiting. More than a few heads turned to eye the skinny kid in the belligerent outfit.

"Hey now!" Big Bill said as he stood to shake hands. "We was startin' to worry you'd signed with Fitzgerald-Hartley or something. C'mon, sit down. Thanks for joining us."

"Thank you for inviting me." Whitney turned to Franklin and shook his hand too. "I mean, both of you. I appreciate it." Whitney generally wasn't the nervous type, but he felt out of place. Here he was, shaking hands with two people who were, by his reckoning, among the most influential in Nashville. He didn't know what to say. He spoke best through his music and never had to talk business with anyone more influential than the bar owners who usually hired him. He sat down and looked around. He'd never seen a crowd of people like this. Whitney sensed the disdain.

Big Bill saw Whitney was unsettled. "I gotta tell ya, I haven't been able to get your song outta my head since I heard it."

"Which one?"

"Oh, the, uh, slow, pretty one," Big Bill said.

" 'Night's Devotion'?"

"That's it," Big Bill said. "You know, it all starts with the song. Sure does. A great song can do a lot more for a mediocre performer than a great performer can do for a mediocre song, if you know what I'm sayin'. And your song is great."

"Well, thank you," Whitney said. "I got more of 'em too."

"You got a gift," Big Bill said. "No doubt about it." After seeing Whitney in a better light, Big Bill made a quick career decision for him. It wasn't fair, but, given the importance of videos in marketing music these days, he sometimes had to steer kids toward songwriting from the beginning so they didn't get it in their heads that they might be on a big stage someday. "You are one helluva songwriter."

"I appreciate that," Whitney said. "Especially coming from you." He began to relax and enjoy the unlikely situation where he found himself the center of attention. Big Bill pulled a bottle from the bucket of ice next to the table. "Wine?"

"Uh, sure." Whitney had never been a big drinker, and he preferred beer on the occasions when he did drink, but he didn't want to seem like a rube. It was bad enough he felt like one.

"You like chardonnay?"

"You bet," Whitney said, not knowing chardonnay from Shinola. "It's . . . real nice."

For the next hour, Herron and Peavy blew enough balloon juice to float Whitney over the Cumberland River and into Adelphia Coliseum on the other side. They predicted his songs would be at the top of the charts, and he was looking at a big-money future with more beautiful women than you'd find at a Miss Mississippi pageant. The two industry giants poured it on thick, insisting over and over that Whitney had that something special. Actually, the only thing they were sure of was that Whitney had a couple of songs, one of which Big Bill felt was a hit. If it turned out the kid had more than that, well, there might end up being some truth to what Herron and Peavy were saying. But for now they just wanted the one song.

Whitney absorbed everything, including the chardonnay. He found that sipping the wine only accentuated its bitterness, so he took to gulping it. "Well, that's flattering and all, but—"

Big Bill held up his hand and gave Whitney a serious look. "Son, we're not in the flattery business. We're in the music business, so don't think we're here to blow smoke up your skirt and buy you dinner. We wanna sign you as a client."

Big Bill poured more wine while Franklin reached into his briefcase and pulled out a contract—one that Big Bill had already

checked for covert producer credits. "This is our standard agreement." Franklin flipped from page to page, pointing as he spoke. "It
covers publishing rights, mechanicals, sync rights, compulsory
license, all the boilerplate that's in everybody's contracts." Franklin
pulled a pen from his coat and clicked the push button with his
thumb. "By the way, what's the name of your publishing company?"

Whitney shrugged. "Uh, I don't think I have one, really. Should I
get one?"

Big Bill smiled broad as a double-wide. "It's no big deal. Some
writers use publishers, most of 'em just let their managers handle
that kind of stuff."

"All this is real standard," Franklin said.

Whitney nodded. "I'm just a songwriter and a singer. I figure you
guys know all that other stuff."

Franklin could barely hide his contempt. One of the few things
he and Big Bill agreed on was that it wasn't their job to educate anyone who wasn't their client. In fact, the way they saw it, it was
against the basic tenets of business to do so. As far as they were concerned, it was the potential client's responsibility either to learn
about the business or to hire an attorney to handle his affairs. Otherwise it was in Herron and Peavy's best interest to operate under
the assumption that the potential client was a competent party. It
was like football. Each team arrives at the field assuming the other
understands how the game is played. If one of them doesn't, they
get their butts kicked and learn a valuable lesson for next time.

From a contract law perspective, Franklin felt they were on solid
ground. If a client didn't know any better and felt like he got a good
deal earning $30,000 even when he could have earned $100,000,
well, in Franklin's experience the courts tended not to consider the
adequacy of the consideration in most contract situations, unless
the difference was startling. Of course, for obvious reasons, once
Herron and Peavy signed a client it was in their best interest to continue not educating him, lest he go back and read his contract.

Whitney flipped through the thick document. "This looks pretty complicated. You think I should get a lawyer to look at it?"

"A lawyer?" Franklin pointed at Whitney. "Absolutely. Best thing you can do."

Big Bill waved the waitress over. "Sugar, could you bring me the Yellow Pages?" He passed the hors d'oeuvres to Whitney. "Have you tried these little ham-and-goat-cheese things? Man are they good!" He picked up the bottle and refilled Whitney's glass. "And try 'em with this wine. It's a great combo."

The waitress returned with the phone book. Big Bill opened it to "Attorneys" and slid it in front of Whitney. He ran his finger down a column of names. "I know all these fellas. They're all real smart. This ole boy went to Vandy with Franklin. That one went to Ole Miss. I betcha dolla there's even a Harvard guy or two in there. And I'm tellin' you, these guys know their contracts." Big Bill leaned across the table to share a secret with Whitney. "But I tell you what, every last one of 'em'll charge you five grand just to tell you this is all standard stuff."

"Five thousand dollars?" Whitney turned to Franklin. "Just to read this?"

"Up front." Franklin shrugged. "That's pretty standard." He held the appetizers out to Whitney. "Care for another?" Whitney ate another one and gulped some more chardonnay. It was starting to taste pretty good, especially with the salty ham-and-cheese things.

They ordered their dinners. The waitress talked Whitney into the pan-seared catfish with okra and fig chutney. Franklin got the pasta with crawfish and andouille in a heavy cream sauce. Big Bill ordered prime rib with the crabmeat topping, then held up their empty bottle. "Honey, could you bring us another one of these?"

Franklin took the contract from Whitney, turned back a few pages, and pointed at a long obfuscating paragraph. "Here's the most important part of this as far as you're concerned. The standard song-writer royalty for Herron & Peavy Management clients is five percent. Of course, after a little success, we'll negotiate that up, but for starters, you gotta admit, that's good money."

Whitney looked unsure. "Five percent doesn't seem like much."

"You'd be surprised," Big Bill said, picking up his pen. He took the contract, turned it over, and started doing the math. "Say you sell a million records at an average price of, well, let's just say ten dollars to make the math easy, right? I mean, otherwise you gotta go through the calculation of suggested retail list price, recoupable advances, packaging deductions, and all that, so five percent of ten dollars is fifty cents, right? Times a million units is half a million dollars."

Bill circled the $500,000 several times for emphasis. "Can you imagine? The heck would you do with five hundred thousand dollars? And that's just one record."

"Wow." Whitney smiled and shook his head. He'd never allowed himself to think such thoughts, and now not only were these guys telling him it was possible, but they were making it sound like it was more likely than not. Whitney didn't know what had him feeling better, the wine or the endless promises, so he slugged down the rest of his chardonnay and urged them on.

Big Bill refilled Whitney's glass while Franklin flipped the contract over and turned to the back. "Have you already got a personal services corporation set up?" He made it sound like this was something every songwriter should have done a long time ago.

"No sir. You know, I just got to town and . . . is that something where I just go down to the courthouse and fill out some forms?"

Big Bill pushed the Yellow Pages back in front of Whitney. "Any one of these fellas will help you set it up. Probably cost another five or seven thousand, no more than that. But most of our clients save the money by running their income through our corporation, since we already got it set up for that sort of thing."

"Well, that makes sense," Whitney said. "It sure does."

The waitress brought their dinners and, before long, a third bot-

tle of wine. Herron and Peavy eased off the contract talk while they
ate. Instead, they regaled Whitney with ribald tales of country
music celebrities. Big Bill ticked off the names of famous players
and singers who were serious cocaine and heroin users, then
Franklin shocked Whitney with news of the sexual orientation of
one of the industry's biggest stars.

Whitney stared drunkenly at Franklin, his mouth agape.
"He's . . . gay?"

"Queer as a blind guide dog," Big Bill said.

"But I read where he was datin' that TV actress."

Big Bill arched his brows. "Oh yeah, we got some fine public relations firms here in Nashville. Don't let anybody tell you otherwise."

Later, as the waitress cleared their plates, Franklin rolled the
contract into a tight tube and wagged it at Whitney. "Think about
this," he said. "We want to sign you and we've only heard two of your
songs. You know how many other artists we've signed after hearing
just two songs? None. Not a one. Now, that must mean we see
something in you we don't see in others, right?"

"I got a whole lot more than just those two," Whitney said. "If
you want, we can go back to my place and I can play some of the
others." Whitney wondered if they were ever going to ask him to
sign the contract.

Big Bill ordered brandies all around. He was surprised Whitney
hadn't offered to sign the contract yet. Most newcomers signed
before dinner was brought to the table. Big Bill swirled his brandy
around his snifter for a moment, then looked up. "Franklin, show
him page eight."

Franklin flipped through the contract. "This is something else
we don't do very often," he said, pointing to the clause in question.
"We're prepared to offer you a one-thousand-dollar signing bonus if
you'll let us manage and produce you and publish your songs."

Whitney took a deep breath. He couldn't believe it. "You'll pay
me to be my manager?" He could get his truck out of hock and get

his boots fixed with that kind of money. He smiled and started to think maybe he'd come to the right place after all. "Where do I sign?"

*   *   *

It was another sleepy, dusty Delta day when Jimmy arrived in Quitman County. He had lunch with two of Eddie's childhood friends, then met with his high school algebra teacher. After that he went to see two of Eddie's former employers. There was no one at the Hegman farm, where Eddie used to help out during harvesting, so he went over to the Lytles' property. Lamont Lytle said Eddie had been a good worker, tending their small peach orchard. "He mostly did pruning and fertilizing and keeping the bugs away," Lamont said. "Some folks don't like that kind of work, but Eddie didn't seem to mind. And I'll tell you, we never lost much crop when he was here." Mr. Lytle said he wasn't surprised to hear Eddie had moved to Nashville. He pointed to a rickety outbuilding down by the grove of peach trees. "That boy used to set down there by the toolshed and play his songs whenever he was waitin' on me. He's got talent, they ain't no question 'bout that."

Jimmy went to take some photographs around the old toolshed. Inside were ancient rusting shears and rakes and peach-picking tools. A network of spiderwebs connected everything. Rat traps were stacked on the shelves next to a dozen old brown glass gallon-size bottles and some big rusty cans containing an array of pesticides and fertilizers and other tools of the trade. Jimmy noticed a beam of sunlight blooming through the colored glass, casting amber light on an old pair of boots with high Cuban heels. He took a couple of shots of that and several from the exterior before heading off to track down the public records on Tammy's death.

The county clerk's office and the sheriff's department shared a new one-story brick building with thick tempered-glass windows and good air-conditioning. Walking in the front door, Jimmy could smell fresh paint and caulk that was still curing. Behind the counter was a skinny man wearing a maroon knit polo shirt. Jimmy introduced himself and explained why he was there. The man looked at Jimmy with suspicion. "So, what is it you want?"

"I just need to take a look at the coroner's report and the death certificate for Tammy Long," Jimmy said. "She died about—"

"Oh," the man interrupted. "That's something you need, is it? Not just something you want, but need." The man squinted in Jimmy's direction. "Well, if that don't tear the rag off the bush, you comin' up here nosin' around other people's affairs. You might as well be peepin' in windows far as I'm concerned." He leaned on the counter that separated him from Jimmy. "I'm not sure I'm gonna let you see 'em. Whaddya think about that?"

Jimmy was surprised by the man's aggressive attitude. He could understand if he was at the Pentagon trying to get some compromising federal documents, but a Quitman County coroner's report? "I'm writing a book on her husband, and I just want to get the facts right."

"Oh, I see." The skinny man pulled a stool over to the counter and sat down. "You wanna get the facts right 'cause you're so concerned for the families and all, is that it?"

"I just want to get the facts," Jimmy said. "What do I have to do?"

The man looked at Jimmy for a moment. "Well, I tell you. You're entitled to get a look at them documents according to Title Five, U.S.C. Section five-five-two." He leaned across the counter again. "But I guess a big-city writer like you knows all about the Freedom of Information Act, don't'cha?" He pointed at Jimmy. "Guys like you enjoy pokin' around in the files and gettin' everybody's dirty little secrets, ain't that right? Does it get you excited? Is that it?" The man seemed to be rubbing against the other side of the counter.

"No, that's not it." Jimmy tried to see what the man was rubbing against. "Like I said, I'm writing—"

"A book, I know. You told me already. What do you think I am, stupid?" The man backed away from the counter slightly.

"Look," Jimmy said, "the public has a right to information concerning—"

"Oh, now you're gonna lecture me on the fundamental rights of a constitutional democracy, is that it?" The man smiled in an odd way.

"I'm not lecturing about anything. I just want to know what I have to do to get a look at the public records."

"Same as everybody," the man said. "Fill out some forms. I need to see copies of a thirty-seven dash one thirty-one and the federal FOIA request form along with your tax returns for the past three years and two forms of photo identification."

Jimmy made an involuntary face. "What? That's insane. I'm not asking for sensitive federal information here, I just—"

The man behind the counter slowly opened a drawer and pulled out a small, dirty pistol, which he laid gently on the counter. Jimmy's eyes opened wide. What sort of nightmare had he stumbled into here? He half expected the man to open another drawer, pull out a banjo, and start playing the theme to *Deliverance*. The man's face tensed like a dam holding back an emotional reservoir. Jimmy couldn't decide whether to go for the gun or the door. When the man made a sudden move, Jimmy snatched the gun and skittered backwards on the tile. That's when the dam burst and the man started laughing. "Ewww-weee! You shoulda seen your face!" he cackled. Then he got all serious again. "I'll need to see your last three tax returns." He laughed some more. "I'm just having fun with ya, man, relax. I don't get to have a lot of fun here."

Jimmy was unable to see the humor. He felt the heft of the gun in his hand and wondered if the skinny guy was the sort of person who ought to be in possession of a weapon.

"Gone and shoot me if you're mad," the man said. "Ain't nothin' but a starter's pistol." He chuckled some more as he imitated himself. "Thirty-seven dash one thirty-one and two forms of photo ID." The skinny man turned and headed for the filing cabinet. "What was the last name again?"

Jimmy stared at the man for a moment before answering. "Long," he said. "Tammy Long." Figuring the best thing to do was play along with this lunatic, Jimmy faked a laugh and pointed the gun at the man. "You had me going there," he said. "I was ready to go get my tax returns for you."

The guy was rooting through a filing cabinet now, not paying attention to Jimmy. He mocked himself again as he stood there: "Plus your tax returns for the past three years." He laughed. "I wish more folks came in here so I could do that," he said as he walked back to the counter holding up the file. "You'd be surprised at how dull this job can be." He stopped short of handing the file to Jimmy. He cocked his head to one side. "What kinda book you writin'?"

"Biography," Jimmy said. "You ever hear of Eddie Long?"

The man said he'd seen Eddie perform once at the casino up in Tunica and thought he did a good show. "I didn't realize he was from around here, though." He put the file on the counter, then looked around like a naughty schoolboy. "You better not let the sheriff walk in here and see you holding that gun on me."

Jimmy slid the pistol across the counter in exchange for the file. It contained crime-scene photos along with copies of reports from every county agency that dealt with the matter. The newspaper reports Jimmy had seen said only that Tammy had been found dead in her house. There had been no details about cause of death, only that it was under investigation.

The coroner's report filled in the blanks. It said Tammy had died of poisoning and the death was listed as a suicide. But there was also mention of a gunshot wound to the head. Jimmy looked at the skinny man. "Doesn't that seem strange to you?"

"Yeah," the man said. He looked over to his desk, then back at Jimmy. "And you wanna see something past strange?" He went to his desk and picked up a printout of an e-mail. "This came in a few days ago from the state police in Terrebonne Parish, down in Louisiana."

Jimmy took the document. The information had come by way of the National Crime Information Center, a federal clearinghouse of malfeasance. It said a man by the name of Fred Babineaux, first assumed to have died in a single-vehicle automobile accident, had actually died of sodium fluoroacetate poisoning. According to the investigating officers, the poison appeared to have been put intentionally into a dose of Dr. Porter's Headache Powder which Mr. Babineaux had ingested moments before crashing his car. According to a receipt found in the wreckage, Mr. Babineaux had bought the powder at an EZ Mart in Shreveport the day prior to his death. The Louisiana State Police was investigating his death as a homicide and making routine inquiries about any similar poisonings in the region on the chance that this was part of a pattern.

"My guess is they're thinkin' it's a serial killer like that Tylenol pois'nin' back in the eighties," the man said. "That'd be a pretty good chapter for your book if Eddie's wife turned out to be a victim of a serial killer, wouldn't it?"

Jimmy nodded. It certainly would be interesting, he thought. In fact, a good serial killer story might be a book unto itself. Jimmy's publishing career couldn't seem to stay on one track. He already had a possible biography or a novel, depending on how Eddie's future played out, and now he suddenly had the start of a true-crime book. Except for the fact that Megan had dumped him, he was having a good week. He held up the fax. "Did you respond to this?"

The skinny guy looked wounded. " 'Course I responded. I called and told 'em we had a pois'nin' and that we'd found a box of the Dr. Porter's stuff in the medicine cabinet." He rifled through the crime-scene photos and found one taken in the bathroom. It showed the open cabinet with the box clearly visible on the shelf. "We sent 'em the box, and sure enough, there was poison in every one of the little doses, you know, those little envelopes." He indicated the size of the envelopes with his thumb and index finger. "And you wanna know something else weird?" The man found the part of the coroner's report detailing the contents of Tammy's stomach. "Says she'd eaten Chinese food 'fore she died—didn't even get digested that poison killed her so fast."

Jimmy saw that she'd eaten orange beef, one of his favorites. "What's weird about that?"

The man spread the sheriff's report on the counter, then slapped his hand down on top of it. "Where'd it come from? You know what I'm saying?" He pointed at the photos. "Ain't nothing in the pictures. No Chung King cartons in the trash, no take-outee boxes on the counter, nothin'. Not a dirty dish in sight, and ain't a decent Chinese restaurant within fifteen miles of Hinchcliff. I think they oughtta be looking into that, is what I think."

"That's weird all right." Jimmy collected the sheriff's and coroner's reports. "Can I get copies of these?"

The man pointed at the copy machine. "Go on." As Jimmy made copies, the guy took a phone call. Jimmy stapled the coroner's report to the death certificate, then made a note to find out what sodium fluoroacetate was. After a few minutes of saying "Uh-huh" and "Issat right?" into the phone, the man hung up and looked at Jimmy. "Well, talk about scratchin' where it itches." The man pointed at the phone. "That there was a detective from Tuscaloosa, Alabama." He walked to the fax machine just as it started to ring.

"What did he want?"

The skinny man didn't answer. He just stood by the fax machine, grinning. When the fax finished printing, he handed it to Jimmy. "Seems somebody down there had a headache too."

*   *   *

Eddie picked up the phone to make a call, but there was no dial tone. He pushed the button a couple of times, trying to hang up, but to no avail. Finally he said, "Hello?"

"What?" The woman on the other end sounded startled. "I never heard it ring," she said, then paused. "Eddie?"

The voice was familiar, but he couldn't place it. "Yeah," he said. "Speaking."

"Surprise! It's me. Megan."

"Hey, girl! What's going on with you?"

Megan moved her lips close to the mouthpiece and slipped into her earthiest radio voice. "Guess who's working nights at one-oh-six-point-nine FM in Nashville?"

"Get outta town!" Eddie said. "But don't stop talking that way." He knew flirting when he heard it.

Megan lilted the station's tedious slogan, "Givin' you everything you want . . . and more."

"Wow," Eddie said. "You oughta forget radio and go into phone sex."

"Probably pays better," Megan said, "but you don't get all the free CDs and T-shirts."

"So what's the deal?" Eddie asked. "How long've you been in town?" He hoped Jimmy hadn't come with her, but he wasn't sure if he should ask or wait to see if she dropped it into conversation. "Where're you livin'?"

"Some apartment complex way the hell out past Brentwood. It's pretty tacky, but at least my commute's a bitch."

Eddie laughed. He could picture Megan behind the control board at the radio station wearing a too-short T-shirt revealing her flat stomach. "Man, I'm glad you called when you did. You came close to missing me," he said. "Just now, I was pickin' up to call the phone company about getting an unlisted number. I mean, one second later and, hell, I don't even have call waiting."

"Well, like they say, timing's everything." Timing was one of the things on Megan's mind at the moment. She was wondering how long Eddie planned to wait before he started dating, and she wondered how long she should wait before making a move. "You gettin' an unlisted number 'cause you got girls stalking you?"

"Not hardly." Eddie told her all about signing with Herron & Peavy.

"Ohmigod, Eddie! That's fabulous! Congratulations! I knew you were going to make it. And just think, I knew you when." *Wow*, she thought, *timing is everything*.

"The unlisted number's part of this whole marketing plan we got." He paused. "Listen, I'd love to tell you about it."

"And I'd love to hear."

"Hey, listen," Eddie said. "Uh, did Jimmy, I mean is he—"

"Oh, we broke things off," Megan said, real casual. "I mean, we're still pals, but he didn't want to try the long-distance-relationship thing. So I guess he sort of dumped me in that sense. But, you know, no harm done. No blood, no foul. I'm a big girl."

"Well, I'm, uh, sorry, you know. So, uh, how're you doing?"

"Hey, I'm over it," Megan said. "New city, new apartment, new start."

Eddie knew the door had just been opened. "That's cool," he said. "Listen we're going in to record this weekend. You wanna be my date?"

"I'd love to."

8

*E*ddie and Megan arrived at Big Bill's house an hour before the start of the recording session. The three of them sat in the six-hundred-square-foot kitchen sipping sweet tea. Megan was playing it cool, but she was agog at the proportions of Big Bill's Belle Meade estate. This was exactly the sort of place Megan could see herself living. "I just love your house," she said.

Other than that, Eddie was doing most of the talking. He was excited, and not just about the recording session. He had some good news. "Silicon and copper," Eddie said cryptically. "Connects the whole world." After a brief rumination on the wonders of the micro-processor, Eddie gave Big Bill an update on the Internet marketing scheme. He had explained the strategy to Herron and Peavy the night he signed his contract. Herron and Peavy had agreed to fund the plan as long as the costs were as low as projected and only if Eddie managed it. They'd figure out later how to make it recoupable against Eddie's royalties, assuming he ever had any.

Meanwhile, Eddie had hired eight net-savvy Vanderbilt under-graduates for minimum wage plus promotional copies of CDs from

Herron & Peavy Management's stable of artists. Their job was to create buzz by spreading the word on the Frances Neagley website and the search for the mysterious musician who had stirred her still heart with his song "It Wasn't Supposed to End That Way." The Vandy crew was in the process of visiting every e-zine, bulletin board, and chat room related to pop music, country music, or free downloadable music files.

"You can't be serious." Big Bill was looking at a document Eddie had handed him. "You're telling me that more'n five thousand people've already heard the song?"

"Well, half of it, anyway," Eddie said. "And it could be two or three times that many. The only thing we can track is the number of times it's been downloaded from the site. Once it's downloaded, people can forward it to others who can forward it and on and on. It's electronic word-of-mouth. So far we've left footprints at over two thousand sites on the web. Like I said, we can't track how many of those have started telling others who have told others—"

"It's called mushrooming," Megan said, just to participate.

Eddie nodded. "Right. But we know that inquiries about the Frances Neagley website have started to pop up independently in chatrooms and message boards."

"That sounds like a good thing." Big Bill was clueless.

"It's fantastic," Megan said. "It means people are talking about it. Somebody's even trying to sell it on eBay! Can you imagine trying to sell cassettes of half a song?"

Big Bill nodded knowingly despite not knowing what an eBay was. "It sounds like it's going good."

"It's going great," Eddie said. "These numbers are unreal. If it keeps up like this . . ." Eddie leaned back and put his hands behind his head. ". . . we're talkin' double platinum."

Big Bill couldn't resist the enthusiasm. "Well, then," he said, suddenly drumming his hands on his belly. "I guess we better produce a goddam record!" He pushed back from the table and stood

up. "Let's head on down to the studio." Bill led the way through the
cavernous house. "Oh, by the way, Franklin sends his regrets he
can't be here tonight. He had to attend the Class of '89 Awards in
Atlanta. One of our clients got nominated for Best New Hat Act,
but he'll be here tomorrow. In fact, he's bringing our newest client
with him, kid named Whitney Rankin, real talented songwriter. I
think you'll like him."

As they walked down a hallway, Megan counted the gold records
on the wall. "You know, Mr. Herron, I just started working at Hot
Country one-oh-six-point-nine, and like I told Eddie, when the
time's right I'm going to work on the promotion director about running a 'Where's Eddie Long?' contest or something to increase
awareness within the industry."

Big Bill allowed as how he thought that was a good idea. "Never
hurts having somebody in radio on your side," he said, turning to
Eddie with a nudge. "I'd hang on to her if I were you."

They arrived at a large, heavy door, which Big Bill pushed open.
They stepped inside the studio. It was warm and smelled faintly of
cedar. "You can keep your silicon and copper," Big Bill said, gesturing at the bank of tubes that pushed his Pulltech midrange EQs and
his Teletronix leveling amp. "Iron and gas are the things that connect me to the universe." He smiled.

"Wow," Megan said as she laid her hands on the mixing console.
"Is this whole room analog?" She was amazed anyone was that much
of a dinosaur.

Big Bill nodded. "Damn right, and I don't care what Don Cook
says about all that fancy digital crap. I've done blind tests too, and
believe me, nothin' sounds as good as analog, period. End of story."
He showed them around the studio. It was a thing of beauty and a
technical wonder, though not in the modern Nashville sense. This
was a working museum of vintage recording equipment. "That's an
original Marshall eighteen-watt combo." He said this with the sort

of pride usually reserved for parents talking about their Harvard-graduated children.

Megan pointed at some equipment. "What are those?"

"Those, my dear, modern, FM girl, are 1954 Fairchild compressor/limiters that I bought from an AM radio station that went out of business in 1969. The transformers were still in pretty good shape, but I had 'em refurbished and had all the tubes replaced. Cost a fortune, but worth every damn cent." He showed off his API console, his Neve EQs, and his Manly Vox Box. "That's a five-way, class A piece of gear," he said.

Eddie acted impressed. "Are those tube mics?"

"That's a Neuman U47 and those're AKG C-12s. Better microphones have yet to be built." Big Bill put his arm around his client. "Eddie, I'm telling you, this is going to be a helluva record. Nobody in town can reproduce the sound you're gonna get in these rooms."

Behind the main board, the control room floor was elevated and appointed with two sofas and matching overstuffed chairs. The lighting was recessed and the bulbs were soothing blues and grays. The main studio was a large room with mic stands and a Steinway D grand off to the side. Surrounding that were five isolation rooms, all with perfect line of sight throughout the studio. Big Bill's only concession to modern studio design was the acoustic treatments for the walls and ceiling. They were fixed with fabric wall systems, diffusers, and absorbers. By anyone's standards, the room had some of the best acoustics in the city. And for nearly $600,000, it had better.

Over the next fifteen minutes, the session players began drifting in, greeting Bill, Eddie, and Megan. They were all middle-aged men, all members of AFM Local 257, all accomplished pros. They'd all been in earlier to get sound for their instruments. The engineer for the session was a Music City veteran by the name of Ed Simmons who, for reasons even Ed couldn't articulate, was known as Porky Vic.

As the session guys were setting up, Eddie overheard the pedal steel player complaining to the keyboard guy. "Hell," he said, "I don't know anybody in town who's making any money these days." It was an oft-repeated phrase and explained why all these guys were here, working "off the card." Not too many years ago they'd all been making double scale along with fancy catered meals and other union-negotiated perks. But with the country music industry in its post-Garth tailspin, that sort of gig had dried up for all but a few. And since all these guys still had bills to pay, it was easy to find topflight players willing to work cheap.

Megan had expected a bunch of cowboy-boot-wearing good ole boys, but instead they looked like balding ex-hippies—short pants, baseball caps, Hawaiian shirts, Birkenstocks. Not a cowboy boot in the bunch.

Big Bill was talking to the bass player. They were looking at Bill's newest piece of old equipment. "It's got a tube boost with a passive cut. It's a nice little box," he said. "You know how piano gets all washed out in the middle?" He pointed at the device. "This thing fills it in, makes it sound like it's all around you."

The bass player nodded solemnly. "Beautiful."

Before Nashville entered the digital age, a producer could get in and out of the studio with a complete album in a couple of days. One reason was that the playback equipment and the listening environments in the old control rooms weren't great, so they couldn't hear all the blemishes. They recorded their song, then listened to them. If they sounded good, they moved on. But with the equipment available now, producers and artists—and consumers—could hear even the tiniest mistake. Coupled with the introduction of computerized systems like Pro Tools that were capable of correcting pitch errors and other flaws, the technology led everyone to believe perfection was attainable. As a result, producers and artists tended to spend more and more time trying to achieve that goal, which in turn ran up the cost of making a record. What used to take a couple of days and a few thousand dollars now took weeks and cost closer to a quarter million, all of which was charged against the artist's royalties and, whenever possible, cross-collateralized.

But Big Bill thought he had a way to get around Nashville's current economic model. His recording plan was as bold as Eddie's marketing scheme, and if it all played out, Big Bill would rise once again to the top of Nashville's Power 100. Looking out from the control room, Big Bill felt the time was right. He nudged Porky Vic, then took his seat behind the console and clapped his hands. "Hey now! What say we get this show on the road!"

As Eddie turned to go into the studio, Megan surprised him by taking his hand. She leaned toward him and kissed his cheek. "For luck," she said, lingering close. Eddie breathed in her scent and let her wild red hair brush his face. "Now go make me some music."

Like everything else in life, a recording session can go good or it can go bad. When it goes bad, it's as ugly a thing as exists in nature. But when it goes good, it's like dreaming out loud. Now, there's no way to control which way a session goes—otherwise they'd all go smooth as a new stretch of blacktop. It's all about the chemistry between the people involved. Fortunately, Big Bill had a knack for picking people who would mesh. Earlier in the week, Bill had introduced Eddie to the musicians, and they'd hit it off. They'd rehearsed Eddie's songs and were ready to do it, as Big Bill said, the old-fashioned way. Instead of having everyone lay down tracks individually and then putting them together in postproduction, they would record the songs as a band would perform them live. It was either risky or downright nuts, depending on your point of view, and they could have wasted a lot of time waiting until they got it right, but, as everyone would later agree, the force was with them.

Before each song, the players huddled around Eddie in the main studio. They each had their sheets with the Nashville Number System notations showing the chord progression for every song. They discussed solos and reminded each other of things that they'd come up with in rehearsals, then they broke their huddle and moved to the isolation booths like flankers to the line of scrimmage. Eddie would count 'em down and they'd do the song, usually without any significant errors. After each take they'd talk it over.

"Hey, Eddie, let's switch parts between the first and the second," the other guitar player said. "You do it up to the do do do's, then I'll take it the second time to the do do do's."

"Good idea," Eddie said.

"I don't know if it's good, but it's different anyway."

From his throne in the control room, Big Bill nixed some of the ideas and promoted others. He did it all with enough diplomacy to make everyone feel free to toss in their two cents. The result was usually several conversations going on at the same time in everyone's headset.

"Is that a vocal tag?" Porky Vic asked.

"You want to do that on all three bars?"

"We're tagging the second ending."

"No, do it at fifteen, eleven."

"What key is this in?

"Boy."

"Good. Boy's good."

"Got it. Are we ready?"

And just like that, they'd do another take, creating the song anew each time, filling out the corners, trimming a bridge or repeating a chorus with a variation on the lyrics. Eddie tapped out the count on the soundboard of his Gibson. "One . . . two . . . uh one . . . two . . . wait a second . . . wait, wait, wait." Eddie waved his hands until everybody stopped playing. "Sorry, guys. I don't know what made me think about this just now, but does anybody know who said, 'Writing about music is like dancing about architecture'?" He looked to the control room and saw Megan smile.

"Yeah," the bass player said. "I just read that somewhere." He plucked a few low notes as he thought about it. "That book by Bruce

Feiler, I forget the title, but I think he quoted Martin Mull saying that."

The pedal steel player disagreed. "No, it was Tom Waits."

"I don't think so," the piano player said. "Tom Waits said, 'The big print giveth, and the small print taketh away.'" Everybody laughed at that.

Eddie shrugged, then looked to Megan. "What do you think, Martin Mull or Tom Waits?"

Sitting next to Big Bill, Megan reached over and pushed the mic control button. "I still think it was Zappa," she said.

Eddie shrugged again. "Just curious. Sorry to interrupt the flow, guys. Are we ready?" He looked around and got thumbs up from everybody. "Well, all right then." Eddie pulled his guitar up close. "One . . . two . . . uh one . . . two . . . three . . ." They launched into one of Eddie's outlaw country tunes, which fit perfectly with the relaxed living-room atmosphere of the session. It was an edgy country rocker that could have passed as something cowritten by Robbie Fulks and Kinky Friedman. It was about a guy running from the law who was lusting for a girl he'd just met in a bar. *"You know what I'm thinking,"* Eddie sang, *"and you know that it's true."* He was looking straight at Megan with a devilish smile. *"Ain't no gun in my pocket . . ."* The music stopped cold, Eddie paused, then spoke in an exaggerated baritone: ". . . I'm just damn glad to see you." The drummer hit a rim shot and the rest of the band kicked back in and took it home.

By two in the morning they had five good songs in the can and a camaraderie that was inescapable. The fiddle player tried to organize an excursion to Estella's for shrimp plates. Porky Vic and the pedal steel player signed up, but the others reluctantly begged off, citing potentially irate spouses and lovers.

Megan slinked up next to Eddie as he was putting his guitar away. She let out a little sigh.

"S'matter?" He stopped what he was doing and looked at her.

"I've got a staff meeting tomorrow morning and I really don't want to drive all the way back out to Brentwood, 'cause I'm just going to have to turn right around and drive right back into town in a few hours."

Eddie snapped the latches on his guitar case, trying not to respond too quickly. "Well, it ain't exactly the Vanderbilt Plaza," he said, "but you're welcome to stay at my place. We can stop off and grab you a toothbrush and whatever on the way."

Megan moved closer. "Oh, we don't need to do that," she said. "I packed an overnight bag." She pressed her lips against his ear and whispered, "Just in case."

*   *   *

The skinny oddball at the Quitman County clerk's office ended up being quite helpful. In addition to showing Jimmy the National Crime Information Center bulletin, he handed over a list of law enforcement contact names and numbers. The next day, driving back to Jackson, Jimmy ran up his cell phone bill talking to various people with the Louisiana State Police as well as investigators in Tuscaloosa. Jimmy learned of a fourth suspicious poisoning death that had occurred several months earlier in Gulfport. The deaths had two things in common, the type of poison used and a locally manufactured headache remedy that appeared to be the poison delivery system.

Jimmy now had ninety minutes to kill as he drove east out of Jackson. He had a two-o'clock appointment with a representative from Okatibbee Pharmaceuticals, which was based just east of Meridian, near the Alabama border. Oak Pharm, as it was known locally, was the maker of Dr. Porter's Headache Powder and had once been the biggest employer in Lauderdale County. But over time the market for headache powders had shrunk considerably, even in the South.

The drive from Jackson to Meridian was a straight shot east on

I-20, a hundred miles of concrete walled on both sides by tall, thin pine trees. Jimmy would have preferred a dangerous winding road, some god-awful weather, or a series of road rage incidents—anything to occupy his mind, which was otherwise engaged. He was fixated on what it said about him that Megan could dump him so easily. Was he that uninteresting, that unattractive, that disposable? Maybe, he hoped, it wasn't him so much as it was Jackson. Maybe Megan was right about moving to a bigger city. Maybe he should move to Nashville too. He could live anywhere and write; it was one of the profession's few benefits. Come to think of it, a fresh setting was probably what their relationship needed. They were stagnating in Jackson. They needed new friends, new circles in which to circulate, a more exciting social milieu.

Jimmy didn't believe that, but it was less humiliating to blame Jackson than to accept being dumped. But maybe "dumped" was too strong a word for what had happened. Sure, Megan had moved to Nashville without saying goodbye, but maybe she hadn't had time to call. Maybe she was so busy packing and having her phone disconnected . . . Okay, maybe "dumped" was accurate, but couples got back together all the time after one dumped the other, right?

Then it hit him. *Why do I even care? We weren't together long and she never even hinted that she loved me. Why the hell can't I stop thinking about her? This is nuts. Shouldn't I hate her? Shouldn't I at least forget about her? She leaves town without a word, making me look and feel like a fool, but I can't get her out of my mind!* Jimmy knew reason had nothing to do with it; emotions always trump intellect. *Why do I miss her? How can I miss something I never really had? Am I pathetic or what? Hey, maybe that's the title of my love song.*

By the time he passed the exit for Pelahatchie, Jimmy realized he was obsessing. He turned on the radio, hoping to get Megan off his mind. It didn't help that Clay Walker was singing that he didn't know how love started but he sure knew how it ended. Jimmy tuned to a different station only to run into another familiar song. He couldn't remember where he'd heard it before, then it hit him like a punch in a barroom brawl. It was Eddie's song. Jimmy got honest to God goose bumps. He slapped the dashboard and turned up the volume. This could only be good news for Eddie. And anything good for Eddie was good for Jimmy's book. Eddie's Internet scheme was obviously working. Jimmy laughed out loud and started humming along. Then, halfway through the refrain, the song stopped cold.

The disc jockey came on immediately. "I know it's the name of the song," he said, "but I just don't think the *song's* supposed to end that way either, but it does. Just that like, ever single time. Now, I been in the radio business for twenty-five years, and I've heard a lot of good songs. But I'd put that *half* a song up against anything I ever liked." The announcer talked about the Frances Neagley website, the MP3 file, and how no one knew who the artist was. He asked listeners to call and let him know what they thought about the song and to speculate who the mystery singer-songwriter might be. "And don't worry, we'll keep playing what we got until we can find the back half of it. Meanwhile, let's get back to songs with beginnings, middles, and ends. Here's a little something from S-K-O on Country Mixx 96. . . ."

Jimmy grabbed his cell phone and dialed the station's number, but it was busy. Just as well, he realized. Since the plan was to pique curiosity, Jimmy shouldn't be revealing the answer this early. He couldn't wait to tell Eddie. He punched in the Nashville number. After a few rings, a familiar voice came on the line. "I'm sorry," she said. "The number you have reached is no longer in service." *Shit! Not again.* "If you feel you have reached this recording in error—" Jimmy disconnected. He tried Nashville information but was told Eddie Long now had an unpublished number.

Jimmy couldn't imagine why Eddie would have done that, but there was nothing he could do about it. "Try Megan Taylor." He heard the operator typing into her computer.

"I'm sorry, sir, that's unpublished too."

Jimmy sucked at his teeth and tapped his fingers on the steering wheel. "All right," he said, "how about Herron & Peavy Management?" He wanted to talk to these guys anyway, get their perspective on their client and the Internet marketing plan, that sort of thing. Besides, they could put him in touch with Eddie. The operator gave him the number, then connected him.

A second later, Jimmy was on the line with Big Bill Herron. Jimmy explained who he was and why he was calling. "Listen," Big Bill said brusquely. "Eddie told me all about you and this book you're supposed to be writing. And I'm going to tell you something, and I'm only going to tell you once, so you better listen. Stop. Harassing. My. Client." He said each word as if there was a period after it. "Eddie wants nothing to do with you or your book, and we will get a restraining order to keep you away from him if you won't stay away voluntarily."

Jimmy was flabbergasted. His foot inadvertently eased off the gas pedal. "I think there's been a misunderstanding, Mr. Herron. Eddie signed off on this a few months ago. I've been covering his shows for a couple of years now, and the book's under way. Maybe you—"

"Get this right, friend, there ain't no misunderstanding." His tone bordered on menacing. "As Eddie's manager, I'm tellin' you that you're treading on some damn thin ice. Any publishing rights to Eddie Long's story belong jointly to Eddie Long and to Herron & Peavy Management, and if you persist with this project, we'll slap you with a cease and desist order."

"Well, now, hang on—"

"No. You hang on," Big Bill said. "Further, if you represent to any publisher that you have the rights to this story or if you submit any proposals with such representations, we will sue you into fiscal year 2020. Do we understand each other?"

"Well, no, I . . ." Jimmy had no idea what to say. He had to speak to Eddie. "Could you just give me Eddie's number?"

"Try to get this through your head," Big Bill snarled. "I do not

give out my client's unpublished phone number." His voice was rising. "If and when we decide the time is right for a biography on our
client, we will get in touch with our publishing industry contacts
and we will hire a professional biographer and we will do the book
professionally." He was yelling now. "We don't need some freelance
clown trying to cash in with some piss-ant memoir!" He calmed
down a few decibels. "Now, I am very busy and I don't have time to
discuss this any further. If you pursue this, I will turn the matter
over to our attorneys." Click.

Jimmy was dumbstruck. What the hell had just happened?
This had to be a mistake. He stared at the phone until he heard his
tires drifting onto the gravel shoulder. He looked up just in time to
see a large wooden sign on the roadside in front of him, but not
soon enough to avoid it. He yanked the steering wheel, but he
clipped the sign and sent it flying. It landed in pieces on the side
of the road behind him. The part that landed face-up said: *Welcome to Meridian—Home of the Singing Brakeman.*

Adrenaline fueled Jimmy's agitated system. His mind and body
bristled. Goddammit! What the hell was going on? A month ago,
Jimmy'd been in tall cotton. He'd had a girl he loved and a project he
was passionate about. Now all he had was a new dent in his front
quarter panel. As he drove though Meridian, Jimmy tried to assess
the situation. Had Eddie betrayed him on the book deal or was this
a case of gatekeeper interference? Either way, Jimmy was pissed.
He'd put in too much time and invested too much of himself and his
future on this book. He wasn't going to bow up and die like a cut-
worm on a cabbage leaf just because Eddie's manager was playing
hard-ass. Hell, he was probably putting words in Eddie's mouth, but
there was nothing Jimmy could do about that for now.

But what if Eddie really had turned on him? What if Herron and
Peavy had blown so much smoke up Eddie's ass that he was taking
their advice on the book deal? The fact that he had an unpublished
number all the sudden, just like Megan, didn't help. And, come to

think of it, it wasn't like Jimmy hadn't noticed the way Eddie and Megan had looked at each other in the past. Maybe Eddie had betrayed him. Well, screw him, Jimmy thought. If Eddie was too much of a coward to say it to his face, fine. If Eddie didn't want Jimmy to write his official biography, fine. He'd write the unofficial biography. They couldn't stop him from doing that. And even if they could, Jimmy could always fall back on writing his fictional version of the story as well as the book on the serial killer. So, ha! Jimmy's plate was still full and the rest of them could just kiss his ass.

Jimmy was blown up like a toad by the time he pulled off the freeway. A few minutes later he pulled into the parking lot at Okatibbee Pharmaceuticals. The building, like the business itself, was in need of a facelift it would never receive. The sign was sun-faded and the whitewash on the bricks was flaking off like dandruff. The company spokesman met Jimmy in the lobby. He was a handsome man, a few years older than Jimmy. He seemed nervous the way people do when the smell of downsizing is thick in the air. After introductions, the man led Jimmy down a hallway. "Okatibbee Pharmaceuticals has long held an important position in the economy of Lauderdale County." He stopped and gestured at a large portrait hanging on the wall. "The company was founded by—"

"Whoa," Jimmy said. "I'm not here for the tour."

The man turned and looked at Jimmy. "No?"

"No. I'm here to ask questions."

"Questions?"

"Yes, the opposite of answers," Jimmy said.

"Questions about what?" The man seemed uneasy with Jimmy's prickly attitude.

"Questions about Tammy Long and Fred Babineaux and a couple other folks."

The man looked at the portrait, then back at Jimmy. "Uhhh, do they work here?"

"No, they were customers."

"They're customers?"

"Were," Jimmy said. "As in now they're dead."

"Dead customers?"

"Yes, quite dead," Jimmy said, "and all with Dr. Porter's Headache Powder in their systems."

The spokesman paused, thinking. He gestured toward a door. "Perhaps we'd be more comfortable talking in my office." He showed Jimmy into the room. "Can I get you something to drink? Coffee? Co-Cola?"

Jimmy shook his head. "I just need some information." He pulled a file from his satchel.

"I don't have any information about dead customers, I can assure you." The man sat down behind his desk and began fidgeting. "Perhaps I could answer some other questions, like how many boxes of Dr. Porter's Headache Powder we make in an hour, something like that?"

Jimmy looked at the man and shook his head. "No, that wouldn't do me any good." He pulled a sheet of paper from the file. "This is a lot number," he said, handing the paper over. "I want to know exactly when and where this lot was shipped."

The man looked at the list, then at Jimmy. "Are you sure I can't get you a Co-Cola or something? Tastes real nice on a day like this."

Jimmy cleared his throat and set his elbows on the desk. "No. Thanks." He steepled his fingers and stared at the man. "Look, this is very simple," he said. "I'm writing a book about a guy, okay? The guy's wife dies suddenly, so I have to look into the death, right? Turns out she died from poisoning after taking your product. So I have to look into that, right? To my surprise, I find out about similar deaths in Louisiana, Alabama, and the Mississippi Gulf Coast. Now, I know you've been contacted by all these police agencies, and you've given them this information. Now you just have to give it to me."

The man looked genuinely confused. "I do?"

Jimmy pulled out his wallet, which got the man's attention. "Let me ask you a question," Jimmy said. "Does the press know about this?"

The man looked around nervously. "I don't think so." He was starting to imagine a hefty bribe. Maybe he'd be able to get that jet ski he'd had his eye on.

Jimmy pulled out his laminated press credentials and tossed them onto the man's desk. "Do you want to keep it that way?"

The man looked at the credentials and nodded. "Maybe you'd like a Mountain Dew instead of a Co-Cola?"

"I'm not thirsty," Jimmy said. "But thanks. Now, here's the deal. This book I'm writing? It might not get published. And if it does, it won't be for a while. Meanwhile, you guys will be very quietly recalling everything on the shelves and implementing new safety packaging, right?"

The man continued to nod, keeping a hopeful eye on Jimmy's wallet.

"By then the police might have already caught the perpetrator, in which case the news won't hurt your sales too much."

The man shifted in his seat, thinking Jimmy would reach into the wallet again at any moment. *A Jet Ski would be real nice,* he thought.

"Alternatively," Jimmy said, "in the interest of public safety, I could make a few phone calls to my friends in the news business and break the story. This would probably push your crumbling little enterprise here over the brink into financial ruin." Jimmy smiled as he slipped his press credentials back into his wallet, all the while thinking that Big Bill Herron wasn't the only guy who could play hard-ass. "Like I said, it's very simple."

Disappointed he wasn't being bribed, the man looked at the lot number, then at Jimmy. "That's blackmail."

Jimmy held up a finger, then reached into his pocket and tossed a coin on the man's desk. "Here's a quarter—call somebody who cares."

*   *   *

Megan opened with the traditional "Oh my God, Eddie, you're sooo big," which never failed. Combined with an unnecessary readjustment of her hips and a practiced look of amazement, it was a solid confidence booster for her new sexual partner. About halfway through she started in with the "give it to me's" and the short gasping breaths as if it was the best thing she'd ever had and she wasn't sure how much more she could take it was so unbelievable but please don't stop. Then, toward the end, Megan called his name with each turgid thrust. "Eddie. Eddie. Eddie." Each call matched the flimsy percussion of the headboard tapping the wall. And then, as he achieved, "Oh, Eddie! Yes!" She just hoped it sounded like she meant it.

Megan could have been reciting a cornbread recipe as far as Eddie was concerned. He just didn't want things to end too quickly, which was a distinct possibility given how long it had been since he'd had any. He tried thinking about NASCAR standings and fishing lures to delay the countdown, but even visions of Kyle Petty in his Nomex jumpsuit couldn't keep Megan's expert coaxing from triggering the launch. The mattress dance was over less than ten minutes after it started.

"Oh my God, Eddie. That was un-be-lieve-able!" Megan sprawled across the bed, huffing like she'd just finished a four-minute mile.

Eddie couldn't remember ever feeling this good. He was still thrilled by the recording session and was excited about returning the next night. To top that off with a steamy horizontal mambo, well, hell, he was fine as frog's hair. Thinking maybe he should do some cuddling, Eddie leaned over to kiss Megan, but she was already snoring. Eddie smiled. *Could things get any better?* he wondered.

9

ig Bill was in a pensive mood. He was thinking about how
great ideas often come from the strangest places. Specifically
he was thinking about the phone call he'd received from the
guy calling himself Jimmy Rogers. Because of the name, Big Bill
assumed the guy was a crackpot, but still, it set Big Bill to thinking
that a biography of Eddie Long was a terrific idea, assuming Eddie
ever had a hit. Of course, if you were going to do a book, Big Bill
thought, now was the time to get started. You wanted it ready so you
could rush into publication and cash in on what might turn out to be
a flash in the pan. To that end Big Bill was thinking he would write
the book himself. After all, how hard could that be?

He'd been sitting at his kitchen table for an hour trying to think
of a good title when Eddie arrived. Big Bill looked up and saw the
satisfied face of a man who not only had got laid the night before but
figured he had it coming again tonight. "Hey now!" Big Bill said,
pointing at Eddie. "Betcha dolla I know who got some gravel for his
goose!" He slapped his hand down on the table and laughed. "You
ready to make some music?"

Eddie tipped his Stetson back and smiled his best Eddie Long smile. "If nothin' breaks or comes untwisted," he said. "How you doin'?"

"Well, I feel more like I do now than I did when I got here," Big Bill said. "And I felt pretty good to start with."

"Well, all right then." Eddie set his guitar case down and sat at the table with his producer. "You decided when we're gonna do 'Wasn't Supposed to End That Way'? I think we oughta do it third or fourth, after we're warmed up a bit, but not too late that we might be tired."

"Whatever you want. We'll do it when it feels right," Big Bill said. "That's the key with a song like that, you gotta do it naturally. See, the great thing about that song is it's, uh, what's the word I want? It's organic. Not a false note or an untrue word in it. And we gotta capture that." Bill shook his head. "We can't do it on a schedule. It's not like a bought single. I bet you didn't write it on a schedule, did you?"

Eddie thought about it for a second. "No, sir, that's true." He grew serious all the sudden, looking at his hands and where his wedding band used to be. "That song came out of me like I don't know what. Most of my songs I have to think about and work on, but that one . . . it was like . . . it was hard."

"Like splittin' gum logs in August," Big Bill said, nodding his giant round head. "I know. I could tell the first night I heard it." Bill reached across the table and touched Eddie's chest. "It came from in there." He reached up and touched Eddie's forehead. "Not there."

Eddie felt comfortable with Big Bill. They were kindred. In a way, he was a father figure and Eddie just opened up to him. He told Big Bill about Tammy's death and how he'd moved to Nashville afterwards. He told him all he could remember about the five days he'd spent trying to get the song to come out, and how it had felt when it was over. "I'm tellin' you," Eddie said, "it was rough."

Big Bill took it all in, thinking it would be good material for the book. He'd heard others tell similar stories. Songwriting was a mysterious process even when it consisted more of steady hard work than out-of-the-clear-blue inspiration. It was mostly day-in, day-out spent working with a theme, or taking a common phrase, putting a twist to it, and building a song around it, or telling a story with perfect economics. It was poetry with the complication of being set to music. But every now and then a song would force itself on a writer, make his life hell for some time, then present itself when it was ready. This was how many of the best songs were born. Knowing this served to bolster Big Bill's belief that Eddie's song was a classic. He couldn't wait to get it on tape. Big Bill stood up. "Come on," he said, putting his arm around Eddie. "Let's go make some music."

An hour later, Porky Vic and the players were back and it was like the night before had never ended. It was a recording session the likes of which everyone dreams. And it wasn't just that everyone was playing well and getting along, though both of those things were true. The thing was, they could tell they were making a great record. They didn't know if it would be a commercial success or not, but they could tell it was something to be proud of. The confidence and camaraderie that followed from that were palpable. Each player was in perfect sync with the others, requiring no more than eye contact or body language to communicate ideas in the middle of a song. It was a fast break with guitars. They started with a sort of rocking west Texas shuffle that sounded like it had been filtered through an early Doobie Brothers hit. After running through it a couple of times, they compared notes.

"How 'bout we do three bars on that to the downbeat to the chorus," the bass player said.

The pedal steel guy held up his hand. "Wait, wait, wait! You wanna make it four minors? That might be cool."

Eddie thought about it for a second. He looked at his charts, tilted his head. "Eleven, fifty-five, forty-four, eleven? That's different from what I was thinking of, but it might work. Let's try it."

The pedal steel guy smiled as they played a few bars that way before pausing. "Yeah," he said, "that works, doncha think?"

"Yeah, four." Eddie smiled back and nodded. "I'm diggin' that." He looked to the control room. "Boss?"

Big Bill pushed the mic button. "I got special tape rolling. It captures magic. Now go!"

Eddie counted it down and they nailed it in one take. Absolutely nailed it. It was impossible, but they did it. There was a pause as the last note faded and Eddie looked from one face to another. They ranged from sublime smiles to shit-eatin' grins. Eddie leaned into his microphone and spoke softly, like an announcer on a classic music station. "Gentlemen," he said. "I believe we have our mojo working." Everybody let out with hoots and hollers and high fives.

The door behind Big Bill opened. Megan stepped into the room and waved. "Hey, everybody! That last one sounded good even through the door."

The sight of Megan's wild red hair sent a charge through Eddie. "Hey girl! Glad you could make it," he said with a wink. "We're on a roll. Just make yourself comfy while we knock out another one." He turned to the guitar player. "How about 'Homeless in Love Town' next?"

The guitar player shrugged. "I'll follow you anywhere, man." So Eddie counted it down and they did a run-through. It was a mournful, lovesick ballad that would have been at home on a Clint Black or a Randy Travis record. Afterwards, they listened to a playback and did their postmortem.

"Something's hinkey," Porky Vic said.

The guitarist agreed. "Yeah, there's a seventh on the fiddle."

"It might be duckable," someone suggested.

"You don't like the seventh?" The fiddle player sounded a little hurt.

Big Bill jumped in. "No," he said, "but only because of the harmonies we're going to do. Can't have that and the seventh, right?"

The fiddle player nodded understanding. "Cool." After three more takes, "Homeless in Love Town" was in the can, save the harmony tracks Bill would record and mix in a few days.

Megan sat in the control room admiring her new man. Even though Eddie was the youngest one in the studio, she could see the rest of them were glad to have him lead them to the promised land. She kicked back on the sofa and began to imagine a plush future at Eddie's side.

"Hey, Bill," Eddie said. "I think the time's right." He'd been waiting for Megan, for inspiration. "I'm feelin' organic, if you know what I mean."

"You rascal, I know what you mean." Big Bill was about to give a thumbs-up when the door behind him opened again and Franklin walked in with Whitney. Big Bill turned around. "Hey now! Look who we got." He waved everybody in from the studio. "Let's take five, fellas. Eddie, we'll do it when we come back."

The players emerged from the isolation booths and headed for the control room. The pedal steel player stopped the guitarist as he passed by. "You bring your two-fifteen?"

The picker smiled slyly. "Yeah, you got an idea for something?" He set his guitar down and pulled his 1955 Martin Style 2-15 mandolin from its case. It was a beauty, rosewood and tiger-striped maple and an unbound ebony fingerboard with seven ivoroid dot-markers. The pickguard clamp was an unusual shade of jade and brown. The instrument made sounds that might have come from heaven, if angels played mandolins. The picker pulled a stool up next to the pedal steel guitar. "What'ja have in mind?"

Out in the control room some of the players chatted with Franklin, whom they knew from prior business dealings. Franklin made a joke about Big Bill's studio being the Jurassic Park of Nashville. "I'll take a digital rig any day," he said. "But what do I know, right? I'm just a lawyer."

Big Bill introduced Whitney to everyone. Whitney tried not to look too astonished at where he found himself. After some small talk, Porky Vic and a couple of the players headed out for smokes. Big Bill corralled Eddie and brought him over. "Eddie, I want you to meet Whitney Rankin, the writer I told you about. He's our other newest client, wrote a song that's going to be a big hit. Whitney, this is Eddie Long."

Whitney was a little disappointed Big Bill had introduced him as a writer only. He thought of himself as a performer too, but he didn't think now was the time or place to bring that up. Eddie and Whitney shook hands, each looking at the other with a vague sense of recognition, though neither remembered they had played at the Bluebird that same night. "Good to meet you," Whitney said.

"Likewise." Eddie wondered what was up with the earrings and the bandanna tied around Whitney's wrist, but he wasn't going to say anything. He turned and introduced Megan as his girlfriend.

She looked at Eddie in mock surprise. "When did I become your girlfriend?"

Eddie smiled, pulling her tight to his side. "Last night, if I'm not mistaken."

"Oh, that was you." Megan smiled. "I knew you looked familiar." She arched her thin eyebrows and smiled at Whitney. "It's nice to meet you."

Whitney tipped his black hat. "Ma'am."

"Oh, my," she said in her Southern Belle voice. "There *are* some real cowboys left." She looked Whitney up and down. Nothing prefabricated about this guy, she thought. He was authentic something, though she wasn't sure what.

"So," Eddie said, "where you at with your song, the one Bill's talking about? You shopping a demo?"

"Supposed to record a bunch of my stuff here next week. Tell you the truth"—Whitney shrugged meekly—"I'm not real sure what the whole process is, but Mr. Herron says he's out there pluggin' me." Eddie nodded as if he cared. Whitney twisted the bandanna around his wrist. "You know, I play too," he added. "I mean, I'm not just a writer." He wanted Eddie to know he was a member of the club, hoping to gain a little acceptance. "Mr. Herron didn't mention it, but, uh—"

Just then Big Bill rumbled by and slapped Eddie on the back. "All right," he said. " 'Nuff of this socializin'. Let's make us some music." Bill sank into his big chair behind the console and rubbed his hands together like he was about to do a magic trick. "Where's Porky?"

As the players filed back into the studio, Whitney and Megan moved to the sofas behind Big Bill. Franklin walked over and leaned onto the mixing console, watching the musicians. He spoke to his partner without looking at him. "By the way," Franklin said, "our boy didn't win Best New Hat Act. Probably won't get his deal picked up now."

Big Bill was busy adjusting something on the tape machine. He shrugged off the news. "Tough break," he said. "Maybe he'll pick up something at the Viva Nash Vegas Awards."

Franklin nodded. "Yeah, everybody wins something there."

Big Bill punched the mic control button. " "Whaddya say, fellas? We ready?"

"Hey, Bill?" It was the pedal steel player. "Before we get started, we got a little something we worked out during the break. Might work good with the song."

Big Bill looked to Eddie. "It's your session. Whaddya say?"

Eddie smiled. "I ain't in no hurry."

Big Bill held his hands up, surrendering to the musicians. "Let's hear it."

The pedal steel player nodded to the picker and they began to play. It was just the two instruments, a pedal steel guitar and a mandolin, their voices combining to create a third. What they played wasn't strictly a melody; it was more of a mood or a setting or an emotion in chords. The fiddle player stood by, arms folded gently over his instrument, nodding his head solemnly as if to say, *Yeah, I've felt that way too*. Megan and Whitney sat forward on the sofa, listening intently. Franklin stood there, hands clasped behind his back, wishing Eddie hadn't cut him out of the producing credit. The passage lasted only fifteen or twenty seconds but left everyone marveling. When it ended, you could've heard a pin drop. Porky Vic sat there smiling.

Big Bill broke the silence when he punched the mic button. "Play that again," he said as he hit the record button. So they did. As they approached the end of the piece, Eddie and the fiddle player made eye contact and joined in with what used to be the opening parts. The bass player and drummer fell in a couple of bars later and they did a complete run-through. Eddie sang his heart out. Big Bill sat at the console, riding the gain, his head tilted back slightly and poised perfectly between the monitors. He closed his eyes and listened. When it was over, Porky Vic stopped the tape machine. Bill hit the mic button again. He paused, not knowing at first what to say. "I don't think we can improve on that," he said finally, "but let's do another take, just for grins." He pointed at the pedal steel and the fiddle player. "And at the end, I want you to come back in with that same thing and we'll fade it out."

They did the song two more times, each as affecting as the one before. When they had the take they wanted, Eddie went over and shook the pedal steel player's hand, thanked him for his contribution, and said, half joking, that he might be willing to give up a quarter of a point of the publishing for the intro. "That's not necessary," the slide player said, though he didn't mean it.

"All right," Eddie said quickly. "If you insist. But I'll mention it in the liner notes."

No one said another word about what they had just recorded. It was as if they all knew it was a monster, but no one wanted to jinx it by saying so. "You wanna take a break or move on?" Big Bill asked.

"Long as the spirit's with us," Eddie said, "let's go on and do

'Dixie National.'" The players shuffled through their charts and toyed with the chords for a few minutes, warming up. "Dixie National" was Eddie's tribute to the rodeo he used to go see as a kid at the Mississippi Coliseum at the fairgrounds in Jackson. The song was two parts Chris LeDoux, one part Charlie Daniels, and just enough Eddie Long to make it his own.

In the control room, Franklin worked on Whitney. "For example, say you play a midsize venue and they want to record your show and pay you five thousand dollars for the right to sell copies of that performance *in perpetuity*." He paused, tilting his head the way he remembered one of his law professors doing. "Would you sign that contract?"

"For five thousand dollars?" Whitney thought about it for a moment. He looked at Megan, then back at Franklin. "Sure." He shrugged. "I guess. I mean, why not?" Whitney hated talking about business. He'd come here to play music, to record, to do his craft. If he'd wanted to talk about contracts, he'd have gone to law school.

Franklin assumed a fatherly demeanor. "See, that's why you need me. I'd never let you sign that contract. Never. Everybody in this town'll tell you, I can't scratch the words 'in perpetuity' out of a contract fast enough."

"But it's just one show," Whitney said. "Five thousand's good money to me, especially for one gig. You know what I mean?" He looked to Megan for her thoughts. She smiled politely and shrugged as if to say she couldn't argue. She thought that was nicer than coming out and just calling him a shortsighted clodhopper.

"Now don't get me wrong," Franklin said, "five thousand's not bad, but stick with me and Big Bill and you can probably do better'n that. That's all I'm sayin'."

Whitney nodded thoughtfully, figuring Mr. Peavy was right. After all, he and Mr. Herron had been in the business a long time. A guy like Whitney was probably better off sticking to what he knew and letting the big dogs with the brass collars handle all that business stuff.

Eddie and the band finished "Dixie National" and had started talking about what to cut next when Big Bill suddenly slapped the arms of his chair and spun around. "Hey now! I just had a wild idea," he announced. "What do you think about having Eddie record your song?"

A moment passed before Whitney realized Big Bill was talking to him. "What do you mean?"

"That's a great idea," Franklin said, hands held wide in well-practiced wonder.

Big Bill held his own hands out as though they were a part of his argument. "We need a demo to take the song around anyway, right?" He gestured at the players in the studio. "Long as we got a band, why not kill two birds?"

"It'll save you some money too," Franklin said, nudging Whitney. "Demo session with a band'll usually run you five or six grand. This is a good opportunity."

Big Bill looked at his watch, then at Whitney. "Whaddya say, hoss? We'll just record it as a demo, full band, no charge."

Whitney felt the pressure as they waited for his decision. He always thought he'd be the first one to record his song, but maybe he misunderstood the purpose of a demo. He could ask, but he didn't want to look stupid in front of all these people. And he sure didn't want to get anybody mad just when he felt he was getting a foot in the door. He looked around, unsure about what he should do.

"Whitney?" Big Bill looked at his watch again.

In the acoustically perfect room, he could hear the watch ticking. "This would just be a demo," Whitney said tentatively, "so I could still record it, right?"

"Absolutely," Big Bill assured him. He pointed toward the studio. "Go on in there and play it for 'em so they can get a feel for it." He pushed the mic button. "Fellas, we're gonna do Whitney's song next."

"We got charts on it?" the bass player asked.

"Nope, you'll have to roll your own," Big Bill said.

A moment later Whitney was in the studio with a borrowed Martin, playing his song while the musicians charted it for themselves. Whitney sang it a couple of times while Eddie wrote out the lyrics. It was an elegant ballad, sweet and aching, with a beautiful chorus. The bridge was simple and forgiving. The lyrics were straightforward and honest and conveyed the tender security of true, unconditional love. It timed out at just over three minutes and left you wanting more.

"That's a terrific song," Eddie said. "What's it called?"

" 'Night's Devotion,' " Whitney said.

"That's nice. I'll try not to mess it up too bad." Eddie winked at him.

"Thanks," Whitney said. "I, uh, I appreciate it." He didn't know what else to say. He put the Martin back in its stand and returned to the control room to watch his song come to life. He'd never heard anyone else—let alone an entire band—do one of his songs, and he wasn't sure how he felt about it.

Eddie and the band ran through it a few times with Big Bill making suggestions here and there. He turned to Whitney every time he made a change. "You see why I did that?" Whitney would always nod, even if he didn't really understand. But at the moment, he didn't care, because they were playing his song and, honestly, it sounded better than it ever had.

Whitney sat back on the sofa and took it all in. Here he was at the home studio of one of Nashville's most storied producers. Sitting on one side of him was his own manager, and on the other side was the very attractive girlfriend of the recording artist who was in the studio recording one of Whitney's songs. For the first time since moving to

Nashville, Whitney felt he belonged. His elusive dreams seemed to be coming true. He just wished his mama could see him now.

*   *   *

Jimmy got back from Meridian late and went straight to the Dutch Bar and Lounge, a seedy beer joint that served up a good plate of fried pickles and cheap draft beer. He chose the DB&L not only for its atmosphere and menu, but also because it was close enough to his apartment that he could stumble home afterwards if it came to that. And Jimmy was thinking after the day he'd had, it just might.

On the upside, he'd gotten the information he wanted from Oak Pharm, but the deal with Eddie still had him concerned. Cease and desist and restraining orders? What the hell was that all about? Jimmy could think of three possible explanations, none of them auspicious. The worst-case scenario, the one composed of both personal and professional humiliation, was that Eddie was now sleeping with Megan. In that case Eddie would likely be unable to visualize himself working side by side with the guy from whom he stole the girl. But that raised other questions. Had Eddie stolen Megan or had she gone after him? Jimmy knew Megan better than he knew Eddie, and he had to admit the latter was entirely possible.

As Jimmy sucked down a second draft and ordered a third, it occurred to him that he might be jumping the gun. It was possible Eddie and Megan hadn't even been in contact with each other. It could be that Big Bill Herron had convinced Eddie that Jimmy was simply the wrong guy to write the book. There were certainly other writers—proven biographers, for example—with whom publishers would rather be in business. Given Eddie's ambitions, it was easy to imagine him buying that argument. The final possibility was that Eddie had never even mentioned the book idea and that Big Bill was simply caught off guard by Jimmy's call. In that case his threats might have been a knee-jerk reaction to buy some time while he checked with his client or tried to find a way to work it more to his advantage. So Jimmy didn't know if Eddie had really betrayed him or if his manager was just being a dickhead. Worse, the only way he could find out for sure was by going to Nashville, finding Eddie, and asking him. And right now Jimmy didn't have the time for that.

There was only one thing that didn't pass the sniff test no matter which way Jimmy approached it. That Eddie hadn't called after getting his unlisted number told Jimmy where he stood more than anything else, just as it did with Megan. With that in mind, Jimmy finished his third beer and fried pickles and headed home.

He lived in a two-bedroom unit at the River Wood Oaks Townhouses, one of a hundred unimaginative apartment complexes in Jackson with the sort of name that made you expect better construction than you got. The wafer-thin walls were actually a convenience, inasmuch as they allowed Jimmy to hear, in exquisite detail, the vocal sex life of his neighbors, which in turn allowed Jimmy to masturbate without having to overuse his limited store of sexual memories.

Perhaps he'd get to that later, he thought, but right now Jimmy was more interested in the information he'd picked up about the poisoned Dr. Porter's Headache Powder. It turned out that all of the tainted boxes had come from a single lot shipped to a store in Little Rock, Arkansas, eight months earlier. The killer apparently bought several boxes from that lot, added the poison, resealed the packages, then put them on store shelves in at least three Southern states. So far, the police had found nothing to connect the victims other than sodium fluoroacetate and Dr. Porter's. No debt problems, no common lovers, nothing.

The only death Jimmy and the feds didn't know about was Hoke Paley's in Lee County, Alabama. Sheriff Herndon had never seen the National Crime Information Center bulletin about the other poisoning deaths, and besides, he already had two good suspects. So he didn't feel the need to see if similar crimes had been committed anywhere else.

Jimmy put one set of the Oak Pharm documents into his file labeled "Serial Killer Book Proposal." He then pulled out the file labeled "Eddie Long Biography." He picked up a black pen and angrily modified the label with the word "Unauthorized." He put the second copy of the Oak Pharm documents in the "Unauthorized Biography" file, then reviewed the autopsy report on Tammy. He'd glanced at it once or twice since Quitman County, but this time he read it in detail. Among the other contents of her stomach was MSG, monosodium glutamate. *Hmm.* MSG triggered two associations in Jimmy's mind. The first was Chinese food. The second was headache, which in turn triggered an association with Dr. Porter's Headache Powder. *Hmm, again.* Jimmy remembered the skinny guy at the county clerk's office saying he wondered where the Chinese food had come from. It seemed like a good question, the answer to which was probably back up in Quitman County. Jimmy closed the file, grudgingly accepting the fact that he had to drive back up to the Delta the next morning.

He sat at his desk for a moment, making notes about the things he still needed to find out. *Where did the Chinese food come from? How come no food containers were mentioned in police reports? Was Tammy allergic to MSG? What is sodium fluoroacetate?* As he sat there trying to think of other questions, he heard his neighbors giggling in the bedroom. "Trust me," he heard the man say. "It only seems kinky the first time you do it." It suddenly occurred to Jimmy that he had all the questions he needed, so he doused the light and went to his bedroom.

*   *   *

Big Bill was in such a high and palmy state after the recording session that he took everybody out to Estella's. He was hunched over his plate biting a shrimp off at the tail secure in the knowledge that this time next year he wouldn't have to put up with industry people constantly assaulting him with Barbara Feldon jokes. He looked over toward the jukebox where Eddie was standing with Megan and he smiled. Big Bill Herron wasn't going to be ninety-nine next year, that was for damn sure.

Estella's was crowded with its usual late-night congregation. The Staple Singers were on the jukebox endorsing self-respect. Franklin, Whitney, Big Bill, Porky Vic, and all the session players had pushed a couple of tables together not far from the kitchen. It wasn't long before Franklin was again arguing the merits of Pro Tools over Big Bill's archaic methods. "Now you have to admit, most sessions aren't as perfect as Eddie's, right? All I'm saying is the computer saves a lot of time and lets you assemble a perfect take even if you don't get one in the studio."

Big Bill was in too good a mood to let Franklin bother him. "That's true," Big Bill said, "and if you don't mind putting out records of performances that never happened and can never be reproduced live, then it's the way to go. But I like the idea of something more authentic, that's all. Call me old-fashioned."

Franklin didn't want to push the Pro Tools issue too far and spoil the mood, but recently he'd taken a couple of weekend seminars on modern recording techniques. Franklin was enamored of the technology, and like anyone else he liked to talk about things he'd learned.

Just then, Otis slid two shrimp plates across the ledge of the service window and rang the little bell. Estella picked up the plates and shambled over to Big Bill's table. "Here we go." She set one plate in front of the pedal steel player and one in front of the fiddler. She pulled a bottle of hot sauce from one apron pocket and a pint of scotch from the other. "Here you are, Mr. Peavy. You need more ice?"

"No. Thank you, Estella," he said, "I'm fine." He unscrewed the cap and tipped the bottle over his glass.

"All right, then. Ya'll enjoy." Estella turned her attention to Big Bill, who was busy with his fingers, herding the remainders of his potato salad onto his fork before stuffing it into his roly-poly face. Estella watched him chew for a moment. She half wished he would choke and die facedown on one of her plates, but he just swallowed and looked at her, smiling, like he knew what she was thinking. Estella didn't bat an eye. She just pointed at his plate, which held little more than crumbs and shrimp tails. "Mr. Herrons, you gonna eat them scribbles or you done?"

"I'm all topped off," he said, leaning back with his mouth full. "You can take that."

Estella took the plate and headed for the kitchen. As she crossed the room with the plate in her hand, Estella's eyes landed on Eddie, and everything but her thoughts suddenly seemed to decelerate, as if life had slipped into slow motion. She recognized Eddie from the night he had signed with Herron and Peavy, right over there at that table. The handsome young man was with a pretty redheaded girl tonight. They were standing by the jukebox. Estella looked to her right and saw Otis through the service window. His face was still and peaceful as he watched the angry oil cook another batch of shrimp. She could hear him saying, "Just let it go," and she wondered where they might be if things had been different. If Herron hadn't given up so quick. If Otis had had another hit. If he hadn't drunk too much. If she hadn't gone out in that alley.

And then the switch flipped again and everything was full speed ahead and she smelled the shrimp frying and she heard booze splashing on ice and she felt the plate in her hand and she was standing right next to Eddie all the sudden. He looked at her and she looked right back and she said, "Mr. Herrons says you finished makin' your record." She sort of pointed at Eddie with the plate in her hand. "That's real good," she said. "You should be proud."

"Yes, ma'am, thank you."

Estella glanced over her shoulder at Big Bill's table, then back at Eddie. "Don't tell him I said it, but you be careful with that man."

Eddie smiled, almost chuckling. "Yes, ma'am. I sure will."

She wagged a stern finger at him. "Don't you be they fool."

"No, ma'am, I won't."

Sensing she wasn't going to be included in this conversation, Megan cleared her throat. "Excuse me," she said. "Ladies' room?"

Estella pointed the way and waited until Megan was gone before turning back to Eddie. "You not careful, you might end up where you don't want. You gotta take care of your own bidness."

Eddie flashed a knowing smile. "That's the truth." He sensed this woman knew what she was talking about. They thought along the same lines.

Estella seemed to relax as she measured Eddie's handsome young face. "I got a good feelin' about you," she said. "You'll do all right." She nodded several times like a little hammer driving a nail. "You'll be fine." Her eyes drifted away, and a moment later she stepped over to the service window to set the plate down.

Eddie looked back at the jukebox. He didn't notice Estella come back. "You want my advice?" She didn't wait for his reply. She just pointed. "C nineteen and twenty."

Eddie looked at the titles, then back at Estella. "They good?"

Estella ducked her head to one side. "Chiiild yes they good."

Eddie squeezed a hand into his tight jeans and pulled out two quarters. He dropped them in the coin slot, punched in the numbers, and waited as the machine whirred and clanked. He heard the needle drop into the groove and a few scratchy seconds later "Lookin' for Ruby" jumped into the room with a scream that could've split James Brown's pants. Otis's head jerked sideways to see who was playing his song.

"Even if you're country," Estella said, "you needs your soul."

"Yes, ma'am," Eddie said with a nod. "That's the truth too."

"Lemme axe you somethin'." Estella folded her arms and leaned forward from the waist up. "You know the secret to the music bidness?"

Eddie turned sincere, nodding modestly. "You gotta write your songs from your heart."

Estella shrugged as if she took that for granted. Then she shook her head and looked Eddie in the eyes. "You keep control of all the publishin' you can."

* * *

Born tired and raised lazy, the typical country music fan was a backwards, tobacco-chewing, snaggle-toothed, inbred, beer-swilling boob who couldn't pour piss from a boot with directions printed on the heel. This crude portrayal, probably a creation of the liberal East Coast media elite, might once have contained a grain of truth. However, thanks to the reams of research compiled by country radio programming consultants, we now know better. Today we know the typical country music fan is a home-owning, college-educated, city-dwelling, constantly-on-the-cell-phone Suburban driver, earning between $40,000 and $100,000 a year.

In the not-too-distant past, country music was the exclusive domain of those with a genuine rural heritage. It was made by and for—and was about—Americans who had suffered the exacting nature of rural life, whether it be in a Kentucky coal mine or an Oklahoma cornfield. The songs were about hardship and heartbreak, black lung and drought, desperation and doing time. But as the nation moved from an agricultural and industrial-based economy to an information-based economy, the audience changed and the original artists and their fans lost their death grip on the music. It was fair to say that most of today's country music fans were all hat and no cattle in terms of their rural heritage. Oh, sure, they might own a pickup truck, ride a horse on the odd weekend, or speak with a drawl or a twang, but for most of them, that's as far as it went. As such, it had become a generally accepted fact in the country music industry that even the catchiest tune about black lung disease would have a hard time getting radio play.

The programming consultants who tracked changes in market demographics identified dozens of trivial differences between fans of country music and fans of pop and rock. But for Eddie Long, there were three differences that weren't trivial at all. The first of those was "level of education." Contrary to the stereotyped perception, country fans were more educated than fans of pop or rock (with fourteen percent more holding postgraduate degrees). The second difference followed from the first. On average, country fans had a higher per capita income than fans of other forms of popular music. The third difference related to "computer literacy." Research showed that the more education and money a group had, the more they used computers. And the more they used computers, the more familiar they were with the Internet.

In other words, the demographic profile of the modern country music fan correlated neatly with the demographic profile of the typical Internet-savvy computer owner. So it was no surprise, really, that Eddie's marketing strategy was causing such a stir.

As it turned out, a decade or so after America went country, country went America . . . Online. Of course, Eddie's band of web surfers was taking full advantage of this fact. They had sent a steady stream of hyperventilating "listener" e-mails to more than half of the nation's 2,600 country radio stations, sometimes pleading for a complete version of the song, other times pretending to be local musicians offering to record an ending for it. They visited hundreds of country-music-related chat rooms and bulletin boards, where they posted a variety of theories on the real identity of this Eddie Long character ("It's probably Garth trying another Chris Gaines stunt"). At other sites they carried on scripted discussions about the song's meaning and whether it was the best country song ever written. They also started a dozen fan sites, a mailing list, a web ring, and a Usenet group.

The result of all this was remarkable. The extent of Internet penetration in the country radio industry was illustrated by the fact that seventy-five percent of the country stations in the United States had downloaded the MP3 file. One third of those stations had played the half-song at least once, and two dozen stations were actually playing it in light rotation by the end of week three of the campaign. Nearly twenty million people in America had heard the tune—or had at least heard of it—by that point. The major radio and music industry trade papers, *Billboard* and *Radio & Records*, had all either mentioned it in passing or had devoted an article to the mystery songwriter. And *Country Weekly* was running a weekly update about "the search for Eddie Long" on its "Cyber Country" page.

By the end of week four, no fewer than thirty-five country radio station music directors were under orders from management to get the entire song on the air or find a new job. It was an idiotic demand, of course, but it was a well-established fact that radio station managers didn't have as much sense as you could slap in a gnat's ass with a butter paddle.

All this excitement about an unknown singer-songwriter was seen as a mixed blessing on Music Row. The good news was there was a song and an artist out there that the audience wanted. The bad news was twofold. First, obviously, was the fact that no one knew how to find the artist. Secondly, if and when they ever found him, there was going to be a serious bidding war for his services.

And all this was good news for Eddie Long.

10

Jimmy wasn't worth a milk bucket under a bull when he first woke up. The randy couple next door had kept at it late into the night, long after Jimmy had satisfied his own needs. He finally drifted off around two in the morning. Unfortunately his four-button neighbor started laying pipe again at six sharp, so Jimmy didn't get half the sleep he needed. He lay there for a while, listening as the neighbors worked to perfect their dawn coupling.

"A little higher," she said.

"Okay," he replied.

"But hold that in your other hand, then push and twist at the same time."

After about fifteen minutes of this, Jimmy dragged himself out of bed, fixed a large thermos of coffee, and headed back to Quitman County.

By the time he was halfway to Greenwood, the caffeine had him agitated and thinking bad thoughts about Eddie. In fact, he was so pissed off at the whole turn of events he was thinking about writing an article exposing the truth about the Internet scheme in the hope of ruining Eddie's strategy. But Jimmy realized he wouldn't even be allowed that satisfaction, since his own success depended on Eddie's.

Jimmy arrived at the Quitman County sheriff's station, explained what he knew so far, then said he had a few more questions. The sheriff, a calm, patient man in his fifties, figured since Jimmy already had the coroner's report and the other information, there was no good reason to keep any other facts from him.

"One thing I can't figure out," Jimmy said, "is where the Chinese food came from." He held up his file, fanning the air. "There's nothing in these reports about it."

The sheriff nodded, looking mildly dismayed but not quite embarrassed. "First on the scene saw a girl with a hole in her head," he said. "Didn't think a couple Chinese food takeout boxes in the garbage were real important." The sheriff opened a file drawer as he spoke. "Didn't know it mattered until a coupla days later when we found out she'd been poisoned, and even then it turned out the poison was in the headache powder, not the food." The sheriff looked at his own file, then up at Jimmy. "It's a place called Feng Shang's in Memphis. Never been there myself. I always go to the Rendezvous for ribs when I'm in Memphis." He pointed vaguely out the thick glass window. "For Chinese I like Chow's down in Clarksdale." The sheriff pulled a document from the file and showed it to Jimmy. "We checked Eddie's credit card activity. He'd been at Feng Shang's two days before and a few other times too." The lawman sat back in his chair and thought about sending a deputy for some twice-cooked pork.

Jimmy made a note: *Why Memphis if local egg rolls good?* He looked at the sheriff and broached the final subject. "How would you characterize the status of your investigation into Ms. Long's death?"

The sheriff didn't hesitate. "Closed," he said, sliding the file drawer shut.

Jimmy was no homicide investigator, but that seemed premature to him. "What about the National Crime Information Center bulletin? Are they still looking at this as part of a pattern?"

"Can't really say. 'Bout all I know is, Louisiana State Police are talking to law enforcement in Tuscaloosa and Gulfport, and a 'course I sent 'em everything we got, but until somebody somewhere proves something . . ." The sheriff shrugged, thinking about his friend Henry Teasdale. "My case is closed."

Jimmy thumbed through his notes to see if he'd forgotten anything. Satisfied that he hadn't, he stuffed his file back in his briefcase. "You have a Memphis phone book?"

The sheriff shook his head and again pointed vaguely out the window. "But there's a library just down the street."

Jimmy made the short walk to the library and found the Memphis Yellow Pages. He turned to Restaurants and found a quarter-page ad for Feng Shang's. It featured a serpentine dragon breathing fire and spouting the words NO MSG! That can't be right, Jimmy thought. He checked the coroner's report again. It said Tammy had had MSG in her system, though Jimmy had no idea if the concentration in her blood was consistent with what you'd expect from a typical Chinese restaurant meal. He pulled out his cell phone and dialed.

"Feng Shang's!" a woman yelled into Jimmy's ear. In the background, he could hear the din from the kitchen, scraping metal, leaping flames, screaming.

"Yes, this is Jimmy Rogers with the, uh, *Memphis Commercial Appeal*. We're doing a story on local Chinese restaurants and I need to know if we should list you under the MSG or the no-MSG banner."

The woman became hysterical. "No MSG! Nevva!" Her screaming drowned out the chaos of pots and pans behind her. "You come look! No MSG, okay? Spell name right! F-E-N-G S-H-A-N-G! No MSG! You come look!"

"No, that's okay," Jimmy said. "I believe you." The woman continued yelling as if Jimmy had accused her of peeing in the egg drop
soup. "I'll put you down as a no-MSG establishment," he said. The
woman was still screaming as Jimmy flipped the phone shut. He
wondered where the MSG had come from if not Feng Shang's. He
also wondered if it mattered. To answer that, Jimmy would have to
find out if Tammy was allergic to MSG in the first place. But in any
event, it seemed odd it was in her system when the restaurant was
so adamant they didn't use it.

Until he had that squared away, Jimmy needed to find out about
sodium fluoroacetate. He pulled a copy of the *U.S. Poison Control
Center Guide to Toxic Substances*. The USPCC used a six-point
scale to rate poison toxicity. Substances with a rating of 1 were
almost nontoxic, those with a rating of 6 were called supertoxic.
Sodium fluoroacetate had a no-nonsense rating of 6.1. It was a
botanically derived pesticide in the form of a fine white powder with
no smell or taste. It blocked cellular metabolism in the entire body,
including the central nervous system. Depending on dosage and
means of exposure, death occurred within minutes as a result of res-
piratory failure due to pulmonary edema or ventricular fibrillation.
Sodium fluoroacetate was used as a rodenticide in some cases, but
was mainly an insecticide used on fruits to combat scale insects,
aphids, and mites.

Jimmy's mind seized on something. Fruits? His blood chilled.
The peach orchard. Was it possible? He drove straight out to the
Lytles' farm and went directly to the shed where Eddie used to sit
and play his guitar when he wasn't tending the peach trees. He
looked at the shelf with all the large brown bottles and the rusty
cans, but all he found was Benzahex, Ortho-Klor, ethylene chlorohydrin, and Compound 1080. No sodium fluoroacetate.

Jimmy was relieved. He was also a little embarrassed for thinking, even for a moment, that Eddie was a murderer, let alone a serial
killer. It wasn't until he was driving back toward town that another

thought, perhaps slightly more evil, occurred to him. If he'd found the poison, and it turned out that Eddie was a killer, he just might be sitting on a best-seller.

* * *

Big Bill was nearly done. It was two in the morning and he was alone in his studio, lights dimmed, doing the final mix. Earlier, a cello player had laid down a track for "It Wasn't Supposed to End That Way." Big Bill put it way in the back, lurking, whispering something dark and sad. The instrument blushed a lucid warmth so low you could hear more wood than strings. It was perfect.

As Big Bill listened to a playback, he remembered the moment he was first touched by music. He was ten years old and the teacher had Bill and his little classmates arranged in a tiny choir. They were singing a hymn, a dozen guileless voices, free of self-consciousness, united and soaring. Bill was in the middle row, his eyes closed, his soul open, and the music moved him. It was a spiritual moment and he was fully aware of it. He knew it was something special, a gift from a higher plane. And he knew, from that point forward, music would be his world.

He listened to the radio and he bought records and he went to local shows to hear and, just as important, to watch people play. He always got as close to the stage as he could. He wanted to see how it was done, how someone could take wood and strings and coax emotions from them. They were magicians, and it thrilled him that he couldn't see how they did their trick, no matter how close he stood. He watched the players communicate without speaking and he wanted to learn how it was done. He loved watching the guitar players especially, their faces contorting as they reached for notes and chords and meaning.

Bill saved his money and bought a guitar. He took lessons and he practiced every day. But he could never get beyond the notes and the chords and the mechanics. He could never do the alchemy he had seen others do. Still, he knew his place was with music and he could work with those who had the gift and that would have to be enough.

The playback ended and the sudden quiet eased Bill back to the present. The only sound in the perfect room was the hiss of tape racing across the heads at thirty inches per second. He hit a button and the room went silent. Big Bill sat in the dim light, a tired old man far nearer the end of things than the beginning. He tried to recall when his life had become more about the business than about the music. Sad enough, he couldn't remember; worse, he realized he no longer cared.

*   *   *

It was dark by the time Jimmy left the Lytles' farm. He wanted to go by Eddie and Tammy's old house before returning to Jackson, but he didn't have time this trip. He'd go by next time he was here to take some photos, even if he had to break in to do it. The place was still considered a crime scene, since the National Crime Information Center bulletin had piqued FBI interest.

Jimmy was sitting in a booth in the local diner. He was working on his fourth Budweiser and starting to get angry with himself for thinking about how much he still loved Megan and how much he missed her despite how she'd done him wrong. *What the hell happened to my self-respect?* He was just drunk enough to think he should write a song about it. But before he could get started, the waitress stopped by to take his order. "I'll have the catfish and the dinner salad." He handed her the menu. "And another beer when you have a chance."

Jimmy toyed with some lyrics for his been-done-wrong song: *You left without a word, and got a number unlisted; love flew off like a bird, just ceased and desisted.* He shook his head, deciding he was either way too drunk or not near drunk enough for country songwriting, so he turned his attention back to his book. Looking over the sheriff's report, Jimmy found something he thought might be helpful. The sheriff had made a list of everyone they'd interviewed after Tammy's death. Jimmy hoped to find someone on the list who might be willing to answer a few more questions. The Teasdales were at the top of the list, but Jimmy wasn't prepared to pester the parents of the deceased, so he skipped down a bit. There was a Steve Teasdale, an uncle, way the hell over in Fulton, but Jimmy didn't think his questions warranted the two-hour drive to Itawamba County. Next on the list was one of Tammy's coworkers, Carl. He circled the name just as the catfish arrived.

* * *

Jimmy got to the Dollar Store late the next morning. He found Carl lining up a putt on the little AstroTurf green in the middle of the sporting goods section.

"Excuse me," Jimmy said.

Carl never broke concentration. "Be riiight with you," he said. He reset his feet, looked at the cup, then addressed the ball.

Jimmy waited for Carl's backswing before speaking. "Sheriff tells me you knew Tammy Long." Carl's putt soared across the green and disappeared into cosmetics. Jimmy looked off in that direction. After a pause, he looked back at Carl. "Bad case of the yips."

Carl's right leg suddenly got the weak trembles. He'd thought all this was behind him. Ever since Tammy's death, he'd been going to church regular, had been faithful, more or less, and was starting to feel better about himself. Until now. "You shouldn't talk when a man's fixin' to putt," Carl said. "It's bad manners."

"Yeah." Jimmy nodded. "I guess that's why they won't let me join the country club." Jimmy glanced at Carl's leg and wondered what had triggered the sudden palsy. "You seem a little tense," he said. "Have you tried decaf?"

Carl spoke through clenched teeth. "Well, you come up in here messin' up my putt and talkin' about what the sheriff said and . . .

what's this all about, anyway? You with the FBI or something?" He feared Jimmy was about to ask for a semen sample.

"I'm just doing a little investigative work is all," Jimmy said. "Relax."

Oh God, Carl thought, *they've caught me. I'm done for. When the truth gets out, I'm gonna get it from all directions. Mr. Teasdale's gonna wrap this putter around my neck and my wife'll use the driver to cave in my testicles. How did they find out? I thought the investigation was all over. Maybe I should call a lawyer. No, wait until he makes an accusation, otherwise I look guilty. Meanwhile, I better say something instead of just standing here.* "What kind of investigative work?" Carl's voice cracked slightly.

Jimmy looked at his notepad. "Well, I figured since you and Tammy worked together you might be able to answer some questions."

"I already answered the sheriff's questions. Besides, I'm married and have a new baby."

Jimmy nodded slightly, unsure what to make of Carl's nonlinear thinking. "Were you and Tammy close?"

"Were we close?" Carl leaned up against a display case trying to get his leg to stop trembling. "Close for working in different departments, I guess." Carl suddenly read a little something extra into Jimmy's question. "What do you mean by close?" He squinted at Jimmy.

Jimmy thought poor Carl was going to have a stroke. "Listen, I'm not with the police or anything. I'm writing a book about Eddie. I'm just trying to find out a few things."

Carl's eyes flashed skyward in a *thank you, Jesus* glance. "Not with the police" were the sweetest words Carl had ever heard. He took a deep breath and leaned forward on his putter. His twitchy leg began to settle. "A book about Eddie, huh?" Carl's rusty wheels began to grind. It seemed like there might be some way to turn this whole thing to his advantage. He just hoped he could figure out how before it was too late. "What kinda book you writin'?"

"Biography," Jimmy said.

Carl nodded sagely. "What kinda biography?"

Jimmy hesitated, unsure how best to answer such a question. "Oh, uh, all about his life, his music career, major events, like his wife's death, that sort of thing."

"What makes you think people wanna read about Eddie? He ain't never done nothin'."

"I'm thinking he might, now that he's moved to Nashville."

That's when it occurred to Carl. "Lemme ask you a question," he said. "You talked to the sheriff. Are they still looking into this? I mean I'd hate to think they'd stopped looking for who killed her."

"Sheriff said as far as he was concerned the case was closed in Quitman County. I think the FBI still considers it open but I don't know how active their investigation is."

Carl nodded some more. He figured if the feds were still poking around on this thing, they might end up talking to this fella writing the book about the husband of the deceased, in which case Carl figured this would be a good chance to direct attention away from himself and cast it in other directions. "All right," Carl said, "I'll answer your questions, but you gotta promise not to use my name or nothing if I tell you anything."

"Fair enough."

"So what kind of things you wanna know?"

Jimmy glanced at his notes. "Well, for instance, I was wondering if you knew why Tammy and Eddie used to make a two-and-a-half-hour round trip to Memphis for Chinese food. I mean, I hear that place in Clarksdale's pretty good."

"What, Chow's?" Carl shook his head. "Nah, Tammy liked that Hunan food what they serve up at that place in Memphis, real spicy you know, with them little peppers." Carl curled up a pinkie finger to indicate the size of the peppers in question. "Things're stronger'n horse piss with the foam farted off," he said. "Turns out you're not supposed to eat 'em." Carl looked a little embarrassed. "Anyhow, Chow's serves that Mandarin style. It was too bland for Tammy."

"Do you know if she was allergic to MSG?"

Carl shook his head. "No, we weren't so close I'd know stuff lack 'at. But I'll tell you somethin' else I do know . . ."

*   *   *

Every day for five days e-mails were sent to the head of every record label in Nashville, their A&R departments, and members of the local music press. The content of the e-mail changed each day. Monday's e-mail said: "We found him!"

Tuesday's said: "You'll want to meet him!"

Wednesday's: "He's more than the next 'It Boy.' "

Thursday's: "We've got the whole track!"

Friday's: "Vanderbilt Plaza. Acuff Conference Room. 5 P.M. Today. Open Bar."

Whereas the level of intrigue generated by the e-mail campaign promised to put a lot of butts in the seats, the open bar guaranteed an SRO crowd. There was, of course, a great deal of speculation within the industry as to the nature of the event. All week long theories floated up and down Music Row, but by Friday the good money was on this being the culmination of an elaborate promotional campaign by a new dot-com set to introduce a new Internet music delivery system or some clever new way to control the sale of MP3 files. The assumption was that the Eddie Long character was the mythical spokesperson for the company. Everyone agreed the campaign had been handled expertly, probably out of Atlanta.

By four forty-five the Acuff Conference Room was near capacity. At one end of the room there was a dais with a podium in the middle. Behind the dais, heavy maroon curtains dropped from the ceiling. Centered in front of the stage was an array of tables draped in white linen and dotted with tealite candles floating in crystal bowls filled with icy blue water. The room was equipped with an elaborate sound system, which was playing something at a hush. Listening closely, one could just hear a cello lurking in the background, but it was mostly drowned out by the sounds of people enjoying themselves.

At the other end of the room, adjacent to the bar, was a buffet of boiled shrimp, crab fingers, roast beef on buttermilk biscuits, and crudités vinaigrette. And no one was being shy about it. At odds with the fact that a great deal of the conversation seemed to revolve around claims that nobody in the music business was making any money, the mood was prosperous, upbeat, and friendly. In fact it was like a locker room with cocktails, especially given the eight-to-one ratio of men to women.

"Not that it says anything about the state of the business," one well-dressed woman was overheard saying to a reporter, "but out of the twenty-five record labels, I'm the only female label head." Using a crab finger, she pointed across the room at another woman, who happened to be talking to Megan. "And she's the only head of A&R in this town who doesn't have a dick." She lowered her voice slightly and winked at the reporter. "But she's got brass balls."

The head of A&R for one of the major labels, who had been eavesdropping, elbowed his way into the conversation. "Well now, to be fair, little lady," he drawled, "just let me point out that a lot of the girls here tonight work in all those A&R departments." He smiled as if that settled that.

"Well, of course to be *really* fair, sugar," the woman replied in a condescending tone, "there'd have to be a few more girls *running* those departments."

Just then, the lights in the room dimmed, the cello faded, and a disembodied voice came over the sound system. "Ladies and gentlemen." The crowd fell silent as a spotlight hit the podium. "Big Bill Herron and Franklin Peavy." As the maroon curtain parted and the two men took the stage, the crowd broke into spontaneous applause—a knee-jerk reaction from having attended so many awards ceremonies. While the applause continued, the guests looked at one another with expressions ranging from curiosity to suspicion. Big Bill took the podium, Franklin hovered at his side. Both wore dark, tailored business suits with matching cowboy hats.

Big Bill held up a hand asking for quiet. "Thank you very much for coming this afternoon, ladies and gentlemen. For anyone who doesn't know us, my name is Bill Herron." He held a hand out toward Franklin. "And this is my partner, Franklin Peavy." Franklin took a slight bow. "Now, I suspect the question most of you are asking yourselves is, what the hell has gotten into Herron and Peavy that they're giving away crabmeat and cocktails?" The crowd laughed and nodded collectively. "Well, don't worry about that, Franklin'll find a way to make it recoupable against somebody's royalties." The crowd laughed again, this time less perfunctorily.

"Okay, so now you're asking yourself, what's this all about? Well, I'll tell you." Big Bill took the mic from the stand and, followed by the spotlight, began pacing. Franklin moved to the far end of the stage, where the sound gear was stacked. "Over the past several weeks," Big Bill said, "there's been a lot of talk about a certain song drifting around out there in the ether . . ." He waggled his free hand in the air. ". . . otherwise known as the Internet, the World Wide Web. The dubya-dubya-dubya." His bug eyes bulged a bit more than usual. "Most of you have already heard half the song." Big Bill pointed across the stage to Franklin, who was standing at the controls. "Right now, we are pleased to play the rest of it for you."

The spotlight winked out and the overheads faded to black. The only light in the room came from the tiny candles floating in the crystal bowls. Franklin hit the play button and a moment later the tones of a mandolin and a pedal steel guitar merged to remind the room of the feeling of loss. The fiddle and Eddie's guitar joined in a few seconds later and everyone suddenly and inexplicably felt buoyed by hope. The piano, bass, and drums gave them strength, and Eddie's voice, singing words they'd all heard before, helped them feel release. It was an incredible and visceral response, all the more remarkable because of the nature of the audience. These were hardened music professionals who heard and dismissed a hundred songs a week, people whose response to music tended more toward calculation than celebration. But still, there it was.

From his place on the dais, Big Bill could see the wonder in the candle-lit faces as the song played. But he knew it wasn't just the song. He knew it was also the sound of the recording itself that had heads tilted in awe toward the monitors. There was a warmth and immediacy to it that they hadn't heard in years. It was free of digital sterility and binary exactness and was all the more accessible because of its slight imperfections. Big Bill also knew part of the effect came from hearing a full arrangement of the song for the first time. Once one was familiar with the solo guitar version, there was something fulfilling about hearing it with a complete band. And when the cello slipped in under the bridge, it seemed familiar, like something subtle from a favorite old song. No one realized they'd been listening to the cello track on a tape loop for the last thirty minutes. All these elements combined to create the exact effect Big Bill had intended. *Number ninety-nine my ass.*

When the song ended, there was a moment of silence before one of the A&R executives said to Franklin, as seriously as he'd ever said anything, "Play it again." So he did. This time, as the song played, the executives from each label huddled together to discuss strategy. They knew Herron and Peavy hadn't called them together just to hear this thing.

When it ended the second time, the crowd just stood there, mute. The house lights came up and Big Bill looked out to measure the stunned faces. He took the microphone and waited. He wanted them to think about it for a moment. "Well," he said, "I guess the silence speaks for itself." Big Bill knew every executive in the room wanted the song, but he wasn't interested in selling Eddie off in pieces. Herron and Peavy had a package deal in mind, and they intended to wade deep in the revenue streams. "Franklin and I have had the good fortune to sign the young artist who wrote and sang that song," Big Bill said. "His name is Eddie Long, and before I bring him out I want to talk a minute about the changing nature of our business." Bill paused a moment to sip his drink.

"I think everyone in this room will agree that it's just plain remarkable that so many people in this country already know about this song. It speaks to the power of the Internet, certainly, but it also speaks to the power of the song itself. In fact, I betcha dolla that it's a lot more about the song than the dubya-dubya-dubya thing. And lemme tell ya what makes me say that. Franklin showed me a website the other day with a database of nearly two hundred 'n' fifty thousand MP3 files. A quarter million songs, and not a one you've heard of. But half the country music fans in America know about this one—and they wanna buy it too."

Big Bill walked over to Franklin, who handed him a couple of boxes with master recording tapes in them. They both smiled. Big Bill held the boxes up for all to see. "The album's already in the can, twelve tracks, so right off the bat you know we've got something unorthodox in mind." He smiled and set the tapes on the podium. "Now, you've heard the first single. Believe me when I tell you there are at least two more. Of course, you'll be able to hear the whole thing before we execute any contracts, but trust your instincts based on what you just heard. You've got a rough idea of the value of that one song. Now add a couple of zeros to that and we can talk."

It would be an understatement to say this was not how most record deals came about, especially for an unknown artist, but then "It Wasn't Supposed to End That Way" was not most songs. On the one hand, the executives couldn't believe how good the song was. On the other, they were afraid to imagine the deal Herron and Peavy were going to propose. Were they so brazen as to think they could command the Garth deal right out of the box? It crossed more than a few minds that they should just leave in a huff to show that their label didn't let artists dictate to them, but they had to wait to see if anyone else did it first, lest they screw themselves out of this record based on nothing more than principle. No one budged.

"Well, then, you're still with me," Big Bill said. "That's good." He nodded to his partner, who picked up a stack of documents. "Now before Franklin passes out his memo covering the main points of the deal, let me introduce to you the young man who's made this all possible."

The curtain parted and Eddie came up the stairs from backstage. He was wearing pressed Wranglers and a denim work shirt unbuttoned to reveal a white T-shirt underneath. He had his big flattop Gibson in his hand and he was wearing his tan Stetson. He kept his head down until he reached Big Bill's side. "Ladies and gentlemen, it's my pleasure to introduce Mr. Eddie Long." A second spotlight jumped on him and he looked up flashing his best smile. Several of the women in the crowd actually gasped. He looked that good.

Eddie bowed modestly and pulled his guitar into position. He looked out at the crowd, found Megan, and winked. Then he counted it down, "One, two, uh-one, two, three . . ." He busted into a rowdy version of "Dixie National" and played the crowd like a seasoned pro. Meanwhile, Franklin circulated among them, distributing the pages outlining the proposed deal points.

When Eddie reached the second chorus, he stopped singing, but he kept playing the guitar. Big Bill talked over the music. "As you can see from the memo Franklin's handing out, we're not exactly proposing a standard deal," Big Bill said. "The numbers in the right-hand column are the minimums for today's bidding. The maximums, well, that's up to you." The executives were still absorbing the deal points when Eddie suddenly stopped playing the guitar and Big Bill raised the microphone to his lips. "Now, who'd like to start the bidding?"

Big Bill Herron might've been fixin' to fall off Nashville's Power 100, but everyone knew he still had an ear for great songs. They'd just heard proof of that. Or had they? No one stopped to ask that question, and that's what Big Bill was counting on. Whether it was a great song or not didn't really matter at the moment, though. The only thing that mattered was that the people in this room, at this moment, *believed* it was a great song. That was the genius of this gathering. There was no time for doubt or focus group surveys. Big Bill was relying on pack mentality, plain and simple. All he needed was one major label to start off in the right direction and the rest of the herd would follow. Big Bill pointed at one of his old friends, the head of a major label. "James? Whaddya say? You know that's a hit."

James figured he didn't have anything to lose by making the minimum bid. If no one countered, he got the record as cheap as it could be gotten. If someone did counter, he was off the hook. And in his gut he felt Big Bill was right; it was a hit. So he made the bid, and that was all it took. In a matter of minutes, the Acuff Conference Room looked like the trading floor of the Chicago Mercantile Exchange. Fueled by alcohol and driven by greed and fear, the label heads bid higher and higher. Once it achieved a certain momentum, the thing simply fed on itself. There were frantic cell phone calls to corporate headquarters. The smaller labels either fell by the wayside each time the bid jumped by ten or twenty or fifty thousand dollars or they tried to forge ad hoc alliances to outbid the majors. It was a thing to behold.

The reporters for *Billboard* and *Radio & Records* would later recall in breathless terms how the historical auction played itself out over the course of a frenzied forty minutes. When it was over, there were photo ops and lots of champagne. The press release out of Nashville the next day was picked up by all mainstream media. Some of the articles that followed were steeped in hype—"The new Garth!" and "Country music's twenty-first-century savior," that sort of thing. But there was one element in the stories that wasn't hype.

It was plain and simple and true: Eddie Long had signed the most lucrative rookie contract in the history of country music. Bar none.

* * *

Carl opened up like a magnolia blossom once he realized the opportunity Jimmy's book afforded him. It occurred to him he could attribute all sorts of statements to Tammy—some true, some not— and it would be impossible for anyone to know which was which. "Tammy told me more than once she wanted Eddie to settle down and take a job at the Dollar Store so they could start raising a family." Carl held his putter in the air and wrapped his fingers perfectly around the grip. "Of course, Eddie resented that real bad. He had his own dreams, you know, the country music thing, and he told Tammy it was gonna be a cold day in Jew-lie before he got tied down in Hinchcliff." Carl tapped the heel of the putter on the floor, then leaned toward Jimmy, propping himself up by the club. "I think he beat her too. She never said anything about it, but I saw a bruise on her leg once." Carl reached into his pocket and dropped another ball onto the putting green. "Now I hate to tell on her, but this might be helpful." He tapped Jimmy's chest with the grip of the putter. "Just don't tell nobody you heard it from me."

Carl was acting like he was a key figure in some sort of international espionage intrigue. Jimmy figured he'd play along if that's what it took to get Carl to talk. He grabbed the putter and assured Carl that he was bound by a journalist oath of confidentiality and protected by the First Amendment guarantee that sources don't have to be revealed. "Carl," he said in all seriousness, "I'll take your name to my grave."

"All right," Carl said, wrenching the putter away from Jimmy. "Tammy told me she'd been seeing another man. A feller from Grenada, I think. She never said his name, but . . ." Out of the corner of his eye Carl saw his boss heading toward sporting goods. "Hey, listen, I think I've said enough." Carl put the putter back in its stand. "And if you quote me, I'll deny we ever talked." He walked off toward his boss. "Hey, Mr. Teasdale, how you doin'?"

Notwithstanding the fact that Jimmy hadn't found the right kind of poison out at the Lytles' farm, his earlier suspicions returned. If Eddie felt Tammy was standing between him and his dream, that might amount to motive. Of course there was the matter of having to explain the other poisoning deaths and the gunshot wound, but, well, he was new at this. He'd just have to take things one step at a time.

Jimmy looked at his watch. It was four-thirty. "Shit!" He raced out of the store, dove in his car, and headed south. He'd been hired to cover a Foghat concert at a casino in Vicksburg in four hours, and it was going to be close. Highway 61 through the Delta wasn't exactly the Autobahn, and if he got caught passing too many tractors between Quitman and Warren Counties, he'd probably end up writing a story about the appalling conditions at the jail in Panther Burn or Nitta Yuma.

11

o be charitable, one could have argued Megan was simply being experimental with her foreplay. She was wearing nothing but a pair of pink silk panties while sitting in bed next to Eddie with a calculator between her legs. "All right," she said, "let's add up how much money you're going to have a year from now." She took a swig off her beer, then leaned way over to put it on the bedside table. Eddie peeked at her underside and did what he had to. Megan shrieked and nearly fell off the bed before she started laughing. "Hey! You pinch that again and I'll retaliate." She grabbed the toenail clippers that were sitting next to her beer and brandished them at Eddie.

He covered his giblets with one hand and pointed with the other. "I was just trying to get that piece of lint, I swear."

Megan looked at her crotch. "That's not lint!" She looked up and wagged a finger at Eddie. "Okay, later tonight I'll give you a lint identification lesson, but first we've got some accounting to do."

Truth was, they'd both taken drunk. And, as if the alcohol and the promise of a lint identification lesson wasn't enough, Eddie was still plenty high from having deposited $250,000 into his checking account. It was an unheard-of situation for any recording artist, but especially for a first-time record deal. The way it normally worked in Nashville was very different. After a label signed an artist to a recording contract, they advanced the artist money for various expenses—legal fees, wardrobe, video production, and the biggest expense of all, recording an album. It wasn't unusual for an artist to be $350,000 in debt to the label before the record was actually released. The good news for the artist was that he or she didn't owe the label anything if the record bombed. The bad news, in a sense, was the artist didn't get to spend all that advance money on fun stuff.

The label made back the advance only if the record sold well. Once it started selling, the label applied the artist's royalty income against the amount advanced. It was only after the advance was recouped that the artist started seeing money from record sales *as the artist*. Income from songwriting and publishing was a whole different animal. To see any profit from record sales, the artist had to sell at least 500,000 units in less than six months lest the "mechanical" income be offset by long-term overhead. There were probably hundreds of well-known country artists with good careers who made next to nothing on their record sales, even after going gold. The bulk of their income came from touring and, if they wrote their own songs, from publishing and radio play.

Now, ask anyone on Music Row and they'd tell you the same thing—the standard royalty rate for a new artist in Nashville was twelve percent of the retail price of the record, with three or four of those points going to the producer. Of course, that was really just a screwy way of saying the standard royalty rate for a new artist was eight percent, but that's how they talked in Nashville. And of course, all this was a vast oversimplification of how money was accounted for in the industry. The real business practices were far more convoluted and deceptive than this.

But after all the fancy accounting, which involved a Byzantine schedule of retailer discounts, packaging costs, "free goods," mysteriously discounted royalty rates, and the split with the producer, a new artist might earn sixty-six cents for each CD sold and about forty-four cents on each cassette sold at retail outlets. And that's before the lawyers, managers, agents, and government took their cuts, ultimately leaving the artist with little more than a bewildered expression.

As a guide, consider this example. A well-known country artist's recent debut record sold 500,000 units, thereby grossing $4 million for the label. Of that, the artist earned less than $200,000, all of which was applied against his advance of $350,000, leaving the artist still in the hole to the tune of $150,000. Most young artists lucky enough to have a gold record were genuinely surprised to find they were in such debt after becoming so famous. But Eddie wasn't most young artists. Thanks to his astute marketing scheme, a couple of good songs, and the negotiating skills of Herron & Peavy Management, he had a quarter million in the bank, a record that hadn't even been released, and nothing to recoup before seeing royalties.

"Where should we start?" Eddie asked. "Mechanical and songwriting royalties? Record sales? Touring? Merchandising?"

"How about endorsements?" Megan said. "What do you think, Gibson or Fender?"

Eddie shook his head. "Why limit ourselves? I mean, why not go after somebody with deeper pockets? Maybe a company that could sponsor a tour. Somebody we could cross-promote with, like, General Motors or Kmart or Seagrams. I bet we could get a hundred K a year from somebody like that."

"A hundred thousand?" Megan sounded disappointed. "Eddie, you gotta start using bigger numbers. You gotta be more positive!

Plus, think about it, those Fortune 500 people have so much more money than good sense. Soon as you've got a number one single, I bet you can get a million-dollar endorsement." Megan keyed in 1,000,000 on the calculator.

Eddie laughed and drained his beer. "Talk about your easy money." He burped. "Okay, let's do mechanicals." He leaned over and whispered in Megan's ear. "Thanks to our little bidding war, we'll earn a mechanical royalty of about ten cents for every song on every copy of the CD we sell." He burped again. "Oh, sorry." He twisted up part of the sheet and stuck it in Megan's ear.

"Oh, how gallant." She sat there with arms folded as Eddie dried her ear. "You know, most guys? They'll just belch in your ear and think they're done." She pointed her finger at the tip of Eddie's nose. "But you . . ."

"Yes, I know, I'm a full-service sort of guy." He untwisted the sheet and smoothed it onto the bed. "Now, where were we? Ahh, yes, mechanical royalties at ten cents a song. But of course I have to split each of those dimes fifty-fifty with my publisher." Now Eddie sounded disappointed.

"Hey," Megan said in her upbeat tone, "cost of doing business."

"You're right," Eddie said as he pulled another beer from the six-pack. "You're totally right." He gestured at the calculator. "So put us in for a nickel per song and we'll be happy about it."

Encouraged by Eddie's use of the word "we," Megan keyed in .05 on the calculator. "Okay, what's a gold record," she asked, "five hundred thousand units?" Megan thought about that for a moment. "Nah, that's not enough. Let's say it goes platinum, okay? So let's see . . ." Megan keyed in the new numbers. ". . . five cents times eleven songs times a million equals . . . Woo-hoo!" Megan kicked her bare legs up and down on the bed. "Five hundred fifty thousand dollars. Plus the million from the Fortune 500 people plus the two-fifty nonrecoupable advance brings us up to a million eight." She clapped her hands together. "This is fun. What's next?"

Eddie looked down at the calculator poised between Megan's ivory thighs. "I'm gonna have to do an audit on you pretty soon," he said.

"First things first," Megan said. "Let's look at touring income."

Eddie reached to the side of the bed, grabbed his Gibson, and started playing. "On the road again . . ." As Eddie did his warbling impression of Willie Nelson, Megan went through a series of calculations based on highly inflated estimates of income from touring, publishing, merchandising, songwriting, and coproducing deals.

When she had added everything she could think of, Megan turned to Eddie, who still had his guitar in his lap. "A drumroll please," she said. Eddie obliged on the soundboard of the guitar. Megan hit the calculator's total button, then leaned close to read the number. "Holy eight-hundred-pound Jesus!" She showed Eddie the calculator. "Sixteen billion dollars and forty-two cents!"

Eddie looked closer. "I think you hit an extra zero or something." Laughing, he flopped back into the pillows and reflected on how well his life was turning out. It occurred to him that his one-of-a-kind record deal was exactly the sort of thing Jimmy would want to put in the biography. Eddie's expression changed as he realized how long it had been since he'd spoken to Jimmy. He realized he'd never given Jimmy his new unlisted number. But what could he do now? Call Jimmy and say, "Hi, how's the book going? Thought you'd want to know I just signed a fantastic deal with Big World Records. Oh, and by the way, I've got my hands in Megan's pink panties and she sends her best." He thought about asking Megan if she'd talked to Jimmy lately. But there was something peaceful about her expression that stopped him.

Megan looked like she was lost in a dream. She was still toying with the calculator, trying to figure what her cut of the total might be if she managed to secure the position as the second Mrs. Eddie Long. She made a mental note to find out if Tennessee was a community property state and, if not, how she might get Eddie to move to one. She turned to look at him. "Have you ever thought about living in California?"

* * *

Jimmy made it from Hinchcliff to the casino in Vicksburg in just under three hours, arriving just as Foghat hit the stage. The show was everything he expected, except that the band consisted of something less than the original lineup, owing to the untimely death of Lonesome Dave Peverett. Actually this "Foghat" turned out to be fronted by a guy who had played cowbell on one song on the *High on the Hog* album. He had licensed the rights to the band's name and had been playing around the country for several years without anyone noticing that only one of the band members was over the age of thirty. Of course that really wasn't surprising when you figure the only people interested in seeing Foghat now had to be so stoned that they wouldn't have been able to do the math. But the upside was that compared to Foghat's '77 live album, these guys were fabulous. Jimmy enjoyed the free show, took his notes, then headed back to Jackson.

He was back at his apartment by eleven and slugged out the review in less than an hour. He e-mailed it to the editor who had hired him, then he poured himself a big drink and crashed on the sofa. He was hoping to drift off to sleep, but a question had been nagging at him ever since he left Quitman County, plus he couldn't get "Slow Ride" out of his head. Jimmy finally surrendered. He sat up and looked at the clock. He knew someone who could answer his question but he didn't know if he should call this late. Screw it, he thought, she shouldn't have become a doctor if she didn't want to get paged late at night.

Five minutes later, Jimmy's phone rang. He picked up. "Hellllloooo, Dr. Glick."

"Jimmy? What are you doing calling so late?"

"Sorry, Cris, I just—"

"Wait, lemme guess. You just got back from covering some lame concert where you had too much to drink, and you want to talk dirty again."

Jimmy paused. "Boy, one lapse in judgment and you're labeled for life. I wish you'd let that go."

"Can't," she said with a smile in her voice. "It's too much fun."

"Still with the cheap shots, huh?"

"I know, I should be ashamed, but you're so darn cute when you squirm. Are you squirming?"

Cris and Jimmy had dated during high school. They'd drifted apart during college, but reconnected one night a few years later when they ran into each other at Hal and Mal's during Christmas vacation. The following week, after covering a B. J. Thomas show at one of the casinos, Jimmy, slightly toasted, called to invite himself over to Cris's apartment for a late-night get-together. When she declined, he tried steering her toward a little smutty conversation. Cris told him to call her back when he was sober, then hung up. He called the next day to apologize. She accepted. But she still enjoyed giving him grief about it.

"You know, it doesn't speak well of you that you still hold that over my head," Jimmy said, "but I'll let it go, since I need a favor."

"Get over it," Cris said. "What do you need?"

"I need you to interpret a coroner's report for something I'm writing."

"Really?" She sounded surprised. "Sounds like you've wandered off the old entertainment trail, Jimmy. What're you working on?"

Jimmy told her about Eddie's biography and Tammy's death. "So can I fax it over?"

"Sure. Give me half an hour," Cris said. "I'll meet you in the cafeteria on the third floor."

*　*　*

Jimmy faxed the coroner's report, then left for the hospital. It was only a five-minute drive from his apartment, but, by Jimmy's reckoning, the University of Mississippi Medical Center was one of the largest medical facilities in the universe. It was a sprawling, ponderous puzzle of tedious architecture, and Jimmy knew he'd need at least twenty-five minutes to find the particular third floor and cafeteria Cris was talking about.

Dr. Glick was finishing a cup of coffee when Jimmy burst through the door ten minutes late. "Sorry," he said. "They've added a few new wings since the last time I was here." He sat down across from his old flame. She was still the beauty with the curly reddish-brown hair he'd had such a crush on, except now she was an M.D. with a husband and two children, so he had to remember not to make goo-goo into her brown eyes the way he used to. He leaned toward her. "Just between you and me," he said, "how many patients go missing in this rat's maze every year?"

"I'm not allowed to say." She smiled.

Jimmy smiled back. "Have I ever told you how great you look in scrubs?"

Dr. Glick clicked her fingernails on the coroner's report. "Let's try and focus. I've got real work to do."

"Right. So, what's the answer?"

"Well, actually, you asked the wrong question," she said. "People who show the sort of adverse response to MSG you're thinking of aren't having an allergic reaction. They're showing an intolerance. By that I mean it doesn't trigger a histamine cascade or anything like that. The common reaction is what's known in the literature as Chinese restaurant syndrome."

"Get out."

"It's also known as MSG symptom complex, but how much fun is that?" Dr. Glick looked at her watch. "All right, I've got time for the short course on MSG intolerance versus allergic reaction, so take notes. Monosodium glutamate is the sodium salt of glutamic acid, which is a form of amino acid, plus a form of glutamate, okay?

It's found naturally in the human body and in things like cheese, milk, meat, peas, and mushrooms."

Jimmy pretended to hit his Jeopardy buzzer. "What are protein-containing foods? I'll take medical mumbo-jumbo for two hundred, Alex."

Dr. Glick rolled her eyes sweetly, then proceeded to talk for five minutes about glutamate in its "free" form, lymphocytes, antibodies, antigens, and immunoglobulin E, followed by another five minutes on hydrolyzed proteins, protein hydrolysates, and enzymatically treated proteins which contain salts of free amino acids, like glutamate.

Finally Jimmy held up his hand to stop her. "You are amazing," he said. "How do you keep all that from spilling out of your head and staining your shirt? And more important, how can you possibly say all that without answering my question? That's what I really want to know."

"I had to learn it. You gotta hear it. Okay, in a nutshell, the brain, among other organs, is rich in glutamate receptors." She made a hand gesture representative of a glutamate receptor. "Glutamate's in constant flux with the amino acid gluta*mine* through several very boring biochemical reactions. The interesting thing is, these two chemicals play an important role in clearing the waste product of protein metabolism, which is ammonia. And ammonia is a bad dog for anyone's neurons, and thus causes headaches."

Jimmy pointed to the results of Tammy's blood screens. "So you're talking about this ammonia count? Is that high?"

"Seriously high."

"And that makes my deceased a textbook case of Chinese restaurant syndrome?"

"Not necessarily. Ammonia levels tend to go high postmortem."

"Damn."

"But—"

"I like but," Jimmy said. "Go on with the but."

"Okay, but don't quote me. I'm a little out of my field. I've never seen an ammonia count this high postmortem, so I think your MSG theory is sound. Your deceased probably had a headache the size of Hinds County when she died."

Jimmy slapped the table and smiled. "Thank you. I really appreciate your help." He looked at Cris and tilted his head slightly. He waggled a finger at her outfit and lowered his voice. "Seriously, though, what are you wearing under those scrubs?"

■ ■ ■

The front pages of *Billboard* and *Radio & Records* are usually given over to news from the radio and record industries. A story about a company's stock split might compete for space against a story about a Senate subcommittee hearing on music piracy issues. But this week both industry trade papers featured headlines about Eddie Long's unprecedented deal with Big World Records. "Big World Takes Long Shot" scrolled across the top of *R&R*. *Billboard*'s headline was "Going Deep—Big World Throws Long."

Everything, the saying goes, is negotiable. And the articles in the trades bore that out. It was all there. The two-points-higher-than-usual royalty rate, the six-figure nonrecoupable signing bonus in lieu of the standard advance against royalties, the guaranteed marketing budgets, and the not insignificant gross profit participation. But the most incredible aspect of the deal was the one that approached Garth status. Eddie actually shared in control of the masters. He didn't own them outright and license them back to Big World Records the way Garth did with Capitol, but he shared ownership, which was unheard of until Eddie Long showed up. There were other unusual clauses in his contract, but what really mattered was that Eddie Long and his management team ended up with a deal that earned them roughly two dollars for every record sold, more than twice what anyone in their right mind would've expected.

The front-page articles were continued in the "Country" sections of each of the trades, where they featured photos of the parties in question. One picture showed Eddie and Megan smiling deliriously, flanked by Herron and Peavy and the Big World Record executives. Another showed Eddie shaking hands with the president of Big World while the others looked on.

Asked about the street date of Eddie's record, Big World's president said, "We're sending parts to both our East and West Coast duplication facilities. We're having to 'cut in line,' so to speak, and that's going to delay a couple of our other projects, but Eddie's got the heat, so we hope to have him in stores in two to three weeks."

It was a fantastic projection. Typically, the process of going from a master tape to having CDs on retail shelves took a couple of months, but only because they scheduled it that way. And that made sense on an ongoing basis where a steady stream of product was coming down the pipeline. But when something big had to happen fast, that time could easily be cut in half, since any major-label CD duplication facility could turn out 500,000 copies of a new CD, in jewel box, with artwork, shrink-wrapped and ready to ship, in a day. It was shipping those units to retailers that took most of the time.

The articles also contained an analysis of the incredible industry buzz resulting from the spread of the MP3 file. It was this, the writers pointed out, that had led to the frenzied auction at the Vanderbilt Plaza and the unheard-of contract. There were insinuations that the Internet business might have been, at least partially, contrived. And, they went on to say, if that was the case, it signaled the triumphant rebirth of Big Bill Herron as one of Nashville's principal players.

█ █ █

Whitney had just finished working the lunch shift at the Smoke House. He was sitting at one of the tables counting his tips, nursing a beer, and trying to fend off a sense of discouragement. Since moving to town he'd spent all of his time either working or writing songs.

As a result he'd made no friends, so he spent most of his free time alone. To make matters worse, nothing was happening with his career. It seemed like it had been forever since Big Bill recorded his demo, but he hadn't heard a word about it. On top of that, between rent, food, and a new set of guitar strings, Whitney hadn't been able to save a dime to get his truck back. And Herron and Peavy still hadn't paid the $1,000 "signing bonus" they'd promised. He was starting to wonder if he'd made a mistake coming to Nashville. As he picked up his beer someone walloped him on the back, sloshing Whitney's draft onto the table.

"Hey now!" Big Bill said. "Gotcha some good news there, son." He grabbed a chair and pulled it up across the table from Whitney, a smarmy smile smeared across his fat face. "You're gonna wanna kiss me."

Whitney doubted it. Still he couldn't help but get his hopes up. "You got me a deal?"

"What, a record deal?" Big Bill waved a hand to erase the thought. "No, but believe me, I'm workin' on it. Gotta walk before we run, am I right?" He stopped a passing waitress and asked for a sweet iced tea. "Tell you the truth, I'm running into a little resistance on your songs. They don't exactly fit what country radio's looking for, if you know what I mean. But I think this might help." Big Bill pulled some papers from his coat pocket and handed them to Whitney.

"What's this?"

"*Row Fax,*" Big Bill said. "Comes out every week." *Row Fax* was a weekly newsletter "Serving Nashville's Creative Community." It noted which record executives had left which labels and which ones had been promoted. It announced artists' television appearances, trumpeted hallmarks in record sales, and otherwise acted as a vehicle for press releases. Big Bill pointed at one of the feature headings: "The Cutting Edge." "Check that out," he said. Whitney studied it for a moment but wasn't sure what to make of it.

"The Cutting Edge" was the weekly listing of the types of songs artists were looking for at the moment. It might say Collin Raye was looking for "uptempos only" or that Trisha Yearwood was looking for "great songs" or that Amber Marie was trying to find a "power ballad à la Martina McBride."

Big Bill wagged a finger at Whitney. "I think it'll help you get more in step with what the labels and the artists are looking for."

Whitney's face coiled in skepticism. "Lynyrd Skynyrd meets Alan Jackson?"

"Yeah," Big Bill said, "I think that's a good one for you. Put a little more Muscle Shoals into one of your Texas troubadour things, see what happens. Maybe we can get somebody interested. Irregardless, I think we need some new songs to shop you around. But you really gotta write stuff that's more . . . accessible. You know?"

Whitney read a little further down the list. A lot of them just said they were looking for "great songs." "What do they mean by that?" he asked. "That doesn't seem real helpful. I mean, how can I know what they want if that's all they put in here?"

Big Bill poured some sugar into his sweet tea. "Well, like my daddy used to say, don't worry about the horse being blind, just load the cart."

Whitney kept reading and suddenly he sparked to one of the descriptions. "What about this one?" He pointed at the list. "This 'alternative country'?"

Big Bill shook his head and gestured toward the street with his glass of tea. "You might as well just go play on the sidewalk for all the money you'll make with that stuff." He pointed at the list. "Trust me," he said, "try that Lynyrd Skynyrd, Alan Jackson thing and just see if something good don't happen."

Whitney folded the *Row Fax*, stuffed it in his back pocket. "So what's this good news you were talking about?"

"You're gonna love this," Big Bill assured him. "Remember how we recorded your song at that session with Eddie? Well, I don't know if you heard, but we got Eddie a deal with Big World Records. And after they listened to the tapes from that session, you're not going to believe this," Big Bill chuckled lightly, "but the folks at the label demanded we include your song on the record." This wasn't strictly true. Big Bill had planned on including it from the get-go, but he didn't want to admit to that.

Whitney was dumbfounded. "But I thought you said—"

Big Bill threw his hands up. "Nothing I could do about it," he said. "They absolutely loved your song. Kept asking about you too after I told 'em you were the original writer on it. Said they weren't going to sign Eddie's deal unless your song was on the record." Big Bill slapped his hand on the tabletop. "So, guess what, my friend? You're fixin' to be a published songwriter."

Whitney figured this was at least some progress. "So when they asked about me, did you give 'em my demo tape?" There was a glimmer of hope in his voice.

Big Bill frowned and shook his head. "No, and I'll tell you why. Based on the feedback so far, I figured that would hurt more than help. That's why I wanted to bring you the *Row Fax*, get you started on some songs that suit what they're lookin' for. Then I can go back in."

The phrase "published songwriter" began to sink into Whitney's consciousness. He decided it was more than just a little progress. It might be just the break he needed. "Well, so I get paid for my song being on the record, right? I mean, how's that work?"

"Way it works is simple," Big Bill said. "You're gonna make what's called a mechanical royalty for every one of Eddie's records that gets sold. Of course, by law, mechanicals get split with the publishing company."

"That's what you got set up through your business, right?"

"That's right," Big Bill said, pointing back and forth between the two of them. "We've got what's called a copublishing agreement between you and our company, just like we talked about. But that ain't all. See, on top of the mechanical royalties, you'll also get paid a little sumpin' every time your song gets played on the radio." Big Bill leaned toward Whitney. "And I wouldn't be surprised if your song is the third or fourth single." He sat back and shot Whitney a can-you-believe-it look.

Whitney smiled for the first time since Big Bill sat down. "Are you kiddin' me? Well, damn, that's great." Whatever disappointment he felt about not being the artist was overpowered by the feeling he got from hearing his song might get released as a single and that he was going to get paid for it to boot. Whitney felt a surge of confidence and looked at Big Bill. "Well, let me ask you about something else, Mr. Herron. I was wondering when I might get that signing bonus we talked about."

A look of disappointment suddenly clouded Big Bill's face. "Oh, shoot! Talk about bad timing. I forgot to tell you. The day you signed your contract, my damn accounts payable department switched to a ninety-day pay cycle. I'm real sorry, I should've told you sooner, but I just forgot, I been so busy out trying to sell your songs and all." Big Bill pulled out his money clip and peeled off fifty dollars. "Here, lemme give you this," he said. "We'll consider it an advance on what we owe you."

*   *   *

In order to accommodate Eddie Long's debut disc—*Long Shot*—Big World Records pushed back the street dates for a dozen of their established acts. They also redirected a significant percentage of the marketing budget from each of those projects to make a huge media push on Eddie's record. The managers of the bumped artists were so mad they couldn't spit straight, and the artists themselves, understandably more concerned with their own careers than that of the latest "It Boy," were fit to be tied. In public, of course, every one of them talked about how excited they were to have such an exciting young talent on their label and how they were looking forward to the record and how the business was all about honoring the music and no, they weren't at all concerned about the delay in their own release date, not in the least. Don't be silly. No point in speaking your mind and running the risk that the label would give you shorter shrift than it already had. Oops, did I say that out loud? What I meant was, shucks, I'm just glad to be with Big World Records.

Meanwhile Big World had to solicit sales at the wholesale level in order to determine how many units of *Long Shot* to produce on the first run. Thanks to the extensive trade magazine coverage and the Internet buzz, demand was astounding. Based on orders, Big World could have set the initial run at a million units. But Eddie had other ideas. He persuaded the label to try a high-risk marketing strategy. And damned if they didn't buy it. They set the first run at 350,000 units. It was enough to ensure they got at least a few of Eddie's discs into just about every outlet in the country, from truck stops to Wal-Marts to Sam Goody's stores, but at the same time it almost guaranteed that not everyone who wanted the disc would get it right away.

Eddie's thinking was that an initial undersupply of product would increase demand by creating in consumers a sense of urgency for buying the product immediately, whereas an oversupply would tend to make people think there was no hurry to go buy it. The strategy was designed to create Beanie Baby–like hysteria in record stores. Naturally Big World's marketing department would arrange to have television crews there to record the madness. The footage would be broadcast on the news and would create interest in the record for consumers who otherwise never would have considered buying it. As Eddie explained it, "When you see fifty people fighting in the aisles over something, you start thinking to yourself, 'Shit! I need to get me one of those!' "

When the head of marketing asked how Eddie could be sure such a group of people would break into a fight when a television crew was at a store, Eddie just smiled and said, "Temps."

Before starting on the *Long Shot* disc, the duplication facilities cranked out a few thousand copies of "comp" singles for radio and shipped them overnight. The album version of "It Wasn't Supposed to End That Way" was also made available as an MP3 file for any station with MP3 capability.

The last piece of the marketing puzzle was put together out at Willow Street Studios. Eddie knew as well as anyone that it was possible to sell a country artist without a music video, but it wasn't very smart. They shot it in two days. The set was the interior of a modest home, presumably Eddie's. All the furniture was covered in sheets and the walls showed shadows where pictures used to hang. Eddie wore black, befitting a man in mourning. They shot him as he wandered through the house, sitting on the arm of the covered sofa, touching the wall where a cherished photo had hung. All the while Eddie played his guitar and sang. Most of the video was shot from a voyeuristic point of view as the camera followed Eddie and caught glimpses of his face from a respectful distance. But about two-thirds of the way through, as he sat at the foot of the bed, looking down at his guitar, the camera pushed in and Eddie slowly looked up all sweet and sad as he reflected on the unexpected loss of someone he had once loved. And then, with what looked like a tear in his eye, he sang the words "it wasn't supposed to end that way." It just broke your heart.

Country Music Television and The National Network put the video in heavy rotation immediately, and "It Wasn't Supposed to End That Way" became the "most added" song on country radio its first week out. It debuted at number seven on both *Billboard* and *R&R* country charts and put Eddie Long on the map.

*   *   *

Jimmy was in his kitchen having breakfast and reading the paper. After glancing at the news and sports, he turned to the Southern Style section, where he was blindsided by a photograph. The cup of coffee stalled on its way to Jimmy's lips. "That cocksucker." It was all Jimmy could say as he stared at the paper. It was the photo of Eddie and Megan that had run in *Billboard,* the one taken at the Vanderbilt Plaza the night Eddie signed his record deal. And now it was running in the *Jackson Clarion-Ledger* along with a story about how another Mississippi boy had gone to Nashville and hit the big time. The caption read, in part, ". . . seen here with his girlfriend, former Jackson radio personality Megan Taylor." "That cocksucker," Jimmy repeated.

While he could have been referring to Megan with a literal use of the pejorative noun, he was actually using it in the figurative sense and was thinking of Eddie when he said it. It didn't matter that Megan was draped all over Eddie in the photo, Jimmy still hadn't gotten over her. He blamed Eddie for stealing her.

The *Clarion-Ledger* story said *Long Shot* had sold 350,000 units in its first week, making it the best-selling record in the country. In fact, according to the article, a near riot broke out at one store in Atlanta when a group of customers started fighting over the last copy of the disc. There was even a photo of the event. It looked like fifty amateur wrestlers throwing punches and pulling hair. It was the sort of PR you couldn't buy—well, you could, actually. In fact, not only could you buy it, you could choreograph it too. Jimmy could see Eddie's fingerprints all over the stunt. He might be a cocksucker, but he knew marketing. The story and the photo had been picked up by half the papers in the country, and it was helping make Eddie Long the hottest thing out of Mississippi since Faith Hill.

Ironically, it was just what Jimmy needed. Energized by a combination of jealousy and aspiration, he spent the rest of the day and night working on a book proposal for *The Long and Short of It: The Eddie Long Story.* Jimmy already had several sample chapters, so all that was left was to finish an outline for the remainder of the book and put together a section on audience and marketing. Knowing it would be pointless to submit the proposal directly to publishers,

Jimmy wrote a query letter, then pulled out his directory of literary agents and started addressing envelopes. By midnight he was at Kinko's making copies.

Jimmy stood by the machine as it hummed and rocked and spit out the warm, collated sets of documents. It was a good proposal on a hot subject, but he was having second thoughts. He wondered if he should go back and rewrite it to include his speculation that Eddie killed Tammy. What else could he think? The MSG in the Chinese food from a restaurant that didn't use MSG indicated that someone else had to have put it in the boxes with the leftovers. The fact that Tammy was MSG-intolerant, which meant it probably gave her headaches. And the fact that the only headache remedy in their house was poisoned. Add to that Carl's claim that Eddie felt Tammy was holding him back and it was just too much to shrug off.

But while all that seemed to point at Eddie, there was still the matter of the troublesome evidence pointing elsewhere. The gunshot wound, for example. Eddie obviously couldn't have done that, since he was on the Gulf Coast at the time. And then there was Carl's comment about Tammy's affair with a man from Grenada. Maybe something had gone wrong there and this mystery lover was the one with blood on his hands.

Jimmy mulled all this over on the drive home and decided not to include his theory about the identity of Tammy's killer. Sure, it would have made for a more titillating proposal, but he had no proof, only circumstantial evidence. He figured publishers would see that as the easy road to a hard lawsuit, and who needs that headache? No, he'd leave the proposal as it was, hoping to sell it on the merit of his writing and the fact that Eddie was heading for stardom. Meanwhile, Jimmy had to return to Hinchcliff to look for some direct evidence. Then maybe he'd go to Nashville and confront Eddie with his theory. Or Megan.

Back at his apartment, Jimmy glanced again at the picture in the *Clarion-Ledger*. Seeing Megan and Eddie together hurt the way betrayal always did. But he took comfort in the fact that now he knew where he stood with Megan. Now he knew it was a matter of trying to win her back, and, ironically, Eddie's sudden success looked like it might be the thing to allow Jimmy to do just that— especially if he could prove the cocksucker was also a murderer.

*   *   *

"I'm cooter than Drunker Brown!" the man hollered, half laughing. "And I wannanuther beer!"

The bartender shook his head and looked at the clock. It wasn't noon yet. "Go home, Chester. I ain't serving you no more."

Chester Grubbs didn't seem to hear the bartender, and for the moment he seemed to forget that he wanted another beer. His attention span had suffered as much as his liver from three decades of drinking. Not that he was always this drunk this early in the day. His drinking spells came and went. He'd go on a high lonesome for a while, then he'd hit bottom, straighten up for a month, get some half-assed job doing shit work for shit wages, then he'd start drinking again, do something stupid, and get fired. This circle had remained unbroken for thirty years.

Chester was in a juke joint on a back road outside Broken Bow, Oklahoma. Over the years he'd been in similar roadhouses in Texas, California, Tennessee, Kentucky, Alabama, Georgia, Louisiana, and maybe a few other states, he wasn't sure. He just moved around, hoping to remain anonymous until he died. Chester had screwed up his life and he knew it. No point in arguing with the truth, he'd say. Better just to keep out of its way.

Chester looked harder than two summers in hell. His face was all dirty crags and dull gray whiskers and there was something about the trouble in his eyes that made it look like he'd spent more time in jail than he really had. It was hard to say if he was a fifty-year-old who'd aged badly or a seventy-year-old who looked pretty good for his predicament. A long time ago Chester had had a lot of promise.

But he hadn't kept the promise and the guilt seemed to gnaw on his face.

That's what first got him to drink too much. Guilt over things he'd done and things he'd failed to do. Then of course it was guilt over things he forgot he'd done until someone reminded him the next day. After enough of those nights he'd have to move on and find somewhere else to drink.

"Hey!" Chester yelled again. "I said I wannanuther beer!" He threw his empty bottle across the room. It broke against the wall.

That was all the bartender would tolerate. "Goddammit! That's it," he said. "You're eighty-sixed, you sorry-ass drunk." He pointed at the door. "Get outta here!"

"I just wannanuther beer." He sounded pathetic.

"I said get out!" The bartender stormed around the bar, grabbed Chester by the belt and collar, and forced him out the door.

Chester put up a drunk's fight on the way. "I didn't come here and I ain't leavin'!" he yelled as the bartender threw him into the dirt. Chester pulled his head up and spit a small rock. His mouth was muddy where the dirt had mixed with beer and spit. He rolled over and yelled at the sky, "And I want my money back!"

12

*E*ddie was on the phone with the program director of WUSN-FM in Chicago making promises he intended to keep. "I swear! I will do your morning show," he said. "I will play at your listeners' party, whatever you want. I love you guys!" Earlier that morning Eddie had made pretty much the same promises to the program directors at KYCY-FM, San Francisco; WXTU-FM, Philadelphia; KPLZ-FM, Dallas–Fort Worth; and WYCD-FM in Detroit. "Yeah, we're on our way to New York. I'll have my assistant call when we get in and make the arrangements." By the time the plane landed, Eddie would have spoken to eight or ten more country stations in the top twenty markets. He looked out the window at mid-America and was wondering if someone down there was listening to his song when the program director asked him a question. "Sure, I'd be glad to," Eddie said. "Is tape rolling? Hey everybody, this is Eddie Long and you're listening to WUSN-FM!" He couldn't have been happier.

Neither could Megan. She loved flying first class. She was made for it. Prior to takeoff, she sat there, casually flipping through *Archi-*

tectural Digest, periodically casting a disdainful eye over the top of the magazine at the coach-class fliers as they filed past. *Yeah, that's right, I'm somebody. Now move along, you're slowing the champagne service.*

The members of "Team *Long Shot*" were living a rare dream. "It Wasn't Supposed to End That Way" had gone from number seven to number four in its second week. And now, in its third week, it was the number one song on country radio. The reviews were sparkling, four-stars, pick-of-the-week, preordained album-of-the-year. Many of the reviewers commented on the remarkable overall *sound* of the record. "Like nothing you've heard in years," one reviewer wrote, "as full, rich, and warm as a living-room guitar pull." It was on all 149 of the top country stations reporting to *Radio & Records* and was getting spins on roughly 2,300 of the 2,600 country stations in the United States. The album had sold a total of 620,000 units in just under three weeks, the media requests were pouring in, and Eddie's accounts receivable were getting fat in a hurry.

Big Bill, Franklin, Megan, and Eddie were on their way to New York for three days to kick off a national media blitzkrieg. In addition to six magazine features and three newspaper interviews, Eddie was scheduled for *Good Morning America* and *Late Night with David Letterman*. Then he had to do the morning show on New York's number one country station, WYNY-FM. After New York they were headed for Dallas to start a thirty-five-city tour in support of his album. The tour would take them to Los Angeles, where he'd do the *Tonight Show* as well as *Entertainment Tonight* and *Access Hollywood*. He'd also meet with film agents interested in looking at him with an eye toward roles in upcoming features.

Megan was next to Eddie, in the aisle seat, tickled pinker than a salmon. Two days earlier, in Nashville, Big Bill had called to tell them *Long Shot* had been certified gold and was on track for platinum. Being the kind of girl who adhered to the old adage "Them that don't pluck don't git feathers," Megan rushed out to buy some champagne before returning to pluck Eddie's lights out. Aftcrwards, with Eddie lying next to her sweetly drunk and satisfied, Megan picked up the phone, dialed the radio station, and quit her job. Then, gently stroking Eddie's champagne flute, she convinced him that the smartest and sweetest thing he could do right then was get Big Bill to hire her.

"I'll be your road manager and your personal assistant," she said as she began kissing his chest. "You need somebody to schedule all the media stuff and coordinate with the travel agents and the promotion people and the label. And you don't want Herron and Peavy doing it. You want them out making deals." Megan's kisses began migrating south as she continued "I'm perfect for the job." She kissed his stomach, making it quiver. "I've got radio credentials and I know enough about the record business and concert promotion. And besides . . ." She gave little Eddie a kiss on the head. "I take dictation."

Eddie smiled as he looked down. He was as drunk on his new-found fame as he was on the champagne. In fact, his hat size had probably doubled in the last week. "Why don't you go ahead and finish what you're doing," he winked, "and I'll see what I can arrange." He grabbed the phone and dialed. "Hey, big buddy, just wanted to call and thank you for hiring my new assistant."

"What're you talkin' about?" Big Bill said. "I didn't hire anybody."

"Sure you did. She's here takin' dictation right now." Megan performed some sort of fancy oral maneuver. "Whoa! And we need to give her a big raise." Eddie explained the deal while Megan continued her work.

Big Bill hesitated only slightly before agreeing to the terms. He knew women like Megan. He was still paying alimony to three of them. He considered saying no but he didn't want to piss off the golden goose. He played everything upbeat. "Hey, tell her she's got the job. 'Specially if she gives good dictation." Big Bill tendered a fraternal chuckle. "Hard to find an assistant willin' to do that these days. Now if you'll excuse me, I'm trying to sell some synchronization rights on your behalf."

* * *

Two days later, Team *Long Shot* had four seats in first class heading for New York.

The sudden success had an interesting effect on Franklin and Big Bill's relationship. They'd become almost chummy, at least as far as you could tell by looking. Sitting side by side across the aisle from Eddie and Megan, they were working on several things at once. Big Bill was on the phone hammering out tour details with concert promoters while Franklin was finalizing a merchandising agreement. Later, while Franklin checked in with the record label, Big Bill was hunched over a legal pad, tapping the pen against the paper, apparently unable to articulate his thoughts. After a moment he elbowed Franklin, who put his hand over the mouthpiece. "What?"

"You have any idea who said 'Writing about music is like dancing about architecture'?"

Franklin shook his head, then returned to his phone call.

Big Bill had been working on his version of Eddie's biography ever since the call from Jimmy Rogers put the idea in his head. After nearly two months, he almost had a first draft of the opening line written. He was starting to think a better use of his time might be to farm out the actual writing of the book while retaining the "written by" credit and the royalties. He stuffed the legal pad into the pocket of the seatback in front of him, then grabbed his phone book. He'd put in a call to someone he knew in publishing, see if he couldn't find an eager young writer. Big Bill knew he could always make a good deal with somebody whose stomach was growling.

Eddie hung up with the guy from WUSN-FM and opened his laptop. He figured he'd try to get started on songs for the second album, which thcy planned to record in about six months. Just then Megan eased a real estate flyer onto the keyboard. "Sweetie, I think this is the best we're going to find in Belle Meade. Six bedrooms, five baths, four fireplaces. Gourmet kitchen, three acres, gated, video security. It's only two point eight. I spoke with Colleen Michie, the listing agent, and she says we need to get an offer in real quick at that price." Megan snuck a glance over her shoulder at Big Bill and Franklin, then lowered her voice. "But have you thought about what I said about California? Better media access, and if you're going to be doing TV or features it makes sense. I mean, you can live anywhere you want and write songs." She looked at Eddie as he glanced at the flyer, head nodding. "I'm sorry," she said. "I shouldn't bother you with this. Get back to writing." She leaned over and bussed his cheek. "Just leave everything to me."

*   *   *

As he waited for a response from the literary agencies, Jimmy moved forward on the book. He'd covered Eddie's early years in Quitman County, the first show he reviewed, Tammy's death, the debut of "It Wasn't Supposed to End That Way" at the bar in Starkville, the Internet marketing scheme, the phenomenal record deal, and the rise to the top of the country charts. Jimmy had finished two hundred pages and he knew he was going to sell it, especially now that Eddie had the number one country song in America and was on his way to setting sales records for a debut album. *Of course, if I could come up with some direct evidence that Eddie was a killer, I'd have a best-seller and Megan would come running back like a hungry pup. And with my corner on the lack-of-self-esteem market, I'd welcome her with open arms.* He gave that a moment's thought. *I really need to work on that.*

Jimmy looked into the file of all the reviews he'd ever written on Eddie's shows. Inside, he found a document Eddie had given him, listing every club, casino, and frathouse he'd ever played and the dates he'd played them. He was about to create a timeline of Eddie's early years on the road when the phone rang. Jimmy picked up. "Hello?"

"Jimmy Rogers, please. This is Jay Colvin in New York." Jimmy recognized the name as one of the literary agents he'd sent his proposal to. He had an off-key-nasally-talking-at-the-speed-of-sound thing going with the voice.

"This is Jimmy Rogers. How are you, Mr. Colvin?"

"How am I? I'll tell you how I am," he said. "I'm excited. I'm very excited. That is, unless you've already signed with another agent, in which case I'm depressed. Very depressed. Obviously I've read your book proposal. First of all, I've got to tell you, you're a very gifted writer. Extremely talented, no question about it. Second I've got to tell you, this is the mother of all book proposals. I'm talking mother with a capital M. Forty points, all cap. And third I tell you these things not only because they are true, which they are, but also because, as we like to say in the publishing game, 'timing is everything.' And you, Mr. Rogers, have excellent timing. Excellent. Best timing I've ever seen. I saw in the trades today that your friend Mr. Long has the number one song on country radio, but I suspect you already know that. So tell me, Mr. Rogers, have you signed with another literary agent? No, wait, let me rephrase that, please tell me you haven't signed with anybody else."

The guy talked so fast Jimmy could only pick up about half the words, but he got the gist of what Mr. Colvin was saying and he liked it. "No sir, I haven't signed with—"

"Fabulous! Do me a favor. Do you have a fax machine? Can I fax you a contract? I want to represent this book, Mr. Rogers. And not just the book. I want to represent you, the writer. I'm not in this just for the project. I believe you have a future and I want to be your agent. What's your fax number there, Mr. Rogers? Would you at least consider signing with me? Are you there, Mr. Rogers, did we get cut off? Hello?"

"Hey, listen," Jimmy said, "I work on a first-come-first-served basis. Send me the contract and I'll take a look at it. If it looks—"

"It's a standard contract. I sell your work to publishers and I take a fifteen percent commission. If my foreign co-agents make foreign publishing deals, assuming I don't sell worldwide publishing rights to a U.S. publisher, I split a twenty percent commission with the foreign co-agent on all overseas deals. If I can scare up interest in the film rights, I'll co-agent with someone in L.A. and we'll split a fifteen percent commission on those sales unless there's a manager involved in which case there goes another five percent and if you have an attorney there that's another five. Absent any sales, either party can terminate the contract with thirty days' notice."

"Fine," Jimmy said. "Fax it over." While the frantic Mr. Colvin was rattling off the details of the contract, Jimmy looked him up in his agent's directory. The Colvin Agency represented some big hitters in publishing. He gave Colvin his fax number.

"I'm faxing right now," he said. "You won't regret this, Mr. Rogers. Listen, how much of the book is finished? I think it has to cover up through wherever this first record takes him. He'll have some more singles we'll want to track, plus he'll be touring. Maybe you can cover the tour. I'll try to negotiate expenses into the advance. Oh, yeah, one more thing. I assume you approached Long's management on being the official biographer, am I right? They turned you down, said they'd find a big-name biographer, am I right?"

"That's pretty much it," Jimmy said.

"Well, fuck them, if you'll pardon the expression. They're six or eight months behind us," Colvin said. "Plus you're the only one with the early show reviews and insights. That's not a problem. But let me ask you, this Eddie Long, is he as squeaky clean as you make him out to be? I mean, a little dirt on the guy would be nice for us. They do an official bio, they'll make him look like some guy in a Chevy truck commercial. All hard work and clean habits. If you can dig up any dirt on the guy, great. If not, don't worry about it. I can sell this either way, but any kind of gossip or scandal is good."

Jimmy smiled. "You know, Mr. Colvin, it's funny you should bring that up."

*   *   *

Eddie hit the Big Apple out of the park. With the combination of his Southern charm, his songs, and his disarming smile, even the cynics came around. Since arriving in New York, Eddie had played "It Wasn't Supposed to End That Way" on three network talk shows and one local TV news program. His next stop was the morning show on New York's number one country station. Eddie played along as the DJs had some fun at his expense doing a send-up of Eddie's song which was retitled 'It Wasn't Supposed to *Bend* That Way.' Afterwards they worked the phones.

"Hi, Eddie? My name's Wayne Jackson. I just wanted to tell you how much I love *Long Shot*, and not just me, everybody I work with thinks the whole disc is great, top to bottom, not a bad song on there. Best record since Allison Moorer's last one."

"Well, thanks," Eddie said. "Where do you work?"

"I'm the manager of the Tower Records on Broadway in midtown. Now I know you're busy and all, but I was wondering if you'd consider dropping by the store to play a couple of songs and sign some autographs?"

"Well, I . . ." Eddie looked quickly to Big Bill, who shook his head and shrugged indifferently. He wanted to get out to the airport and relax before catching their flight to Dallas. As Eddie was about to beg off, Megan banged on the glass separating the hallway from the studio. She waved her arms and pushed Big Bill aside, nodding emphatically to Eddie while urgently mouthing *Yes!* With eyes wide and nostrils flaring, her expression was clear. *Don't take Herron's advice! He's an idiot! Do this!*

"Wayne, I tell you what," Eddie said. "I'll be by right after lunch. How's that?"

"That'll be great. Thanks a ton!"

By two that afternoon, traffic in the 1600 block of Broadway had ground to a halt. Eddie was inside the packed store doing a solo show. The speakers outside had drawn hundreds more. The sidewalk crowd spilled into the street, and soon there were people standing on the roofs of cars and trucks listening and dancing and whooping it up. The original plan was for Eddie to do three songs, sign a few autographs, then fly. But now, six songs later, Eddie was still playing encores, since it seemed like the only way to keep the show from turning into a riot.

"Betcha dolla they gonna have to call the cops," Big Bill said, looking out the window at the crowd.

"You say that like it's a bad thing . . . Big Bill." Megan said his name with enough sarcasm to put a fine point on it. Her smile was wide as Junior Samples as she watched the throng of fans press against the front of the store. "This is fabulous."

Franklin glanced at Big Bill. He could see the irritation. Franklin checked his watch. "I hope we can get out of here in time," he said. "Flight's in three hours, and we still have to go back to the hotel." They were due in Dallas that night for the beginning of Eddie's thirty-five-city tour.

Franklin nudged Big Bill. "Oh, did I tell you Whitney Rankin called again." He shook his head in mild amusement. "Kid really wants to talk to you about his song."

"Ain't surprised," Big Bill said. "I think he'll get over it when we send him a little check."

Megan suddenly clapped her hands together. "Jesus!" She grabbed Franklin's arm. "Give me your Palm Pilot," she said. "Fast!"

Franklin pulled away from her grip. "What for?"

"PR! Now give it to me!"

Franklin reluctantly pulled the Palm Pilot from its carrier. Big Bill waved his hand calmly in the air. "We're doing fine, Megan. We don't need anything else." He made the mistake of using a patronizing tone.

Megan shook her head. "Jesus, you two . . ." She grabbed the Palm Pilot out of Franklin's hands. She punched in the URL and the site blinked onscreen. "Okay, here we go."

Franklin watched as she began punching in numbers. "Hey," he said, "that's our corporate AmEx number. How the hell did you get that?"

"I'm Eddie's road manager," Megan said. "I pay attention to important details." Megan scrolled down through her options, made a few selections, then submitted the form for credit card clearance.

"What is that?" Franklin asked.

"PressCon dot-com," Megan said. "They do instant press releases to all national news outlets and wire services." She froze Franklin with a nasty look. "You *are* willing to spring for some good press coverage, aren't you? I'm sure you'll be able to find some way to make it recoupable against Eddie's royalties." Megan didn't wait for a reply. She was too busy typing. *Broadway turned into a pedestrian mall for an hour as the handsome new country star Eddie Long lit up midtown with his bright smile and his hit song. . . .* Franklin cast a worried glance at Big Bill, who was shaking his head, annoyed at their common enemy. *Organizers estimate the crowd at fifty thousand.* Megan thought about it for a moment, then deleted the figure and typed *seventy-five thousand. Police in riot gear were called in to end the show to prevent complete midtown gridlock. Eddie Long's debut album,* Long Shot *is the best-selling record of the year and certain to take home some statues at next year's Country Fanfare Awards.* Megan gave it a quick proofread, then submitted it. She handed the Palm Pilot back to Franklin by poking him in the stomach with it. "That's a handy little unit, but it helps if you know how to use it," she said with a smart-ass smirk. "Now let's get Eddie and get ready for Dallas."

*   *   *

Jay Colvin was beside himself. "Unfuckingbelievable" was the first thing he said after Jimmy explained his theory about Tammy's death. "Why didn't you tell me before? My God! This is a best-seller!" he screamed into the phone. "Get to work. Find out all you can and write the book *with the accusations in it!*"

"Listen," Jimmy said, "I appreciate your enthusiasm, but don't you think we have some pretty big exposure on this? I mean, aren't publishers skittish about publishing unproven accusations? Slander, defamation of character, that sort of thing?"

"Trust me," Jay said. "I know what I'm doing."

"But—"

"What's it going to take to earn your trust? Jimmy, I promise you two things. One, I will get you a fat six-figure advance, and two, you will get in your contract a 'hold harmless' clause bigger than Al Sharpton's mouth."

Jimmy couldn't imagine how that was possible but figured he could write the book in such a way that his theory could be pulled out without causing a major rewrite. "Okay, if you're sure."

"I'm sure already," Jay insisted. "Now go dig."

"All right," Jimmy said. "I'm going back to Quitman County."

*   *   *

Jay Colvin dropped the phone into the cradle with a smile. A notion had popped into his head while he was talking to Jimmy, and now he had to do some research. He called his attorney and had him to do a Lexis search for civil suits featuring Bill Herron as defendant. Meanwhile, Jay scoured the Internet for all references to the man once regarded as "one of Nashville's most powerful manager/producers." Among the results was the Power 100 list from *Nashville Scene*.

Next Jay called a contact at *Good Morning America*. He needed to know the hotel where Herron was staying. "They're gone," his contact said. "Starting a tour in Dallas tonight."

Jay called information in Nashville to get the number for Herron & Peavy Management. A second later, Jay's attorney called back. "You want me to fax all this over there or just give you the *Reader's Digest* version?"

"Nutshell it," Jay said.

"The guy's a weasel. Unwashed."

"Perfect," Jay said. "Thanks." He clicked off, then started dialing again, trying to think of how to finesse the information he needed.

"Herron & Peavy Management," a woman said.

"Hi, this is Jay Colvin in New York. Mr. Herron and I met yesterday while he was in town. We discussed a publishing deal for his client, Eddie Long. I know he's on his way to Dallas, but could you do me a favor? When he calls in for messages, would you ask him to call me as soon as possible? I have some good news for him. Thank you so much."

*   *   *

Halfway to Dallas, Eddie was still staring at the screen on his laptop. He was trying to get started on a new song, but nothing was coming to him. Out of the corner of his eye he noticed Megan looking at him. After a moment, he turned and looked into her violet eyes. "Can't seem to get started on this song," he said.

Megan nodded. "Don't worry, it'll come to you." She looked at him for a moment before leaning toward him slightly. "You know what? There's something I've always wanted to do. . . ."

Eddie closed his laptop. He wasn't getting anything written anyway. "What's that?"

Megan leaned closer still and whispered something in his ear. Eddie blushed and his eyes popped wide. "Get outta town!"

She winked as her right hand slid down to his lap. "Give me five minutes, then knock twice." She gave him a gentle squeeze, then casually got up and went into the lavatory nearest the cockpit. By the time she threw the latch Eddie was so hard a cat couldn't scratch it.

Five minutes later he was at the door. He looked around to be sure no one was watching. He knocked twice and a second later he was inside. Megan was wearing a short skirt and a sleeveless pullover knit top. Eddie saw her panties on the counter by the sink. He took that as a good sign.

Megan started rubbing against him. "Good Lord," she said, "is that a gun in your pocket?" She offered up a sultry smile.

Eddie rubbed back. "No ma'am. I'm just glad to see you." He looked down and Megan pulled her skirt up. "Damn glad," Eddie said. She unhitched Eddie's big rodeo belt buckle and popped the buttons on his jeans like a pro. A second later she had one foot on the toilet seat while the other was braced against the wall.

"I don't have a condom," Eddie said as he—"Oooohhhh, baby."

Megan gasped. "Ohmygod, I don't care. Yesssssss." She pulled him in as close as she could and started breathing harder. "Just like that, Eddie. Just like that." Her arms reached out for something to hold on to. She grabbed the handicap grip.

Eddie was watching everything in the mirror. He started to preen, like a star in his own porn film, only this one was going to be a short. Without warning, Eddie grabbed the hot water faucet, rounded third, and headed for home. "Ohhh! Ohhh! Ohhh . . ."

Megan bucked and squeezed for all she was worth. "Yeaahhh." Then she threw in a few sexy noises to make Eddie think he'd done his part. She was considerate that way. Afterwards, they huffed for air as their tensed muscles began to relax. The intimate confines of the lavatory made the postcoital moment somewhat awkward. It really hadn't been designed for cuddling. Fortunately, the plane hit some turbulence and the FASTEN SEAT BELT sign came on.

Like a gentleman, Eddie handed Megan her panties. "Here you go, cutie." Then he bent over to retrieve his jeans. The instruction for passengers to return to their seats hastened things. As Eddie buttoned up, Megan leaned over and kissed him. "Me and you, babe." She looked into his eyes. Then she tilted her head just so and smiled. "Some things are just meant to be."

*   *   *

Big Bill was on the phone when Eddie slipped out of the bathroom. He could see Megan in the background. Eddie knew he was busted, so he looked over at Big Bill and winked. He figured that sharing the conquest, one good old boy to another, was the best way to avoid a you-need-to-think-about-your-image speech. Eddie needn't have worried, though. Big Bill played along instinctively, winking back and flashing a low-key thumbs-up. But he didn't like what he'd seen. Megan was shaping up as a major pain in the ass, he thought, potentially a very disruptive force. Big Bill had seen this sort of thing dozens of times in his career, and he knew it rarely worked out good for the manager. Unfortunately he couldn't afford to bump the jukebox at the moment, so for now he'd let Megan have her way. He'd find a way to undermine her later.

"Mr. Herron, are you there?" The voice came from the phone. It was Big Bill's assistant in Nashville.

"Yeah, sorry," he said. "Any other calls?"

"Whitney Rankin called three more times," she said. "He sounds upset."

"I bet. Anything else?" He listened for a second, then wrote, *Jay Colvin*. "A publishing deal, huh? What's his number?" Big Bill figured this Colvin guy was calling to get the rights so one of his authors could do Eddie's story. Well, he was in for a surprise. *Sorry, Mr. Colvin, I've already started the authorized bio.* Big Bill gave him-

self a psychic pat on the back for being so far ahead of the publishing curve, then he made the call.

"Mr. Colvin? Bill Herron." He softened his good-old-boy tone
and went with more Southern gentility. "I understand you want to
talk to me about a publishing deal of some sort?"

"Yes sir, Mr. Herron, thank you for returning my call," Jay said.
"First I have to say it's an honor to speak with the man who produced so many great records."

"Thank you, Mr. Colvin, I—"

Jay cut him off. "I've read all about you, Mr. Herron, and I think
we might be able to do some business together."

"Maybe we can, Mr. Colvin, because it turns out I've started—"

"Let me just get right to the point, Mr. Herron, and I'm sorry to
cut you off again, but I don't want to waste any of your time. I represent a writer named Jimmy Rogers. You recognize that name?"

"Yeah," Big Bill said slowly as it came to him, "a guy called me
one day, said that was his name. I thought it was a prank, you know,
father of country music and all."

Jay Colvin had no idea what Herron was talking about and he
didn't care. "It's no prank, Mr. Herron. Mr. Rogers has nearly completed a biography of your client, Eddie Long. And not everything in
the book is exactly what you'd call flattering. In fact, it's so inflammatory I expect to place it at one of the top three publishers in the
city for a good six-figure advance. But that's only going to happen
with your cooperation."

Big Bill was starting to get miffed. It was bad enough this fast-
talking New Yorker—maybe a queer, maybe a Jew, hell, maybe a
queer Jew—had cut him off twice, but now come to find out this
Rogers kid was about to beat him to the bookstores. He dropped
back into truculent good old boy. "Well, now, that's all well and
good for you, Mr. Colvin, but I'll tell you the same thing I told that
client of yours. We intend to rigorously defend against any unauthorized—"

"Mr. Herron, there's no need for any of that. Let me tell you what I have in mind."

At this point, Big Bill was about to cut loose on this guy. He didn't have to put up with anybody cutting him off three times in a single conversation. Big Bill was the one with the hottest country music artist in the world and he was supposed to be the one doing the cuttin' off. But as Jay Colvin outlined his strategy, Big Bill began to reconsider.

Jimmy's book would essentially accuse Eddie of being a murderer. This would generate massive publicity for both sides. In response, Herron & Peavy Management would file a huge lawsuit on behalf of their aggrieved client. This would generate even more publicity for both sides. Book and record sales would benefit from all the attention. After a few weeks of milking the press with the inflammatory accusations and a $90 million lawsuit, Herron & Peavy Management would announce that they had reached an out-of-court settlement with the publisher. There would be a gag order so no one could discuss the terms of the deal. In reality no money would change hands as a result of the alleged settlement. But Big Bill would receive a two percent royalty on Jimmy's book in exchange for orchestrating things at his end. "Atlas Publishing has signed off on this if I can get you to agree to it," Jay said. "So what do you think?"

It was such a cagey arrangement Big Bill was forced to take a look at the big picture. Whereas he'd written only half a page of his biography, Colvin's client was almost finished with an entire manuscript. Big Bill knew he'd never get a whole book finished in time to compete with the Rogers book—at best he'd be picking up the book market scraps—so participating in Mr. Colvin's innovative deal was clearly the best way to go. "Well, I'll tell ya," Big Bill said, "it reminds me of me."

"I'm delighted to hear you say that, Mr. Herron."

"Yes, sir. It's a fine idea. Works for both sides." Big Bill thought about asking for a higher cut of the book's royalties, but he figured Mr. Colvin would counter by asking for points on any increase in record sales, and he knew that wasn't in his favor, so he kept his mouth shut.

"Terrific," Jay said. "And I think you'll agree neither of our clients needs to know about this arrangement."

"Oh, I believe that goes without saying." Big Bill looked across the aisle at Megan as she whispered something to Eddie. "Makes us both look more . . . indispensable if our clients think we pulled 'em out of a fire."

* * *

That night, at a sold-out Texas stadium, Eddie stood poised to go onstage for the first show of his thirty-five-city tour. There were 45,000 frenzied fans waiting for their new hero to come out and sing his song. In the semidarkness, the band strode onstage. The crowd saw the silhouettes and began to scream. It was the moment Eddie had been waiting for all his life.

Megan was with him, brushing some fuzz from his hat and primping his glittery Manuel jacket. "My God," she said. "If you aren't the handsomest man I have ever seen." She put her hands on his arms and looked into his eyes. She smiled. "You nervous?"

Eddie looked around the backstage area. The place was crawling with local radio people, print and television media, the promoter's staff, groupies. Groupies, for crying out loud! And some fine-looking ones at that. "Nervous?" He shook his head. "This is what I was made for."

The stage announcer came over the loudspeaker system. "Ladies and gentlemen . . ."

Megan primped Eddie's coat. "You ready?"

Eddie snugged his hat on his head. "Tail up and stinger out," he said.

She kissed him. "Save a little of that stinger for me."

"From Nashville, Tennessee, the man with the best-selling record in the US of A, please give a hot-dang-you-all Texas welcome to Big World Records recording artist . . . Mr. Eddie Long!"

*   *   *

"Just so we're on the same page," Jimmy said into the phone, "we're talking about Atlas Publishing. In New York. *That* Atlas Publishing?"

"No, I'm sorry, I talking about the one in Kokomo, Indiana," Jay replied. "They want to turn Eddie's story into an illustrated children's book. Christ! Of course the one in New York!"

"No way," Jimmy said. "I don't believe you." It seemed like the natural thing to say in such a unique circumstance.

What sounded like a tire going flat on the other end of the line was Jay Colvin venting some frustration. "Jimmy, we have to work on the trust in our relationship, I can see that. But you've got to understand, I wouldn't lie about this sort of thing."

"But six hundred thousand dollars?" Jimmy paused and sat down. "It's just hard to believe."

"What's hard about it? It's a great book and your timing's miraculous. It's very easy when you look at it that way. Easy, easy, easy. Atlas pays half on signing, half on publication. And they want to rush to print as soon as you deliver the manuscript."

"And the catch?"

"There is no catch!" Jay sucked some air through his teeth. "Were you born distrustful or do you train? Because you have it down to a fine art."

"You've gotta understand—"

"Wait, don't tell me. This is some sort of Mason-Dixon thing, right? Tell me the truth, Jimmy, has the word 'carpetbagger' crossed your mind in the past two minutes? Never mind. I don't care. I've gotta tell you, I've never had such a hard time delivering good news. Now I want you to sit down, because if you're having a hard time with that, you may be unable to come to grips with this next part."

"What part?" Jimmy could hear Jay punching in a phone number on another line.

"Atlas wants you to include your theory, all the 'evidence' of Eddie's culpability in Tammy's death."

"What? That's insane! Eddie and Herron'll sue my pants off. And Atlas will hang me out to dry." Eddie's fax machine began to ring.

"Do you know how much it hurts that I don't have your trust? I'm sending something that might help. Check your fax machine."

As Jimmy walked to his office, he began to let himself believe the good news. "It's not that I don't trust you," he said, "it's just this is happening so fast. Six hundred thousand's a lot of money. I don't want to get all excited, then find out it's not what it seems to be." His fax machine spit out a letter on Atlas Publishing stationery. "Okay, I got whatever you sent."

"That's a deal memo," Jay said, "signed by the president of Atlas. In the third paragraph it states that not only will Atlas not hang you out to dry but they have also agreed to some extra language in the standard 'hold harmless' clause. And in the extremely unlikely event the plaintiff should win a judgment against you, you are covered by an Errors and Omission policy bigger than the National Democratic Party's soft money fund. And, as if that's not enough, Atlas has also agreed to pay you ten-thousand-dollar bonus if we *do* get sued."

Jimmy read the applicable paragraphs. "Well, that's just plain damn crazy," he said. "Why the hell would they do that?"

"Because they love the book! Jimmy, I'm telling you, you get the editorial staff of Atlas Publishing on a jury in a libel suit against you, and you'd end up with a murder conviction against Eddie on the evidence you already have."

"No charges were ever brought—"

"Jimmy, look, the cops don't know everything you do. That's the only possible explanation for why Eddie hasn't been arrested. You are sitting on a stack of gold bars. I'm just trying to get you to look down and see what you've got."

"It feels more like dynamite." Jimmy paused and thought about the $600,000. "Ahhh, but what the hell," he said. "Long as we got it in writing, make the deal. I'll finish the book."

13

The *Long Shot* tour moved east out of Dallas like a storm front. In eleven days they played Tiger Stadium in Baton Rouge, the Horseshoe Casino in Bossier City, the Coliseum in Biloxi, the fairgrounds in Mobile, the Daytona International Speedway, Taladega Super Speedway, the Palace Theater in Myrtle Beach, Harrah's Cherokee Smoky Mountain Casino, and Jamboree in the Hills in Wheeling, West Virginia.

They were averaging 18,500 a show at forty bucks a pop. After ten shows they'd brought in nearly $7.5 million in ticket sales. The merchandising was a whole other cash cow. The Eddie Long T-shirts, sweatshirts, and baseball caps were hard to keep in stock, and the *Long Shot* mouse pad and the "It Wasn't Supposed to End That Way" screen saver were kicking ass. Of course, there were expenses—rental on two decked-out tour buses and a big equipment truck, the band, backup singers, equipment manager, sound engineers—but even when you finished doing all the subtraction, there was no way around the fact that Eddie was just flat broke out with money.

Recording artists and their managers would tell you the great thing about touring income was its immediacy. Money from radio play, publishing, and record sales was all delayed by a minimum of six months and it was chipped away at by suspect accounting practices, but every night after a show there was a brand-new pile of folding money to count. Of course it wasn't like the good old days when everybody carried handguns and walked off with a suitcase of cash, but modern country didn't work like that. Now it was all electronic transfers and cashier's checks and no need for a .38. It was safer and perhaps even a bit bland, something the old guard might say paralleled the music, but hey, things change. Still, you needed petty cash for per diems and just generally to keep the skids greased, so, every night after a show, Big Bill came onto the bus with a few thousand in cash in his briefcase.

"How'd we do tonight?" Eddie asked as he opened a beer and settled into a sofa in the back of the bus.

"We got enough money to burn a wet mule," Big Bill said. "That's how we did."

"Thank you, West Virginia." Eddie reached up and got a high five from Herron. "That's ten down, twenty-five to go. Where are we tomorrow?"

Megan looked at the tour sheet. "Heading east," she said. "Medina County Fair in Ohio."

Franklin was outside the bus with one hand pressed to the side of his head trying to keep his earpiece from tumbling out again. While in New York, he had bought a new headset for his cell phone, thinking it made him look like a Silicon Valley hot shot. Sadly, it made him look more like a guy taking orders at the drive-through at a KFC. He was talking to someone at SoundScan. "Good. Good. Wait a second," he said, "let me get that down before you do the rest." Franklin pulled his digital recorder from his pocket and repeated the numbers. "Okay, go ahead. No, wait, I dropped my earpiece."

SoundScan was a company that had helped, however inadvertently, to put country music on the map. They created a computerized in-store system for tracking record sales at the retail level. Before SoundScan, artists and managers had to rely on the notoriously corrupt charts in the industry trade papers, which were compiled from the reports of easily bribed radio programmers and record store managers. Historically, the pop music industry used this system to control the charts to their advantage but SoundScan changed all that. With the implementation of their system in 1991 came numbers that were immediate and reliable and surprising to a lot of folks. The numbers showed country was selling a lot more than anyone thought—certainly more than the record companies were letting on in royalty statements. This public acknowledgment of country music's popularity had an interesting side effect. Once it got out that country music wasn't solely the realm of hideously inbred hillbilly defectives—that is to say, once the stigma of buying country records was lost—the citified middle classes began buying more and more country music. In effect, SoundScan made country appear "hip," and this in turn increased sales even further. Of course, there was always a backlash to popularity of this magnitude, thus the post-Garth dip in sales. But according to the numbers Franklin was hearing, the drought was over.

"Thanks," Franklin said. "I'll be sure to pass that on to Eddie." He turned off the phone and stepped onto the bus. "Anybody interested in the latest SoundScan numbers?"

"Talk to me," Eddie said.

Franklin wore a grim expression. "Bad news is we haven't hit the million mark yet." Then he broke into a grin. "Good news is we will before we cross the state line."

"Yesss!" Megan pumped a fist in the air, then did a little bump and grind.

Franklin continued, "The official numbers are nine hundred sixty-eight thousand units in just over four weeks. And it's still trending up. They're projecting it out as double platinum. Also, I spoke to Debbie at the label. She said the single's in hot rotation on two thousand five hundred and forty-nine of the twenty-six hundred stations. The others, she assures me, will follow next week. We," Franklin said loudly, "are number ONE!"

Big Bill stood, faced Eddie, and started to applaud. Everybody on the bus followed suit. Eddie waved them off at first, then tipped his hat. Finally he picked up his beer and put his thumb over the mouth of the bottle. He shook it up and sprayed it everywhere in celebration to the hoots and hollers of the band and crew.

Big Bill stepped into the spray, then sat back down next to Eddie, wiping the beer from his face with his shirtsleeve. "Well, as much fun as this number one record's been, I think it's about time to pick the second single." Getting to choose the singles and their release dates was yet another of the unheard-of aspects of Eddie's deal with Big World Records.

Eddie stuck his tongue out to snag a large drop of beer that was rolling down his face. "Okay," he said, "I'm new at this. What's the conventional wisdom?"

"Conventional wisdom says we go with 'Dixie National,'" Big Bill said. "It's upbeat, skews more male than female, broadens our audience. I think it's the way to go."

Eddie pointed at Franklin. "Your turn."

Franklin shook his head and pointed at Big Bill. "That's his area," he said.

Eddie looked at Megan. "What do you think, puddin'?"

Megan was already shaking her head. "'Dixie National.'" She rolled her eyes. "Christ a'mighty," she said. "Did we get to where we are by following the conventional wisdom?"

"Well, first of all," Big Bill said, "it's customary to—"

"Bullshit," Megan said, stamping her foot. "Screw what's customary. Look, they say an artist's first single shouldn't be a ballad, right? Well, Eddie's was, and guess what? Nine hundred sixty-eight thousand units later I think we can put that rule to rest. Then they say, well, you shouldn't follow one ballad with another, right? Well, ask Vince Gill what he thinks about that. He did all right. I say we change the damn rules. Go with our other ballad as the second single. And what's more"—Megan turned to Eddie—"I think we ought to put it out while the first one's still number one."

Big Bill snorted derisively. "Well that's just foolishness," he said. "You'd never do that. You're just being contrary. I don't care how far you get being unconventional, there are some things that you just don't . . ." Big Bill was getting so frustrated he couldn't finish his thought. "Eddie," he said, "I been in this business long enough—"

"Long enough to work your way down to number ninety-nine on the Power 100," Megan said. "That says all you need to know about conventional wisdom, don't you think?"

Big Bill wanted to slap Megan in the worst way, and if she'd been within reach, he'd have done it instinctively and probably lost his biggest client. His carotid artery looked like a blue garden hose running up the side of his neck. Bad enough the bitch had interrupted him twice, now she was insulting him. "All due respect," he hissed, "but I don't recall ever seeing your name anywhere on that list, Megan, so I wouldn't be talking so loud." He stepped closer to her as he spoke, hoping his size would help intimidate. "Now, as to your iconoclastic release strategy, keep in mind that the most likely result of releasing a second single while your first one is still at the top is that you bring the first one down before it's done." He stepped closer. "Now as far as I know, Lonestar still holds the record for consecutive weeks at number one. I think we've got a shot at breaking that," he said, putting his face in Megan's, "if we don't do anything to screw it up." The last words came out louder than the others.

Eddie stood and casually walked between the combatants. "Nothing like the free exchange of contrasting ideas," he said. "But you know what?" He turned to Big Bill. "I like taking chances, and as long as we got a contract that lets us do things that ain't been

tried, I think we ought to look at setting a new kind of record."
Eddie looked out the bus window and saw thousands of fans
streaming out to the parking lot. "You know, you see a lot of artists
with two songs in the top forty at the same time, but I think we
oughta see if we can't get two in the top five at the same time.
Maybe even get the top two slots!"

This was really starting to chap Big Bill's ass. "Please! That hasn't
happened since . . . hell, I don't know, since Dill Scallion, for cryin'
out loud."

"Well, I think it's time we changed that," Eddie said. He sat
down and took a pull on his beer. "Okay, I think that seals it. 'Pothole in My Heart' is our second single and it ships next week." He
pointed at Big Bill. "Make it happen."

*   *   *

Whitney sat on the edge of his bed, eyes fixed on the ragged bandanna tied around his wrist. He was consumed by discouragement
and a sense of betrayal that had started just after *Long Shot* was
released. Whitney had waited for the comp disc Big Bill had
promised but it never came, so he went out and bought a copy. As he
stood in the aisle of the record store, his excitement dissolved into
surprise, then confusion and disappointment. "Night's Devotion"
wasn't on the disc. He didn't understand. He took the disc home
and listened. When it got to a song called "Pothole in My Heart,"
Whitney suddenly felt ill. He grabbed the liner notes and frantically
searched the writing credits. When he saw it he got sick enough to
throw up his socks. It said "B. Herron/E. Long/W. Rankin." He'd
been trying to get Big Bill on the phone ever since.

That was nearly three weeks ago. Since then, Whitney had been
sinking deeper and deeper into despair. When the phone rang Whitney barely moved. He just stared at the bandanna. After five or six
rings he slowly reached over and picked up.

"Hey now!" Big Bill said. "I understand you've been tryin' to reach me."

The voice jarred Whitney's mind and stirred some anger. "Yes sir, that's right."

"Sorry it took so long for me to get back to ya. I been on the road with Eddie Long. Man, this guy's hotter'n concrete in July in Houston." Big Bill figured Whitney was pissed about what had happened to his song, so he tried to create a diversion. "Oh, and by the way, I got you some good news," he said. "Your song's gonna be the second single off Eddie's record. Whaddya think about that?"

"That ain't my song," Whitney said bitterly. "What the hell happened?"

"Whaddya mean what happened?" Big Bill tried his best to sound wounded by Whitney's accusatory tone.

"I never wrote a song called 'Pothole in My Heart,' and I didn't cowrite anything with you and Eddie Long." Whitney paused. "You lied to me right outta your mouth, Mr. Herron."

"Now hang on a second there Whitney." Big Bill's tone was firm but fatherly. "You were there when we made a lot of those changes. I remember asking if you understood why we did what we did and you looked right at me and said, 'Yeah.' You're not denying that, are you?"

"I never wrote anything about potholes in my heart and I sure didn't hear him sing it that way when I was there."

"No, I'll grant you that," Big Bill said. "After you left we had a couple more notions on the song, so we went back and did another version. Nothing unusual about that, and there's damn sure nothing underhanded about it, if that's what you're gettin' at. I'm surprised at you, Whitney. I thought you'd appreciate what I did for you, 'specially now that it's gonna be the second single. You have any idea how much money you're gonna make on this?"

"That ain't the point," Whitney said.

"Well, it damn sure is, son. If that song goes to number one, like I think it will, you're looking at twenty to twenty-five thousand dollars just from radio play. Your mechanicals are probably worth another five, maybe ten thousand." All told, the truth was closer to $200,000 for a record that was selling and getting radio play like Eddie's, but Big Bill knew Whitney was clueless about the value of his work. He had counted on it. Herron & Peavy Management stood to make an extra $175,000 or so thanks to Whitney's willful ignorance. "Now, honestly, did you ever expect you'd make thirty thousand dollars on a single one of your songs?"

Whitney tasted acid creeping in his throat. "That ain't my song and you didn't have the right to do what you did." His voice was thick with hostility, his discouragement and depression suddenly displaced by pure anger.

"Whoa now," Big Bill said. "Better read your contract again, son. Now, I can tell you're upset, but you just wait. You'll feel better about it when you cash that first check. Trust me."

"I'm through trusting you and everybody else in Music Fucking City, you fat son of a bitch!" Whitney slammed the phone down. He was shaking. He'd put up with all the Nashville bullshit he could. Big Bill had been lying to him from the start, taking him for a ride. And now Whitney imagined the son of a bitch laughing at his expense. Big Bill might as well have stolen a piece of Whitney's soul. Lies were bad enough, stealing was worse, but this was beyond the pale. This was humiliating and Whitney wouldn't stand for it. It was enough to make him want to kill.

*   *   *

The answer hit Jimmy just north of Jackson. He was heading back up to Quitman County when he saw the sign marking the turnoff for the 220. It was the shortcut to Interstate 20, which took you to Vicksburg, then west to Louisiana and Texas. But Jimmy's answer was on this side of the Mississippi River, and that highway sign reminded him why he felt the way he did about Megan.

It was one of their first dates. They drove over to picnic in the

Vicksburg National Military Park. It was an inspiring spring day, breezy and uncrowded. Halfway through the hilly sixteen-mile tour of the Civil War battleground they found a spot on a knoll with a view of the big river in the distance. They spread their blanket in the shade of an oak tree and ate fried chicken, sweet cornbread, and ripe peaches. Jimmy also brought a thermos full of pink lemonade enhanced with bourbon and triple sec. Megan took one sip and broke into a wide smile. "What *is* this?" She held the glass up to the sunlight to examine the colors swirling around the chunks of ice.

"Secret recipe," Jimmy said. "I call it patio lemonade."

Megan took a gulp. "Oh, I like this." She held her glass out for a refill. Jimmy obliged.

They ate and drank and talked and laughed until they were both sweetly drunk. Megan curled up in Jimmy's arms and let herself be held. Her self-consciousness dissolved in the sugary bourbon and lemonade and she opened up about her dreams and fears and sorrows and things she rarely shared. As he looked down at her, touching her perfect skin, Jimmy knew this was the person he could love forever.

Megan sighed, all contented. "I hope you plan to kiss me pretty soon."

Jimmy smiled. Then he leaned down. It was the sweetest kiss he'd ever tasted, her lips soft as the shade. They lay back and felt the sun dance through the tree's leaves and they fell asleep. It was the sort of day most people look back on and recognize only from a distance as one of the best in their lives. But part of the wonder of this day was how they both embraced it as it happened. The difference between them, Jimmy now realized, was that he still cherished the moment, whereas Megan seemed to have let it go without regard.

The turnoff for Vicksburg vanished behind him just as she had, and Jimmy suddenly realized he was worried about something. But what? That he wouldn't get Megan back? No, he had almost come to accept that as a given. It was something else. As he continued north toward Hinchcliff, it occurred to Jimmy that he was worried about Megan's safety. If his theory was right—if Eddie had killed Tammy—Jimmy wouldn't want her around the guy, no matter how badly she'd treated him. Jimmy figured there were only two results to the research he was doing, and he didn't know which one he preferred. If he disproved the theory, the publisher wouldn't be so hot on the book, but at least he'd know Megan wasn't sleeping with a murderer. On the other hand, if he proved the theory, at least he could warn her about him.

Jimmy arrived at Eddie and Tammy's old house around eleven. It was hot. The sun was coming down at the same angle from which one is bludgeoned to death. He parked around back, in the shade, so no one would see his car and so it wouldn't be an oven when he got back. The air was sticky as chewed gum, and Jimmy could smell the Tallahatchie filtered through a hundred yards of pine trees. He grabbed his camera and took some exterior shots of the small brick house plagued as it was by the accusing yellow crime-scene tape.

Because he was about to enter an official crime scene, Jimmy slipped on a pair of gloves. Everything was locked, so he broke a kitchen window. Jimmy lowered his camera bag in first, then shimmied in after it. The place was hot, stagnant, and dead quiet. Dust particles hung in the air, almost motionless. Suddenly there was a noise, a tiny buzzing sound coming from behind him. He turned and saw a fat housefly caught in a spider's web struggling to escape. He hadn't been inside sixty seconds and he was sweating.

Jimmy got the creeps. It was one thing knowing what had happened within these walls, it was another to actually be there. He hefted his camera and looked around. He took photos of the faded "God Bless This House" needlepoint near the front door and the unframed watercolor of the cow in the cotton field hanging above the sofa. He took shots of the taped outline of Tammy's body and the small bloodstain on the floor. He stepped into the bathroom to get a look at the medicine cabinet. The glass shelves were stocked with the typical array of over-the-counter medications, but the box of Dr. Porter's Headache Powder was gone, no doubt to the police lab for testing.

There wasn't much else to see at this end of the house, so Jimmy returned to the kitchen. It was cramped with an avocado-green refrigerator and a rust-brown stove, a dishwasher on wheels still hooked up to the sink faucet, which dripped slowly like the sweat creeping down Jimmy's neck. He recalled Eddie saying he used to sit on the kitchen table while composing his songs. It was large and heavy, like something from a butcher's shop. You had to scoot sideways to get to the chair at the far end. He sat on the edge of the table wondering how much of what Carl had said was true. Jimmy couldn't remember Eddie ever saying anything bad about Tammy, nothing about her holding him back or anything. He frequently made jokes about being married while he was onstage, but they were innocuous and aimed at getting laughs.

Jimmy sat on the table for a few moments taking in the view as Eddie would have seen it. It was less than inspiring—mismatched appliances and a bank of grease-covered kitchen cabinets. Looking down, he saw something wedged in the corner where the wall met the floor. It looked like a shard from a shattered plate or perhaps a serving dish. Across the room was a washer-dryer combo that looked like it got hit by the back door every time it opened. Jimmy sat there for a moment before his attention returned to the cabinets. He slid off the table and went to the pantry. Inside were some dried red beans, canned tomatoes, and a box of beignet mix. There were two cast-iron skillets and a nonstick saucepan in the lower cabinet next to the stove. Next he looked in the small cupboard above the range. It held a lazy Susan. Jimmy gave it a spin—red pepper, chili powder, and a box of shrimp boil circled past like spicy red carousel horses. Old garlic salt, solidified onion powder, and a gooseneck jar of Zatarain's Gumbo Filé chased a five-year-old tin of ground thyme, a jar of chicken bouillon cubes, and, bringing up the rear, a fat, round container of Uncle Randy's Meat Tenderizer. Then the thing stopped.

Jimmy stared at the cylindrical container. It was cardboard with a red plastic top. He picked it up and shook it like a tiny maraca. It was nearly empty. He read the list of ingredients—salt, dextrose, calcium silicate, and bromelain were second, third, fourth, and fifth on the list, but they didn't really matter. It was the primary ingredient that made him shiver in the heat. Big as all get out it said: monosodium glutamate.

* * *

The spring on the screen door screeched like an alley cat when Chester Grubbs walked into the bar. It was lunchtime and he was bad thirsty. He hadn't had a drink in two days and, as he told the bartender, he needed a beer. The bartender wrinkled his nose and went to get a cold one. Soaked in sweat, Chester's clothes were ripe enough to sprout legs and walk. The sweat mixed with dirt and formed muddy troughs in the lines of his face. As he waited for his beer, Chester spotted half a cigarette crumpled in an ashtray. He picked it up, reshaped it as best he could, and lit the thing.

He'd moved from Broken Bow, Oklahoma, to Lake Village, Arkansas, to get some work. A friend had told him about a guy who needed some day labor for a big landscaping project. The pay was decent and the job was supposed to last three weeks. Chester had hoped to get hired on driving a Bobcat or a skip loader, something where he'd be sitting down in some shade, but he'd ended up swinging a pick at the hardest, rockiest acre of dirt he'd ever set foot on. It was nearly ninety-six degrees at noon and Chester was forty years older than the other guys on the job site. One of the kids on the crew summed it up best when he looked at Chester's ashen face after the first hour and said, "You're way too old for work this damn young."

The bartender gave Chester his beer. "You wanna order lunch?"

Chester hoisted the bottle. "Just did." He turned it upside down into his face, mouth-to-mouth resuscitation.

The screen door screeched again when another man entered the bar. He waved at the bartender. "Hey man, how you doin'?"

"Real good," the bartender said. "Whadja bring me this week?"

The man walked over to the jukebox, pulled out a key, and opened it. "Got the new single from Eddie Long," he said. "Real nice song. I'll put it on for you."

Chester waved his empty bottle at the bartender. "Give me anuther one of these?"

The bartender shuffled over to the cooler. Chester looked at the big jar of pickled pig's feet on the bar, wondering if he ought to eat a little something or if he should just drink his lunch. A moment later a song came on the jukebox and Chester forgot whether he was hungry, thirsty, or out of his mind. The hair on his neck stood up and he felt something twist in his bones. He slowly turned around on his stool and stared at the jukebox, listening, humming along in his head like he already knew the song. Halfway through, he stood and walked over to the jukebox, where the man was changing out some of the tunes. "Lemme see that record," Chester said.

"Which one?"

"The one's playin'."

"Sure." The guy shrugged. "Soon as it's done."

Something wild flashed in Chester's eyes and he screamed, "Now, goddammit!"

The bartender reached for his baseball bat while the jukebox man did as he was told. Chester calmly took the forty-five and looked at it. It was called "Pothole in My Heart," and in the paren-thesis under the title, Chester saw something he could hardly believe. He handed the record back to the jukebox guy, all calm and purposeful. "Pardon me," Chester said. "I've got someone to kill."

*   *   *

"Pothole in My Heart" was released as the second single the day Eddie headlined a show at the Cheyenne Frontier Festival. Two days later, as they prepared for a show in Salem, Oregon, "Pothole" was already the number one song on country radio, pushing "It Wasn't Supposed to End That Way" to number two. It was the first time in decades an artist had had the top two singles on country radio. Eddie's album had sold nearly two million copies so far, and with the release of the second single, a big spike would soon appear on the sales graph.

The *Long Shot* tour buses were parked in the lot of the L.B. Day Amphitheater. Some of the guys in the band had gone to see a movie while the roadies set up the equipment. A sound check was scheduled for later that afternoon.

Big Bill was in the back in the bus, a set of headphones pinching his fat round head. He was listening to something on a Walkman, over and over. The expression on his face grew more pained each time he listened to the tape. After the fifth time through, Franklin walked in and motioned for Big Bill to take off the headphones. "We need to talk about Eddie," he said.

Big Bill pulled the headphones off his head and held them up. "No shit."

Franklin pointed at the Walkman. "Are those the new songs?" He sounded hopeful in a desperate sort of way. "Are they good?"

"Let me put it this way." Big Bill popped the tape out of the machine and held it up for inspection. "These things suck worse than a two-dollar hooker."

"Shit."

"Shit about describes it." He tossed the headphones onto a table.

Franklin sat down and rubbed his eyes. "I saw Eddie about an hour ago. He looks worse than I do," Franklin said. "And I look like hell . . . or at least I feel like it. He's been going hard for seventeen straight nights. If we don't start getting him out of these after-show parties earlier, he'll never finish the tour."

Big Bill nodded. "He's not gonna like it."

"They never do."

Franklin and Big Bill had seen it more than a few times. It was a natural response to an unnatural situation. Coming offstage after a show wasn't like leaving the office at five o'clock. After an hour or two in the spotlight, one couldn't simply switch off the power and call it a day. Eddie was swimming in a cocktail of adrenaline, flashbulbs, adulation, sex, and drugs. It was like living in your own personal X-rated music video. Eddie was a young man with appetites. He couldn't help himself and they knew it. They had to help him. That was their job.

Big Bill looked up at Franklin, and their eyes connected. After a second they both smiled. Big Bill half-rolled his eyes while Franklin shook his head. They both laughed a little, but neither said anything. There was no need. After thirty-five years of butting heads with each other, with artists, record labels, indie promoters, and everyone else they had to battle, the two had a bond, like guys who'd been to war together. And now, after all that, they had a goose laying golden eggs, and they knew they'd have to work together to keep 'em coming.

"One of the problems is that damn Megan," Big Bill said. "She's convinced him he has to attend all the after-show parties to schmooze the radio guys."

"Yeah, and then she schedules radio call-ins to the morning shows and has goddam magazine interviews in the afternoons. She's gonna burn him out if we don't do something."

Big Bill placed his hands flat on the table. "I'm open to suggestions."

Franklin nodded. "Look," he said, "from here on out we let him make a short appearance at the after-show for a quick schmooze, get his picture taken with the radio guys then we leave. Just drag him onto the bus and go." He pointed at Big Bill. "And we tell Megan, in no uncertain terms, that she's got to ease up on his goddam media schedule."

Big Bill threw his hands up, then slapped them down on his legs. "Whatever. But we've got to do something, and, more important, we gotta get another record ready while he's still hot." He gestured at the cassette tape. "Problem is he's not writing any decent material."

Franklin looked shocked. "Well, we're not putting a notice in *Row Fax*, if that's what you're getting at. We are *not* going to solicit songs."

Big Bill waved the thought away. "Hell no!" Big Bill leaned over to confide with Franklin. "We'd have to be dumber'n a barrel of hair to put a single song on his next record that we don't publish."

Franklin nodded solemnly. "Might as well throw money out the damn window."

"Okay," Big Bill said as he hoisted himself up. "I'll go talk to him about the songs and—"

Franklin held up a finger. "Another thing," he said, folding his arms. "You're gonna love this. I finally talked to the people at the Country Fanfare Awards." Franklin looked especially oily as he smiled. "They want to give Eddie a special award at this year's show."

"They can't. Record's not eligible till next year."

"Tell them that. Board of governors voted to create a new category. They figure Eddie's hot right now, so right now's the right time to have him on the show. They're calling it the Tall Cotton Award."

"Get outta here." Big Bill snugged his hat on his head.

Franklin shrugged at the silliness of it all. "Henceforth to be awarded to any debut album going double platinum or better. They want to meet with us to discuss some things."

Big Bill chuckled. "Fine," he said. "We'll go back, take care of some business, then rejoin the tour in L.A." Bill headed for the door but paused to look Franklin in the eye. "We need to do whatever it takes to keep this train from derailing," he said.

"Amen," Franklin said.

"Good. I'll go talk to the conductor."

*   *   *

Big Bill walked over to the amphitheater, where Eddie and Megan were waiting for the sound check. He tracked them down in the hospitality suite. They were drinking gin and tonics. "Hey now," Big Bill said. "We ready for another great show?"

Eddie looked up and smiled like the sun was shining in his head. He looked alert, rested, energetic. "Steady ready Freddy," he said. "Raring to go. Man, this is a great venue. I've never been to Oregon, but someone was telling me there's a place on the Columbia River we ought to book on the next tour." He took a sip on his drink. "Oh, I talked to Franklin—"

"Frankie Baby!" Megan interjected. "Frankie goes to Hollywood!" She and Eddie both laughed at what was apparently their new nickname for Franklin.

"Yeah," Eddie said with a chuckle, "that's right, Frankie Baby came by and told us the new SoundScan numbers. Are we the big swinging dicks or what?!"

"Yeah, man," Big Bill said, momentarily confused by Eddie's energy level. "The bottom rail finally gettin' on top. Look, I—"

"Listen," Eddie said, "we decided 'Dixie National' is gonna be the next single. Probably release it in four or five weeks, don't you think, depending on how long 'Pothole' stays strong on the charts. Man, I can't wait for the show tonight. I'm ready to kick some ass and move some merchandise!"

Megan put her arm around Eddie's waist. "I keep telling him we ought to release it sooner and see if we can't get three songs in the top ten at the same time," Megan said, "but I guess some of your conservatism's rubbed off on the boy."

Big Bill smiled and nodded at the two of them. "Seems unlikely," he said, "but we'll do whatever Eddie decides." Big Bill knew what they'd been up to, but he also knew better than to come down hard right now. He just pretended everything was beautiful. "I mean, I ain't proud. I'll be the first to admit your strategy's done us good so far." Big Bill pulled the cassette from his pocket and held it up. "By the way, I been listening to the songs," he said.

Megan finished her drink and went to mix another. "Aren't they fabulous? Eddie and I cowrote all of 'em. We're thinkin' 'Country Voodoo' might be the first single on the next record."

"Yeah," Eddie agreed, "sort of a Neville Brothers meets Brooks and Dunn kinda thing."

Bill's head bobbed noncommittally. "You know, there's an old saying about how you got your whole life to write your first album but you only get about six months to write your second."

"I know, it's unreal, ain't it?" Eddie handed his empty glass to Megan. "At the rate we're goin', we'll have all the songs we need before the tour's over."

"Well now, Eddie, I gotta tell ya, these songs aren't—"

"Aren't what?" Megan said. "Those songs are hits. Nothing wrong with any of those songs. Don't come in here trying to—"

"No, no, no. Don't get me wrong. I'm not saying we can't use some of what's on here," Big Bill said, hoping to slow Megan down. "I just think you need more time to work on 'em is all. Nothing unusual about it, you get on tour with a tight media schedule and show after show. All I'm saying is we need to make sure you get more time to spend on writing, that's all."

A roadie stuck his head in the room. "Hey, Eddie, we're ready for the sound check."

Megan waved the guy off. "Be there in a minute."

"Besides," Eddie said, "at this point I can pretty much do a polka record and go platinum, right?"

"Well, damn near," Big Bill said. "All I'm sayin' is—"

"Trust me," Eddie said. "There's plenty more good songs where the others came from. We're fine. No, we're better than fine!" He started singing in a mock-operatic voice, *"We are the champions,* la la la la la . . . " He kept singing as he headed for the door, then stopped and turned to Megan. "Hey, you comin'?"

Big Bill waved him on. "You go ahead. I need to talk to your road manager for a second." He stood there smiling as Eddie headed for the stage, still singing the Queen song.

"So what's up, Billy Boy?" Megan picked up a wedge of lime and squeezed the juice into her drink.

Big Bill eased over to her and got close enough to make her uncomfortable. He spoke in a low, controlled voice. "I don't know how stupid you think I am, but I been around. I know what's going on. What'd you get a gram? An eight ball? More?"

Megan stepped away from him, scoffing. She looked at her drink. "I don't know what you're talking about."

"No? I'm talkin' about cocaine, sweetheart. Bolivian marching powder. The fastest way to ruin your life anybody ever came up with, at least till they came up with crack. I know a lot of folks you could ask about it if they were still alive, but—"

"You don't know shit about it," Megan said.

"Listen, missy, I spilled more cocaine in my day than you'll ever see." Big Bill grabbed her arm and pulled her close. "Now, Eddie can't write any new songs as it is. You get him all fucked up on cocaine and what do you think's gonna happen?"

"Let go of me!" She tried to jerk free, but Big Bill held tight.

"And by the way, you got no business cowriting anything longer than a grocery list. Now, if you don't straighten up I'm going to get you the hell out of Eddie's life. And make no mistake, I know how to do that." He let go of her arm. "I'm glad we had this little chat."

Megan smiled her prettiest smile. "Bill," she said sweetly, "until you start going down on Eddie? I think he's going to do what I tell him a lot faster than what you tell him." She sniffed her nose at him. "Trust me on that." Megan spun around and headed for the stage.

14

_J_ ay Colvin was screaming into the phone, "You're a genius! I can't believe they haven't caught this guy yet! You oughta be a damn detective!"

Jimmy had called Jay to report his discovery of the nearly empty container of MSG in Eddie's kitchen cabinet. "Well, it's all circumstantial," Jimmy said. "You can't convict on—"

"Hey, it's good evidence supporting the theory," Jay countered. "Listen, just write it up and get it ready. And leave the ending open so you can write something at the last minute, just before publication. We want it as up to date on Eddie's career as possible."

"I'm going through my old files to make sure I didn't miss anything."

"Good. Oh, your editor had a great idea. He wants to do a website where you continue writing on Eddie's career after the book's published. They'll make it so people can pay to download each new chapter. Later we'll compile the on-line chapters and do a follow-up book."

After Jay explained how Jimmy would get paid for the on-line dcal, Jimmy got back to work. He was at his desk, surrounded by all his files and a hundred sticky notes with little memos reminding him to go back and check this or that or another thing. He decided it was time to organize the mess, so he gathered the notes and sorted them by subject. That's when he found a note stuck to the back of one of his files: *Compare Eddie's early tour to Oak Pharm info.*

Jimmy had to think about it before he remembered what the note meant. He shuffled through the files until he found the information he'd blackmailed out of the guy at Okatibbee Pharmaceuticals.

Jimmy found copies of the police reports from the agencies that had investigated the four known poisoning deaths. Thanks to receipts found in Fred Babineaux's car and in the wallet of the victim in Tuscaloosa, the police knew when and where those boxes had been purchased. The Gulfport police had used credit card records to determine when and where that box had been bought. The only unknown purchase date was for the box found at Eddie's, which Jimmy knew had also come from the shipment sent to Little Rock. He made a list of the dates of purchase.

Jimmy then pulled out a document Eddie had given him. It was the list of every club, casino, and fraternity he'd ever played and the dates he'd played them. He put the two lists side by side and compared them. After a second something caught his eye. Not only had Eddie played in each of the cities where the poisoned powders had been sold, but it turned out he had played in each city a few days *before* each purchase. It didn't cinch the case, but, logically, it failed to exclude Eddie as the killer. Jimmy looked at the touring schedule. Eddie frequently played at a club in Little Rock called Little Rock, Little Country. In fact, according to the schedule, he had played there several times a year, and one date coincided with the arrival of the Dr. Porter's lot that had been tampered with and redistributed throughout the South.

Jimmy thought about it for a moment. Something was goofy. Somebody had violated the law of averages, which suggested Eddie would have been in at least *one* of the cities *after* the poisoned dose of Dr. Porter's was sold. But he always arrived before. Jimmy found it impossible to believe someone at Oak Pharm would take several boxes from a lot bound for Little Rock, Arkansas, poison them, and slip them into lots that consistently arrived in those particular towns just before Eddie got there. Coincidence couldn't possibly explain it. The pattern at least hinted at Eddie's involvement.

Jimmy paused to consider a possible alternative explanation. What if Eddie had a psychotic fan—someone who had followed him from show to show and, at the same time, was leaving a trail of poisoned headache powders? Nah, didn't make sense. For example, why would this psychotic fan choose only three of the two dozen cities where Eddie had played? Further, Eddie had never played in Hinchcliff. Okay, maybe the fan was actually trying to kill Eddie. No, that made even less sense. It required too many reasons to explain all the actions. Given a set of facts, Jimmy believed the simplest explanation was probably the right one. Besides, he couldn't think of a more dimwitted way to try to kill someone than hoping the intended victim would get a headache and go to the right store and buy the right box of poisoned headache powder.

Jimmy ran through a few more far-fetched scenarios, but he kept coming back to the one explanation that made sense. Eddie was the killer. But why? Maybe Eddie had found out about the other man. Or maybe it was because Eddie felt Tammy was holding him back. Okay, that might explain Tammy's death, but not the others. Unless . . . "Holy shit," Jimmy muttered. The facts came together in his mind and hit him like a wrecking ball.

First Jimmy had to assume Eddie wanted Tammy dead. And so far he'd heard two possible reasons for that. Second, Jimmy figured that since Eddie knew Tammy was hypersensitive to MSG, after bringing some Chinese food home, Eddie dosed the leftovers with the meat tenderizer before leaving to play the coast. He knew Tammy would eat the leftovers while he was out of town, would get a headache, and would take the only headache remedy in the house, which Eddie knew was poisoned because he had poisoned it. It was nice and neat except that Eddie would be considered the prime suspect even though he was out of town at the time of her death. So how would he get around that? The answer was simple, if macabre. What if Eddie had killed the others to make it look like there was a serial killer roaming the South and Tammy was just one of several unfortunate victims?

"Jesus H. Jones. This is fabulous." Not only did this round out his theory, but Megan was sure to leave Eddie when she heard this. She might even look to Jimmy as the guy who had saved her life. How could she not come back after that? Jimmy looked at his calendar. The Mississippi Coliseum in Jackson was the last stop on the *Long Shot* tour. If Jimmy couldn't reach Megan sooner, he'd be able to tell her then.

Jimmy wheeled over to the computer to start writing up his conclusion, but, with his fingers poised over the keyboard, he realized there was still a flaw in his argument. It was about the size of the hole that .22 had left in Tammy's head. Where the hell did that come from? he wondered. Eddie couldn't possibly have done that. Jimmy thought of the Robert Altman film *Cookie's Fortune* and considered the possibility that someone (Mr. Teasdale? The mystery lover?) had fired the shot for reasons Jimmy couldn't fathom. But he quickly realized the reasons didn't matter except as a bizarre side note, since he knew, from the coroner's report, that Tammy had died from the poison.

But the gunshot wound was only one of the problems. There was also the matter of the sodium fluoroacetate. It wasn't exactly a commonplace product, and Jimmy had never been able to show Eddie had access to the stuff.

Jimmy put his hands over his face. Shit. He just wanted to prove it. Or disprove it. He didn't care which. He just wanted something definite instead of all the circumstantial stuff leading to all the maybes. Jimmy started to rub his temples. All this crap was giving him a headache. He got up, went to the bathroom and looked for an aspirin, an Advil, Tylenol, anything but Dr. Porter's Headache Powder.

* * *

While back in Nashville, Big Bill met with the people from the Country Fanfare Awards. They agreed to make the presentation of the Tall Cotton Award at the midpoint of the show. Prime-time network television exposure was expected to boost record sales by 250,000 units.

Franklin would have been at the CFA meeting except that he was busy negotiating a big endorsement deal with Seagrams. Eddie would get $500,000 and Franklin would never have to pay for a bottle of scotch the rest of his life.

Everywhere Franklin went these days, he was starting to get the respect he craved . . . and not just for the deals he was negotiating. He was beginning to get some credit for his association with the record itself, and he loved it.

After being back in Nashville for a week, Big Bill and Franklin packed their bags and headed for Los Angeles, where Eddie was scheduled to play the Greek Theater. It was show number twenty-five and it had been sold out for weeks. The special services departments at all the major talent and literary agencies had pulled all available strings to get every last ticket for their VIPs. It was the toughest ticket since the Lakers were in the championship.

Big Bill put on the dog for the show at the Greek. He knew the place would be slithering with celebrities, so he stepped out of the limo wearing his $1,000 black cherry brush-off full-quill ostrich boots with the black cherry brush-off goat top, the thirteen-inch full scallop, and the #1212 stitch. He had a special pair of jeans, tailor-made to give him the "relaxed" fit his big ass required. He wore a leather fringe vest over a brightly colored Brushpopper bib shirt with pearl snaps. He topped the whole ensemble off with a silver belly El Patron from Stetson. He looked like the Pillsbury Doughboy dressed as the Grand Marshal for a cartoon rodeo.

And he didn't even stand out.

The whole crowd was a spectacle of Western raiment. Stars from the television, film, and recording industries were there in full country regalia, from $1,000 Stetsons to boots made from rare Burmese speckled lizards. Back in the cheaper seats the fashions were more authentic among L.A.'s vast population of displaced dust bowlers, Bible belters, and Texas panhandlers, most of whom were working on screenplays featuring hard-luck bull riders, struggling farmers, or legendary SEC football players.

Backstage, Franklin was strutting around in his favorite pair of natural-marked Tejo lizard boots with the black kidd top along with his usual dark slacks and sports coat. He wore a gaudy silver-and-turquoise medallion over his black turtleneck. Though not normally a hat guy, he was sporting a black Resistol Lancer with a custom red and green feather headband. The boots hurt like hell, so he had turned to vodka to get him through the night. He was enjoying a Bloody Mary while talking to a young agent. "Well, as of this afternoon," Franklin said, "the thing had sold nearly three million units. It's an answered prayer, no other way to characterize it."

"That's fabulous," the young agent said. He gently took Franklin's arm, leading him away from other ears. "The reason I ask is, I have a client, very talented singer-songwriter. He's not working out in pop music, and I think it's because he's too country. Now, I think with the right producer, and by that I mean you—no offense to Big Bill, he's a certified giant—but I think your sensibilities might be perfect."

"I'd love to get a tape," Franklin said coolly, "because it happens that I'm looking for a project to work on right now."

* * *

Megan and Eddie were off in a corner talking to a development executive from one of the film studios. "Let's see," Megan said, " 'Potholes' is still at number one. 'It Wasn't Supposed to End That

Way' was down to number six or seven this week, but it tied the record for most weeks at number one."

"That's fabulous, congratulations," the development executive said. "Listen, I know I should probably talk to Herron and Peavy first, but I just have to ask, have you considered film? Your smile is pure cinema, and I'm not just saying that."

"Actually," Megan said, "Herron and Peavy just manage Eddie's recording career. I'm his manager for all other media."

"Terrific! The reason I bring it up is I just read coverage on a wonderful script about a kid who gets a football scholarship to the University of Georgia but he has to leave the struggling family farm to do so. Unfortunately he loses a hand in a combine accident his last day on the farm, so he loses his scholarship and ends up on the rodeo circuit as a hard-luck bull rider."

"Interesting," Megan said. "Sort of *North Dallas Forty* meets *The Grapes of Wrath* with a little *Cowboy Way* thrown in. We'd love to see the script."

"Absolutely," Eddie agreed. He glanced over the film executive's shoulder. "I'm sorry, would you excuse us for a minute? We'll talk more, but I just saw someone I have to speak to." Eddie put his arm around Megan and led her away, whispering in her ear, "It's time for a toot, sweetie. I'm starting to flag here."

"Well, you've come to the right place," she said. "Listen, you want me to pick up another eight ball for the rest of the tour?"

*   *   *

Big Bill was watching them from across the room. He stepped over to Franklin, and gestured at Eddie and Megan. "My little speech didn't seem to take," Bill said.

"Yeah, well, he's handling it okay for now. Has he written anything since Oregon?"

"Two songs, both filler, and weak at that."

"Damn." Franklin gulped some Bloody Mary, then let out a sigh.

The two men stood there, silently contemplating their situation. After a moment Franklin noticed Big Bill's expression brighten. "You know," Big Bill said, "it just occurred to me we have at least one great song for Eddie. A big hit in the mid-seventies. Perfect for him to cover." He smiled broadly and slapped his hands together.

"It's ours?"

Big Bill nodded. "Remember 'Good Old Daze'?"

"The Carson Fletcher song?"

"That's the one."

Franklin looked vaguely confused. "I thought we only had half the publishing on that, with what's his name, uh, Buddy Glenn. Whatever happened to him?"

"Buddy hit a rough patch," Bill said. "I understand his wife passed away a couple of weeks ago."

"Sorry to hear that."

"Yeah, there was nothing anyone could do. But the point is we got all the publishing now and it's a damn good song. Perfect for Eddie."

All the sudden Franklin could hear it in his head. "I think you're right. The thing was never too twangy."

"It was really just a pop song with country lyrics and a steel guitar," Big Bill said. "Always reminded me of Pure Prairie League. Country radio'd probably jump on it."

Franklin nodded. "Well, good. We got a song. Now all we need is about nine more."

"Excuse me." Herron and Peavy turned to see a beautiful young woman. "Hi," she said. "I'm Heather Brown with *Country Weekly* magazine. Could I ask you two a few questions?" Big Bill and Franklin kindly obliged, answering the usual questions about how the tour and record sales were going. They also lied about the great songs Eddie was writing for the next record. "I really appreciate your talking to me," Heather said, wrapping up her interview.

"Our pleasure, ma'am," Franklin said with a tip of his hat.

Big Bill looked around cautiously, then subtly gestured at the young reporter. "Heather, can I ask you something off the record? I figure if anyone knows about this, it's someone with connections like yours." He leaned toward her and lowered his voice. "Have you heard anything about an unauthorized biography on Eddie that's about to be published? I heard it was coming from one of the big houses in New York. Supposed to make some wild allegations."

Heather looked surprised. "I haven't heard anything, but I'll definitely look into it."

"If you hear anything," he said, handing her his card, "please call me. I'd appreciate it."

"I'll let you know," Heather said before turning to leave.

Franklin and Big Bill slipped away from the crowd to continue their private conversation. "Where'd you hear about a biography?" Franklin asked.

"Rumor somebody asked me about a half hour ago." Big Bill gestured across the room at no one in particular. "Some guy over there, I forget who he said he was with, said he'd heard something about a book on Eddie. It was bound to happen."

"I suppose. So how much time should we give Eddie before we go outside?" Franklin asked. "For songs, I mean."

Big Bill shook his head. "I hate to do it, but why don't we listen to some tapes. If we find some things we like, we can put a hold on them. If Eddie comes up with something in the meanwhile, we're not out all that much."

Franklin slugged down the rest of his drink. "God, I'd hate not having the publishing."

*   *   *

It was late Tuesday night. The last customer settled his bill and slipped into the dark Nashville night. Estella had gone home, leaving Otis to close the place. He was in the kitchen, making his dinner. He dipped his hands into the big bowl of milk and paprika to gather the shrimp. He let the liquid drain through his fingers, wait-ing patiently so gravity could do its job. He laid the shrimp onto the big board with the spicy flour and carefully dredged each one, like tucking them in for bedtime. When they were ready, Otis put them into the wire basket and lowered them into the fat.

He stared at the bubbling oil and smelled the froth for the mil-lionth time. It was a familiar and relaxing ceremony. It took his mind off things. Otis wiggled the basket once, like he always did, and never took his eyes off the oil. Its heat held his gaze as the sounds soothed his jangled nature.

Bing! The bell in the service window rang suddenly. Otis jerked his head up in surprise. Who the hell would be ringing the bell? *Bing!* He turned and looked. It was an older man, white, looking into the kitchen, ringing the bell. *Bing!* Otis looked at the man, then stepped forward and looked again, disbelieving. He wiped his flour-covered hands on his apron. "Chester?" he said tentatively. "Chester Grubbs, is that you?"

The old guy smiled and tipped his worn cowboy hat. "What's left of me."

*   *   *

Otis gave Chester the first plate of shrimp and made another. They sat in a booth by the back wall with their food and two pints of bour-bon. There were way too damn many lost years for them to talk about things in any kind of order, so the conversation ran loose and wild. At first it was mostly about the old days—the records, the con-certs, the girls. They laughed about all the funny stuff and they tried to be philosophical about all the shit that had gone wrong.

Otis popped a shrimp into his mouth, tail and all. He liked the crunch. "You wanna know what I heard?" he asked. "I heard you was dead."

"Wasn't far from it," Chester replied, leaving it at that.

Otis was still crunching on the shrimp tail as he spoke. "Heard some bad things. Everything from you dying from heroin to hangin' yourself with a guitar string." He shook his head. "Peoples'll say just about anything when they don't know the truth."

Chester was pulling the tails off his shrimp. "Well, there's probably some truth to everything you heard," he said, tossing the tails onto Otis's plate. "Except for the one about me hangin' myself. After things fell apart here, I just couldn't stay, you know, couldn't stand the shame. People didn't want to work with me all the sudden, whispered that I never fulfilled my potential or that I never had any potential in the first place. I got to thinking they were right, so I run off and spent mosta my time drinkin' and movin' around to places where nobody knew who the hell I was so I didn't have to explain why I turned out like I did, you know?"

Otis looked Chester in the eye, nodding slowly. He understood.

"Everything good they can throw at a man and every bad choice a man can make and I made 'em all." Chester just shook his head. " 'Course, some things I did was worse than others." He took off his hat and rubbed his hand through his dirty gray hair. He pushed back his chair, stood, and gestured at himself. He looked worn out and his clothes didn't help—a pair of grease-stained blue shop pants and a plaid shirt from Goodwill. It was a look frequently seen on ex-convicts in the Midwest in the fifties. "Tell me I ain't the sorriest son of a bitch you ever saw."

Otis was shaking his head now. "Things shouldn'ta happened the way it did." Otis hesitated as Chester sat back down and resumed eating. Seeing Chester like this put Otis somewhere he hadn't been in a long time. It made him think about all the shit that had happened to them and to a lot of other people they knew. He almost didn't want to say it, but it came out anyway. "That Bill Herron . . ." He shook his head some more and calmed himself down. "I was real mad for a while, but I learned to let it go." He said the last part like he was still trying to convince himself.

Chester squinted wryly. "Yeah, I heard you let it go on some man in Memphis after I left."

The slightest smile crossed Otis's face. "Yeah, I 'spect that's part of why that happened. But that man was forcin' hisself on Estella. Man can't allow that to happen, you know that. But I did my time." He said it like he'd earned the right. "Woulda been more, but Mr. Peavy, he helped me out on that."

"That's good," Chester said. "But you shouldn't have to do time for defending your woman is all I'm sayin'."

Otis poured a little more bourbon for both of them. They sat there in silence for a while, just eating and sipping their drinks, looking at each other and thinking about the water under the bridge. "It's been a awful long time, Chester." He looked at his old friend. "Why'd you come back?"

Chester put both elbows on the table and fixed Otis with dead serious eyes. "Everywhere I went, I heard people talkin' 'bout your shrimp, Otis. I had to come back and see for myself." He wrapped a couple of the shrimp in a piece of white bread, then took a big bite and chewed a few times. "I just wish I'da come back sooner."

Otis laughed. "You shoulda. Used to put more on a plate than we do now."

They both laughed, then Chester held up his glass for a toast. "Old friends."

"Old friends," Otis said, clinking his glass to Chester's.

They drank. As Otis poured some more, Chester pulled something from a sack he'd brought with him. It was a copy of the *Long Shot* CD, which he laid on the table. "This is the reason I came back, Otis." He took the CD out of the jewel box and pointed at the writing credits for "Potholes in My Heart." "I think this here's my son," he said, pointing to "W. Rankin." "See, we named our boy Whitney. 'Course, I lost touch with his mama, but for all I know she remarried some man last name of Rankin, might've adopted the boy, you know?" Chester stared at the name on the disc. He touched it lightly, as close to his son as he'd felt in decades.

Otis didn't want to dampen Chester's enthusiasm, but he also didn't want his old friend leaning on such a weak reed. "That's not much reason to think it's your son, Chester. I mean, you been gone too long to come back just for that."

"Yeah, I know," Chester said, "it's more'n that. It's the song. The music. I wrote it. A long time ago, for my son. I sang it to him almost every night for I don't know how many years before I . . . left." He looked back at the disc with disdain. " 'Course the words've been changed. I didn't write nothing about no damn potholes in my heart. I suppose that's 'at damn Herron's doin'. Fact, when I first saw his name on the credits I wanted to kill him. Sumbitch screwed me over thirty years ago and now come to find out he's still doin' it to me." He shook his head in amazement. "But I ain't here 'bout Big Bill. I just want to see my boy. Got some things I'd like to tell him. " 'Course I s'pose he might not even live here. But I had to come look, trail's gotta start here."

"How long you think you'll be around?"

"Hard to say. Long enough to see if he's here, maybe find enough work to pay my way back outta town. Speakin' of that, if you hear of any kind of work, I'd appreciate it if you'd steer it my way. I ain't exactly livin' on royalties, if you know what I mean. I can do just about anything on a construction site, framin', roofin', whatever. I'm not bad with a backhoe either."

"I'll keep my ears open," Otis said. "Estella might be able to use some help cleanin' up around here. She gets tired easy these days."

"I don't want you making up a job for me, but if you need the help, I'm for hire. Pretty cheap too." Chester ate a shrimp, then picked up another one and sort of waggled it in front of him. "Damn, Otis, these're some fine little delectables you cooked up." He popped it into his mouth.

Otis smiled. "They draw a good crowd out here. Matter of fact, old Herron and Peavy come by every now and then. They fall up in here late for a bottle and a plate. Mr. Peavy comes more than Mr. Herron, but come to think, they was both in here just—" Otis stopped and looked at Chester. "Oh Lord," he said. "I think I seen him."

"Who?"

"Your boy," Otis said.

Chester leaned across his plate. "When'd you see him?"

Otis's eyes darted left and right like he was searching for an image in his head. "They was all here after they finished that other boy's record." He pointed at Eddie's disc. "This boy here." Then he pointed at Chester and smiled. "He's a good-looking kid, your son. I'll tell you that."

Chester looked proud all the sudden. "I'd sure like to see him." Otis said he'd call Franklin and find out where he could get in touch with Whitney. "I'd appreciate that, Otis, I really would," Chester said. "And you know I'll return the favor any way I can."

* * *

The last stop for the *Long Shot* tour was the old Mississippi Memorial Coliseum in Jackson. Completed in 1963, it had a white roof pitched up in the center as if supported by a big tent pole. The sides were covered in giant panels, alternating yellow, white, and orange. The result was a sort of circus-tent motif that had tremendous aesthetic appeal to anyone under the age of eight. In 1995 the facility received a long-overdue face-lift, replacing the faded carnival look with a new copper facade that had tremendous aesthetic appeal to whoever got the contract to supply the copper.

For Jimmy, the Coliseum was a venue of odd memories. As a child, he'd been dressed in a degrading jester's outfit and forced to participate in the Junior League's annual Carnival Ball fund-raiser there. He was also there when Cliff Finch gave away free barbecued chicken while running for governor from the seat of a tractor, or was it a bulldozer? As a teenager, he'd seen a hundred rock-and-roll shows under its roof, everyone from the Allman Brothers to Yes. And it was there, on the night of August 16, 1987, scarcely stoned on some woeful Mexican weed, that Jimmy officially got to second base with a girl named Terry while Bob Seger played "Shakedown."

Given Eddie's third single, Jimmy figured the Coliseum was a fitting place for the *Long Shot* tour to end, because it was also the place where he—and Eddie, for that matter—had gone to see the Dixie National Rodeo when they were kids. He remembered the inside transformed into something he imagined was straight out of the Old West. The place was decked wall to wall in red, white, and blue bunting, the floor was covered with dirt and sawdust, and the smell of animals filled every crevice in the building. He watched in awe as real cowboys rode the backs of wild bulls while others jumped off speeding horses to wrestle steers to the ground. Jimmy couldn't remember the last time he'd been to the rodeo, but every time he stepped into the Coliseum he remembered the first.

In his twenties, Jimmy had started attending events there as a member of the press. Consequently he knew everybody who worked the shows there. As soon as he heard Eddie's tour was wrapping at the Coliseum, Jimmy flashed his credentials and received a backstage press pass.

He got there about two hours before the show was scheduled to start. With the tour buses parked in back, Jimmy wandered around chatting with old acquaintances, taking photos, and waiting for Megan to show herself. He was talking to one of the concert promoters when she entered his field of vision. She was barking at a roadie, and she looked great doing it. She wore a Wrangler shirt unbuttoned at the bottom and tied in a knot to reveal her pierced belly button and hip-hugging jeans. She had half a dozen shiny Montana Silversmith bracelets on each wrist, and her wild red hair was just visible under a Stetson Caldwell. Jimmy couldn't help but stare.

The moment he saw Megan, Jimmy felt the surge of whatever it was she always triggered in him, like the involuntary secretion of some powerful hormone. He wondered what the hell was wrong with him. She treated him like crap. Why couldn't he get over her? She was an addiction. He had a Jones and he wished it would stop. A possible title for his unwritten song popped into his head: "Doesn't Anyone Have a Cure for This?"

When she finished with the roadie, Megan turned and saw Jimmy. She stopped dead in her tracks as if she was about to pretend she hadn't seen him. But then she perched on her tiptoes, faked a surprised smile, and called out his name. "Jimmy! Haaaay!" She rushed over and gave him a little hug and an air kiss. "How *are* you? You look great. Have you been working out?" She acted like Jimmy was someone she had dated twenty years earlier instead of being the guy she'd snuck out of town on in the middle of the night not too damn long ago.

"I'm good, thanks." Jimmy paused. He wanted to let her know how much she'd hurt him, but all he could think of was that day in Vicksburg. And suddenly all he wanted to do was find a way to make that happen again. "How're you doing? You look great."

"Ohmigod, you wouldn't believe. This has been the wildest tour," she said as though she'd been on a dozen others. "Thirty-five shows in forty days, sound-system problems in Spokane, Teamster problems in Bakersfield, blahblahblah. It's endless, but it's been great fun. But what about you? What have you been up to?" Megan suddenly put a hand to her cheek. "Ohmigod, are you still working on the book?"

Jimmy told her he had spoken to Big Bill about it. "He made it pretty clear he'd never let Eddie sign a contract to let me do the official biography, so I decided to go the unofficial route."

"That ass." Megan indignantly stomped one of her cowboy boots. "You wouldn't believe that fucking dinosaur. I can't believe . . . you want me to talk to him? I bet I could—"

"Too late," Jimmy said. "I've already got a publishing deal for the one I'm writing." He looked at her lips and remembered the sweet bourbon kisses.

"Ohmigod! Congratulations! I knew you'd do it. Didn't I tell you? That's great, Jimmy. When's it due out? I can't wait to read it. Can we get an advance copy?" She sniffed slightly and discreetly pinched her nose.

The depth of Megan's insincerity finally crushed Jimmy's fond memory. He folded his arms and looked her in the eyes. "You know, I tried to call you after you moved, but your number's unlisted. I wanted to tell you about the book."

Megan looked to the ground. "I know, I'm sorry, Jimmy, I just, well, I got the job in Nashville and we were, well, you know . . ." She reached over and gently touched his arm, as if confirming her sincerity. "I should've called, but, I know, I'm terrible." She looked up to see if Jimmy had a forgiving look on his face. He didn't. He was looking at her as if he thought she ought to continue talking about how terrible she was. But Megan didn't have all day and she sure wasn't going to stand around groveling for no good reason, so she returned to her perky showbiz demeanor. "But tell me about the book and your deal, I am so *excited* for you."

"I found out some things about Eddie." He paused. "And about how Tammy died."

"Really? What kind of things?"

"I think he killed her."

Megan looked at Jimmy blankly. "What?" Like she misunderstood.

"And two or three other people."

Megan looked at Jimmy in all seriousness. "Are you crazy?"

Jimmy went through all the evidence, piece by piece. "I tried to come up with alternative explanations, but nothing else works. I think you should leave him. He's not the guy you think he is. He's not the guy *I* thought he was. And its a pretty safe bet if you dig Tammy up and ask her, she'll say he's not the guy she thought he was either."

Megan looked genuinely shocked. "I don't believe you, Jimmy. I mean, I can understand you being jealous, but this? This is what's in your book?" She looked up at the ceiling for a moment, then back at Jimmy. "Nobody's going to publish a bunch of, I don't know, it's all . . . coincidental evidence."

"Circumstantial."

"Whatever." She lowered her voice and wagged a finger at Jimmy. "Nobody is going to publish a book accusing a major star of murder based only on circumstantial evidence."

"I got the contract." He shrugged. "Deal's done." He couldn't help it. He had to say it. "Got a six-hundred-thousand-dollar advance."

Megan's face went slack. First she'd learned that she might be sleeping with a murderer, then the boyfriend she'd left for the murderer announced he'd signed a six-hundred-thousand-dollar book deal. Talk about your bad judgment. "Jimmy," she said disapprovingly, "I am so disappointed. After what we had, all we shared, this is how you pay me back?"

"I didn't realize we'd been engaged in a transaction."

She rolled her eyes. "First of all, Eddie's a killer? Puh-lease. . . ." She shook her head. "You'll get sued all over hell and half of Georgia if you publish that nonsense."

"You'll have to talk to my publisher about that," Jimmy said.

Megan's face suddenly softened. She seemed to be thinking, then she smiled. "Wait a second." She put her hands on her hips and cocked them to one side. "Ohhh, this is so sweet," she said. "You want me to leave Eddie so bad you're willing to come in here with this silly story?" She made a "tsk" sound with her tongue and teeth. "You are so adorable. You'll find someone else, don't worry." Megan glanced at her watch. "Listen, I've got to go check on some stuff, but it was great to see you again."

As Megan turned to leave, Jimmy grabbed her arm and fixed her with an incredulous stare. "I'm sorry, what part of 'serial killer' don't you understand?"

* * *

There were a couple of things Big Bill didn't understand. One was how Eddie had lost the ability to write a decent song. Forget about great songs, Big Bill would have been satisfied with a pretty good one. Something that didn't stink would've been nice. For the last thirty minutes he'd been sitting on the bus listening to Eddie's two newest songs, both cowritten with Megan. He put his finger on the stop button of the cassette player and pressed so hard the plastic snapped.

The other thing he didn't understand was a recent ruling in a Nashville civil court tripling the monthly amount of alimony and child support he was required to pay. His ex-wives had banded together to petition the court for higher payments in light of Big Bill's recent windfall. The court handed down the ruling faster than you could say *just when I was getting ahead.*

All things considered, Big Bill knew he was a lucky man. He'd produced a hit record late in his career—and a huge one at that. He had his name on the best-selling debut record in history, and even if Eddie never wrote another decent song, Big Bill would probably have a little money for his golden years. At least that's how it had looked before the lawyers showed up.

While it would be nice, Big Bill thought, if his three ex-wives suddenly died, he didn't think the odds favored such an exceptional event happening without his involvement, and he just wasn't up to that. But was there something he could do to get a good song out of Eddie? The publishing money on the next record alone, well, Big Bill hated to think about not having it. But he knew he'd rather go out with a good record he didn't control the publishing on than a bad one he did. It was a close call, but that's how he felt.

Still, he thought, if he could get Eddie to write one good song for the second album, Big Bill would be satisfied. Then no matter how much money his ex-wives bled him for, he'd be fine. All he needed was to figure out a way to make that happen. He thought about it. First of all, he knew time was an issue. Between the tour and the media schedule Megan had arranged, Eddie hadn't had time to write. With the tour over, that problem would be solved. Next, Big Bill knew he had to get Megan out of the room while Eddie worked. As a songwriter, Megan was somewhere between useless and a complete idiot. But Big Bill knew that trying to remove her from the process would lead to conflict and maybe to a power struggle that he could lose, so the remaining question was how to solve that.

Something in the back of Big Bill's mind started to push forward. He began thinking about a conversation he had had with Eddie the second night of their recording session. They were in Big Bill's kitchen talking about the difficulties of songwriting when Eddie made a comment about what had led him to write "It Wasn't Supposed to End That Way." Big Bill remembered Eddie saying the song came to him as a result of the tragic death of his wife.

Big Bill squinted as he considered the implications of Eddie's comment. After a few moments, Big Bill's pinched, pug face settled into a smile. He had an idea. A kill-two-birds-with-one-stone idea. He knew it was appalling, but at the same time it was perfect, or close to it. He mulled it over for a moment and decided to knock over the first domino and see what happened.

15

espite her doctor's orders, Estella fried herself up half a chicken for lunch. *But I took off most of the skin* was her rationale. She balanced her plate with the usual side of potato salad and two slices of white bread. She sat at a table near the kitchen, said grace, and then, as they say, she crammed it in with both fingers and stomped it down with both feet. No question about it, Estella could put it away. When she was done, her belly was tight enough to crack a tick on. She sat back and let out a long satisfied sigh.

A few minutes later, Estella got busy cleaning the place the way she always did. She pushed all the tables to one side of the restaurant and swept up before she started to mop. Estella kept the place spotless. Her name was over the door. She was proud of it. She kept the cleanest linoleum in Nashville. She sang while she worked. Somebody once said Estella had a voice like a finely tuned V-8 engine. Otis always gave her a solo slot during his shows, and people always compared her to Aretha. There was talk of a solo career, and Estella let herself dream big dreams. But things never quite worked out, and Estella had been carrying that with her ever since. A chance so close she could touch it. But Otis went to prison and Estella had to let the dream go. It still ate at her.

Estella was halfway done with the floor when she pulled up short of breath. She figured she was just putting too much elbow grease behind that mop. She pulled up a chair to catch her breath and let her stomach settle.

Estella's mistake was a common one. She dismissed the pain as an upset stomach at first. It would pass. But it didn't. It got worse and she started to sweat. She tried to convince herself it was just gas. She needed to get a Co-Cola and burp it up, then she'd feel better. But that didn't help either. Finally she had to accept that the pain wasn't so much in her stomach as it was in her chest and it was starting to radiate out. Estella knew what that meant. *I can't be havin' no heart attack,* she told herself. *I already had one.*

Estella sat there with a growing sense of anxiety. She was alone and didn't know when Otis would arrive. She got up to go to the phone but collapsed halfway across the room. The plaque in a coronary artery had ruptured and a blood clot had formed. She lay on the floor, trying to breathe. Unable to do anything to help herself, she began to pray.

Otis walked in a few minutes later and found her. He called 911 and administered CPR the way they'd showed him at the hospital the last time Estella was there. The ambulance got there quick and carried Estella to the hospital. She was still alive, but unconscious, they said. They didn't know if she'd make it.

*   *   *

Megan loved the new house. It had so many possibilities. It was a ten-thousand-square-foot Belle Meade Colonial, once owned by Wanda Jackson. A gated property, it sat on three and a half rustic acres. Megan had rented some furniture to use while she worked on the interior scheme.

She'd read part of a book on Feng Shui and had done her own element analysis. The house would be a haven for the creation of music. This was clearly related to the harmony element, which was used to sweeten the music. Thus, Megan figured, it was important to enhance this aspect. She decided the harmony element would be energized by blues and light greens. These colors, in turn, called to mind the water element. So Megan was in the kitchen looking through magazines for an indoor fountain to go with the blue-and-green sofa.

Eddie was in the living room just glad she was working on something other than one of his songs. He was sitting at the big wrought-iron-and-glass table in the center of the room thinking he was just one good line from having a great song. His big flattop Gibson leaned against a chair while Eddie leaned over the table to the line in question. It was a long sparkling stripe he hoped contained his inspiration. He snorted it and threw his head back, putting a finger to his nose so he wouldn't lose anything. He sniffed once or twice, grabbed the Gibson, and tried to think of another rhyme for "heart." "Cart . . . smart . . . apart . . . Kmart . . . shit!" He grabbed the legal pad, ripped off the page, and crumpled it. The floor was littered with yellow paper balls. Eddie told himself to relax, that he still had plenty of good songs inside. He just needed something to pry them out. He set his guitar down, hunkered over the glass-top table, and snorted another line. Maybe that would do it.

"Save some for me," Megan said. She breezed into the room with fabric samples draped over one arm and a catalog for indoor fountains tucked under the other. She crossed to the table, picked up the straw, and snorted the remaining coke.

Eddie saw her at the last minute. "Heyheyhey! What're you doing? That was the last of it, goddammit!"

"Would you relax? I got a call in for more." Megan sat down and looked at all the crumpled yellow paper. "I got an idea. How about we write a song—"

"How about you leave the goddam songwriting to me, huh?" Eddie bolted to his feet. "How about that?" He grabbed the pad of paper and started circling the table. "Jesus."

Megan threw her hands up. "Sure, whatever. I was just trying to help. Christ."

Eddie jabbed the pencil in Megan's direction. "Goddammit, I haven't written a decent song in four months! And you know what? If I don't have some hits on the second record I'm fucked."

"Hey! What about the songs we wrote? You said—"

"I know what I said, but they're all crap and Bill agrees. He said A&R at the label hates every one of 'em. Called 'em amateurish and derivative." Eddie figured this bit of humiliation would shut Megan up for a while, let him get back to work. He shrugged. "Not a single one we can use, simple as that."

Megan exploded. "Well fuck them!" Standing in a fury, she snatched the big Gibson by the neck. "When did you start giving a shit about what those idiots think, huh Mr. Long Shot Hot Shot?"

"Calm down," Eddie said derisively.

"Don't you tell me what to do!" Megan suddenly turned and smashed the Gibson into the wrought-iron leg of the table. The solid flamed maple split on impact. Strings popped and coiled up the rosewood fingerboard.

Eddie snapped. "Goddammit, bitch!" It happened quick. Eddie landed an open hand against the side of Megan's head. She dropped the busted guitar and staggered backwards, feeling the sting of it. "Oh God," Eddie said immediately. "I'm sorry." He reached out and put his arms around her. "Are you all right? I didn't mean to . . ."

Megan struggled to maintain her composure. She didn't want to do or say anything to set him off again. She had too much to lose. She made a small whimpering sound, then slowly lifted her head. "Eddie," she said, her eyes clear and sweet. "It's okay, I love you."

"I'm sorry I hit you." Eddie felt terrible. "I'm just under so much pressure. I never have any time alone anymore. I'm feelin' all penned in, you know? Just trapped."

"I know. I'm sorry."

Eddie took a couple of steps away, looked outside. "I've been thinking," he said. "Maybe it'd be better if we kind of cooled it for a while, me and you."

Megan tried to stay calm. "No, it's okay, sweetie, I forgive you. It didn't really hurt." She reached down and picked up the shattered guitar, which sounded a damaged note. "I shouldn't have done that. We'll get you a new one."

Eddie stared at the guitar for a moment, then blankly walked across the room and dropped into the La-Z-Boy. "It's just that I'm used to being alone more. I work better that way, you know? That's how I wrote all my old songs. And after being cramped up on that bus for a month and a half, hell, I just need some space, that's all. I just need my space."

Megan couldn't believe her ears. This country prick was trying to toss her after all she'd done for him? Hell, she'd practically made him. And this was her thanks? "Eddie?" She said it in a small, almost childlike voice. "There's something I have to tell you."

"About what?"

Megan bit her lip and looked like she might cry. "I just didn't know how to. I didn't want to mess things up for you."

"What're you talking about?"

"Remember on the plane? To Dallas before the first show?"

"What about it?"

"In the bathroom. You didn't have a condom?"

"Yeah." Eddie started to get a bad feeling about the direction of the conversation.

"I didn't want to do anything without telling you first."

"Megan, what the hell're you talking about?"

"It's all my fault, I'm so sorry."

"Sorry about what?"

She hesitated, looking down at her belly. "I think I'm pregnant."

*   *   *

Jimmy felt like a proud papa as he held the complete draft of the manuscript in his hands. Three hundred forty-seven pages, double-spaced, one-inch margins all around. It was well written. It was thorough. It was something you could thump against a desk. It was a lot of things, but it wasn't finished.

After reading it cover to cover for the first time, Jimmy knew it was missing something. He had failed to show Eddie had access to any sodium fluoroacetate. He reviewed his notes from his visit to the Lytle farm. The shed there had all sorts of chemicals on the shelf. According to his notes there was Benzahex, Ortho-Klor, ethylene chlorohydrin, and something called Compound 1080. But no sodium fluoroacetate.

The link was too important to ignore. If he couldn't show Eddie had access to the poison, the rest of the evidence seemed considerably less compelling. Problem was, Jimmy had looked at all the obvious places the poison might be. In addition to the Lytles' shed, Jimmy had been to the Hegman property, and he'd looked in Eddie's garage. Of course, if Eddie really was the killer, there was no reason to think he'd leave the stuff somewhere it could be found. So Jimmy decided to take one last look at where he'd been. If he didn't find what he was looking for, so be it. He'd go to print with what he had.

The coroner's report confirmed sodium fluoroacetate was the cause of Tammy's death. The documents from the National Crime Information Center said the same thing about the three other victims. Jimmy went online and linked to the National Poison Control Center website where he read about the various substances in the shed.

Benzahex was a trade name for benzene hexachloride, a synthetic pesticide soluble in oily and fatty solutions, but not water.

Highly toxic, it was especially deadly if ingested after a fatty meal, making it that much more hazardous in the deep South.

Ortho-Klor was a trade name for chlordane, a chemical commonly used against termites during the 1950s, 60s, 70s and 80s. It was banned by the EPA in March of 1988 after the manufacturer was forced to acknowledge chlordane was a carcinogen.

Ethylene chlorohydrin had a wide range of industrial uses, but down on the farm it was used to speed up the sprouting of potatoes and to treat seeds to inhibit biological activity.

That left Compound 1080, a substance that occurred naturally in the African plant *Dichapetalum cymosum*. Its synthesized cousin had been used in the United States as a rodenticide since 1945, as well as being an insecticide used on fruit trees to combat scale insects, aphids, and mites. According to the website, most mammals were fatally poisoned by less than 1 mg of Compound 1080 per kg of body weight. Compound 1080 was also known as Fratol, sodium salt, sodium monofluoroacetate, and sodium fluoroacetate.

"Bingo." Jimmy grabbed the phone and dialed. "Jay, it's Jimmy. Guess what?"

* * *

Big Bill knew he lacked the gumption to do what his plan called for. He also knew better than to have any hands-on connection to the thing. He required outside help and, given his history in Nashville, there was only one person in town Big Bill could trust. He picked up his phone and punched in the number.

Franklin was sitting in a booth at the Pancake Pantry in a fine mood. Ever since the end of Eddie's tour, Franklin had been getting the sort of respect he felt he deserved. In the ten minutes he'd been at the Pantry, a half-dozen music industry veterans had stopped by his table to pay respects. He was pouring cream into his coffee when his cell phone rang. "Franklin Peavy."

"Hey, it's me," Big Bill said. "Got a minute?"

"Sure," Franklin said. "What's up?"

"Well, I've been thinking," Big Bill said. "Thinking about how you played such a critical part in getting Eddie signed, and getting his endorsement deal, and working out the merchandising contract, and, well, it occurred to me that if anybody in this town was on their toes, they might just try to lure you away from the company."

Being an experienced attorney, Franklin sensed a good opportunity to distort the truth. "Well, I'd be lying if I told you I hadn't had a few offers."

"I don't doubt it," Big Bill said. "But I can't afford to lose you, so I've got a proposition I hope might interest you."

"I'm listening."

"I want to talk to you about coproducing Eddie's next record. Me and you, whaddya say? It's gonna be a big record."

Franklin was speechless. This was huge. It meant a ton more money with the producer points he'd get plus a producer credit on what might turn out to be one of country music's most important records. What a way to cap off a career. "I think it's a great idea," Franklin said.

"Long overdue," Big Bill replied. "So let's talk about it."

"Great. Your office or mine?"

"Tell you what, uh, things are so crazy around here these days, let's meet somewhere we won't be interrupted. Say, Owen Bradley Park in an hour?"

*   *   *

As a favor to Chester, Otis called over to Herron & Peavy Management and spoke to Franklin's assistant. He explained he was trying to track down a client. "I believe his name is Whitney Rankin." The assistant said Whitney worked at the South Side Smoke House.

Chester got there as the lunch hour was starting. He sat at the bar and ordered the meat-and-three and a beer. He hadn't been there five minutes before Whitney walked out of the kitchen with a big tray of food hoisted over his head. It took Chester's breath away. He knew the instant he laid eyes on the boy that he was his son. And he was a fine-looking young man, just as Otis had said.

Chester watched as Whitney carried the tray of food to a table full of office workers. He was tall and lanky and moved with an awkward grace. He wore Wranglers, a black T-shirt, and a worn pair of black Tony Lama ropers. Chester noticed the ragged piece of red bandanna around his wrist. He smiled at his long dark hair. It reminded him of Whitney's mother. His face was innocent, narrow, and boyish, but not without troubles. Chester could see a whisper of himself in Whitney's face. He watched every move and strained to hear his voice, but he was too far away.

Chester ate his lunch, then sat there for an hour watching his son. He wanted to go over and tell Whitney who he was, but he knew this was neither the time nor the place. He wanted to put his arms around his boy and tell him how sorry he was for what he'd done—or more specifically, for what he'd failed to do. More than ever Chester felt the guilt that had dogged him all his life. He was ashamed, not because he'd failed as a singer, but because he'd failed as a father. He'd walked out and left a young boy and his mama to fend for themselves. He was a coward, or worse.

Chester also wanted to know about the song. He had no doubt it was the one he'd written for his son so many years ago. It wasn't that Chester felt he was owed anything for it. But since Big Bill Herron had his name attached to it and Whitney was in Nashville toting pork ribs for tip money after the song had gone to number one, well, Chester knew someone had been fucked and he knew from experience it hadn't been Big Bill.

But as much as Chester wanted to go over and say something, wanted to ask Whitney a million questions and tell him how ashamed and sorry he was and how he didn't deserve to be forgiven after what he'd done, Chester couldn't bring himself to do it. He didn't think he deserved to satisfy his own desires at the expense of his son, so he just put some money on the bar and slipped away, happy for having just seen the boy.

■ ■ ■

Franklin took his time. He sat there and enjoyed his waffles, his bacon, and his coffee. He was enjoying everything these days. He'd been asked to be the keynote speaker at several major record industry functions. There was talk about a profile in *Gower's Nashville Magazine*. And if he wasn't mistaken, that attractive marketing executive at the label had been flirting with him. Yet despite this parade of blessings, Franklin refused to believe his luck. No matter how dazzled he was by his newfound celebrity, Franklin knew Big Bill wasn't inclined to feeling charitable even in the best of times. He suspected there was more to his generous offer than he was letting on.

Franklin reached into his pocket and pulled out his digital recorder to make sure the memory card was clean. No matter what else, if Big Bill was going to make him a bona fide offer to coproduce Eddie's next record, Franklin was damn sure going to get proof of it.

Owen Bradley Park was at the north end of Music Row, a five-minute drive from the Pancake Pantry. Franklin parked on 16th Avenue, near the old Hall of Fame. He slipped his recorder into his breast pocket. He could see Big Bill sitting on one of the benches reading *Billboard*. Franklin hit the record button, got out of his car, and crossed the street.

"Hey now!" Big Bill said when he saw Franklin. "Thanks for coming."

"You kiddin'? Your invitation was too tempting to ignore."

"Good." Big Bill smiled. "Real good." He gestured for Franklin to sit, and they settled down on the bench together. Big Bill looked toward downtown. "Nice day, huh?" Franklin nodded. It wasn't too hot. There was a breeze and the blue sky was busy with clouds drifting toward Memphis. Big Bill took a deep breath and exhaled peacefully as he gazed at the clouds. "It's been quite a ride so far, hasn't it?"

"You mean the whole thing or just the Eddie Long part?"

"Whole thing," Big Bill said, spreading his arms wide. "But especially the Eddie Long part." He clapped his hands together, turned to his partner, and winked.

"Can't argue with that," Franklin said with a cock of his head.

"What'd we move this week, three hundred fifty thousand units?"

"In that neighborhood."

"Yes sir, a helluva ride," Big Bill said. "Whole thing's got me thinking a lot lately about how you and me've pretty much spent our entire professional lives together." He shifted in his seat to speak more personally. "Now I know we hadn't always got along great and we've passed some words now and then, but I figure that's just business and it doesn't rightly signify the respect we have for each other." Big Bill's eyes swept the park, then settled on his partner. "Look," he said, "let me just put this on the front porch. Way I see things is, we got two problems standing between us and a mighty prosperous future. One is the fact that Eddie's run dry with his songs." Big Bill paused before continuing in a tone of disgust, "The other's that damn Megan Taylor."

"I don't disagree," Franklin said, "but what's that got to do with me producing Eddie's next record?" He leaned slightly closer to Big Bill to make sure the tiny microphone could pick up every word.

Big Bill nodded, understanding Franklin's concern. "Don't worry, I meant what I said. I want you to coproduce Eddie's next record with me, use that damn Pro Tools or whatever you wanna do. But if we don't do something about Megan, and quick, we might not be in a position to be makin' any more Eddie Long records."

"I'd like to see her try. We've got a solid contract."

"I know, and you write as good a contract as can be written. But she's got him all fucked up on coke and he still hasn't written a single song I'd put on anybody's next record, much less his. Hell, *ours!* You want to be coproducer on a record that flops?" Franklin shook his head. Big Bill gestured vaguely toward Belle Meade. "The bitch is probably back at their house right now filling him with all sorts of ideas about how he needs to sue to get out of our deal and hook up with some young, hip manager, and all things considered I think we'd all be better off without her in the picture."

Franklin wasn't surprised at the pitch so far. This wasn't the first time he'd heard Big Bill talk about driving a wedge between an artist and an outside adviser unsympathetic to the goals of Herron & Peavy Management. "What're you proposing?"

"Well, like I said, I think we got two problems, and I had an idea that just might solve both of 'em." Big Bill's expression suddenly grew dark. "You might think I'm crazy—and I damn well might be, but you remember how Eddie said he wrote 'It Wasn't Supposed to End That Way' after his wife was killed?" Big Bill waited for that to sink in before continuing, hoping it would brace Franklin for what was coming. "I think the key here for this is we got to give him some . . ." He lowered his voice. ". . . emotional turmoil." He gave a look of I-didn't-come-to-this-decision-lightly before continuing. "He's got a huge hit record and he's fixin' to be honored at the CFAs. He knows he ain't got a trouble in the world. So I'm thinking we have to . . . create some."

"Emotional turmoil." Franklin's expression changed, as if he could all of a sudden sense where this was going.

Just as suddenly Big Bill had second thoughts, unsure if Franklin's expression conveyed approval or not. "Now this is just talk, mind you," Big Bill said, trying to inoculate himself against what he was about to say. "Just some 'what ifs.' "

"I understand," Franklin said. "Now *what if* you just tell me your idea."

"All right." Big Bill looked around the park. They were alone. He leaned toward his partner and said, "The girl has to die." He said it right into Franklin's pocket. It was only when the words actually came out of his mouth that Big Bill truly embraced the callousness of his idea. "Think about it," he said with a salesman's enthusiasm. "First of all, it gives Eddie the emotional turmoil he might need to write a decent song or two. Secondly, it gets her outta our hair. And the publicity?" He waved a hand in the air. "The outpouring of public sympathy for a man who lost his wife and now loses a lover? Betcha dolla that'll sell some records." A pained expression quickly clouded Big Bill's face. " 'Course there's no guarantee that just 'cause we kill her Eddie'll write a good song, but it does guarantee that we're back in control of the client."

Franklin sat there, his head nodding slowly. He was thinking about the nature of ideas. *Where do they come from?* he wondered. *It must be like this for songwriters. You can be sitting around talking about one thing when BAM!—an idea about something entirely different forms in your head.* Franklin couldn't help but smile. The idea he'd just had was a doozy. It had an immediate million-dollar payoff plus a series of long-term payments that would elevate Franklin to the tax bracket in which he felt he'd be most comfortable.

Big Bill interpreted Franklin's smile favorably. He figured since Franklin hadn't responded to the idea with a gasp or an indignant speech they were on the same page. He tapped his partner's arm with the back of his hand. "Obviously it can't be me or you since it's not exactly our line of work. But I figure we can hire somebody to do it and I thought you might . . . know somebody."

Franklin feigned offense. "Why? Because I'm a lawyer?" He chuckled. His idea had given him a thrill he'd never experienced.

Big Bill smiled. "Well . . . yeah."

Franklin leaned toward Big Bill and nodded like he had connections. "As a matter of fact, I do know somebody."

"Well, shit, you rascal, whaddya say?"

Franklin looked at his partner with all seriousness. "I think it's a damn good idea," he said. "I'll take care of it and let you know the plan."

Big Bill suddenly closed his eyes and stuck his fingers in his ears. "No, no, no. I don't want to know a thing about it," Big Bill said. "I don't care how you do it, long as you can trust whoever it is, and long as you keep our names out of it. This ain't no damn prank we're talkin' about. This is serious. We can't afford to mess it up. Just get somebody you trust to do the killin'."

*   *   *

Franklin called ahead and made arrangements to meet the man he knew would help. He arrived at Estella's around five. Otis was waiting for him. They sat in a booth and poured sweet tea from an old plastic pitcher.

"How's Estella doing?" Franklin asked.

Otis pursed his lips and looked down at the tabletop, his head shaking slightly. " 'Bout the same, Mr. Peavy." He thought of her, lying in the hospital bed, unresponsive to his voice. "She's weak, but she ain't give in just yet."

Franklin nodded at the news. "That's good, Otis. I'm glad to hear it. Place ain't the same without her."

"No, sir, it's not." Otis sipped his tea, waiting for the other shoe to drop. Ever since Mr. Peavy called and asked to meet about something important, Otis had felt something ominous coming.

Franklin leaned onto the table and put both hands around his glass. "Otis, you remember way back after your trial, you said you owed me a favor?"

Otis nodded once. "Yes, sir, I sure do. And I meant it." Lord, this was serious, he thought, maybe even dangerous. Small favors get asked over the phone.

"I know you did, Otis, and I'm sorry this has to happen now, with

Estella in the hospital and all, but now's when I've got to ask."
Franklin could see that Otis sensed the seriousness of the matter.
His usually peaceful face had grown hard.

Otis took off his beret and rubbed the top of his head. He tried
to brace himself for whatever was coming. "Just name it, Mr. Peavy."

Franklin felt like God testing Abraham, knowing all along how
things were going to turn out. Still, he wanted the drama to convey
the grievous nature of things, because no matter how good
Franklin's idea was, they were still talking about killing somebody.
"Mr. Herron came to me the other day and asked me to take care of
some business."

"Yes sir, what was that?"

"Otis, he asked me to find somebody to kill this girl."

Otis felt his skin crawl. After five hard years at Fort Pillow State
Penal Farm, Otis had sworn he'd never go down that road again, but
he'd given Franklin his word and intended to keep it. He looked at
his hands. "Is that what you want me to do, Mr. Peavy?"

Franklin was impressed. Otis hadn't flinched, at least not out-
wardly. Franklin was used to dealing with weasels who routinely
broke even small promises, yet here was a man apparently willing to
risk everything to repay a debt. Franklin eased into a cunning smile.
"Well, Otis, let me put it this way." Franklin looked him in the eye.
"After Big Bill asked me what he did, I got to thinking. . . ." He told
Otis how his idea had come to him out of the blue and how he'd
worked out the details and how he was confident it would work.
Though obviously, it wasn't without risk. On hearing the plan, Otis
felt some relief, but still, it wouldn't be easy. Killin' was killin', after
all. And somebody wasn't going to just walk away when it was over.
"But we gotta find somebody else to do it," Franklin insisted. "Somebody to keep us at arm's length from the thing."

Otis considered it for a moment. "It's a good plan, Mr. Peavy, but
somebody's going to end up on the inside."

"Maybe," Franklin said. "But maybe not. District attorney'll be willing to do a little horse trading on something like this. And either way, I got a hundred thousand dollars a year that says whoever you get will be taken care of. You got my word on that, Otis. But whoever it is has got to be willing to take the medicine if that's what happens."

"Yes, sir, I can see that."

"And don't worry," Franklin said. "I'm going to take care of you too. I don't expect you to do this for nothing. This is more than a favor."

Otis seemed to chew on the inside of his cheek for a second. "All right."

"It's gotta be somebody you can trust with your life, Otis, 'cause that's what we're doing. We're puttin' our lives in somebody else's hands." Franklin punctuated his words by stabbing the tabletop with an index finger. "This'll work if it plays out right, but you got to get somebody willin' to stand in the hedge and take up the gap, you understand?"

Otis nodded solemnly.

"Do you know somebody, Otis?"

"Yes, sir, I believe I do."

▮ ▮ ▮

Atlas Publishing got Jimmy's book on shelves faster than anything since the Starr Report. *The Long and Short of It: The Eddie Long Story* didn't make any direct accusations, rather it enumerated a set of facts about Tammy's and the other deaths and simply let the reader draw his or her own conclusion. It was half biography, half murder mystery, and as a result of its innuendo that America's biggest country music star had committed not just one but several murders, the book received a staggering amount of press coverage and uniformly great reviews.

What followed was a scandal of colossal proportions that arrested the nation's attention. The debate over Eddie's innocence or guilt consumed and divided the country more than the Presidential Election of 2000. You couldn't turn on CNN, MSNBC, Larry King, Geraldo, Chris Matthews, Headline News, VH-1, TNN, or anything else without hearing somebody talking about whether Eddie Long did or didn't do it. On Court TV, a panel consisting of F. Lee Bailey, Willie Nelson, Gerry Spence, and Hank Williams, Jr., debated whether Eddie should be honored at the Country Fanfare Awards or sentenced to death. Greta Van Sustren moderated the panel with the seriousness one might accord discussions on the Middle East peace process.

A spokesman for the Country Fanfare Awards issued a statement. "The awards show will proceed as scheduled on CBS at nine eastern, eight central, with special appearances by Chuck Norris and John Schneider. And of course we're still going to honor Mr. Long," he said. "These are nothing but unfounded allegations. We here at the CFA are shocked that a reputable publisher, and I use that word reluctantly, that a publisher like Atlas would go to print with such scurrilous charges. In fact, I understand Eddie Long's representatives are filing a lawsuit of appropriate proportions in response to the slander contained in this book."

The CFA spokesman was right. Herron and Peavy screamed bloody murder in the press as well the courtroom. They filed a $60 million lawsuit claiming libel and defamation of character. On top of that was a claim for another $30 million for intentional infliction of emotional distress. *Time, Newsweek*, and the *Wall Street Journal* gave it maximum coverage. Franklin Peavy, who had to brush up a little on these areas of the law, responded by saying the claims in Jimmy's book constituted a tortious act so utterly shocking and outrageous as to not only meet but to wildly exceed the court's high standard for prevailing in such cases.

The lawyers for Atlas Publishing scoffed. "They can scream as loud as they want," one of them said. "Mr. Long is no longer a private citizen. He is a celebrity and as such he cannot recover any damages unless he can prove Mr. Rogers knowingly wrote untruths about him. It's what the Supreme Court calls 'actual malice.' And unless the great state of Tennessee no longer recognizes the authority of the United States Supreme Court, I feel certain we will prevail in this matter. As to the claim that in writing this book Mr. Rogers's actions meet the standards cited by Mr. Peavy in their claim for punitive damages, keep in mind that in this day and age it takes a hell of a lot more than the mere insinuation that one may have committed murder to qualify as utterly shocking and outrageous."

Thanks to all the publicity and the positive reviews, *The Eddie Long Story* shot to number one on the *New York Times* best-seller list its second week out. Not surprisingly, sales of *Long Shot* surged as well. According to SoundScan, the album sold another 435,000 units the week following the book's release. People who somehow had managed never to hear of Eddie Long before now suddenly had to hear the songs by the guy who might turn out to be a serial killer.

The press naturally turned its attention to the police in the cities where the crimes had been committed. The police said their investigations had dead-ended and all their evidence had been turned over to detectives with the National Crime Information Center. The feds would say only that they were not free to comment on open investigations. But one anonymous source with the NCIC said that after the book was released, an investigator returned to Eddie's old house but was unable to find the container of Uncle Randy's Meat Tenderizer that Jimmy mentioned in the book. According to the anonymous source, it appeared that someone had recently broken into the house and tampered with the crime scene. The NCIC investigator also returned to the Lytles' property, only to find the pesticide shack had recently burned down in the middle of the night. Asked about this, the local fire marshal said, "We know it was arson. We just don't know the arsonist."

*   *   *

"By God, you were right. He's a handsome kid," Chester said with more than a little pride. "I could see part of myself in him, 'cept of course he's better-lookin'."

Otis nodded. "I'm glad you got to see him. You thinking you'll go back to talk to him?"

Chester rubbed his chin, smiling wistfully. "Can't decide. One part of me wants to, but hell, for all I know he'd like to kill me for runnin' out on him and his mama. That's not really the way I wanna go. But I hadn't ruled it out entirely. I figure I'll go back, see him again, see if it feels right. Maybe I'll introduce myself, maybe I won't. Least I know where to find him."

Chester and Otis were sitting in the kitchen at Estella's. Otis had called Chester that morning to say he might have some work for him. Now it was late afternoon and the place was empty except for the two men. They'd been sitting in the kitchen for half an hour talking about Whitney and, before that, about how Estella was doing. Chester could see the burden on Otis's face. Doctors had told him there'd been no change in Estella's condition, no brighter prospects for recovery. "I'm awful sorry to hear that," Chester said. "She's a fine woman, Otis."

"I know and I'm afraid I'm gonna lose her." The thought made Otis feel smaller than he was. He needed her all day and all night. She started where he ended, and if she was gone, Otis might as well be too. "I've been spending time at the hospital," he said, "just sittin' with her, you know? Thinkin'." Otis shrugged his narrow shoulders. "Thinking about things she said to me that I never listened to." He smiled halfway and his little tuft of whiskers pointed at Chester.

"You know, she never much cared for old Bill Herron. I don't know how many times she told me I shoulda got more money outta that man for my records and everything, and, well, I probably shoulda listened, but you know I never listened good as I talked."

Chester looked across the table and wondered where all the time had gone. He was thinking about how young and alive they all used to be and how it all seemed to have passed in a wink. He wanted to say something to prop Otis up but he didn't know what words to use. "You let me know if there's anything I can do."

"Tell you the truth," Otis said, "that's why I called you."

"Just name it."

"Mr. Peavy came to see me the other day about something."

"What'd he want?"

Otis told Chester the same thing Mr. Peavy had told him. Chester listened, disbelieving at first. But every word Otis said chipped away at the disbelief until there was a feeling of inevitability about the thing. "I told him I knew somebody who would do it," Otis said, "but I never said your name, so you're not obliged." Otis paused a second. "I just thought you might at least wanna know about it."

Chester looked at Otis for a few moments without any expression. "How much time you think there'd be, Otis?"

"Mr. Peavy thinks they'd be willin' to negotiate pretty good after they hear that evidence he's got, but there's no guarantee. You still might go inside for a little while."

Chester sat back in his seat, his hands flat on the tabletop. He had to think about it, but he didn't have to think for long. "That's pretty good money, even if you had to do a nickel."

"That's a long time, Chester. Longer'n you think."

Chester thought about the whole thing a little more. He took a deep breath, exhaled, then smiled. "Otis, I'd do it just for the satisfaction," he said, "but I'll take the money too."

16

*E*ddie was screaming into the phone. "Under control? How the fuck is it under control? There's a goddam book on the *New York Times* best-seller list says I killed four people! Including my wife! Christ on a crutch, how can he get away with that?" Eddie had been yelling so loud he was going hoarse. "My career's over! And it barely got started!"

"Relax, son. You're spittin' like a goose shittin' by the moonlight. The guy never actually says you killed anybody. It's all implied, and nobody believes it anyway. Besides, look at, uhhh, I dunno, oh, what's his name? Marv Albert. Press dragged that clown through the mud for what he did, but he was back on network TV in no time. Nobody remembers these things."

"Goddammit, Bill, they said he liked wearing women's panties, not that he killed four people. There's a difference."

"Granted, but think about it, Eddie, the cops haven't come to see you, right?"

Eddie peeked out the window. "True." He saw several television vans down at the gates of his estate, but no cops.

"The guy's just a damned opportunist, Eddie. You gotta expect this sort of thing now that you're a public figure. It's part of the fame game. People just find ways to make money on your back, that's all. And you know the old saying 'There's no such thing as bad publicity,' right? Well, we sold another four hundred thirty-five thousand units thanks to this yahoo's book. Hell, you oughta send him a thank-you note."

Eddie was pacing the living room, a beer in one hand, the phone in the other. "What about the Tall Cotton Award? What are the CFA people saying?" He peeked out the window again. "Are we still up for that?"

"It's under control, Eddie. I talked to the CFA people ten minutes ago. They have every intention of giving you the award as planned. Like I said, hardly anybody believes what's in the book, and those who do are afraid of you, which is always a good thing. Now I've got a conference call with the attorneys at Atlas in about five minutes, tryin' to get this whole thing resolved. I'm fightin' for ya, Eddie. You just try to get some writin' done. I'll call you after the conference call and let you know what happened."

"Fine. I ain't goin' nowhere." Eddie slammed the phone down, then crossed the room to the glass-top table, where he had half a gram laid out in a series of lines. He snorted one, grabbed his guitar, and started pacing the room waiting for the inspiration to hit. But his mind was too cluttered with a stampede of paranoia. *How the hell did this happen?* he wondered. *I worked my ass off to become a star and now this. My own manager is telling me not to worry about a best-selling book accusing me of murder, a book written by a guy I thought was my friend. What the hell kind of management is that? What the hell kind of friend would write those things, even if he thought they were true? And what about the police? Even if Jimmy's book doesn't prove anything, surely the Nashville police are about to come crashing through the front door. There's nothing they love better than bringing down the rich and famous. Hell, it's practically sport for those goons.*

And Megan. Somehow she's gone from flirty, enthusiastic fan to worming her way into the center of my damned life. Then she tricks me into fatherhood and now she's plowing through my money quicker 'n a dog can lick a dish. Well, she's going to have to terminate the pregnancy, he thought, *it's simple as that.* He paused. *Or maybe she's not even pregnant.* Eddie slapped the soundboard. *I have got to be the king of fools. There's no way she's pregnant. Just isn't possible. She's taking me for a ride. Wait a second, a song idea. Something about crowning the king of fools?* He sat down, snorted another line, and wrote it down. *King of fools. Crown. Oh, shit.* He threw his pen across the room when he remembered somebody had already done it.

Eddie jumped when he heard the kitchen door open, followed by two voices. There was a moment when he considered bolting for the front door out of fear it was the cops. But just as quickly he realized it was Megan and Sean, the image consultant she hired to help deal with the aftermath of Jimmy's book. They traipsed into the living room, chatting about the importance of media spin.

Sean was a self-impressed little prick in his late twenties wearing a suit with a single-breasted jacket. It looked to Eddie as if someone had accidentally sewn two extra buttons near the top of the coat and, making matters worse, Sean had them fastened, resulting in a look so laughable it had to be intentional.

"Hey, we're back," Megan said. She had several large shopping bags with her. "I can't wait to show you the dress I got for the CFA's. Sean helped me pick it out."

"I'm not in the mood for a damn fashion show," Eddie said. He watched as Sean casually dabbed his finger into the coke on the table, then rubbed it on his gums. "Hey, do you mind?" Eddie shooed Sean away from the table. "I just talked to Herron. He's acting like Jimmy's book's the best thing that could've happened to me, if you can believe that."

"Well," Sean said, "he's right insofar as it gets your name in the press, which never, I repeat never, hurts." He looked to Megan. "Is now a good time to talk about this?"

Megan was pulling clothes, shoes, and jewelry from the bags. "Sure. Tell him about the research."

Sean perched on the arm of the sofa. "We've finessed some terrific information out of our polling data," he said. "Seventy-two percent of those polled who identified themselves as country music buyers said they'd buy the next Eddie Long CD, even though they knew about the claims in the book. Twenty-two percent said they'd wait to see if charges were brought before deciding whether they'd buy it, and the remaining six percent said they could forgive you but wouldn't buy the new CD."

"Forgive me?"

"The focus groups we did indicate we need to spin your image to the right." Sean pinched his thumb and forefinger together. *"Tant soit peu."* He arched his plucked eyebrows.

"What?" Eddie looked at Megan, who nodded as if she knew what Sean had said.

"I suggest we go with a hint of Christian facade." Sean made a gentle brushing gesture with his hands over his face. "Not too far right, of course, nothing extreme enough to alienate urban country buyers." He contorted his face and wagged his tongue. "Nothing Pentecostal or anything, but in your next interview you might want to work in something about how your faith in God has always pulled you through hard times, that sort of thing."

"What?"

"You know," Megan said, "talk about how Jesus had to deal with false accusations and doubting Thomases and Judas and blahblah-blah, all that stuff. Oh, and wear a cross on a chain or something, maybe a St. Christopher."

Sean nodded. "A lot of our Nashville clients use this very effectively."

Eddie had never been particularly religious, so it wasn't Sean's suggestion that bothered him. It was a culmination of other things—the book, the lawsuit, the press, the image consultant, the pregnancy (or not), Megan's leeching, Jimmy's betrayal—everything. It simply added up, and Eddie snapped. "Get the fuck out of here," he yelled at Sean, gesturing violently with his Fender. "Get out!"

Megan turned, a pair of bright red pumps in her hand. "Eddie, calm down."

Eddie turned and pointed at her so hard the bone almost came out of his finger. "You shut up!" He tossed his guitar onto the sofa, grabbed Sean by his goofy lapels, and forced him toward the foyer, popping the top buttons along the way. "You and your stupid fucking suit are fired." Eddie shoved him out the door and slammed it behind him.

"What the hell's wrong with you?" Megan sounded like a demanding housewife. "We've got to get the right spin on this thing. You can't just stick your head in the sand and hope it goes away." She dropped the pumps and came at Eddie wagging a finger. "If you don't start listening to what I tell you—"

"I thought I told you to shut the hell up!" Eddie wheeled to face her and landed a fist to the side of her head. It spun Megan around and she stumbled, falling across a small end table and landing awkwardly on the floor. "So just do it!"

■ ■ ■

"How the hell can it be under control if they're suing me for ninety million goddamn dollars?" Jimmy asked his agent. "I am screwed six ways to Sunday!"

"Jimmy. Please. Meditate. Ommm, whatever. I told you I'm on it. I'm not going to let you down."

"I don't have ninety million dollars, Jay. I don't even have the three hundred thousand Atlas owes me on the first half of the advance. I'm sooo fucked. I can't believe I let you talk me into putting that stuff in the book."

"Are you through?" Jay asked. "I wanted this to be a surprise, but if you're going to be a crybaby, I'll tell you now. It's going to be in the news tomorrow anyway."

"Be gentle."

"We had a conference call with Eddie's people and the Atlas attorneys. We settled. It's a compromise but you come out fine. Herron and Peavy dropped the suit in exchange for an undisclosed sum to be paid by Atlas's underwriter. We will issue a statement explaining how you were simply experimenting with a new form of biography and you never intended to say Eddie was guilty of anything other than having a remarkable set of circumstantial events in his life—"

"What?"

"There's a gag order on the settlement. The underwriter insisted on it, so I can't even tell you the details, but suffice it to say you not only *aren't* fucked but, with the sales all this publicity generated for the book, you are probably looking at a two-to-three-million-dollar royalty when all the money's counted. Plus you get the bonus for getting sued."

That shut Jimmy up. The whole scenario was so far-fetched he couldn't think of what to say. The words "two-to-three-million-dollar royalty" were rattling around his head so loudly he could hardly think.

"I told you to trust me, but did you?" Jay's tone was both smug and joking. "Listen, I'm overnighting a check to you for a hundred thousand. So pack your bags and get to Nashville. I booked you a suite at the Vanderbilt Plaza."

"What the hell for?"

"You're covering the Country Fanfare Awards."

* * *

Franklin was at Owen Bradley Park on the same bench where he and Big Bill had spoken days earlier. It was a nice day, not too hot, a breeze still coming from the east. He was enjoying the Nashville skyline when he noticed a man approaching.

"You Mr. Peavy?" The man's face was hard as a prison wall. "Otis sent me."

"Sit down," Franklin said. "You know why you're here?"

Chester nodded. "Otis said we needed to have a little conversation 'fore we could do this thing."

"That's right," Franklin said, pulling his recorder from his breast pocket. "You understand there's no guarantees this'll work."

"Otis told me everything," Chester said. "I'm here. So talk."

"All right. I'm going to ask you some questions and make some statements," Franklin said. You just respond any way you want, doesn't matter how. Just don't step on my lines." He handed Chester a piece of paper with some phrases typed on it. "Then you read these. Understand?"

Chester looked at the words. "Uh huh."

Franklin pushed the record button. "You ready?"

Chester shrugged. "Go on."

Franklin slipped the recorder back into his pocket. "Thanks for coming," he said.

Chester looked at him with coal-black eyes. "No problem," he replied. They talked for about ten minutes before Franklin had Chester read from the piece of paper. "I understand you wanna take out a contract," was the first line he read. A few minutes later Franklin had all he needed. He handed Chester an envelope containing some cash and an all-access pass for the Country Fanfare Awards.

* * *

Later that afternoon, Franklin was at the controls of his Pro Tools rig feeling inspired. His system featured a d24 audio card, a DSP Farm card, TDM and AudioSuite Plug-Ins including high-quality multi-band parametric EQ, dynamics (compressor, gate, peak limiter, etc.), digital delay, and lots of other computerized goodies. It was a digital beauty and capable of feats recording engineers would have considered science fiction fifteen years ago. And all for less than the cost of a brand-new pickup truck.

Pro Tools did all the things they used to do with multitrack tape recording, only much faster. For example, both recording methods allowed you to take a verse from one take of a song and put it together with a chorus from another take and then let you go back and stack guitars and background vocals and so on. But with Pro Tools you could do it about ten times faster, because there was no waiting for reels of tape to rewind and locate before starting work on the next track.

The magnitude of the benefit of computer manipulation was like the difference between writing a book with a typewriter versus a word processor. If you wanted to move a paragraph from page six to page two hundred you just pushed a few buttons and it was moved. There was no need to retype the thing, no literal cutting and pasting with scissors and tape. And with all the fudging of information that computers made possible, Pro Tools also allowed you to do things like make an off-key singer sing on key. With its advanced editing features, like its nonadjacent region selection, command key focus, TC/E while trimming, scrub while trimming, clip replace, fit to marks, fill paste, and other innovations, a reasonably adept engineer could do remarkable, almost magical things.

Franklin downloaded the recording of his conversation with Chester into the Pro Tools system just as he had done with his recording of Big Bill. He compared them. The ambience matched. Then he did the same thing engineers did all over Nashville. He created a recording of something that had never happened.

* * *

After his last conversation with Big Bill, Whitney had entertained some violent notions. He had vivid thoughts about how he would kill the fat son of a bitch, but his hostility eventually waned. The anger remained but the urge to act on it gradually submerged in the rest of Whitney's emotional soup. He realized he wasn't capable of the violence he wanted to visit on Big Bill, and he wondered if that proved he was rational or if it just made him a coward like he'd been before.

Whitney was unloading empty boxes from the bed of his truck when the first limousine drove past. The windows were tinted so he couldn't see inside, but he despised whoever it was. He couldn't help it. His mood was black as the windows. Whoever was in the back of that limousine was a member of the club that wouldn't let him in despite his qualifications. For Whitney, the proof of his worthiness lay in the fact that even a bastardization of something he had written had reached number one. The fact that his song survived such whorish meddling confirmed his talent. It never crossed Whitney's mind that the song was a hit because of the changes, not in spite of them. He'd never buy that.

The Country Fanfare Awards wouldn't begin for a few hours, but the celebration had already started. It was Nashville's big night. The night they celebrated the music and the artists who made it. Viva NashVegas! Limousines had to be brought in from surrounding states to meet the demand, and every couple of minutes one would roll down the street in front of Whitney's place, stretch reminders of his failure in Music City USA.

Whitney carried the boxes inside and started packing. He'd had it. After years on the road honing his skills, he'd come to town offering his talent and had been fucked for his trouble. He took a lot of pride in what he was and felt he deserved better than what he'd got so far. Whitney reached into the paper sack that was sitting on the end of the bed. He pulled out another sixteen ounces of friendship and loyalty the likes of which he'd failed to find on Music Row. He drank half of it and resumed packing. It wouldn't take long. He didn't have much.

When it came time for the awards show he would turn on the television. He wouldn't be able to help it. It would gnaw at him to watch the less talented strut to the podium like they were better than him, but he'd have to watch.

An hour or so later, Whitney's life was tucked away in the boxes. There were five empty cans lined up on the bedside table and the show was set to start in ten minutes. Whitney sat at the foot of his bed with his guitar. He looked around the forlorn room. Reminded of one of his favorite songs, Whitney strummed a chord. *"Hello walls . . ."* he sang slowly. His arrangement was darker than Faron Young's and his voice bleaker than Willie Nelson at his most hopeless. He sang about his fear, about losing his mind, and about ruin.

Whitney played the song out, then sat a minute looking at the ragged bandanna tied around his wrist. Eventually he reached over and removed it. Underneath was the silky scar that proved his cowardice. He'd been too scared to do it deep enough. He touched it and thought about trying again, but decided he didn't want to give them the satisfaction that they'd beaten him. *As if they'd even notice. Fuck 'em,* he thought. He had to face the music—this just wasn't where he belonged. He'd go elsewhere, try to find people who appreciated him. Maybe they were down in Austin. They damn sure weren't here.

*   *   *

Eddie's punch left Megan sprawled on the floor. It wasn't a particularly hard hit, but it caught her off guard. She stood up slowly, her mouth half open, her hand on her cheek. She tried to think what she could do or say to fix things, to take them back the way they were. She didn't know how much more of this she could take.

Eddie was just as shocked as she was. He knew better than to do something that would leave a mark. It was plain stupid. The moment seemed to last forever as the two of them stood in the middle of the living room. Eddie wondered what Megan would do now. All of a sudden he saw her face twist into confusion and pain. Her eyes drifted down and her mouth opened wider. She made a weak moaning noise before slowly bending over, grabbing her gut.

"What's wrong?" Eddie had a sick feeling about it. This might finish him off.

"Oh God." Megan began stumbling toward the bathroom.

"What the hell's wrong?" Eddie took a tentative step toward her, reaching out, but she swung at him.

"Get away!" Megan rushed into the bathroom, whimpering, and slammed the door behind her.

Eddie got there just as she flipped the dead bolt. He was beginning to worry she really might be pregnant. "Megan, are you all right? What's going on?" She didn't answer. All he could hear was a harsh cry, apparently in pain. Then he heard the toilet seat going up or down, he couldn't tell which. He banged on the door. "Megan! Let me in!" She made the noise again and it made Eddie sick. This wasn't what he wanted.

"Oh God," she moaned.

"What's going on?" Eddie yelled. "Tell me what to do!"

"We're . . ." It sounded like she was crying. "We're losing it."

"I'm calling 911!" He didn't want to but it would look better than if he didn't.

"No, Eddie, don't! It'll be okay. There's nothing they can do. It's okay. We won't tell anybody," she said. "We'll just say it hap—" Suddenly it sounded like every muscle in Megan's body was contracting to squeeze the life out of her.

"Oh God." Eddie slumped into a heap by the door, his face buried in his hands, wondering how this was going to look. He sat there for a long time, finally overwhelmed by his life.

After a while Megan began to speak again. Her voice was growing raspy and tired. "You don't need this in the press," she said. "I'll protect you. I won't tell anyone. I swear."

* * *

Chester arrived at Opryland USA four hours before they were scheduled to open the doors to the public. He was stage-fright nervous but he wasn't scared. He parked his beat-up Impala near a couple of RVs in the Little Jimmy Dickens section of the vast Opryland parking lot for no other reason than he always like the song "Country Music Lover." Besides, it didn't matter where he parked. Chester knew he wouldn't be returning to the car after the show.

He pulled a guitar case from the trunk and headed for the Opry itself. It was a long way to the auditorium, and, realizing it might be his last free walk for a while, Chester tried to enjoy it. Along the way he saw a few reminders of his past. He stopped to read a plaque with names of some of the old-timers he knew. A little further on he paused to look at some hand prints set in the concrete by Country Music Hall of Famers, some of whom he had mingled with at Tootsie's Orchid Lounge, where he'd tried to make connections with someone who might've helped him back then. That's where he'd met Big Bill two weeks before he signed with Herron Management and Promotions.

Looking up from the hand prints, Chester was startled to see Minnie Pearl strolling with Porter Wagoner, but it was just some actors dressed that way. They wandered the grounds of Opryland giving tourists photo ops.

At the backstage entrance a young security guard saw Chester approaching. He didn't recognize the haggard old man with the guitar case, but he assumed Chester was one of those who had come before his own country music heros. The kid had once made the mistake of stopping a poorly dressed older man at the door only to find out he was a member of the Opry. He wouldn't make that mistake again. "You're here early," the kid said.

Chester hefted his guitar case slightly. "Gotta run scales," he said. "I'm a little rusty." Chester showed his pass and slipped inside. There were all manner of technicians, record company personnel, and media coordinators scurrying around the auditorium. They were all so busy they didn't pay Chester the slightest attention. He was neither legend nor "It Boy." He passed through the backstage area and smiled when he saw the famous barn facade and WSM logo that was used each week for *The Grand Ole Opry*.

Chester had never been to the new Opry. It was a beautiful and modern 4,400-seat auditorium. Tradition being the sort of thing that was honored in the culture, there was an eight-foot circle of hardwood taken from the stage at the Ryman and placed center stage here. It gave Chester pause to think of the people who had performed on that very surface. He'd never made it there himself, so he walked out on the stage and stood there for a moment before moving on to what he had to do.

He spent nearly an hour studying the layout of the building, starting down in the trap for the hoists and scenery lifts. Eventually Chester headed back up through the parterre, past the control room, up a flight of stairs to the balcony, then to the gallery. There he found what he needed—a secluded wall-mounted ladder leading up to the catwalk. It wasn't an easy climb with the guitar case, but Chester managed to get up without being seen. Once there he had to find a spot where he wouldn't be discovered.

About sixty feet away he saw a camera operator setting up behind the front lights, and there were a few spot operators clambering around the lighting grid, but none of them appeared to have need to pass where Chester was going. He found a safe spot, sat down, and settled in for the wait.

He opened the guitar case and pulled out the savage bolt-action
.30-06. It had a 6X Redfield scope mounted on top. Chester had
hunted a lot of deer with a rifle like this and was still a fair shot at
two hundred yards. He figured from his current vantage point,
which was more like fifty yards from center stage, even Ronnie Mil-
sap could hit the target. Chester slipped a round into the chamber
and checked the safety. Then he sat back, closed his eyes, and
waited.

* * *

The crowd began drifting in a couple of hours later, filling the seats
in the back of the gallery and balcony. As curtain approached, more
and more stars took their seats in the parterre. Jimmy had been
drifting around the foyer for the last forty-five minutes making notes
for his first e-stallment for the Atlas website. He spent most of his
time judging attire. Unlike the elegant CMA gathering with its
emphasis on designer fashions, the crowd at the Country Fanfare
Awards dressed in an array of styles ranging from would-you-take-a-
look-at-my-cleavage gowns to prom-night-at-*Hee-Haw* tuxedos.
About half the crowd was wearing cowboy hats, and there were so
many exotic animal skins stretched into the shape of Italy you'd
have thought some oversnuffed bootmaker had used the endan-
gered species list to make up his catalog.

About fifteen minutes before curtain, Jimmy headed for his seat
in the middle of the auditorium and read through the program. This
year's Country Fanfare Awards called for thirty performances and
twenty awards, starting with Best Male Vocal Performance and ending with Record of the Year. Eddie's Tall Cotton Award was scheduled for the midpoint in the show, right after a performance by
Mary Maggie Mason, a hot new band whose music was best
described as hip-hop country. M3, as the group was known, was also
up for the Best New Nontraditional Primarily Female Trio Award.
The band featured the traditional country instrumentation of two

guitars, a pedal steel, fiddle, bass, keyboards, and drums, but they also featured a DJ. They were the first country act to use the rap technique of scratching and sampling old records as part of their music. They incorporated bits of Hank Williams, Bob Wills, the Louvin Brothers, and Tammy Wynette recordings in their popular debut album. Contemporary country fans loved M3's hipness, and a surprising number of pop music fans had embraced the group as well. Predictably, traditionalists were appalled by what they considered the group's shameful disrespect for the classics. Jimmy overheard one member of the Opry say he thought Mary-Maggie-Mason was the surest sign he'd yet seen of the coming Apocalypse.

At eight o'clock, the lights dimmed, the curtains rose, and the announcer came over the sound system. "Ladies and gentleman, welcome to the sixteenth annual Country Fanfare Awards!" The show opened with an ill-conceived dance number set to a medley of all the songs nominated for Song of the Year.

The master of ceremonies was a popular country comedian who opened the show by saying, "You might be a redneck if you're here."

The show was only twenty minutes behind schedule as they neared the midpoint. Mary-Maggie-Mason had just been introduced to wild applause and was ripping through their new single, which drew on fragments of Johnny Cash, Ferlin Husky, and Doug Kershaw.

The presentation of the Tall Cotton Award was four minutes away. Eddie and the rest of Team *Long Shot* were back in Eddie's dressing room having a last-minute discussion about acceptance speech strategy.

"I think Bill's right," Franklin said. "It looks better if you walk out there holding Megan's hand."

"It humanizes you," Big Bill explained. "You walk out there with your girl who's proud to be with you, who's at your side during your time of adversity, and then you get that award?" He shook his head. "Nobody'll care what's in that damn book."

Megan tentatively reached over and took Eddie's hand. "And I am proud, Eddie. You know that," she said.

"Okay," Eddie said. "I think you're right. We'll hold hands. Now, what if I just make a joke about the book? Sort of dismiss it as the price we have to pay, that sort of thing?"

"Don't even bring it up," Franklin said. "Bringing it up just means you feel you have to defend yourself, which implies there's some truth to it, even if you're doing it in a joking manner. Just ignore it." Big Bill nodded agreement.

"Okay," Eddie said. "Fine." He was bouncing on his toes, full of nervous energy. "No book jokes. Don't even mention it."

There was a knock on the door. "Two minutes," a voice said.

Big Bill slapped him on the shoulder. "See you onstage." He and Franklin turned and headed out the door.

Megan ran her hand down Eddie's arm. "How you doin' there, champ?"

"I'm a nervous wreck," he said. "And I'm a terrible person who doesn't deserve to have someone as good as you holding my hand. I don't know why you put up with me."

"What else am I gonna do? Miss Wynette said, 'Stand by your man.'" She shrugged. "Who am I to argue?" Megan primped the front of Eddie's coat, then she got on her tiptoes and kissed him on the cheek. "Now let's go get us a statue." She winked at him.

*   *   *

As the members of M3 took their bows, a new backdrop descended onto the stage in front of them, arousing soft ooohs and aaahs from the crowd. It was an exquisite wall of billowy cotton, some of which had been subtly shaded ivory to spell out "Tall Cotton Award" against the bleached white background. "And now," the announcer said, "the Country Fanfare Association is proud to present the newest jewel in our crown. Brought to you by the Cotton Farmers of

America, here to present the inaugural Tall Cotton Award, ladies and gentlemen, Mr. Franklin Peavy and Big Bill Herron." The audience responded with enthusiastic, if insincere, applause.

As Big Bill and Franklin walked toward the podium from opposite sides of the stage, Chester prepared. Doubt never entered his mind. He was settled on what he was going to do and, dispassionately, he set about doing it. He took a sponge-sized beanbag and draped it on one of the pipes that formed the guardrail of the catwalk. He carefully raised the .30-06 and laid the barrel onto the beanbag, his bench rest. Chester switched the safety off, then rolled his neck once. He put his cheek near the stock, closed his left eye, and peered through the scope with his right.

Big Bill and Franklin, both wearing modestly sequined tuxedos, met behind the podium at center stage and took small bows as they waited for the applause to die down. When things had settled, Big Bill leaned toward the mic and read stiffly from the TelePrompTer. "We work in a business built by and blessed with exceptional artists," he said. "And it's on nights like this one that we rightfully take the time to recognize their artistry and their contributions to the country music industry." Big Bill stepped back from the podium slightly.

Franklin leaned in toward the microphone. "But every now and then someone so special comes along that we have to find a new way to acknowledge their gift."

Big Bill continued, "So when this next artist exploded onto the scene, takin' the world of country music by storm, the board of governors of the Country Fanfare Association realized they'd be tryin' to cut the big hog with the little knife by honoring him with any of their existing awards."

"So they created a new award to commemorate any debut album which achieves double platinum status in less than six months." Franklin paused again for applause while Big Bill hoisted the trophy and stepped out from behind the podium. "It is our pleasure here tonight to present the inaugural CFA Tall Cotton Award to the one and only . . . Mr. . . . Eddie . . . Long."

The chorus of "It Wasn't Supposed to End That Way" came soaring from the sound system as Eddie and Megan walked out from the wings holding hands, country music's hottest new couple. The fans in the backs of the balcony and gallery shot to their feet in a wild burst of applause. Eddie's fellow artists rose and gave him a standing ovation. Some of them even meant it. Eddie waved modestly, then tipped his hat just so. He did his best to smile in an aw-shucks-I'm-not-sure-I-deserve-this-but-thanks sort of way. Megan basked in the moment as they crossed the stage to where Big Bill stood waiting with the trophy.

Jimmy couldn't believe how beautiful she was. She was wearing a sheer amber gown cut low in the front and the back. Her wild red hair crowned her magnificently, and she carried herself like she belonged on the stage. From the moment Jimmy saw her walk out there he felt an ache of jealousy he never could have imagined, much less understood.

Chester had Megan's head square in his sight as she floated across the stage with Eddie. "Pop," he said quietly. The thunderous applause continued as Chester watched through the scope.

Eddie let go of Megan's hand as he reached out to receive the trophy from Big Bill, who was so overwhelmed by emotion he had to blink back a tear. He had come to think of Eddie as the son he never had. He was proud of his boy. Eddie looked at the trophy, then at Big Bill, the man who had made it all happen. The two men embraced. "Congratulations," Big Bill said. "You earned it."

Eddie turned and set the trophy on the podium. He waited for the crowd to take their seats again so he could speak. Megan was on his left, her hands clasped in front of her. Big Bill and Franklin stood on his right. Once the auditorium was quiet, Eddie leaned toward the microphone. "First of all," he said, "I want to thank the CFA

Board of Governors for giving me this tremendous honor. Of course, I have to thank all the fans and everybody in country radio. Without them this never could've happened." Eddie turned to his left. "I owe a special thanks to my road manager and . . . more, Megan Taylor." She blew him a kiss. Eddie turned to his right. "And finally, to the two guys who let me in the door to this business. My legal eagle, Franklin Peavy. And my manager. My producer. My mentor. And my dear friend . . . Big Bill Herron." Eddie gestured for them to take a bow as the audience applauded.

Big Bill suddenly felt an overwhelming surge of magnanimity. He reached out to put an arm around his partner, but Franklin took two nervous steps sideways, leaving Big Bill to stand there, facing the audience, one arm awkwardly extended, all alone. He looked half crucified.

It was the shot Chester had been waiting for most of his life, so he squeezed the trigger. It sounded like a bomb exploding in the rafters. The pristine cotton wall behind Eddie was suddenly spray-painted a gory, dripping crimson. And before you could say "There'll Be No Teardrops Tonight" Big Bill's prediction came to pass; he wouldn't be #99 anymore.

17

It took a few moments, but once the crowd realized what had happened, all hell broke loose. The divas up front were screaming and stampeding over anyone standing between them and the exits. A few of the men reached for the pistols in their boots, but decided against. Why shoot someone just for killing Big Bill, they reasoned.

Back in the control room the director was screaming, "Cut to commercial! Cut to commercial!" Someone accidentally hit the wrong button and the chorus of "It Wasn't Supposed to End That Way" began playing again over the sound system.

Jimmy was as stunned as anyone. He was paralyzed at first, but then instinct took over. He pulled out his camera and started taking photos. He zoomed in on the stage. *Click*. He got a shot of Eddie hovering over Big Bill. *Click*. Megan frozen onstage, hands over her mouth. *Click*. Blood and membrane on the cotton wall. *Click*. An empty place onstage where Franklin used to be. *Click*. Last year's Female Vocalist of the Year throwing an elbow to get out the door first. Jimmy tried to work his way toward the stage for a better angle, but he was a salmon swimming upstream against a flash flood. He stepped back into a row of seats to avoid being swept out to the foyer. Suddenly his cell phone rang. Instinctively he answered. "Hello?"

"Jimmy! I can't fucking believe it! This is fabulous!" It was Jay Colvin. "I'm sitting here watching the damn awards and bam! I'm suddenly sitting on another great book! Get all the photos you can! Hang up the damn phone and get to work!"

A dozen cops and several security guards had fought their way into the auditorium with their guns drawn and aimed at the catwalk. The guys handling the big spots had the lights trained on Chester. He was sitting there, legs dangling, casually smoking a cigarette.

No one paid attention to Jimmy, as he snapped a series of exclusive photos. *Click.* The killer in the spotlight. *Click.* The cops with guns drawn.

"Nashville PD," one of the cops barked. "Hands up! Now!"

"Slow down, Dick Tracy," Chester drawled. "I'm willin' to go nice and quiet."

*   *   *

They took Chester into custody without a fight. They read him his rights, stuffed him into the back of a patrol car, and took him back to the Metro Police Department in downtown Nashville. Chester took advantage of his right to remain silent. He simply refused to talk. He'd been in the interrogation room for eight hours without making a peep except to ask to use the bathroom. There was a video camera aimed at him and a stack of tapes next to it, testimony to his silence.

A new detective arrived to take over the questioning. He looked through the one-way glass at Chester sitting at the table, smoking a cigarette. "Who is he?" the detective asked.

The patrolman threw his hands up. "Didn't have any ID, and he hasn't said a word since he's been in custody."

"Fingerprints?"

"Nothing on file. We got no idea who he is or why he did it."

"Maybe he's one of those traditionalists," the detective said with a chuckle. "You know, some people still like the Possum a lot more than what you hear on the radio all the time."

The patrolman was confused. "Why're we even questioning this guy? We tested the gun and confirmed it fired the bullet that killed Herron. This guy's prints were the only ones on the gun. What else is there? We got the who, the when, and the how—who the hell cares about the why?"

The detective looked at the patrolman. "Me and the district attorney," he said. "We're funny that way."

"What difference does it make?"

"One never knows," the detective said. "That's why we like to get to the bottom of things. Folks coulda stopped poking around after they caught Lee Harvey Oswald, but they didn't, and look what all they turned up. Big conspiracy conviction goes a long way if you're in an electable position." The new detective walked into the interrogation room and went to work. He questioned Chester for another eight hours, but Chester never said a word. The detective tried every technique he knew, but Chester just sat there and watched him like a TV cop show. The last thirty years of his life had been far worse than anything the Nashville police could put him through.

They provided a public defender, but Chester never said boo to the man, who just sat there and listened as the detective badgered the suspect. Toward the end of the second day of questioning, when the detective started talking to the public defender about just putting the suspect in jail to await trial, Chester stubbed out the cigarette he was smoking and cleared his throat. "I wanna meet with Mr. Dupree," he said.

"The district attorney?" his lawyer asked.

The detective smirked. "DA's kinda busy right now," he said. "Workin' on cases that aren't as easy as this one."

Chester shook his head like he didn't care. "He's a only one I'm gonna talk to."

"Is that right? Well, let's see about that." The detective thought he'd finally broken Chester, but after three more hours of silence, he put in a call to the DA's office.

An hour later Mr. Dupree walked into the room. He was a tall, handsome man in a nice gray suit. "Well, hello, mystery killer. I heard you wanted to talk to me."

"Yes sir, that's right."

Mr. Dupree glanced at his watch. "Well, I got thirty seconds, old man." He leaned onto the table with both hands and copped an attitude. "Whadda you got, other than the deck stacked against you?"

Chester stared him down. "What if you was to find out I was hired to do the killin'?"

Mr. Dupree shrugged indifference. "We might be interested to know who did the hirin'."

"How interested?"

"Depends."

"Mr. Dupree, let's me and you step back and take a look at the bigger picture," Chester said. "You ain't exactly had a banner year. First you botched that Garnetts case real bad, then your office was sued for having prosecuted twenty-two defendants with what your office, as far as anybody can tell, knew was planted evidence, and I believe you recently got wind of a federal grand jury investigation about some shenanigans pulled by one of your assistant DAs."

Mr. Dupree wondered who the hell this guy was and how he knew so much about his office's track record, let alone a federal grand jury investigation. "What's your point?"

"Point is, you could use a little somethin' to prop you up this fall. Somethin' like the conviction of a high-profile individual who's been known to support the other party."

Mr. Dupree pulled up a chair and sat down. He was starting to warm up to the suspect's line of reasoning. "Keep talkin'," he said.

"Well, sir, how interested would you be if you was to find out the person who hired me to do the killin' was somebody on that list of Nashville's most powerful people?"

Mr. Dupree squinted slightly. "Very interested."

"Very interested?" Chester lit another cigarette. "Could you be more specific?"

Mr. Dupree reached over to turn off the video camera.

"Leave it runnin'," Chester said. "Just for the record."

The district attorney folded his hands on the table in front of him. "Well, I think we could look at a reduction of the charges against you in return."

"I want a sentencing recommendation too. Plus I gotta be free on bail until sentencing so's I can attend a funeral."

Mr. Dupree shrugged. "All right. But you'd have to be willing to testify against this person, and I'll need proof. Some evidence, you know? 'Fraid I can't just take your word on this sort of thing. I'm sure you understand."

"All right," Chester said. "Let's pretend for a minute there's some evidence. Hypothetically speaking, what kinda deal we talkin' about?"

"Well," Mr. Dupree said, "we always like to get at whoever's behind these kindsa things. Don't wanna leave 'em out there where they can do it again." He paused briefly. "If your evidence proves your claim, and you're willing to testify, I'd be inclined toward offering you something you can live with."

"Could you be more specific?"

Mr. Dupree thought about it for a moment. He figured getting the goods on a high-profile supporter of his political opponent and securing a conviction in a big conspiracy-to-commit-murder case was exactly the sort of thing that would be useful come campaign time. "You'll have to do some time," Mr. Dupree said, "but I can make sure you don't miss more'n one Christmas."

"I can live with that," Chester said. He turned to his public defender. "You oughta write up some kinda paper to document all this, doncha think?"

The public defender dashed off a quick deal memo based on the conversation and showed it to Mr. Dupree, who signed off on it.

"All right," Mr. Dupree said. "Where's this evidence?"

Chester leaned over and whispered something to his lawyer. The man stood up. "Mr. Dupree, if we can meet back here tomorrow afternoon, I'll have everything you need."

*　*　*

The next day they gathered in the interrogation room. A microcassette player was sitting in front of the public defender. The videotape was recording. Mr. Dupree looked at Chester. "All right, mystery man, time for the chin music. Who hired you to do the killin'?"

"Big Bill Herron."

Mr. Dupree cocked his head like he was hard of hearing. He spoke slowly. "Big Bill hired you to kill him?"

"No sir. I wouldn't say that."

Mr. Dupree's face tensed. "What exactly are you sayin', then?"

Chester's attorney raised an index finger. "Why don't we listen to the evidence," he said as he put a tape in a cassette player. "My client recorded this at Owen Bradley Park," he said. "It's a conversation between my client and Big Bill Herron." He pushed the play button.

"Thanks for coming." It was Big Bill's voice.

"No problem," Chester replied. "I understand you wanna take out a—"

"A contract," Big Bill said. "And in a hurry." A car alarm began sounding in the distance.

"Fine with me," Chester replied. The alarm stopped. "Just tell me when and where."

"The awards show," Big Bill said.

"All right, and who's the lucky winner?" Chester asked.

"That damn Megan Taylor."

There was a short pause before Chester continued, "And what's in it for me?"

"A mighty prosperous future."

"You mind bein' a bit more specific?"

"Fifty thousand," Big Bill said in a clipped voice. "I don't care how you do it, just kill the bitch."

"All right," Chester said, "here's what I'm thinkin'."

"No, no, no," Big Bill said. "I don't want to know a thing about it. Just do the hit."

Chester's lawyer punched the stop button and smiled. He produced a document and handed it to Mr. Dupree. "This is an independent expert's affidavit authenticating Big Bill's voice against recordings of him in the studio during the recording of Eddie Long's album."

Mr. Dupree looked at Chester. "Sounds to me like Big Bill wanted you to kill Eddie's girlfriend," he said. "Not him."

"Yes sir," Chester said. "That's right. He hired me to kill that girl." There was a long pause during which everyone ended up staring at Chester. Chester took a final drag off his cigarette, then stubbed it out. "I guess I missed." He shrugged.

Mr. Dupree started waving a hand. "Wait, wait, wait. You said somebody hired you to kill Big Bill."

"No sir, I said somebody hired me to do the killin'." He pointed at the videotape. "See for yourself. You just assumed the rest. I can't help that." He stood up from the table. "Of course, like I said, I'm willing to testify against him. You can count on that." Chester walked to the door and paused. "Now if you'll excuse me," he said somberly. "I gotta go bury somebody."

* * *

Due in large part to his spectacular death on national television, Big Bill's funeral was a certified media event. TNN covered it from visitation to burial. There were so many people dressed in black a

passerby might've mistaken it for a Johnny Cash fan club convention. Everybody who was anybody in country music was there. Just
about everyone who had worked with Big Bill during the past thirty
years stood side by side with those who had never met the man but
were compelled to come say farewell to the legend. It all went to
prove the old Hollywood adage that if you give the people what they
want to see, they'll come out for it.

Of course, people said respectful things as they talked about Big
Bill's long and storied career and about how he had represented and
produced some of country music's biggest stars. In an attempt to
inject some humor into the otherwise somber proceedings a few
people told funny stories about how Big Bill had been known to
stray on occasion from the Rotary Club notion of good faith and fair
dealing. Others went so far as to make up stories about all the time
he had given to charitable causes. Out of respect for the newly
departed, no one mentioned Big Bill's posthumous conviction on
charges of solicitation of murder. However, a reporter for one of the
networks did ask an attorney attending the funeral about the conviction. "Well, it's highly unusual," the attorney said, "since due process guarantees the accused the right to be present to participate in
the proceedings and help with his own defense. But the way I
understand it, the district attorney was adamant they try Big Bill *in
absentia*. Damnedest thing I ever heard of," he said with a rueful
shake of the head. "Solid grounds for appeal too, though I understand no one from the Herron estate is particularly interested in
pursuing it."

Franklin spoke last, remaining stoic as he made a short, heartfelt
speech about his partner. "I learned a lot from Bill over the years,"
Franklin said, "about life, about music, about business, and about
the importance of seizing every opportunity that presents itself, no
matter what the arena." Franklin paused and looked out at the sea of
familiar faces, most of which were smiling at him like he'd brought
good news. "Big Bill leaves behind a legacy that won't soon be for-

gotten," Franklin said. "And I betcha dolla that's exactly the way that old rascal would've wanted it."

As the crowd gathered around the open grave, they sang beautiful songs—splendid and stirring renditions of "What a Friend We Have in Jesus," "Walk in the Garden," and "The Old Rugged Cross." Their voices were strong and the harmony was a thing to behold.

The songs brought tears to everyone's eyes. Big Bill's ex-wives cried the most. The alimony train wouldn't be pulling into their stations anymore. Still, they wondered, as they wiped their eyes, if they'd been included in his will.

*   *   *

Estella's funeral was less of an event. There was no press coverage. There was no throng of mourners. It was just Otis, Doreen, Maurice, and Chester, along with a dozen other old friends gathered in a small cemetery in the countryside on the outskirts of Nashville. There was a warm breeze and the clouds were floating past like soft memories against a blue sky.

Otis listened to what the preacher had to say and then rose to say a few words himself, struggling against his emotions. "She had a voice like two angels singing," Otis said. "And a laugh bright as sunshine. And she loved to dance." A tender smile crossed his face as Otis saw Estella in his mind's eye dancing to Slim Harpo. "She just loved to," he said.

"That's right," Doreen said softly. "She sho did."

Otis nodded slowly. "Everybody who heard her sing knew she could've gone a long way on her own, a lot farther'n I ever got. And she had the chance too," Otis said, "but she stayed with me instead and blessed my life." He wanted to say more but he couldn't manage another sound except to cry.

Maurice put his arm around Otis and started to sing an old song.

I know moonlight, I know starlight, I lay this body down.

The others joined in, one by one.

I walk in the graveyard, I walk through the graveyard to lay this body down.
I lay in the grave an' stretch out my arms, I lay this body down.
I go to the judgment in the evenin' of the day when I lay this body down.
An' my soul an' yo' soul will meet the day I lay this body down.

When the song was over, Otis leaned over and gently kissed Estella's casket before they lowered it into the ground. Then he picked up a handful of dirt and gently sprinkled it on top. "Goodbye sweet baby," he said quietly.

 #   #   #

With the press corps camped at the gate of his Belle Meade estate, Eddie holed up inside waiting for the chaos to pass. Except for Big Bill's funeral, Eddie hadn't been out for a few weeks, and the rumors were starting to get weird. Local TV news vans with microwave transmitters lined one side of the street while network trucks with their huge satellite transmitter dishes were on the other. Radio station reporters mingled with writers and photographers from magazines and newspapers from around the world. At its peak the crowd was nearly five hundred people, but in the past few days it had dwindled to about a hundred hard-core reporters, most of whom were still pressing at the gates of the driveway hoping for a glimpse of the reclusive artist.

Suddenly there was a small commotion at the back of the crowd. "Excuse me," a man said. "Trying to get through here. Pardon me." The man's progress was slow until the crowd realized who he was.

Then they stepped aside and made a path to the gate, which was manned by a beefy security guard. "I'd like to speak to Mr. Long," the man said. The crowd closed in behind the man, anticipating the guard's reaction.

The security guard smirked. "You don't say."

"Seriously."

"Mr. Long doesn't wish to be disturbed."

"Tell him Jimmy Rogers is here to see him."

A moment later Jimmy was hiking up the driveway, halfway surprised Eddie was willing to meet. Jimmy didn't know what to expect. He'd read some lurid stories in the past few weeks about his old friend, most of which portrayed Eddie as a country version of Phil Spector wandering through his mansion late at night. The glow of candlelight roving from window to window. Had he snapped? they wondered. Was he a madman? Jimmy stopped for a moment and considered what he'd do if Eddie had bloomed into full-fledged psychopath. He wasn't worried that Eddie would gun him down in the driveway, since he apparently preferred poison, but he figured anything was possible. After a minute Jimmy realized there was no solid plan for dealing with a lunatic, so he just moved toward the house hoping for the best.

To his surprise Eddie met him at a side door wearing his best smile. "Hey man, c'mon in," he said. "It's good to see you." His tone was warm and welcoming. The same guy Jimmy had always known. Eddie showed him into the kitchen and gestured at the table. "Take a load off." He poured two cups of coffee from a fresh pot.

"I take it black," Jimmy said, watching to see if Eddie slipped anything into his cup. There was an awkward silence before Jimmy asked. "So, how's Megan? Is she here?"

"Hell no," Eddie said with a grim chuckle. "She's long gone. Tell the truth, I figured she went crawling back to you." His right hand mimicked a spider crossing the tabletop.

Jimmy shook his head. "I haven't seen her since the CFA Awards."

Eddie nodded slightly and slipped into good-old-boy mode. "Well, I tell you, if I was you and she showed up after all this, I'd take her in for a grudge cut, then show her the door." He winked but noticed Jimmy wasn't amused. "Of course, that's just me," Eddie said. "You might just wanna take her back, I dunno." He sipped his coffee.

"Why'd she leave? I thought she was an integral part of Team *Long Shot.*"

"Who knows?" Eddie shrugged. "I guess she figured the upside of being with me just wasn't worth the trouble. Not that she left empty-handed. Last thing she said was she figured she could sell the rights to her story for a couple hundred thousand bucks." He chuckled slightly. "Is that just like her or what? I told her not to let the door hit her ass on the way out." Eddie suddenly slapped the tabletop. "Hey! I almost forgot." He jumped up and left the kitchen, returning a moment later holding up a copy of Jimmy's best-seller. "Congratulations on the book," Eddie said. "Could I get you to sign my copy?"

Jimmy looked at Eddie like he'd just asked him to tell knock-knock jokes at a funeral. Then, after a moment, he said, "What the hell, why not?" Jimmy took the book from Eddie, then pulled a pen from his pocket and wrote: *For Eddie—I guess you pulled it off. Jimmy.* He slid the book back across the table.

"Thanks, man." Eddie laughed a little when he read the inscription. "Listen," he said, "I'm sorry Big Bill cut you off the way he did. I never knew about it until it was too late. I'da liked to've worked on it with you, but, hell, I guess it don't really matter, does it?" He leaned on the table and smiled. "Me and you made out like banditos on the deal, didn't we?" Eddie laughed. "I believe it's what they call a win-win situation." He arched his eyebrows.

"Unless you count Tammy and Big Bill and the others who died."

"Well yeah, a'course there's that," Eddie said. "But that wasn't our fault, was it? That was just a weird coincidence, fortuitous even, given how things worked out. I mean, without all those funerals, I bet your book wouldn't've sold half as good as it has. And it hadn't exactly hurt record sales either. Ka-ching!" Eddie was relishing the self-congratulatory nature of the chat and wanted Jimmy to join him.

Jimmy just stared at him. "So you're sticking with that story?"

"What, that I'm not guilty? Got to, don't you think?" Eddie cocked his head to the side and pointed at Jimmy. "But I'll say this. That book of yours damn near convinced me that I was guilty. It really is a good read. Nice pacing, all those fine details, and some keen speculation. All that MSG stuff, Compound 1080, the deaths in Terrebonne Parish and Gulfport and Lee County all tied to my old touring schedule. Man, I was impressed." He put his hand on the book. "That's a good piece of work."

Jimmy paused as he thought about something. "Lee County?" He consulted a map in his head. "Mississippi?" He started to wonder if Eddie had killed somebody in Tupelo, but of course every state south of the Mason-Dixon line had a Lee County.

"No," Eddie said. "Alabama. Isn't Tuscaloosa in Lee County?"

Jimmy thought about it for a minute. "No, Tuscaloosa's in Tuscaloosa County. Lee's on the other side of the state. That's where Auburn is."

"Whatever." Eddie stood abruptly and went to get another cup of coffee.

"You used to play at Auburn, didn't you? Frat parties?"

"Matter of fact, I did." It sounded like Eddie was smiling, but he was facing the other way, so Jimmy couldn't say for sure. "But that's not the point." Eddie sat back down at the table.

"So what is?"

"The point is I didn't kill nobody. But I'll say this: whoever did kill those folks, you gotta admit, he was smart. No two ways around that. That's what I was thinking as I read your book. Man, that is one smart son of a gun. And you know what else I was thinking?" Jimmy stared at Eddie without answering. "All right, I'll tell you. It was almost like somebody was trying to frame me. You know what I mean? All that evidence was just too damn perfect, considering I didn't do it. So I started wondering who would know enough about me to make it look like I was a killer. And you know what? I could only think of two people, you and Tammy. And since she's dead, that left me thinking it mighta been you. I mean, who better to frame me than my biographer?"

Jimmy couldn't believe it. Eddie almost sounded like he believed what he was saying. "You bother to assign a motive to my crime?"

"Well, jealousy seemed like the best bet," Eddie said. "You were pissed that Megan left you for me, and, well, you acted out. Is that it? Is that why you tried to frame me, Jimmy?"

"Well, Eddie, that makes perfect sense except for the fact that most of the victims were dead before Megan left me."

Eddie looked at Jimmy for a minute. "Well, you got a point there," he said. "But I can't figure out who else might've done it. Guess it's just one of life's mysteries."

"I guess." Jimmy looked at his reflection in his coffee. He was thinking about his contract for the continuing web version of Eddie's biography. He figured this was probably his last opportunity to get some first-person material. "So what now? You about to start your next album, or are you still writing songs?"

"Funny you should ask," Eddie said. "Turns out I finished the last song a few days ago. And I tell you what, it was worse than giving birth." Eddie told Jimmy how he'd slipped into an emotional tailspin after Big Bill's murder. "It's all a big blur," he said. "I can't even remember the sequence of events after that shot was fired. One second I was onstage receiving the award, then all hell broke loose. Screaming women and cops and blood and paramedics, and the next thing I remember is being stuck here in the house, all alone, trying to forget something I didn't think I ever could." Eddie fixed his eyes on Jimmy's. "I was looking square at Big Bill when it happened. I couldn't erase that image no matter how hard I tried. His expression . . . it was a terrible thing to see." Eddie looked down at his coffee again and shook his head slowly. "For a while afterwards, every time I closed my eyes I saw Bill's head snap back just as that white cotton wall turned red." Eddie looked up. "Every time I fell asleep that rifle would fire again." He slapped his hand on the book, startling Jimmy. "Woke me up like a cannon shot. It was like being haunted. I mean it seemed like Big Bill looked at me just before he fell down, like he wanted me to undo what'd happened, like it was my fault or something. That's not the sort of thing you want burned into your mind, right?"

"I can see how that might become bothersome."

"Damn right it was bothersome. And making matters worse was the media out there." He gestured toward the front gate. "They've had me trapped in here for weeks. After the funeral, I started drinking, you know, trying to get some sleep, trying to forget what happened, trying to erase that image in my head. I disconnected the phones and the TV and the computer. I just wanted to be alone. It felt like I'd lost my own father and they wouldn't give me time to grieve. And then I started seeing Bill's face whenever I closed my eyes, and hell, I thought I was going crazy."

"Funny, I would've expected you to be seeing Tammy's face."

Eddie smirked. "Except of course I didn't see her die, did I?"

Jimmy shrugged. He was looking for something in Eddie's eyes—remorse, guilt, pleasure, something. But they revealed nothing.

"Anyway, it took me a while to figure out what the hell was going on."

"Which was?"

"I finally realized it was another song trying to get out." He held up a hand. "I swear, it was worse than after Tammy died."

"So you wrote a song. Then what?"

"Been sleeping like a baby ever since." Eddie jumped up from the table. "Hang on a second," he said on his way out of the room. "Let me play it for you." Eddie came back a second later with his old Fender.

Jimmy spent the afternoon listening to Eddie play the songs he'd written for the new record. He had to admit they were pretty good. Finally Eddie got around to the new song, the one triggered by Big Bill's death. It was a beauty.

It would be the first single off the second record and it would go to number one, just as Big Bill had planned. Except of course that Big Bill was supposed to be alive to hear it.

* * *

Franklin was waiting on his last appointment of the day. He was sitting at his desk looking over the "key man" insurance policy the company had taken out years ago on Big Bill. The underwriter was Nashville Casualty and Life: They owed a cool million on the death benefit. *It's funny how things work out*, he thought.

Franklin had been busy all week. He'd ordered new stationery and had the old Herron & Peavy Management sign replaced with one that said "The Peavy Company." He'd upgraded his Pro Tools to top of the line and was ready to go into the studio to start work on Eddie's second record. The only problem was he hadn't spoken to Eddie since Bill's funeral. His phone seemed to be out of order and he wasn't answering e-mail. He knew the press was camped out at Eddie's house and he didn't want to deal with that, so he figured he'd just wait it out. It wouldn't be long before some other scandal broke and the press would break camp and move on like a bunch of Bedouins.

In light of Jimmy's book and the rumors that had followed, Franklin had hired a new image consultant for Eddie. They'd been discussing the possibility of repackaging Eddie, going with the all-black thing, and positioning him as the head of a new outlaw country movement. Franklin had put in an exploratory call to Waylon Jennings's people to discuss a collaboration, but so far nobody'd called back.

Franklin propped his feet up on his desk and gazed out at Music Row. The sun was reflecting off the big shiny leaves of the magnolia tree outside the window. He started to think about knocking down the wall that separated his office from Big Bill's, giving himself a little more room. He jumped slightly when his assistant buzzed him. "Two men to see you, Mr. Peavy."

"Thanks, send 'em in," Franklin said. He stood and walked around his desk as Otis and Chester walked in and closed the door behind them. "Come on in, fellas, have a seat." Franklin went to his bar, poured three glasses of whiskey, and served his guests. "Here's lookin' atcha." They clinked glasses and enjoyed the drink before Franklin went to his desk and picked up a file. He pulled some checks from inside. "I put you on the books as 'indie promo' expenses," he said with a chuckle. "Hundred thousand a year for the next three years, right?" Chester and Otis nodded. "Good," Franklin said. "And worth every dime." He looked at Chester. "You want me to put yours in escrow or in the market or what?"

"Buy me some blue chips," Chester said. "Give me something to follow while I'm inside."

"When are you going?"

"They gave me till Monday to 'get my affairs in order,' " he said. "Then I'm gone for about a year. I'm lookin' at it like rehab."

"There you go." Franklin handed another document to Chester. "I also fixed that publishing error we made on your boy's song. He'll get proper credit on future copies and all he's owed on the publishing, mechanicals, and licensing. Of course, there wasn't anything I could do about the lyrics." He pulled a check from the file and held it up. It was for $350,000. "I'll see that he gets this. His landlord had a forwarding address for him down in Austin."

Chester shook Franklin's hand. "I'd appreciate that."

Franklin turned and put his hand on Otis's shoulder. "I'm sorry I missed Estella's service. I had to be at Bill's."

"Yessir, I understand."

"How are you holdin' up?"

Otis bobbed his head a little. "I'll be all right, Mr. Peavy, thank you for asking."

"She was a fine woman, Otis. We were lucky to have her long as we did."

"Yes, sir. We was sure lucky. And I know she's lookin' down with a smile right now."

*   *   *

The Long and Short of It stayed on the best-seller list for eight months. Jay Colvin negotiated $1.25 million for the film rights to the story. He got another $1 million for Jimmy's proposal on Big Bill's biography. Jimmy had a hard time believing any of it, at least until the checks arrived. And when they did, he decided it was time to move. Though he was going to miss listening to his neighbors' sex-capades, Jimmy had discovered that lately he wasn't having such a hard time getting laid. *Funny how that works*, he thought.

Jimmy was loading the last lamp into the back of his rented U-Haul truck when a familiar car pulled into the parking lot of the apartment complex. The second he saw Megan he felt it again. That way she always made him feel. He knew he should just get in the truck and leave, but he couldn't. Megan parked and got out, looking at Jimmy with a bittersweet smile. She was dressed simply in jeans and a T-shirt. "Hey," she said. "Looks like I got here just in time."

"Yeah, I'm, uh, just about done." Jimmy wiped his hands and stuffed them in his pockets. "What're you doing here?"

"Just came by to see if you were still around."

Jimmy didn't know how to respond to that. The thought that she'd come looking for him turned his mind to mush. All he could think about was pulling her close and kissing her. He wondered if

Megan would always have this power over him. *Maybe I should just give in to it*, he thought. *No, show a little self-respect.* "I hear you left Eddie," he said.

She shrugged. "Yeah, I read your book. Decided I didn't want to take the chance of getting a headache being around him so much, you know?"

Jimmy nodded. "Good move," he said.

"It's a great book, by the way. Congratulations. I always knew you'd make it."

"Thanks. So, you going back to radio?"

Megan shrugged. "We'll see. I'm not sure Ken's real keen on having me back. What about you?" She gestured at the U-Haul. "Where're you going?" She held up a hand. "Wait, don't tell me. New York? Seems like a good place for a best-selling author. I was thinking about New York myself."

Jimmy shook his head. "Lake Katherine."

"Really?" Megan tried to sound like she thought that was a good idea. "That would've been my second guess. New York City or Madison County, top two choices." Megan sat down on the truck's bumper. "Oh, by the way, you can add Aaron Copland to your list."

"My list of what?"

"Of people who might have said 'Writing about music is like dancing about architecture.' Somebody told me Aaron Copland said it. I just thought you'd want to know."

"Thanks." Jimmy smiled. "Watch your head." He pulled down the door on the back of the truck. He hoped Megan wouldn't start talking about getting back together. "Well, it was good to see you," he said. "I need to get on out there and unpack before it gets too late." He started to walk around toward the front of the truck. He hoped she wouldn't say anything else, that she'd take the hints and not tempt him. He didn't trust himself to do the right thing.

Megan stepped into his path. "You need some help?" She moved close. "It just so happens I'm free the rest of the weekend." She was inches away, and she smelled as good as she looked. "I could help you unload and then I'll take you out to dinner. Whaddya say? Maybe we could get 'em to make us some patio lemonades." She smiled and looked up into his eyes.

God it was tempting. He could almost taste those bourbon kisses. It would be so easy to say yes. Then he opened his big mouth. "No thanks," he said. "I can manage." As soon as he said no, he had second thoughts. He wanted to grab the words before they reached her ears and replace them with *Hell, yes! Let's go get drunk and christen my new place.* But at the same time he realized saying no gave him a sudden sense of liberation.

Megan's face sagged. She'd never imagined things ending like this. It began to sink in when Jimmy walked past her and climbed into the cab of the truck. She looked up at him sitting behind the wheel. "C'mon, Jimmy. After all we've been through? We're meant to be together."

He looked down at her, considering her invitation with all his might. *Maybe I should take her up on it. Just for a night. A grudge cut.* He thought about it a moment. *Nah, that's too Eddie.* He closed the door, then reached out to adjust the truck's big side mirror.

"You know how much I love you," she said.

Something about the way she said it gave Jimmy pause. *Maybe she means it. Maybe she finally realizes how I feel. How can I not consider it? Those are the softest lips I've ever known.*

"Jimmy?"

Her voice snapped him back to reality and he knew what he had to do. He cranked the engine and put the truck in gear. It inched forward slightly against the brakes.

Megan suddenly looked like a frightened child, something Jimmy had never seen in her before. "Wait!" She reached up and put a hand on his arm. "Don't go yet."

He felt sad for her and he touched her hand. "I gotta go," he said softly.

She looked up anxiously. "Can we talk for a minute?"

Jimmy shook his head, then looked down at Megan. "Good-bye's all we got left to say." He let his foot off the brake and pulled away without ever looking in the mirror. As the truck lurched out of the parking lot, a thought occurred to him. *Hey, now that would be a good song title.*